"Miss Stafford writes with brilliance."

—*Saturday Review*

"This collection will undoubtedly become a textbook for many students of short fiction. Jean Stafford can teach almost anything one could want to know about swiftly and deftly developing characters, balancing them in delicate counterpoint or wrenching conflict, and probing their thoughts and emotions."

—*Newsweek*

"Indispensable. . . . Stories of loss and estrangement that withstand the stresses of time and shifting fashion."

—JAMES WOLCOTT, *Harper's*

The collected stories of JEAN STAFFORD

The collected stories of
JEAN STAFFORD

A Dutton **O**belisk Paperback

E. P. DUTTON, INC.   NEW YORK

This paperback edition of The Collected Stories of Jean Stafford
first published in 1984 by E. P. Dutton, Inc.

Reprinted by arrangement with Farrar, Straus & Giroux.

Acknowledgment is made to the editors of The New Yorker for the following
stories that first appeared in their pages: "Maggie Meriwether's Rich Experience,"
"The Echo and the Nemesis" (originally "The Nemesis"), "The Maiden," "A
Modest Proposal" (originally "Pax Vobiscum"), "Polite Conversation," "A
Country Love Story," "The Healthiest Girl in Town," "The Mountain Day," "Bad
Characters," "In the Zoo," "The Liberation," "A Reading Problem," "A Summer
Day," "Children Are Bored on Sunday," "Beatrice Trueblood's Story," "Cops and
Robbers" (originally "The Shorn Lamb"), "The Philosophy Lesson," and "The
End of a Career"; to The Sewanee Review, for "The Captain's Gift" (originally
"The Present") and "Life Is No Abyss"; to Mademoiselle, for "Caveat Emptor"
(originally "The Matchmakers"); to The Saturday Evening Post, for "The
Children's Game" (originally "The Reluctant Gambler"); and to the editors of
Ladies' Home Journal, Harper's Magazine, Kenyon Review, Partisan
Review, Harper's Bazaar, and Colorado Quarterly, where the other stories in
this volume were first published.

Published in the United States by E. P. Dutton, Inc.
2 Park Avenue, New York, N.Y. 10016

Library of Congress Catalog Card Number: 83-72961

ISBN: 0-525-48101-X

Published simultaneously in Canada by Fitzhenry & Whiteside
Limited, Toronto

10   9   8   7 - 6   5   4   3   2   1

Contents

CONTENTS

Author's note

By the time I knew him, my father was writing Western stories under the *nom de plume* Jack Wonder or, occasionally, Ben Delight. But before that, before I was born, he wrote under his own name and he published a novel called *When Cattle Kingdom Fell*. The other principal book in my family (the rest were memory books and albums of scenic postal cards) was by my first cousin once removed on my mother's side, Margaret Lynn, and this was *A Stepdaughter of the Prairie,* a reminiscence of her girlhood in frontier days in Kansas. To my regret, I have read neither of these books, so I cannot say that they influenced me. However, their *titles* influenced me when my cacoëthes scribendi set in and I wrote about twisters on the plains, stampedes when herds of longhorns were being driven up from the Panhandle to Dodge, and bloody incidents south of the border. All the foremen of all the ranches had steely blue eyes to match the barrels of their Colt .45's. With this kind of heritage and early practice I might have been expected to become a regional writer, but my father's wicked West and Cousin Margaret's noble West existed only in memory, and I could not wait to quit my tamed-down native grounds. As soon as I could, I hotfooted it across the Rocky Mountains and across the Atlantic Ocean. I have been back to the West, since then, only for short periods of time, but my roots remain in the semi-fictitious town of Adams, Colorado, although the rest of me may abide in the South or the Midwest or New England or New York. Most of the people in these stories are away from home, too, and while they are probably homesick, they won't go back. In a sense, then, the geographical grouping I have chosen for the stories is arbitrary. I have borrowed titles from Mark Twain and Henry James (I am a great one for appropriating other people's titles), who are two of my favorite American writers and to whose dislocation and whose sense of place I feel allied.

J. S.

THE INNOCENTS ABROAD

Maggie Meriwether's Rich Experience

There was a hole so neat that it looked tailored in the dead center of the large round beige velours mat that had been thrown on the grass in the shade of the venerable sycamore, and through it protruded a clump of mint, so chic in its air of casualness, so piquant in its fragrance in the heat of mid-July, that Mme Floquet, a brisk Greek in middle life, suggested, speaking in French with a commandingly eccentric accent, that her host, Karl von Bubnoff, M. le Baron, had contrived it all with shears and a trowel before his Sunday guests arrived at his manorial house, Magnamont, in Chantilly. It was quite too accidental to *be* accidental, she declared; it was quite too Surrealist to be a happenstance. Mme Floquet had the look and the deportment of a dark wasp; her thin, sharp fingers, crimson-tipped, fiddled with her bracelets, made of rare old coins ("Oh, Byzantine, I daresay, or something of the sort," she had said carelessly to someone who had admired them; one knew that she knew perfectly well the pedigree and the value of each of them), and through smoked glasses of a rosy cast she gave her lightning-paced regard to a compact that had cunningly been made from a tiger cowrie shell and given by M. le Baron to Mrs. Preston, whose birthday it was today. Mrs. Preston, a Russian, was as Amazonian and fair as Mme Floquet was elfin and swart, and she was the beneficiary of so large a fortune, left to her by an American husband (he had manufactured pills), that in certain quarters she was adored. (Mme Floquet, who was dependent for her livelihood on the largess of a moody Danish lover, had been heard to remark, "I can't say that Tanya carries her money as well as she might, but that sort of thing—money, I mean—can't be ignored. I'd not refuse the offer of the Koh-i-noor, even though it wouldn't be my style." Because of this forbearance on the part of Mme Floquet, she and Mrs. Preston were the best of friends, and the little Greek had frequently accepted presents of slightly worn sables and the use of second-best motorcars.)

It was Mme Floquet's chaffing tone that was immediately adopted by the whole party. The conceit of their host's rising before the dew was dry and arranging this neat tatter and its rural adornment amused them, and, to his delight, they ragged him; someone proposed that he had really done it the night before by moonlight and had recited incantations that would endow this particular herb with magic properties—black or benign, the speaker would not care to guess. Rejoicing in his witty nature, they recalled the Baron's *fête champêtre* of the summer before, when there had actually been jousting and tilting, the knights being jockeys from Longchamp in papier-mâché armor executed by Christian Dior. Someone else, returning to the present joke, said, "If this were Tennessee, we could have mint juleps." But Mme Floquet, who tended to be tutorial, replied to this, "Those, I believe, are made with Bourbon whiskey, and the taste of that, I assure you, is insupportable. I had some one day in America by mistake." She shuddered and her bracelets sang.

Maggie Meriwether, who was from Nashville and was the only American present, and who was abroad for the first time in her young life, blushed at this mention of her native state and country as if someone had cast an aspersion on her secret lover; she was gravely, cruelly homesick. Her French, acquired easily and then polished painstakingly at Sweet Briar, had forsaken her absolutely the very moment the Channel boat docked in Calais, and while, to her regret and often to her bitter abasement, she had understood almost everything she had heard since she had been in France, she had not been able to utter a word. Not so much as *"Merci"* and certainly not so much as *"Merci beaucoup."* She had been sure that if she did, she would be greeted with rude laughter (not loud but penetrating), cool looks of disdain, or simply incomprehension, as if she were speaking a Finnish dialect. Her parents, who had had to be cajoled for a year into letting her go to Europe alone, had imagined innumerable dreadful disasters —the theft of her passport or purse, ravishment on the Orient Express, amoebic dysentery, abduction into East Berlin—but it had never occurred to them that their high-spirited, self-confident, happy daughter would be bamboozled into muteness by the language of France. Her itinerary provided for two weeks in Paris, and she had suffered through one week of it when, like an angel from heaven, an Englishman called Tippy Akenside showed up at her hotel at the very moment when she was about to dissolve in tears and book passage home. She had met Tippy in London at a dinner party—the English ate awful food and drank awful drinks, but they surely did speak a nice language—and had liked him, and she would have been pleased to see him again anywhere; seeing him in Paris at the crucial moment had almost caused her to fall in love with him, though young men with wavy black hair and bad teeth had never appealed to her. He had been wonderfully understanding of her dilemma (he had had a similar experience in Germany when he had gone there for a holiday from Eton), and the evening before, which had begun at Maxim's and ended at Le Grand Seigneur with rivers of champagne, he had proposed this day in the country as a cheerful relaxation. He was a friend of the Baron and knew most of the people who were to be at the party, and he assured her that all of them spoke English. He had promised on his word of honor that he would manage cleverly to make everyone speak it—English was ever so smart these days, he said—and do so without embarrassing her. Tippy's word of honor had proved to be no longer than a nonsense syllable, and his cleverness as a social arbiter evidently existed only in his mind. For English was not being spoken, not even by—especially not by—Tippy. Not one of the company was French, although they looked it; as for their host, M. le Baron was the son of a Viennese father and a half-French, half-Irish mother.

Maggie had loathed Tippy Akenside from the moment they got out of his Renault. Looking back, she saw that he was a poor driver—not reckless but gawky—so that they had made the trip in fits and starts, and he had not paid any attention at all to her except for making introductions.

Not only was she miserable over the death grip in which the cat had got her tongue; she was feeling very country-looking, although she had thought she looked quite smart when she set out from Paris. The other ladies had all brought a change of clothes, had taken off their city dresses and their city shoes and were wearing stunning linen shorts and shirts and Italian sandals. They had not, however, removed their jewels; rubies and emeralds and diamonds were visible at the open necks of their informal shirts; fashionably crude-cut gems of inestimable worth glittered at their wrists and ears; Mrs. Preston wore an ankle bracelet of star sapphires. Maggie, in a tie-silk print and high-heeled shoes (and, oh, lackamercy on us, *stockings!*) and a choker of cultured pearls, could not tell whether they were all really not aware that she was there or whether they thought that Tippy, who was descended from a long line of eccentrics (and, thought Maggie, of traitors), had brought along his mother's tweeny for some sort of awful joke. She did not know, that is, whether she was invisible or whether she was an eyesore too excruciating to look at. Certainly they were managing marvelously to rise above her presence.

Maggie was sorry that she was not enjoying her experience, because she was sure it was a rich one for a simple country-club girl from Tennessee. M. le Baron was a handsome, sparkling man whom many women, according to Tippy, wished to marry. All but a few diehards, mainly girls of a greedy and romantic age, had sensibly faced up to the fact that he would remain a bachelor forever, because he basked in a perfectly rapturously happy marriage to his demesne, this superb Palladian house that confronted a pool filled with blue water hyacinths—a pool that adroitly became a broad and gracefully meandering stream where black swans rode and charming bridges arched to debouch into charming paths, through acres and acres of classical gardens and orchards, up into vineyards, down into cow pastures and paddocks. At some distance behind the house, within a grove of oaks that dated back to Charlemagne, there was a famous, ancient abbey, inhabited now not by clericals—except for the household priest—but by the Baron's aged French-Irish mother, her aged brother, his aged manservant, and a bevy of aged handmaidens. The valet sometimes played the fiddle—badly but with heart—and the maids beautifully crocheted; the brother and sister, who doted on each other, played backgammon almost unceasingly, and both of them cheated without a prick of conscience. It was a supremely contented community. The servants of Magnamont were happy; the tenants were prosperous and exceptionally fecund; the livestock was stalwart; the fruit of the land was unparalleled. And all of this harmony came about because M. le Baron was so faithful to his husbandry.

What he loved best in the world next to grooming and bur-
nishing Magnamont was showing off Magnamont to visitors, but
he was so sensitive to any slight upon his true love that he never
forced her on anyone. This reluctance dated from two episodes,
occurring within a month of each other: Someone had made a
stupid joke about the sheep that were wisely and thriftily used to
keep down the grass of the far lawns, and someone else, who had
had an excess of drink, had gone a little too far about the topiary
garden, which, while admittedly absurd, was heirloom and sacro-
sanct. These boors, needless to say, had never been asked back.
If an invitation to look at his dovecotes or his asparagus beds had
been received with indifference, M. le Baron's heart would have
bled, so he had to be asked—he sometimes even had to be coaxed
—to conduct a tour of the grounds.

Maggie had momentarily warmed to this man, for when Tippy
introduced them he had smiled in the friendliest possible way
and had said, in English, "How nice of you to come," but then,
when rotten Tippy said, "Miss Weriwether is the American girl
I told you about on the phone," the Baron thereafter addressed
her in highly idiomatic French until, encountering nothing but
silence and the headshakes and cryptic groans that escaped her
involuntarily, he began to pretend, as the others had done from
the start, that she wasn't there.

They had had a long ramble, for these guests knew the way
to their host's heart; they had seen everything, including the bees,
including the Baron's mother and uncle, who were swindling each
other and drinking Jamaica rum out of minute silver goblets.
Maggie had not minded the excursion, tiring and baffling as it
had been, half as much as she did this present situation, when
they all sat in a circle on the mat as if they were about to play
spin-the-plate and aim for the clump of mint. They were drinking
martinis made with a European and abominable exorbitance of
vermouth. They were drinking martinis, that is, with the excep-
tion of the Contessa Giovennazzo, who, with enormous originality,
had asked for iced *tilleul*. This woman, a vision in shocking pink
and violet and with phosphorescent streaks of platinum in her
black hair, discomfited Maggie almost more than any of the others,
for she talked so much and so knowingly about the United States;

she had a great deal to say about the United Nations and about Hollywood, and she told a significant anecdote about a senator of whom Maggie had never heard.

From time to time, Maggie tried to catch Tippy's shifty eye, and she unremittingly sent him an SOS by telepathy. But he was engaged in a preposterous recapitulation of scenes of W. C. Fields movies with a Heer Dokter van Lennep, a psychoanalyst who had emigrated from Amsterdam to practice on Park Avenue, and with a man whose name Maggie had not caught and whose nationality or occupation or age she could not begin to determine; he was rather fat and rather fair and rather seedy and rather melancholy of countenance (he was not enjoying the conversation about W. C. Fields at all), but since all these things were only *rather* true of him, their opposites could just as easily have obtained. She had never seen anyone so nondescript; he looked like a bundle that might have contained anything on earth. Because of his very lack of definition, she pinned her hopes on him. At least, he wasn't elegant; he did not look rich; he did not look well-connected; not a single scintilla burst from his soggy, shaggy person. And she began, parenthetically, to send him a distress signal.

The gossip, over these many, many bad martinis, was global. The jokes (they laughed like mad and had to wipe the corners of their eyes with their monogrammed handkerchiefs) presupposed a knowledge of the early peccadilloes of papal princesses and of deposed kings and demoted Prussian generals, the sharp wit of footmen in embassies in Africa, the gaucherie of certain spies and the high style of certain others, the moral turpitude—ghastly, really, but screamingly funny—of a choreographer in Berlin, the lineage of a positively fascinating band of juvenile delinquents that were terrorizing Neuilly-sur-Seine.

Maggie grew hotter and larger.

The interminable day progressed from one disgrace to another, and Maggie Meriwether, who once upon a time had been considered something of a belle, became more and more bedraggled. Her stem, that green and golden tie-silk print, began to look as if it had been dragged in by the same cat that had hold of her tongue; her roots were swollen (looked like potatoes, to tell the truth, thought Maggie wretchedly) in too new shoes; and her hair, which was thick and red-gold (once called "strictly Maggie's crowning glory"), got stringy with the heat and with her emotion and looked, she knew, exactly like a dying dandelion. What a wallflower! The more she drank, the more trembly she got, and she was obliged to refuse several courses at lunch because she could not possibly have handled the serving spoons; she fancied that the butler divined her difficulty and despised her, and she wished that she could say in withering French that where she came from horsewhips were still widely used on uppity servants.

Lunch, which was long, was served at a semicircular table on the veranda, so that the party had a view of the pool and the avenues of lime trees that flanked it. They started with cold sorrel soup and went on to salmon in mayonnaise and capers, to a capon stuffed with truffles and the bottoms of artichokes; they had asparagus; they had salad; they had melon; they had Brie. They toasted the birthday girl in sweet wine, dry wine, champagne; with their coffee, they drank cassis. Everything, except for the coffee beans, had been grown at Magnamont. There were two subjects of conversation; one was the food they were eating and the other was the food they had eaten at other times at Magnamont. The nondescript man, who was sitting at Maggie's right, recalled, or failed to recall, past entrees, in mutters. Mme Floquet chided him for his mood with such intimate ill-humor that Maggie concluded they were related; the others ignored him much as they ignored Maggie. M. le Baron spoke to her once. In English, he said "Do you fly?," and when she said that she did, he grew cordial until, on further inquiry, he learned that she had often been a passenger on commercial airplanes, that she was not a pilot. He said, "Too bad. You might have enjoyed flying one of my gliders later on." At this hideous proposal, poor Maggie's butterfingers dropped the glass they were holding and wine went all over the priceless damask; the accident was Olympianly disregarded except by the butler, who scowled blackly. The Baron turned to Mrs. Preston and asked her to recollect the menu he and she had planned together for the christening party of his godson; it had included a roebuck shot in Bavaria.

After Mme Floquet had smoked a small cigar, the ladies retired into the house, to a boudoir that contained so many mirrors telling the unvarnished truth that Maggie seriously thought she might have a fit. To add to her concern about herself, the ladies discussed their hairdressers and their dressmakers and admired one another's shorts and cuffs and cuff links. Mme Floquet took a bath in the Lucullan chamber that adjoined this one; Mrs. Preston lay down on a chaise with belladonna packs on her eyes; the Contessa removed her maquillage and put on fresh—she was as deft and as thorough as a topflight surgeon. Maggie—poor kid, she thought of herself—applied new lipstick, realizing that it was the wrong color for her scarecrow duds, and ran a comb through her hopeless hair, and observed through tears that her nail polish was chipping squalidly, and then she sat down as far from the others as possible and looked at a copy of *Country Life,* although she had lost her eyesight as well as her power of speech. For a very long time indeed she glared blindly at a photograph entitled "May on the Westmorland fells," in whose foreground there were daffodils the size of umbrellas, sheep the size of buffaloes, and lambs as big as rams, and in whose background there was a Hop-o'-My-Thumb shepherd and a dog to match. She memorized, as she had once memorized the oath of allegiance, the following: "The fellside Herdwick strain is believed to have been introduced by the Norse settlers of a thousand years ago."

When they had completed the reclamation of their pre-lunch faces, had examined one another's jewels, and had finished off some scandal of a dangerous turn, they went outside again and climbed a flight of sturdy steps into a tree house in a massive oak that grew beside the pool. Maggie Meriwether tagged behind like a tug in the wake of an imperial armada. Here, in the tree house, they sat on brocaded poufs around a low, round table on which stood a narghile; they thought about smoking it but decided it was too much trouble. From time to time they glanced casually down at the men, who, in bathing trunks, were practicing tight-rope walking, perilously, along a rope strung across the pool. The rope was low, and a good thing it was, since none of them except the Baron had even a rudimentary skill at this extraordinary Sunday sport. (On seeing the ladies, he had called up that he had decided against the gliders today because the wind was wrong.) They fell into the water frequently and came up splotched with slime, looking as if they were wearing camouflage.

The narghile had led the ladies to a discussion of which narcotics they enjoyed the most, and for some time they vivaciously exchanged memories of their sensations. The Contessa had found her nirvana on the shores of Lago di Garda when she had combined smoking marijuana with drinking champagne and eating apricots. Mme Floquet used Demerol occasionally and achieved noteworthy effects; it tampered in the most bizarre way imaginable with her sense of time, so that she had once arrived for a cocktail party at six o'clock in the morning, thinking it was six in the afternoon, and found no one, of course, but a flabbergasted housemaid—people had dined out on that story for months. Mrs. Preston liked everything; if she had a slight preference, it was for chloral hydrate followed by vodka; whenever she gave herself one of these "Meeky Feens" she had a maid in waiting to remove all matches from her immediate environs, since she had an understandable horror of lighting a cigarette in her delicious coma and setting herself on fire.

All of a sudden the cat turned loose Maggie's tongue, and it behaved like a jack-in-the-box. It said, in English, "Have you-all ever tried snuff? You can lip it or dip it or sniff it. It's mighty good with sour mash and potato chips."

Luckily for her, the tightrope broke just then and there was a good-natured uproar from below, which caused the ladies in the tree house to clap their hands girlishly. The indeterminate man without a name had been halfway across it, and when he came spluttering up out of the water of the pool, he was wearing a hyacinth exactly on top of his head, like a calotte. Mme Floquet exclaimed, "What an oaf! What an ox!" Mrs. Preston said, "He is really a dog in every way," and the Contessa observed, "What bad manners he has to spoil Karl's tightrope." The stumblebum, shaking himself and clawing the flower off his head, wore a look of unspeakable boredom, and Maggie loved him, whoever he was. She even felt a little better off than he; at least she had not excited these recherché dragons to call her names. Who on earth could he be? He looked like a nearly penniless schoolmaster with dyspepsia and a tendency to catarrh, and Maggie resolved, if this day went on much longer, to make friends with him—in sign language, if necessary.

After the men had changed and a great many more people had arrived, from neighboring estates (some bicycled, some came on horseback, a duchess carrying a blue silk parasol arrived in a pony cart, and two beautiful princesses came on motor bikes), the guests returned to the house to sit down for tea around the largest dining table in the largest dining room Maggie had ever seen. A vast three-tiered turntable slowly and automatically revolved, offering a staggering profusion of pastries, fruits, cheese, sandwiches, candies, nuts, hors d'oeuvres; there were tea and coffee and lemonade and orangeade and vinous and spirituous liquors. There must have been twenty-five people at that regal table, and all of them were talking. Though the din was monolingual, it was that of Babel; the laughter was plentiful and it was French; the spoons made a French clatter in the saucers; the bell in the abbey rang *cinq heures;* the Dutch psychoanalyst from New York subjected the duchess, by whom he was impressed, to a Gallic scrutiny through his thick glasses; Tippy Akenside, flanked by the princesses, analyzed Proust.

Not by accident, Maggie found herself next to her shabby counterpart; she had made a beeline for the area in which he was hovering like a rain cloud, and when everyone sat down, she sat beside him. Nearby were her enemies from the tree house. The Contessa, who refused both food and drink, had added a Japanese fan to her costume and oscillated it before her face; it did not disturb a hair of her head. Mrs. Preston fed ravenously and drank deeply. Mme Floquet ate enough to keep a bird alive. And all the time they indulged or abstained, the three of them kept their eyes glued on Maggie's next-door neighbor as if they were waiting to catch him out in some egregious breach of etiquette. They talked of other matters, to be sure, but they plainly had their minds on this poor, dim stick; he appeared to be impervious to their dagger looks, but Maggie suspected that he was only putting up a front, and finally, summoning her courage, she asked him in English, with great compassion, if he had enjoyed the tightrope walking.

"Filthy waste of time," he said, giving her a quick look out of bleary eyes. "I say, are you an American?" Maggie took his accent to be Scotch. Suddenly he looked very Scotch, and she was much comforted, since her maternal grandmother had come from Aberdeen.

Although his question had required a simple yes or no for an answer, Maggie replied at an uncontrolled length, so happy was she to be reunited with her mother tongue, so grateful was she to have her existence acknowledged. She was afterward never able to explain satisfactorily to herself why she had bragged so feelingly about the medical school of Vanderbilt University or why she had delivered a short lecture on the survival of ballad-making among the mountain people in the Cumberland Plateau —nerves, she supposed, a logorrhea coming as the natural result of long privation. The watchful ladies gazed at her as if she were dancing a hula on the tabletop, and this further agitated her compulsive tongue. She talked and talked.

The man did not seem to be terribly interested, but neither did he look away. His tumescent lips were slack and mauve; his pink-rimmed eyes bespoke astigmatism and gin; his skin was dingy, as if he spent much of his time in dingy places—the public bars of railway stations, for example; his fingernails were square and very dirty; he had a huge wart under his left ear; his cheap jacket pinched him under the arms; his shirt was limp and the Kelly-green knit necktie he wore was a disgrace. He was the most unprepossessing of men. Fit company for Maggie in her present condition: Ladies, she implored them silently, please look away.

"I fancy the Civil War," he said when Maggie had finished her recital. And after he had made this surprising statement, not designating what aspect of the Civil War he fancied—whether its literature or its strategy, its ideology or its outcome—he went on to talk volubly about himself, as if, like her, he had discovered that his vocal cords were, after all, not totally paralyzed.

What Maggie learned dumfounded her.

First of all, he was a student at Harrow (she had thought him to be no less than thirty and probably closer to forty), but before Harrow he had flown in the war and had got his "ration of Jerrys." Evidently he had fancied this war, too—had found "mucking up their damned munitions plants not half-bad fun," and had had some "damned good whing-dings with your Commando chaps." He asked her if she knew a damned good cove from Montreal named Agnew MacPherson—they had kicked up one hell of a shindy together in Oxford once, when they were both on leave. Schooling was a bloody bore and he would far rather spend all his time, and not just his hols, in Africa; he made a vague joke about the sport of kings being that of hunting down the king of beasts instead of those tuppenny-ha'penny grouse on the Scottish moors. Give him a safari and then another safari and after that one more safari and then give him a fortnight in Algiers in which to get as drunk as a fiddler and pub-crawl in the Casbah. What could be the possible use of all this damned footling Greek and algebra? The only bearable part of school was going up to town —he had a highly modified Bentley and it was fairly good fun to give the peasants on the road a run for their money. But London was bloody sad; the bottle clubs were mostly a bloody bore and closed too damned early. The floor shows were bloody awful and there were all those damned orchids around.

Orchids were this man's subject. He might be a student of the Civil War, he might be fulfilled by hunting big game, he might like racing cars, he might have all sorts of deep-felt predilections. But what inspired him to oratory was his rabid aversion to orchids, and as he was delivering his vehement tirade against them, he paused once to point his spoon at Mme Floquet as if he were going to shoot her.

"They're not so bad growing in Africa; but they're not my cup of tea even there," he said. "Anyhow, I'm a fauna man, not a flora man—give me a tiger sooner than a tiger lily." He seemed gloomily addicted to this kind of play on words. "And when you have to pay a quid for the damned beastly things for a girl to wear on her dress, it's too thick. They're not worth a bob, let alone a quid. A quid! But do you know there are some women who want you to send them a dozen at once?"

"Serge!" remonstrated Mme Floquet sharply, and tried to sting him with a look.

But his violence had by no means spent itself and he continued, his gray skin taking on an ominous mottle. "I *hate* women who want you to send them orchids," he declared, and savagely devoured the last of his napoleon. "I hate them the most, but I also hate women who drink cold tea in the middle of the night."

"Don't be such an ass, Serge," said the Contessa Giovennazzo calmly. "You'll make yourself ill." She was not as insouciant as she wanted to be thought; Maggie, fascinated, saw that her hand trembled as she fitted a cigarette into a gold holder, and that with one brilliant eye she demolished Serge while with the other she did Mme Floquet in.

"Same to you with nobs on," said Serge, whose face now looked like a garish batik. A vein stood out, thumping, on his temple. Everyone, except a very hungry and very old man, who was interested only in his food, looked at him; all conversation ceased. As if he had been waiting for this, Serge now stood up, arms akimbo. He said, "And I hate women who gorge themselves on fish."

Mrs. Preston, whose plate was littered with the heads and tails of sardines and the rejected portions of eel, touched her low, Slavic forehead with her fingertips; Maggie had failed to notice before that her nails were painted gold.

M. le Baron, directly across the table from Serge, also rose, and faced his guest with a smile of the utmost tolerance and affection. The genial host, the perfect host of this mad tea party, he said, "I wish to propose a toast." A mob of minions materialized to fill glasses with champagne.

"To Serge," said M. le Baron sonorously. "Our beloved prince among princes."

Tippy Akenside uttered his first words of English. He said, "Hear! Hear!" The company drank and cheered, and Serge let his arms fall to his sides; he paled, and his three ladies beamed at him.

"To Sunday at Magnamont!" cried Heer Dokter van Lennep. The exuberant chorus was deafening.

There were further toasts: to Tanya Preston, because of her birthday; to the duchess, because of a fabulous race horse she had just bought; to the doctor, because he had once insulted Jung; to M. le Baron, and to his mother, his uncle, his table, his cellar, his roses; to Mme Floquet, a love; to the Contessa, a beauty; to the princesses and the princesses' fiancés. Throughout this, Serge stood at Maggie's side like a bump on a log except that he was weeping.

Abruptly, it was all over, and Maggie, having no idea how she had accomplished it, found herself beside Tippy Akenside in his car. One of the straps of her slip was hanging halfway down her arm and it terminated in a small gold safety pin. She did not look back and she did not look at her companion. Exhausted, she wondered how on earth the young set of Nashville could have imagined they were lively and original.

Tippy was laughing hard. "Just as well you don't work for the Marshall Plan people, what?" he said.

"It most certainly is," said Maggie, prim inside despite her outward dishevelment. "Who was that man?"

"Serge? Poor Serge. Simply a balmy Georgian prince, only the difference between him and most of them is that he has pots of money. Everyone wants to marry him and *he* wants to marry the Duchess of Kent."

"He must be thirty-five—and still at Harrow!"

"He's thirty-three," said Tippy. "He was held back by the war, and then he went crackers after it and was in the bin for years—harmless but completely ga-ga. How did you like the orchids speech?"

"Oh, it was grand," said Maggie.

Tippy could hardly drive for laughing. "I've heard him give philippics on everything. You should hear him do bubble-and-squeak."

"I liked him," said Maggie.

"Of course you liked him," said Tippy. "Everyone's mad for mad old Serge."

"I liked him because he spoke English to me," said Maggie. Now that she was safely away from those international clothes-horses and had only to contend with a rather puny Englishman whose cuffs, she observed with pleasure, were none too clean, she allowed her dander to get up. "I think you are a stinker."

"Good Lord! Didn't you like it?"

"Drive fast," commanded Miss Meriwether. "Be as competent as you can but drive fast."

"I *am* sorry, Maggie," he said, and he sounded it. "I thought you were having a good time. And you weren't?"

All the way back to Paris, she cried with her face in her hands. "They treated me like an I don't know what," she blubbered, "except for the nutty prince."

"*Noblesse oblige*," said Tippy, with a nervous laugh, and,

realizing that he had put his foot in his mouth, nearly came a cropper with a poultry van.

She bade him goodbye, not *au revoir*, at the door of her hotel.

This appalling day, unlike so many appalling days, had a happy ending. There was a huge bouquet of sumptuous summer flowers in Maggie's room, and under the vase was a *pneumatique* from Roger Carrithers, who was the older brother of Maggie's roommate at Sweet Briar; it asked her to dine that night with him and friends. She leaped to the telephone, which heretofore she had avoided like an instrument of darkness, and in rapid, rebellious French got through to the Meurice and then to Roger's kind Tidewater voice.

The group of six who had dinner together that night were all Americans, and they loved Maggie's story, requiring her to repeat parts of it over again, denying that she had looked the ragamuffin she claimed ("Unthinkable," said Roger Carrithers, who had been brought up properly. "You put them in the shade and they were jealous"), and wholeheartedly sympathizing with her predicament.

Taking the cue from that eccentric Baron, they, too, had toasts. They toasted the tree house and the narghile, the tightrope and the hyacinth on top of Serge's head. And they toasted Maggie Meriwether, the most sophisticated, the most cosmopolitan, the prettiest raconteur of middle Tennessee.

The Children's Game

The wide hanging lamps with beaded fringe and shades of ecru silk cast an unwholesome, joyless light on the watchful countenances of the croupiers and the gamblers at the tables of roulette and *chemin de fer*. Smoke, in this lackluster, was green, not blue, as if it partook of the color of the felt on the tables and it hovered, a sweet effluvium, over the heads that were bent to the study of wheels and cards.

Everyone in the warm, bland, airless room—the tall windows were closed and snuff-brown mohair draperies were drawn over them—looked chronically ill and engrossed with his symptoms. And while the symptoms might vary, the malady was the same in a young Chinese woman, as neat as a cat, who never raised her eyes from a notebook in which she was keeping a system of probabilities; in an aging, florid German whose face was as scarred as the moon, and who wore his monocle like a reprimand; in a cool, queenly Scandinavian whose coronet of golden braids was intertwined with pearls. The common denominator for all of these—and for the rajah in a diapered turban and the two Scots in kilts, for the burghers from Brussels and the wattled old dowagers frothing with native lace and paved with diamonds from Antwerp—was that of the invalid concentrating on the tides of his pain, a look necessarily unsociable.

Indeed, such was the air of apprehension and constraint that the casino could have been a hospital ward save that the uniform was dinner dress, not *déshabillé*. Over the whole Saturday-night throng—five hundred or more, so that the players stood six deep—there was a hush of desperate tension; there was no laughter, there was a little murmured conversation, and except for this, there were only the sounds of the croupiers' muted exclamation,

"Messieurs, mesdames, faites vos jeux!" and the spinning of the wheels, and the croupiers' further admonition, *"Rien ne va plus,"* and a communal sigh as the balls fell into their final, fateful compartments.

Abby Reynolds had left her escort, Hugh Nicholson, playing at the table nearest the bar. Conscientious cicerone that he was, he had offered to wander about with her, but she had replied that she wanted to observe this phenomenon without a guide, and he had not protested, but had at once addressed himself to the wheel. Abby's preconception of gambling derived from scenes in movies, and as she moved from table to table, endeavoring to understand the games, she realized that either her memory was at fault or Hollywood had carelessly added an apocryphal glitter and subtracted an essential gloom. She had expected rich chandeliers, not these morose and fungoid lamps, and the carpet was not dense and darkly red, but was thin, and it bore upon its lugubrious puce background a vapid pattern of flaxen parallelograms.

Vaguely she had imagined balconies, beset with the branches of flowering trees, where, looking down to a moonlit sea littered with the yachts of millionaires, chic lovers confronted the tortures and the consolations of their love. She thought that in the movies there had been the poignant music of stringed instruments, bittersweet, oblique. The bar should have offered a sprightlier aspect: this one, not altogether clean, presided over by two phlegmatic Walloons, looked rather like something to be found in a railway terminal or on a Channel boat. She reflected that probably the gaming rooms of Monte Carlo (or those of cosmopolitan South American cities) had been the ones that she had seen on the screen and that the beatifying lights and airs and blossoms of the Mediterranean (or of the Atlantic in its Southern countenance) had caused her to misconstrue. Here, in Belgium, in Knokke-le-Zoute, the casino perhaps had borrowed its somber look from the dun North Sea, where the skies were low and heavy and the melancholy dunes were gray.

Nor was the clientele what she had anticipated; their tragedy—or their headlong, suicidal folly—if it existed, was masked by that look of malaise, by that look of removal, of being, somehow, behind clouded glass. There was contagion in the atmosphere, and after an hour's roaming, Abby began to feel edgy and glum, although when she had first entered the room she had been exuberant. She and Hugh Nicholson had won handsomely at the races at Ostend that afternoon and had congratulated themselves at length with champagne, and at the height of their gaiety they had decided to hire a car to drive on here. Now the glow of the champagne had been usurped by a headache and Abby's eyes stung with the smoke and the languid light and all her elation had withered away in the silence of this dedicated and unhappy horde and under the practiced, appraising eyes of the croupiers and the officials on their high chairs who could accurately read the physiognomies of knaves and addicts and tenderfeet. Not only did these men stare and classify; so did the players, implacably hostile as if they resented being caught out at their secret vice which they could indulge only in the most public way.

An ancient woman with a cockled, whiskery face, dressed in purple crepe and wearing a purple toque, gazed long at Abby through a jewel-encrusted lorgnette, and Abby, challenged, gazed back, but stage fright overtook her and she lost the battle and moved on to another table where she was once again stared out of countenance by another beldam whose boa of monkey fur was the same texture and color as her poorly dyed hair. Both pairs of eyes had reviled her, had plainly said, "Tripper! Spectator! Who are you to sit in judgment?" And she felt as she did when someone jostled her in a crowd and then gratuitously scolded her for being in the way.

Suddenly, feeling lost, she was assailed by a wild wind of homesickness and she went into the bar, almost weeping, where she ordered a glass of lemonade.

For nearly a year, ever since her husband's death, Abby Reynolds had lived in Europe, moving from a Florentine *pensione* for bereft or virginal gentlewomen to the same kind of asylum in Rome; she had dwelt in rooms in the flats of respectable elderly couples in Vienna and Munich, and she had lived in a borrowed apartment in Paris with a borrowed maid and a borrowed black cat. Although she was only in her early forties, she had begun to feel quaint and wan. She felt that she had become indistinguishable from the thousands and thousands of lonesome American ladies who lived abroad because a foreign address, however modest, had a cachet that a New York or a Boston apartment hotel had not; the cachet was necessary so that they would not be pitied, and their daughters and nephews, their sisters and friends said of them, "Isn't it peppy of So-and-So to go gallivanting off by herself?" Sometimes their excuse for living abroad was that they did not want to interfere in the lives of their married children and for the children of these children they shopped until they were faint and went through horrifying ordeals with the international mails.

Thus, Abby had come to belong to that group who have spent their lives leaning on someone—or being leaned on by—a father, a mother, a husband; and who, when the casket is closed or the divorce decree is final, find that they are waifs. They hide their humiliating condition—for they tend to look on loneliness as inadmissible and a little disgraceful, they tend to regard themselves as wallflowers—by playing bridge on the breezy piazzas of seaside hotels, and writing multitudinous letters, and going to lectures on the excavations of mounds and ruins in Jericho, and applying themselves with assiduity and dismay to the language of the country in which, at the moment, they find themselves.

For years Abby and her husband, whenever they traveled abroad, had seen and grieved for these forlorn, brave orphans, and Abby knew that John would be appalled to see that she had joined their ranks. She did not really know how it had happened; she was by nature gregarious, sanguine and resilient; but she had been so stricken by John's terribly surprising death that she had moved like a sleepwalker and had taken the easiest course. And despite the pleas of her relatives and friends, despite her own judgment, she had rented her apartment in New York and had withdrawn to Europe, following the pattern of cousins and aunts (sometimes, traveling in pairs, they had taken courses at the Sorbonne) and of her own mother, who had faded away on a balcony in Rome as she was painting a water-color of the Spanish Steps.

One warm melodious evening about a month before, when Abby was still in Paris, her inertia had been replaced by an abrupt restiveness, brought on by the sounds of amorous laughter and fragments of song that were borne, together with flowery smells, on the mild wind through her windows, open to a garden. She was playing Canfield—that old-lady game, that game for septuagenarians to whom dusk is the sympathetic time of day—and as she played, the black cat watched her from where he sat on an ottoman beside her so that he had a clear view of the cards. Scornful, chic and French, hugely self-respecting, the cat embarrassed her and made her feel badly dressed and out of place and timid. She really was badly dressed, and she had no need to be since she had flair and enough money, but along with sad looks, she had put on sad clothes; and she really was out of place, and found that she longed to be in her own apartment on the East River.

When the game was finished—she did not win—and she looked up, the black French cat yawned as if the tedium of her sentimental brown study had been unbearable. Unmoved by her predicament, he washed behind his ears. She was aware at last that she despised the flaccid life she was living and that she wanted to be back in the thick of things, among her innumerable energetic friends, in the familiar and surprising streets of New York; she wanted to give and go to parties; she wanted to sit in a box at the Metropolitan and never again go to La Scala alone; she wanted to be back at Bellevue as a volunteer, counting sponges in the operating rooms and, extravagant now, she told herself that she would rather smell ether than all these dense Parisian flowers. To the cat, defiantly, as if he had contradicted her, she said aloud, "I will go home. I shall simply book passage and I'll do it tomorrow."

The following morning, early, she went to a travel agent and took the first passage she could get, two weeks hence, and now, reborn, impatient to be off, the two weeks of waiting that stretched before her seemed an affront. How on earth would she live through them, being eyed by that uncharitable cat? But providence had taken up Abby's cause and the afternoon's post brought her an agreeable reason to leave Paris and leave the cat in the custody of the maid. There was a letter from Hugh Nicholson, a man she had known for many years and had seen from time to time in the course of her recent traveling. He was a Canadian who had lived most of his life in London and he was associated at various times and in various ways with films. He had written and he had directed and he had occasionally acted. When his fortunes rose, he dressed like a peer and lived at Albany in Regency splendor; and when they descended, he moved into obscure bed-and-breakfast establishments and sang for his supper and for weekends in the country.

There was a wife, estranged, who lived in the north of England and bred Kerry blues, and there were two sons at school whom each summer he took to Scotland for a fortnight of bicycling. Abby and John had never met the wife, and Hugh never spoke of her. Once there had reached their ears some nebulous rumor of a scandal, but their affection for Hugh had safeguarded them against investigating its nature or its truth.

They had met him first in New York during one of his prosperous seasons and had been attracted by his warmth and his ebullient appreciation of America, the novelty of which, throughout succeeding visits, never wore off for him. They had seen him, as well, in London both when he was affluent and when he was poor. When he was on his uppers and his shirts did not look fresh, he was understandably less good fun, but he was never pitiable and he was endlessly optimistic: around any corner at any moment, he might stub his toe on the pot of gold at the end of the rainbow.

Hugh's wonderfully opportune letter this morning invited Abby to be his vis-à-vis at a house party in Sussex. The house, he wrote, was enormous and full of history and ghosts, and the gardens had everything Americans expected English gardens to have—"pleasances, ha-has and gazebos and spinneys." The hostess went in for séances, claiming to converse with the shades of Norman ancestors and with Titus Oates.

Abby, charmed with the invitation, did not deliberate for a moment, but at once wrote back to accept. And then, in a burst of euphoria, she went shopping and bought presents and dresses and some superb hats and some marvelous shoes. She packed and two days later left Paris in its August lull and went to London, where, except for the week in Sussex, she meant to stay until she sailed for home.

So she had spent that week in the sweet, misty English country in a house crowded with treasures and white elephants and dogs, and surrounded by gardens and parks and copses of larches where nightingales sang and she began to redeem her spirit, that had so long been mislaid. Hugh had just finished directing a film that was bound to be a smashing success and he was, in consequence, at the top of his form. He and Abby enjoyed each other enormously; they shone at croquet on the luminous lawns and they shone at darts in the murk of pubs, they found that they were perfectly matched at the bridge table, and Hugh surprised and impressed Abby with his bucolic knowledge of mushrooms and sheep. Lady Caroline was a delight; eloquently attired, looking like a Romney, she rode sidesaddle on a gray cob and at every meal she was served a small onion on a Sèvres plate, which she peeled and sliced to eat with apples or muffins or cheese.

Now and then, when they were walking through a meadow or through a tunnel of dark trees on a back lane, Abby and Hugh spoke nostalgically of gala times they had had when John was alive, and one afternoon, as they were drinking bitter in an empty pub, in the midst of a reminiscence that touched her particularly, Abby realized that it was the removal from her life of John's energy that had enervated her, and energy was what she admired and, moreover, required as dearly as food and drink and air. She could burn, that is, with her own flame, but she must be rekindled; she must be complemented so that she could maintain her poise and pride. She was not the sort of woman who could live alone satisfactorily.

She raised her eyes from the dark ale and looked at Hugh, who was looking at her with a questioning and a solicitous expression. The pub had begun to fill and they talked lightly of other matters. But that night when the last rubber of bridge was over and Lady Caroline, with a sigh, had given up trying to get through to her spooks and everyone prepared to go to bed, Hugh asked Abby to go out with him for a breath of air. "Watch out for bats," said Lady Caroline; "they teem in Leo, I can't think why."

There were no bats, but the romantic air quivered with fireflies and smelled of roses, and far away a bewitched owl warned. Beneath a pergola where the purple grapes were ripe, Hugh kissed her and Abby felt as young and tremulous as a schoolgirl.

But she was not demanding and she was not headlong and she counseled herself to look on this tenuous, auroral experience as one that would last only so long as she remained in England, a handful of days before the boat took her home. Like the cat in Paris whose contempt for her negative life had urged her to repudiate it for a positive one, so Hugh was the agent that reminded her that she must seek a husband. His kiss was no more than a symbol, for Hugh was no more than a friend.

When the house party was over, Hugh and Abby were reluctant to quit their fun and games and so, with the abandon of leisured youth, they did not drive back to London, but they went instead to Folkestone and took the Channel boat to Ostend; there were two French fillies running there that Hugh wanted to see.

For three days, in that dowdy harbor, alternately sun-baked and sodden with rain, they went to race meetings at the Hippodrome and rode in hansoms along the *digue* and ate cockles and mussels on the quays as they contemplated the bright shrimpers and the fishwives' bright sunshades and the children's bright balloons that sometimes escaped and went to sea, bobbing along in the wakes of boats.

The kiss in the garden had not been repeated, but their concord had deepened and their joy in each other's society had been so accelerated that Abby lived in a state of heady exultation. She was, indeed, so happy that there came moments when she regretted that the time was running out and she must leave.

And now here they were in this brown and sullen den of dismal, dogged greed, and Abby, drinking warm, sweet lemonade, could not remember any of the fun at all. The whole fabric of the heyday had been riddled and stained and frayed within less than two hours' time. She tried sensibly to attribute her desolation to her headache, tried to think that she was coming down with flu. But her uneasiness was more than physical, and she was frightened by some alien distemper that she could not understand. Why on earth had they come here instead of going, as she had wanted to do, to Bruges?

Repelled by the lemonade, she returned to the gaming room and paused, irresolute, beside a table near the cashier's room. One of the croupiers, a youngish man with a mouth like a knife and eyes like awls, stared at her across the table as he was raking in the profits for the house, and there was in his regard such cynicism that Abby felt contaminated, besmirched with venality, and she fled, looking for Hugh in the hope that he had played enough and that they could go to some cheerful bar and have a drink and recapture their earlier mood.

When she had threaded her way through the quiet jungle (but *this* quiet snarled), she found him just where she had left him, beside the croupier at the left of the wheel. She had the feeling that he had not moved at all except to lean forward through the thicket of people to place his bets. Though she stood so close to him that their arms touched, he was unaware of her and instinct warned her not to call attention to herself. He lost steadily and losing angered him, as she could tell by the flush of his face and the set of his mouth.

Observing him and observing the other players, she began to take in the deadly seriousness of their business here; this was no game, but was a combat in which the enemy was the wheel, as capricious as a windmill.

This kind of betting, she saw, was *sui generis;* in bridge, there were partners, there was an interplay of memory and judgment and intuition; in horse betting there were any number of elements to make up the equations and the permutations, just as there were in playing the stock market. But she could not think of any other kind of gambling—or any addiction—that hadn't a social or at least an organic side to it. In roulette, intelligence was no weapon against the solitary element of random chance. As she thus analyzed, in another part of her mind she recognized a paradoxical circumstance: although Hugh was so remote that he might have been only an apparitional representation of the man she knew, she believed that she had fallen in love with him and, in love, that she was jealous. But of whom?

Rashly she took him by the arm and he wheeled with a mutter of exasperation and then, seeing her, smiled with an effort. It was apparent that he did not want to leave, that he wanted to be here and not with her; and when she said she had a headache and wanted to go back to the hotel, said he need not go with her since it was not far and the beach was well lit, he, usually so well-mannered, agreed too readily, with too perfunctory an apology, and told her good night and turned back to the table.

Abby's room, overlooking the sea and receiving the sea winds and therefore airborne sand, was papered with something nondescript, nubby and bilious, and the linoleum had been designed in the same mean-minded way. There was a varnished wardrobe, too short and shallow to hang clothes in, a wicker table with a crippled leg and a scuffed brown blotting pad and a rusty pen. The bed, with its tumid featherbed and its log of a bolster, was low, although its topography was mountainous. She tossed from peak to valley, invaded by the sound of the sea and distant foghorns and the voices of Flemish revelers and excited dogs loitering on the beach. It was not only the bed and the noises—someone in the next room intermittently snored violently and upstairs a baby howled about a pin or a pain—that kept her awake. It was Hugh's mood and her own perverseness that had caused her to fall in love with him at the very moment she saw that a future for them was plainly impossible, for she knew that the remoteness she had seen tonight was, though sporadic, constitutional, and looking back she remembered that often he had seemed suddenly to disappear, although his flesh remained, in the middle of a conversation, in the middle of a dance.

At last she gave up trying to sleep, turned on the lamp, no brighter than a flashlight, and went to the windows to look out at the sea and the *plage* where the tall cabañas stood as thick as gravestones; the air was damp and still and the moon was hidden and then revealed by dire, swift clouds. One by one the dogs and people left the beach. In the windowsill, on a couch of sand, there were two tiny starfish, left behind, Abby supposed, by some forgetful collector of relics and souvenirs. In the poor light, she studied their fastidious shape and thinking of all the beguilements of the world, starfish and the English countryside and Lady Caroline's idiosyncratic clothes, she recovered from her disaffection and saw that she had been absurd to be upset by Hugh's behavior. At peace with him and with herself again, she allowed sleepiness to overtake her and she left the windows and shut her eyes against the ominous clouds that beset the moon and just before she went to sleep she wished on a non-existent star that Hugh would want her to postpone her voyage home.

On the next day, he was very much with her. Belabored by a cold and sandy wind, they explored the town with the same conjugation of reaction that had made their Roman holiday a supreme contentment. It was a monstrous town. It possessed houses that looked like buses threatening to run them down and houses that looked like faces with bulbous noses and brutish eyes. They wandered, amazed, through street after street of these teratoid villas and they concluded that the architecture of Knokke-le-Zoute was unique and far more disrespectful to the eye than that of any other maritime settlement they had ever seen, worse, by far, than Brighton or Atlantic City. The principal building material seemed to be cobblestones, but they discovered a number of houses that appeared to be made of cast iron. In gardens there were topiary trees in the shape of Morris chairs and some that seemed to represent washing machines. The hotels along the sea were bedizened with every whimsy on earth, with derby-shaped domes and kidney-shaped balconies, with crenellations that looked like vertebrae and machiolations that looked like teeth, with turrets, bow-windows, dormers and gables, with fenestrations hemstitched in brick or bordered with granite point lace. Some of the chimneys were like church steeples and some were like Happy Hooligan's hat. The cabañas, in the hot, dark haze, appeared to be public telephone booths. Even the flowers dissembled and the hydrangeas looked like utensils that belonged in the kitchen and the geraniums looked like comestibles, not altogether savory. The plazas were treeless plains of concrete where big babies sunned and schipperkes patrolled. The kiosks were the size of round-houses; the trolleys, manned by garrulous grouches, made a deafening hullabaloo that was augmented by pneumatic drills which, inexplicably, were drilling in the sand. There was an enormous smell of fish.

They stopped for tea at a pavilion on the beach where the stinging wind was so strong that, as Abby was pouring, a gale redirected the scalding stream and it gushed painfully over Hugh's hand. If the accident had not been so grotesque, he might have felt it more and Abby might have been more compassionate. As it was, they laughed helplessly and Hugh said, "Oh, don't go back to America. This is too much fun."

A sourceless sorrow overcame her and she said nothing. For a while, then, they were silent. The bathers, emerging from their cabañas like troglodytes from caves, furled their umbrellas, collected their hampers and began to leave. The babies were wheeled home, convoyed by little schipperkes. No landscape could have been less pastoral, and Abby was cold and there was sand in her shoes and her ambiguous feeling of love was like sand in her mouth.

"It's too late to get the Channel boat now," Hugh said at length. "Can you endure another night here or should we go back to Ostend?"

She was too listless to care and she said, "Why did we come here in the first place?"

"I got a sudden hankering for roulette, as I do periodically," he said and then, musing, detached, he told her his gambling history.

When he was a student at Cambridge, he had sometimes gone to Monte Carlo; but he had played only casually until twelve years ago when, being in much need of rest and sun after arduous months of making a historical film, he had gone without his wife to the south of France for a long holiday. He had got no rest and he had got no sun because, during that time, he had become altogether obsessed with roulette. At first he had won and had lost equally and, whether he was victorious or was undone, he was obliged to prove himself again and again, to demonstrate that fate could neither coddle nor outwit him.

He said that he had felt like one of those white rats that don't know whether they are going to get the shock of their life or a piece of cheese. In the end he was wiped out altogether; in one night he was reduced to absolute penury and he had to pawn his watch for his fare home. His marriage at its best had been thin and wavering, and when he had got back from France that time and he had told his wife that all his money was gone, they had had their final row and she had left in a glacial rage. It was not only the grievous loss of money, though; it was, he said, "the unfaithfulness to reality."

"Eventually the only need you have in the world is the need to win. You don't need food or drink or sleep or sex—gamblers don't sleep with their wives after they've been gambling, they sleep with numbers."

For some years now he had not gone to Monte Carlo, but had come here because the very grubbiness of the place seemed to him appropriate. "My masochism is extensive," he said, "and I brought you here—you asked me why I did—because I love you and I want to marry you and I know I can't, we can't. But I wanted you to understand."

"I don't understand," she said, close to tears.

"Try it tonight," he said. "I don't mean to proselytize you. I just want you to see what it's like. Do play for an hour or so, just as a clinician."

She could not decide whether he was the cruelest man she had ever known—how cynical, how basely frivolous to state a love in terms of its impossibility—or the most pathetic; but she concluded that she did want to understand him in order more easily to accept the futility of their situation, and so she said that she would play.

It was Sunday and the gaming-room was less crowded than it had been the night before, so that Hugh was able to find a chair for Abby. She sat, shy and self-conscious, beside a croupier at the end of the table, placing her bets where Hugh indicated. At first, confused by the board, she was inattentive and covertly she studied the other players who overtly studied her. They were the same as the ones last night—those hard-faced witches with their beaded bags; those prosperous, stern-visaged merchants with their big cigars and signet rings; those thin men with mustaches whose dinner jackets were well cut but whose cuffs were worn. The Chinese woman was in the same place she had been the night before, still jotting down figures in her notebook; the rajah, in an even more splendid turban, was betting heavily and, when he lost, he was shaken with sighs. There was again that restive silence.

Presently Abby grasped the mechanics of the game and began to situate her counters for herself. Her interest was at last aroused and when, three times in succession, she won, she felt an extraordinary elation and wanted to cry out in triumph, but any display of emotion here would be *outré* and she allowed her face to demonstrate nothing, although she knew her cheeks were pink.

At some point she realized that Hugh was no longer standing behind her, and at another point she was emboldened to pick up a *râteau* that some bankrupt player had relinquished, and with it she arranged her chips and drew in her winnings, afire with defiance; against what, she was not sure. She had beginner's luck and presently she dared to play for the highest stakes; twice she played *en plein,* and won thirty-five to one; it seemed to her, though she was not certain, that the croupier gave her a faint, congratulatory smile, the smile of a veteran to a lucky greenhorn.

Abby was tired, but nonetheless she was animated and she wished this tonic tension could go on forever; the wheel became her quixotic lover, now scornfully rejecting her and now lavishly rewarding her; it became, as well, her ambition, and while she splurged and then economized, rejoiced or lamented, she knew what Hugh had tried to tell her. The faces that had frightened her receded in the miasma of green smoke; the warmth of the room was oppressive, but she did not care; her mouth was parched, but she was too preoccupied to consider how she might slake her thirst. Eventually, as it grew near closing time, the crowd began to thin; the tables of *chemin de fer* were closed and one by one the roulette croupiers collected their gear and disappeared. At last the table where Abby was playing was the only one open and it was with genuine frenzy that she saw her game was nearly over.

She was still ahead when the wheel was spun for the last time; and when everything was finished she was giddy as she struggled out of her cocoonlike trance. The croupiers' fatigue humanized them; they rubbed their eyes and stretched their legs and their agile hands went limp. Abby was a little dashed and melancholy, let down and drained; she was, even though she had won, inconsolable because now the table, stripped of its seductions, was only a table. And the croupiers were only exhausted workingmen going home to bed.

For a long while Abby and Hugh sat on the veranda of the hotel, silent and unmoving, staring at the sea and the overpopulation of the cabañas on the beach. The moon shone palely through the heavy haze; there was no horizon and a slow ship passing by looked like a smudge on a wall.

"Well, you saw what it was like," said Hugh.

"Yes," she said and, reluctant to discuss her sensations which on reflection seemed squalid, she asked him to arrange for a car to take her to Ostend and the Channel boat. There was no mention of what Hugh was going to do or where he was going. Abby had an image of him here, going back night after night to that joyless brown room.

"Would you like me to go along to Ostend with you?" he asked.

"No," she said and, mustering all the gaiety she could, she said, "I think it's vastly more memorable to say goodbye in Knokke-le-Zoute. Besides, partings at boats make me sad. Knokke-le-Zoute—it sounds like a children's game."

They rose and in the ugly, awful dawn Hugh kissed her goodbye; kissed her in the good friend's way, and he said, "I wish it hadn't been a children's game."

She would not have given up so easily; she would have died hard; would, out of vanity and love, said that she could, somehow, save him; she would have staked everything on him if she had not so fully understood him. Sensibly, to comfort herself, she thought of how lovely it would be to see the clean September light on the East River. She told herself that, happy as the interlude had been up until last night, it had been an aberration and that she belonged where she had originated; in alien corn, it was imprudent to run risks. Guiltily, because she was fortunate and he was not, she was now anxious to be away from the spectacle of him. "Goodbye, Hugh; goodbye, I must go and pack," she said.

He was a shadow no more palpable than the phantom ships on the dim North Sea, and his voice, when he echoed her, came from an incommensurable distance.

The Echo and the Nemesis

Sue Ledbetter and Ramona Dunn became friends through the commonplace accident of their sitting side by side in a philosophy lecture three afternoons a week. There were many other American students at Heidelberg University that winter—the last before the war—but neither Sue nor Ramona had taken up with them. Ramona had not because she scorned them; in her opinion, they were Philistines, concerned only with drinking beer, singing German songs, and making spectacles of themselves on their bicycles and in their little rented cars. And Sue had not because she was self-conscious and introverted and did not make friends easily. In Ramona's presence, she pretended to deplore her compatriots' escapades, which actually she envied desperately. Sometimes on Saturday nights she lay on her bed unable to read or daydream and in an agony of frustration as she listened to her fellow-lodgers at the Pension Kirchenheim laughing and teasing and sometimes bursting into song as they played bridge and Monopoly in the cozy veranda café downstairs.

Soon after the semester opened in October, the two girls fell into the habit of drinking their afternoon coffee together on the days they met in class. Neither of them especially enjoyed the other's company, but in their different ways they were lonely, and as Ramona once remarked, in her highfalutin way, "From time to time, I need a rest from the exercitation of my intellect." She was very vain of her intellect, which she had directed to the study of philology, to the exclusion of almost everything else in the world. Sue, while she had always taken her work seriously, longed also for beaux and parties, and conversation about them, and she was often bored by Ramona's talk, obscurely gossipy, of the vagaries of certain Old High Franconian verbs when they encountered the

High German consonant shift, or of the variant readings of passages in Layamon's *Brut,* or the linguistic influence Eleanor of Aquitaine had exerted on the English court. But because she was well-mannered she listened politely and even appeared to follow Ramona's exuberant elucidation of Sanskrit "a"-stem declensions and her ardent plan to write a monograph on the word "ahoy." They drank their coffee in the Konditorei Luitpold, a very noisy café on a street bent like an elbow, down behind the cathedral. The din of its two small rooms was aggravated by the peripheral racket that came from the kitchen and from the outer shop, where the cakes were kept. The waiters, all of whom looked cross, hustled about at a great rate, slamming down trays and glasses and cups any which way before the many customers, who gabbled and rattled newspapers and pounded on the table for more of something. Over all the to-do was the blare of the radio, with its dial set permanently at a station that played nothing but stormy choruses from *Wilhelm Tell.* Ramona, an invincible expositor, had to shout, but shout she did as she traced words like "rope" and "calf" through dozens of languages back to their Indo-Germanic source. Sometimes Sue, befuddled by the uproar, wanted by turns to laugh and to cry with disappointment, for this was not at all the way she had imagined that she would live in Europe. Half incredulously and half irritably, she would stare at Ramona as if in some way she were to blame.

Ramona Dunn was fat to the point of parody. Her obesity fitted her badly, like extra clothing put on in the wintertime, for her embedded bones were very small and she was very short, and she had a foolish gait, which, however, was swift, as if she were a mechanical doll whose engine raced. Her face was rather pretty, but its features were so small that it was all but lost in its billowing surroundings, and it was covered by a thin, fair skin that was subject to disfiguring affections, now hives, now eczema, now impetigo, and the whole was framed by fine, pale hair that was abused once a week by a *Friseur* who baked it with an iron into dozens of horrid little snails. She habitually wore a crimson tamo'-shanter with a sportive spray of artificial edelweiss pinned to the very top of it. For so determined a bluestocking, her eccentric and extensive wardrobe was a surprise; nothing was ever completely clean or completely whole, and nothing ever matched anything else, but it was apparent that all these odd and often ugly clothes had been expensive. She had a long, fur-lined cape, and men's tweed jackets with leather patches on the elbows, and flannel shirts designed for hunters in the state of Maine, and high-necked jerseys, and a waistcoat made of unborn gazelle, dyed Kelly green. She attended particularly to the dressing of her tiny hands and feet, and she had gloves and mittens of every color and every material, and innumerable pairs of extraordinary shoes, made for her by a Roman bootmaker. She always carried a pair of field glasses, in a brassbound leather, case that hung over her shoulder by a plaited strap of rawhide; she looked through the wrong end of them, liking, for some reason that she did not disclose, to diminish the world she surveyed. Wherever she went, she took a locked pigskin satchel, in which she carried her grammars and lexicons and the many drafts of the many articles she was writing in the hope that they would be published in learned journals. One day in the café, soon after the girls became acquainted, she opened up the satchel, and Sue was shocked at the helter-skelter arrangement of the papers, all mussed and frayed, and stained with coffee and ink. But, even more, she was dumfounded to see a clear-green all-day sucker stuck like a bookmark between the pages of a glossary to *Beowulf*.

Sue knew that Ramona was rich, and that for the last ten years her family had lived in Italy, and that before that they had lived in New York. But this was all she knew about her friend; she did not even know where she lived in Heidelberg. She believed that Ramona, in her boundless erudition, was truly consecrated to her studies and that she truly had no other desire than to impress the subscribers to *Speculum* and the *Publications of the Modern Language Association*. She was the sort of person who seemed, at twenty-one, to have fought all her battles and survived to enjoy the quiet of her unendangered ivory tower. She did not seem to mind at all that she was so absurd to look at, and Sue, who was afire with ambitions and sick with conflict, admired her arrogant self-possession.

The two girls had been going to the Konditorei Luitpold three times a week for a month or more, and all these meetings had been alike; Ramona had talked and Sue had contributed expressions of surprise (who would have dreamed that "bolster" and "poltroon" derived from the same parent?), or murmurs of acquiescence (she agreed there might be something in the discreet rumor that the Gothic language had been made up by nineteenth-century scholars to answer riddles that could not otherwise be solved), or laughter, when it seemed becoming. The meetings were neither rewarding nor entirely uninteresting to Sue, and she came to look upon them as a part of the week's schedule, like the philosophy lectures and the seminar in Schiller.

And then, one afternoon, just as the weary, mean-mouthed waiter set their cake down before them, the radio departed from its custom and over it came the "Minuet in G," so neat and winning and surprising that for a moment there was a general lull in the café, and even the misanthropic waiter paid the girls the honor, in his short-lived delight, of not slopping their coffee. As if they all shared the same memories that the little sentimental piece of music awoke in her, Sue glanced around smiling at her fellows and tried to believe that all of them—even the old men with Hindenburg mustaches and palsied wattles, and even the Brown Shirts fiercely playing chess—had been children like herself and had stumbled in buckled pumps through the simple steps of the minuet at the military command of a dancing teacher, Miss Conklin, who had bared her sinewy legs to the thigh. In some public presentation of Miss Conklin's class, Sue had worn a yellow bodice with a lacing of black velvet ribbon, a bouffant skirt of chintz covered all over with daffodils, and a cotton-batting wig that smelled of stale talcum powder. Even though her partner had been a sissy boy with nastily damp hands and white eyelashes, and though she had been grave with stage fright, she had had moments of most thrilling expectation, as if this were only the dress rehearsal of the grown-up ball to come.

If she had expected all the strangers in the café to be transported by the "Minuet" to a sweet and distant time, she had not expected Ramona Dunn to be, and she was astonished and oddly frightened to see the fat girl gazing with a sad, reflective smile into her water glass. When the music stopped and the familiar hullabaloo was reestablished in the room, Ramona said, "Oh, I don't know of anything that makes me more nostalgic than that tinny little tune! It makes me think of Valentine parties before my sister Martha died."

It took Sue a minute to rearrange her family portrait of the Dunns, which heretofore had included, besides Ramona, only a mother and a father and three brothers. Because this was by far the simplest way, she had seen them in her mind's eye as five stout, scholarly extensions of Ramona, grouped together against the background of Vesuvius. She had imagined that they spent their time examining papyri and writing Latin verses, and she regretted admitting sorrow into their lives, as she had to do when she saw Ramona's eyes grow vague and saw her, quite unlike her naturally greedy self, push her cake aside, untouched. For a moment or two, the fat girl was still and blank, as if she were waiting for a pain to go away, and then she poured the milk into her coffee, replaced her cake, and began to talk about her family, who, it seemed, were not in the least as Sue had pictured them.

Ramona said that she alone of them was fat and ill-favored, and the worst of it was that Martha, the most beautiful girl who ever lived, had been her twin. Sue could not imagine, she declared, how frightfully good-looking all the Dunns were—except herself, of course: tall and dark-eyed and oval-faced, and tanned from the hours they spent on their father's boat, the *San Filippo*. And they were terribly gay and venturesome; they were the despair of the croupiers at the tables on the Riviera, the envy of the skiers at San Bernardino and of the yachtsmen on the Mediterranean. Their balls and their musicales and their dinner parties were famous. All the brothers had unusual artistic gifts, and there was so much money in the family that they did not have to do anything but work for their own pleasure in their studios. They were forever involved in scandals with their mistresses, who were either married noblewomen or notorious dancing girls, and forever turning over a new leaf and getting themselves engaged to lovely, convent-bred princesses, whom, however, they did not marry; the young ladies were too submissively Catholic, or too stupid, or their taste in painting was vulgar.

Of all this charming, carefree brood, Martha, five years dead, had been the most splendid, Ramona said, a creature so slight and delicate that one wanted to put her under a glass bell to protect her. Painters were captivated by the elegant shape of her head, around which she wore her chestnut hair in a coronet, and there were a dozen portraits of her, and hundreds of drawings hanging in the big bedroom where she had died and which now had been made into a sort of shrine for her. If the Dunns were odd in any way, it was in this devotion to their dead darling; twice a year Mrs. Dunn changed the nibs in Martha's pens, and in one garden there grew nothing but anemones, Martha's favorite flower. She had ailed from birth, pursued malevolently by the disease that had melted her away to the wick finally when she was sixteen. The family had come to Italy in the beginning of her mortal languor in the hope that the warmth and novelty would revive her, and for a while it did, but the wasting poison continued to devour her slowly, and for years she lay, a touching invalid, on a balcony overlooking the Bay of Naples. She lay on a blond satin chaise longue, in a quaint peignoir made of leaf-green velvet, and sometimes, as she regarded her prospect of sloops and valiant skiffs on the turbulent waves, the cypress trees, white villas in the midst of olive groves, and the intransigent smoldering of Vesuvius, she sang old English airs and Irish songs as she accompanied herself on a lute. If, in the erratic course of her illness, she got a little stronger, she asked for extra cushions at her back and half sat up at a small easel to paint in water-colors, liking the volcano as a subject, trite as it was, and the comic tourist boats that romped over the bay from Naples to Capri. If she was very unwell, she simply lay smiling while her parents and her sister and her brothers attended her, trying to seduce her back to health with their futile offerings of plums and tangerines and gilt-stemmed glasses of Rhine wine and nosegays bought from the urchins who bargained on the carriage roads.

When Martha died, Ramona's own grief was despair, because the death of a twin is a foretaste of one's own death, and for months she had been harried with premonitions and prophetic dreams, and often she awoke to find that she had strayed from her bed, for what awful purpose she did not know, and was walking barefoot, like a pilgrim, down the pitch-black road. But the acute phase of her mourning had passed, and now, although sorrow was always with her, like an alter ego, she had got over the worst of it.

She paused in her narrative and unexpectedly laughed. "What a gloom I'm being!" she said, and resumed her monologue at once but in a lighter tone, this time to recount the drubbing her brother Justin had given someone when he was defending the honor of a dishonorable soprano, and to suggest, in tantalizing innuendoes, that her parents were not faithful to each other.

Sue, whose dead father had been an upright, pessimistic clergyman and whose mother had never given voice to an impure thought, was bewitched by every word Ramona said. It occurred to her once to wonder why Ramona so frowned upon the frolics of the other American students when her beloved relatives were so worldly, but then she realized that the manners of the *haut monde* were one thing and those of undergraduates another. How queer, Sue thought, must seem this freakish bookworm in the midst of it all! And yet such was the ease with which Ramona talked, so exquisitely placed were her fillips of French, so intimate and casual her allusions to the rich and celebrated figures of international society, that Ramona changed before Sue's eyes; from the envelope of fat emerged a personality as *spirituelle* and knowing as any practicing sophisticate's. When, in the course of describing a distiller from Milan who was probably her mother's lover, she broke off and pressingly issued Sue an invitation to go with her a month from then, at the Christmas holiday, to San Bernardino to meet her brothers for a fortnight of skiing, Sue accepted immediately, not stopping to think, in the heady pleasure of the moment, that the proposal was unduly sudden, considering the sketchy nature of their friendship. "My brothers will adore you," she said, giving Sue a look of calm appraisal. "They are eclectic and they'll find your red hair and brown eyes irresistibly naïve." As if the plan had long been in her mind, Ramona named the date they would leave Heidelberg; she begged permission, in the most gracious and the subtlest possible way, to let Sue be her guest, even to the extent of supplying her with ski equipment. When the details were settled—a little urgently, she made Sue promise "on her word of honor" that she would not default—she again took up her report on Signor da Gama, the distiller, who was related by blood to the Pope and had other distinctions of breeding as well to recommend him to her mother, who was, she confessed, something of a snob. "Mama," she said, accenting the ultima, "thinks it is unnecessary for anyone to be badly born."

The Konditorei Luitpold was frequented by teachers from the Translators' Institute, and usually Ramona rejoiced in listening to them chattering and expostulating, in half a dozen European languages, for she prided herself on her gift of tongues. But today her heart was in Sorrento, and she paid no attention to them, not even to two vociferous young Russians at a table nearby. She disposed of the roué from Milan (Sue had read Catullus? Signor da Gama had a cottage at Sirmio not far from his reputed grave) and seemed to be on the point of disclosing her father's delinquencies when she was checked by a new mood, which made her lower her head, flush, and, through a long moment of silence, study the greasy hoops the rancid milk had made on the surface of her coffee.

Sue felt as if she had inadvertently stumbled upon a scene of deepest privacy, which, if she were not careful, she would violate, and, pretending that she had not observed the hiatus at all, she asked, conversationally, the names of Ramona's brothers besides Justin.

The two others were called Daniel and Robert, but it was not of them, or of her parents, or of Martha, that Ramona now wanted to speak but of herself, and haltingly she said that the "Minuet in G" had deranged her poise because it had made her think of the days of her childhood in New York, when she had been no bigger than her twin and they had danced the minuet together, Ramona taking the dandy's part. A friend of the family had predicted that though they were then almost identical, Ramona was going to be the prettier of the two. Now Sue was shocked, for she had thought that Ramona must always have been fat, and she was nearly moved to tears to know that the poor girl had been changed from a swan into an ugly duckling and that it was improbable, from the looks of her, that she would ever be changed back again. But Sue was so young and so badly equipped to console someone so beset that she could not utter a word, and she wished she could go home.

Ramona summoned the waiter and ordered her third piece of cake, saying nervously, after she had done so, "I'm sorry. When I get upset, I have to eat to calm myself. I'm awful! I ought to kill myself for eating so much." She began to devour the cake obsessively, and when she had finished it down to the last crumb, and the last fragment of frosting, she said, with shimmering eyes, "Please let me tell you what it is that makes me the unhappiest girl in the world, and maybe you can help me." Did Sue have any idea what it was like to be ruled by food and half driven out of one's mind until one dreamed of it and had at last no other ambition but to eat incessantly with an appetite that grew and grew until one saw oneself, in nightmares, as nothing but an enormous mouth and a tongue, trembling lasciviously? Did she know the terror and the remorse that followed on the heels of it when one slyly sneaked the lion's share of buttered toast at tea? Had she ever desired the whole of a pudding meant for twelve and hated with all her heart the others at the dinner table? Sue could not hide her blushing face or put her fingers in her ears or close her eyes against the tortured countenance of that wretched butterball, who declared that she had often come within an ace of doing away with herself because she was so fat.

Leaning across the table, almost whispering, Ramona went on, "I didn't come to Heidelberg for its philologists—they don't know any more than I do. I have exiled myself. I would not any longer offend that long-suffering family of mine with the sight of me." It had been her aim to fast throughout this year, she continued, and return to them transformed, and she had hoped to be thinner by many pounds when she joined her brothers at Christmastime. But she had at once run into difficulties, because, since she was not altogether well (she did not specify her illness and Sue would not have asked its name for anything), she had to be under the supervision of a doctor. And the doctor in Heidelberg, like the doctor in Naples, would not take her seriously when she said her fatness was ruining her life; they had both gone so far as to say that she was *meant* to be like this and that it would be imprudent of her to diet. Who was bold enough to fly in the face of medical authority? Not she, certainly.

It appeared, did it not, to be a dilemma past solution, Ramona asked. And yet this afternoon she had begun to see a way out, if Sue would pledge herself to help. Sue did not reply at once, sensing an involvement, but then she thought of Ramona's brothers, whom she was going to please, and she said she would do what she could.

"You're not just saying that? You are my friend? You know, of course, that you'll be repaid a hundredfold." Ramona subjected Sue's sincerity to some minutes of investigation and then outlined her plan, which seemed very tame to Sue after all these preparations, for it consisted only of Ramona's defying Dr. Freudenburg and of Sue's becoming a sort of unofficial censor and confessor. Sue was to have lunch with her each day, at Ramona's expense, and was to remind her, by a nudge or a word now and again, not to eat more than was really necessary to keep alive. If at any time Sue suspected that she was eating between meals or late at night, she was to come out flatly with an accusation and so shame Ramona that it would never happen again. The weekends were particularly difficult, since there were no lectures to go to and it was tempting not to stir out of her room at all but to gorge throughout the day on delicacies out of tins and boxes that she had sent to herself from shops in Strasbourg and Berlin. And since, in addition to fasting, she needed exercise, she hoped that Sue would agree to go walking with her on Saturdays and Sundays, a routine that could be varied from time to time by a weekend trip to some neighboring town of interest.

When Sue protested mildly that Ramona had contradicted her earlier assertion that she would not dare dispute her doctor's word, Ramona grinned roguishly and said only, "Don't be nosy."

Ramona had found an old ladies' home, called the Gerstnerheim, which, being always in need of funds, welcomed paying guests at the midday meal, whom they fed for an unimaginably low price. Ramona did not patronize it out of miserliness, however, but because the food was nearly inedible. And it was here that the girls daily took their Spartan lunch. It was quite the worst food that Sue had ever eaten anywhere, for it was cooked to pallor and flaccidity and then was seasoned with unheard-of condiments, which sometimes made her sick. The bread was sour and the soup was full of pasty clots; the potatoes were waterlogged and the old red cabbage was boiled until it was blue. The dessert was always a basin of molded farina with a sauce of gray jelly that had a gray taste. The aged ladies sat at one enormously long table, preserving an institutional silence until the farina was handed around, and, as if this were an alarm, all the withered lips began to move simultaneously and from them issued high squawks of protest against the dreary lot of being old and homeless and underfed. Sue could not help admiring Ramona, who ate her plate of eel and celeriac as if she really preferred it to tuna broiled with black olives and who talked all the while of things quite other than food—of Walther von der Vogelweide's eccentric syntax, of a new French novel that had come in the mail that morning, and of their trip to Switzerland.

Justin and Daniel and Robert were delighted that Sue was coming, Ramona said, and arrangements were being made in a voluminous correspondence through the air over the Alps. Sue had never been on skis in her life, but she did not allow this to deflate her high hopes. She thought only of evenings of lieder (needless to say, the accomplished Dunns sang splendidly) and hot spiced wine before a dancing fire, of late breakfasts in the white sun and brilliant conversation. And of what was coming afterward! The later holidays (Ramona called them *villeggiatura*), spent in Sorrento! The countesses' garden parties in Amalfi and the cruises on the Adriatic, the visits to Greece, the balls in the princely houses of Naples! Ramona could not decide which of her brothers Sue would elect to marry. Probably Robert, she thought, since he was the youngest and the most affectionate.

It was true that Sue did not quite believe all she was told, but she knew that the ways of the rich are strange, and while she did not allow her fantasies to invade the hours assigned to classes and study, she did not rebuff them when they came at moments of leisure. From time to time, she suddenly remembered that she was required to give something in return for Ramona's largess, and then she would say how proud she was of her friend's self-discipline or would ask her, like a frank and compassionate doctor, if she had strayed at all from her intention (she always had; she always immediately admitted it and Sue always put on a show of disappointment), and once in a while she said that Ramona was looking much thinner, although this was absolutely untrue. Sometimes they took the electric tram to Neckargemünd, where they split a bottle of sweet Greek wine. Occasionally they went to Mannheim, to the opera, but they never stayed for a full performance; Ramona said that later in the year Signor da Gama would invite them to his house in Milan and then they could go to La Scala every night. Once they went for a weekend to Rothenburg, where Ramona, in an uncontrollable holiday mood, ate twelve cherry tarts in a single day. She was tearful for a week afterward, and to show Sue how sorry she was, she ground out a cigarette on one of her downy wrists. This dreadful incident took place in the Luitpold and was witnessed by several patrons, who could not conceal their alarm. Sue thought to herself, Maybe she's cuckoo, and while she did not relinquish any of her daydreams of the festivities in Italy, she began to observe Ramona more closely.

She could feel the turmoil in her when they went past bake-shop windows full of cream puffs and cheesecake and petits fours. Ramona, furtively glancing at the goodies out of the corner of her eye, would begin a passionate and long-winded speech on the present-day use of Latin in Iceland. When, on a special occasion, they dined together at the Ritterhalle, she did not even look at the menu but lionheartedly ordered a single dropped egg and a cup of tea and resolutely kept her eyes away from Sue's boiled beef and fritters. When drinking cocktails in the American bar at the Europäischer Hof, she shook her head as the waiter passed a tray of canapés made of caviar, anchovy, lobster, foie gras, and Camembert, ranged fanwise around a little bowl of ivory almonds. But sometimes she did capitulate, with a piteous rationalization—that she had not eaten any breakfast or that she had barely touched her soup at the Gerstnerheim and that therefore there would be nothing wrong in her having two or perhaps three or four of these tiny little sandwiches. One time Sue saw her take several more than she had said she would and hide them under the rim of her plate.

As the date set for their departure for Switzerland drew nearer, Ramona grew unaccountable. Several times she failed to appear at lunch, and when Sue, in a friendly way, asked for an explanation, she snapped, "None of your business. What do you think you are? My nurse?" She was full of peevishness, complaining of the smell of senility in the Gerstnerheim, of students who sucked the shells of pistachio nuts in the library, of her landlady's young son, who she was sure rummaged through her bureau drawers when she was not at home. Once she and Sue had a fearful row when Sue, keeping up her end of the bargain, although she really did not care a pin, told her not to buy a bag of chestnuts from a vendor on a street corner. Ramona shouted, for all the world to hear, "You are sadly mistaken, Miss Ledbetter, if you think you know more than Dr. Augustus Freudenburg, of the Otto-Ludwigs Clinic!" And a little after that she acquired the notion that people were staring at her, and she carried an umbrella, rain or shine, to hide herself from them. But, oddest of all, when the skis and boots and poles that she had ordered for Sue arrived, and Sue thanked her for them, she said, "I can't think what use they'll be. Obviously there never is any snow in this ghastly, godforsaken place."

There was an awful afternoon when Ramona was convinced that the waiter at the Luitpold had impugned her German, and Sue found herself in the unhappy role of intermediary in a preposterous altercation so bitter that it stopped just short of a bodily engagement. When the girls left the café—at the insistence of the management—they were silent all the way to the cathedral, which was the place where they usually took leave of each other to go their separate ways home. They paused a moment there in the growing dark, and suddenly Ramona said, "Look at me!" Sue looked at her. "I say!" said Ramona. "In this light you look exactly like my sister. How astonishing! Turn a little to the left, there's a dear." And when Sue had turned as she directed, a whole minute—but it seemed an hour to Sue—passed before Ramona broke from her trance to cry, "How blind I've been! My brothers would be shocked to death if they should see you. It would kill them!"

She put out her hands, on which she wore white leather mittens, and held Sue's face between them and studied it, half closing her eyes and murmuring her amazement, her delight, her perplexity at her failure until now to see this marvelous resemblance. Once, as her brown eyes nimbly catechized the face before her, she took off her right mitten and ran her index finger down Sue's nose, as if she had even learned her sister's bones by heart, while Sue, unable to speak, could only think in panic, What does she mean *if* they should see me?

Ramona carried on as if she were moon-struck, making fresh discoveries until not only were Sue's and Martha's faces identical but so were their voices and their carriage and the shape of their hands and feet. She said, "You must come to my room and see a picture of Martha right now. It's desperately weird."

Fascinated, Sue nodded, and they moved on through the quiet

street. Ramona paused to look at her each time they went under a street light, touched her hair, begged leave to take her arm, and called her Martha, Sister, Twin, and sometimes caught her breath in an abortive sob. They went past the lighted windows of the *Bierstuben,* where the shadows of young men loomed and waved, and then turned at the Kornmarkt and began to climb the steep, moss-slick steps that led to the castle garden. As they went through the avenue of trees that lay between the casino and the castle, Ramona, peering at Sue through the spooky mist, said, "They would have been much quicker to see it than I," so Sue knew, miserably and for sure, that something had gone wrong with their plans to go to San Bernardino. And then Ramona laughed and broke away and took off her tam-o'-shanter, which she hurled toward the hedge of yew, where it rested tipsily.

"I could vomit," she said, standing absolutely still.

There was a long pause. Finally, Sue could no longer bear the suspense, and she asked Ramona if her brothers knew that she and Ramona were not coming.

"Of course they know. They've known for two weeks, but you're crazy if you think the reason we're not going is that you look like Martha. How beastly vain you are!" She was so angry and she trembled so with her rage that Sue did not dare say another word. "It was Freudenburg who said I couldn't go," she howled. "He has found out that I have lost ten pounds."

Sue had no conscious motive in asking her, idly and not really caring, where Dr. Freudenburg's office was; she had meant the guileless question to be no more than a show of noncommittal and courteous interest, and she was badly frightened when, in reply, Ramona turned on her and slapped her hard on either cheek, and then opened her mouth to emit one hideous, protracted scream. Sue started instinctively to run away, but Ramona seized and held her arms, and began to talk in a lunatic, fast monotone, threatening her with lawsuits and public exposure if she ever mentioned the name Freudenburg again *or* her brothers *or* her mother and father *or* Martha, that ghastly, puling, pampered hypochondriac who had totally wrecked her life.

Sue felt that the racket of her heart and her hot, prancing brain would drown out Ramona's voice, but it did nothing of the kind, and they stood there, rocking in their absurd attitude, while the fit continued. Sue was sure that the police and the townsfolk would come running at any moment and an alarm would be sounded and they would be arrested for disturbing the peace. But if anyone heard them, it was only the shades of the princes in the castle.

It was difficult for Sue to sort out the heroes and the villains in this diatribe. Sometimes it appeared that Ramona's brothers and her parents hated her, sometimes she thought they had been glad when Martha died; sometimes Dr. Freudenburg seemed to be the cause of everything. She had the impression that he was an alienist, and she wondered if now he would send his patient to an institution; at other times she thought the doctor did not exist at all. She did not know whom to hate or whom to trust, for the characters in this *Walpurgisnacht* changed shape by the minute and not a one was left out—not Signor da Gama or the ballet girls in Naples or the old ladies at the Gerstnerheim or the prehistoric figures of a sadistic nurse, a base German governess, and a nefarious boy cousin who had invited Ramona to misbehave when she was barely eight years old. Once she said that to escape Dr. Freudenburg she meant to order her father to take her cruising on the *San Filippo;* a minute later she said that that loathsome fool Justin had wrecked the boat on the coast of Yugoslavia. She would go home to the villa in Sorrento and be comforted by her brothers who had always preferred her to everyone else in the world—except that they hadn't! They had always despised her. Freudenburg would write to her father and he would come to fetch her back to that vulgar, parvenu house, and there, in spite of all her efforts to outwit them, they would make her eat and eat until she was the laughing stock of the entire world. What *were* they after? Did they want to indenture her to a sideshow?

She stopped, trailed off, turned loose Sue's arm, and stood crestfallen, like a child who realizes that no one is listening to his tantrum. Tears, terribly silent, streamed down her round cheeks.

Then, "It isn't true, you know. They aren't like that, they're good and kind. The only thing that's true is that I eat all the time," and softly, to herself, she repeated, "All the time." In a mixture of self-hatred and abstracted bravado, she said that she had supplemented all her lunches at the Gerstnerheim and had nibbled constantly, alone in her room; that Dr. Freudenburg's recommendation had been just the opposite of what she had been saying all along.

Unconsolable, Ramona moved on along the path, and Sue followed, honoring her tragedy but struck dumb by it. On the way through the courtyard and down the street, Ramona told her, in a restrained and rational voice, that her father was coming the next day to take her back to Italy, since the experiment of her being here alone had not worked. Her parents, at the counsel of Dr. Freudenburg, were prepared to take drastic measures, involving, if need be, a hospital, the very thought of which made her blood run cold. "Forgive me for that scene back there," she said. "You grow wild in loneliness like mine. It would have been lovely if it had all worked out the way I wanted and we had gone to Switzerland."

"Oh, that's all right," said Sue, whose heart was broken. "I don't know how to ski anyway."

"Really? What crust! I'd never have bought you all that gear if I had known." Ramona laughed lightly. They approached the garden gate of a tall yellow house, and she said, "This is where I live. Want to come in and have a glass of kirsch?"

Sue did not want the kirsch and she knew she should be on her way home if she were to get anything hot for supper, but she was curious to see the photograph of Martha, and since Ramona seemed herself again, she followed her down the path. Ramona had two little rooms, as clean and orderly as cells. In the one where she studied, there was no furniture except a long desk with deep drawers and a straight varnished chair and a listing bookcase. She had very few books, really, for one so learned—not more than fifty altogether—and every one of them was dull: grammars, dictionaries, readers, monographs reprinted from scholarly journals, and treatises on semantics, etymology, and phonetics. Her pens and pencils lay straight in a lacquered tray, and a pile of notebooks sat neatly at the right of the blotter, and at the left there was a book open to a homily in Anglo-Saxon which, evidently, she had been translating. As soon as they had taken off their coats, Ramona went into the bedroom and closed the door; from beyond it Sue could hear drawers being opened and quickly closed, metal clashing, and paper rustling, and she imagined that the bureaus were stocked with contraband—with sweets and sau-

sages and cheese. For the last time, she thought of Daniel and
Justin and Robert, of whom she was to be forever deprived because their sister could not curb her brutish appetite.

She wandered around the room and presently her eye fell on
a photograph in a silver frame standing in a half-empty shelf of
the bookcase. It could only be Martha. The dead girl did not look
in the least like Sue but was certainly as pretty as she had been
described, and as Sue looked at the pensive eyes and the thoughtful lips, she was visited by a fugitive feeling that this was really
Ramona's face at which she looked and that it had been refined
and made immaculate by an artful photographer who did not
scruple to help his clients deceive themselves. For Martha wore
a look of lovely wonder and remoteness, as if she were all dis-
connected spirit, and it was the same as a look that sometimes
came to Ramona's eyes and lips just as she lifted her binoculars
to contemplate the world through the belittling lenses.

Sue turned the photograph around, and on the back she read
the penned inscription "Martha Ramona Dunn at sixteen, Sorrento." She looked at that ethereal face again, and this time had
no doubt that it had once belonged to Ramona. No wonder the
loss of it had left her heartbroken! She sighed to think of her
friend's desperate fabrication. In a sense, she supposed the Martha
side of Ramona Dunn *was* dead, dead and buried under layers
and layers of fat. Just as she guiltily returned the picture to its
place, the door to the bedroom opened and Ramona, grandly
gesturing toward her dressing table, cried, "Come in! Come in!
Enter the banquet hall!" She had emptied the drawers of all their
forbidden fruits, and arrayed on the dressing table, in front of
her bottles of cologne and medicine, were cheeses and tinned fish
and pickles and pressed meat and cakes, candies, nuts, olives, sausages, buns, apples, raisins, figs, prunes, dates, and jars of pâté and
glasses of jelly and little pots of caviar, as black as ink. "Don't
stint!" she shouted, and she bounded forward and began to eat as
if she had not had a meal in weeks.

"All evidence must be removed by morning! What a close
shave! What if my father had come without telling me and had
found it all!" Shamelessly, she ranged up and down the table,
cropping and lowing like a cow in a pasture. There were droplets
of sweat on her forehead and her hands were shaking, but nothing

else about her showed that she had gone to pieces earlier or that she was deep, deeper by far than anyone else Sue had ever known.

Sucking a rind of citron, Ramona said, "You must realize that our friendship is over, but not through any fault of yours. When I went off and turned on you that way, it had nothing to do with you at all, for of course you don't look any more like Martha than the man in the moon."

"It's all right, Ramona," said Sue politely. She stayed close to the door, although the food looked very good. "I'll still be your friend."

"Oh, no, no, there would be nothing in it for you," Ramona said, and her eyes narrowed ever so slightly. "Thank you just the same. I am exceptionally ill." She spoke with pride, as if she were really saying "I am exceptionally talented" or "I am exceptionally attractive."

"I didn't know you were," said Sue. "I'm sorry."

"*I'm* not sorry. It is for yourself that you should be sorry. You have such a trivial little life, poor girl. It's not your fault. Most people do."

"I'd better go," said Sue.

"Go! Go!" cried Ramona, with a gesture of grand benediction. "I weep not."

Sue's hand was on the knob of the outer door, but she hesitated to leave a scene so inconclusive. Ramona watched her as she lingered; her mouth was so full that her cheeks were stretched out as if in mumps, and through the food and through a devilish, mad grin she said, "Of *course* you could never know the divine joy of being twins, provincial one! Do you know what he said the last night when my name was Martha? The night he came into that room where the anemones were? He pretended that he was looking for a sheet of music. Specifically for a sonata for the harpsichord by Wilhelm Friedrich Bach."

But Sue did not wait to hear what he, whoever he was, had said; she ran down the brown-smelling stairs and out into the cold street with the feeling that Ramona was still standing there before the food, as if she were serving herself at an altar, still talking, though there was no one to listen. She wondered if she ought to summon Dr. Freudenburg, and then decided that, in the end, it was none of her business. She caught a trolley that took her near her pension, and was just in time to get some hot soup and a plate of cold meats and salad before the kitchen closed. But when the food came, she found that she had no appetite at all. "What's the matter?" asked Herr Sachs, the fresh young waiter. "Are you afraid to get fat?" And he looked absolutely flabbergasted when, at this, she fled from the café without a word.

The Maiden

"I bought the pair of them in Berlin for forty marks," Mrs. Andreas was saying to Dr. Reinmuth, who had admired the twin decanters on her dinner table. "It sickens me, the way they must let their treasures go for nothing. I can take no pride in having got a bargain when I feel like a pirate." Evan Leckie, an American journalist who was the extra man at the party, turned away from the woman on his right to glance at his hostess to see if her face revealed the hypocrisy he had heard, ever so faintly, in her voice, but he could read nothing in her bland eyes, nor could he discover the reaction of her interlocutor, who slightly inclined his head in acknowledgment of her sympathy for his mortified compatriots but said nothing and resumed his affectionate scrutiny of the decanters as Mrs. Andreas went on to enumerate other instances of the victors' gains through the Germans' losses. Evan, just transferred to Heidelberg from the squalor and perdition of Nuremberg, joined in the German's contemplation of these relics of more handsome times. One of the bottles was filled with red wine, which gleamed darkly through the lustrous, sculptured glass, chased with silver, and the other with pale, sunny Chablis. The candlelight invested the wines with a property beyond taste and fluidity, a subtile grace belonging to a world almost imaginary in its elegance, and for a moment Evan warmed toward Mrs. Andreas, who had tried to resuscitate this charming world for her guests by putting the decanters in the becoming company of heavy, florid silverware and Dresden fruit plates and a bowl of immaculate white roses, and by dressing herself, a plump and unexceptional person, in an opulent frock of gold brocade and a little queenly crown of amethysts for her curly, graying hair.

The double doors to the garden were open to admit the

moonlight and the summer breeze, and now and again, in the course of the meal, Evan had glanced out and had seen luminous nicotiana and delphiniums growing profusely beside a high stone wall. Here, in the hilly section of the city, it was as quiet as in the country; there was not a sound of jeeps or drunken G.I.s to disturb the light and general conversation of Americans breaking bread with Germans. Only by implication and indirection were the war and the Occupation spoken of, and in this abandonment of the contemporary, the vanquished, these charming Reinmuths, save by their dress and their speech, could not be distinguished from the conquerors. If chivalry, thought Evan, were ever to return to the world, peace would come with it, but evenings like this were isolated, were all but lost in the vast, arid wastes of the present hour within the present decade. And the pity that Mrs. Andreas bestowed upon her German guests would not return to them the decanters they had forfeited, nor would her hospitality obliterate from their hearts the knowledge of their immense dilemma. Paradoxically, it was only upon the highest possible level that Germans and Americans these days could communicate with one another; only a past that was now irretrievable could bring them into harmony.

For the past month in Nuremberg, ever since Evan's wife, Virginia, had left him—left him, as she had put it in a shout, "to stew in his own juice"—Evan had spent his evenings in the bar of his hotel, drinking by himself and listening, in a trance of boredom, to the conversations of the Americans about him. The mirrored walls and mirrored ceilings had cast back the manifold reflections of able-bodied WACs in summer uniforms, who talked of their baseball teams (once he had seen a phalanx of them in the lobby, armed with bats and catchers' mitts, looking no less manly than the Brooklyn Dodgers) and of posts where they had been stationed and of itineraries, past and future. "Where were you in '45?" he had heard one of them cry. "New Caledonia! My God! So was I. Isn't it a riot to think we were both in New Caledonia in '45 and now are here in the Theater?" Things had come to a pretty pass, thought Evan, when *this* was the theater of a young girl's dreams. They did not talk like women and they did not look like women but like a modern mutation, a revision, perhaps more efficient and sturdier, of an old model. Half hypnotized by the signs of the times, he had come almost to believe that the days of men and women were over and that the world had moved into a new era dominated by a neuter body called Personnel, whose only concerns were to make history and to snub the history that had already been made. Miss Sally Dean, who sat across from him tonight, had pleased him at first glance with her bright-blond hair and her alabaster shoulders and the fine length of her legs, but over the cocktails his delight departed when, in the accents of West Los Angeles, she had said she wished General MacArthur were in Germany, since he was, in her opinion, a "real glamour puss." The woman on his right, Mrs. Crowell, the wife of a judge from Ohio in the judiciary of the Occupation, was obsessively loquacious; for a very long time she had been delivering to him a self-sustaining monologue on the effronteries of German servants, announcing once, with all the authority of an anthropologist, that "the Baden mind is *consecrated* to dishonesty." He could not put his finger on it, but, in spite of her familiar housewife's complaints, she did not sound at all like his mother and his aunts in Charlottesville, whose lives, spun out in loving domesticity, would lose their pungency if cooks kept civil tongues in their heads and if upstairs maids were not light-fingered. Mrs. Crowell brought to her housekeeping problems a modern and impersonal intellect. "The Baden mind," "the Franconian mind," "the German character" were phrases that came forth irrefutably. And the blue-stocking wife of a Captain McNaughton, who sat on Evan's left and who taught library science to the wives of other Army officers, had all evening lectured Dr. Reinmuth on the faults (remediable, in her opinion) of his generation that had forced the world into war. Dr. Reinmuth was a lawyer. She was herself a warrior; she argued hotly, although the German did not oppose her, and sometimes she threatened him with her spoon.

It was the German woman, Frau Reinmuth, who, although her gray dress was modest and although she wore no jewels and little rouge, captivated Evan with her ineffable femininity; she, of all the women there, had been challenged by violence and she had ignored it, had firmly and with great poise set it aside. To look at her, no one would know that the slightest alteration had taken place in the dignified modus vivendi she must have known all her life. The serenity she emanated touched him so warmly and so deeply that he almost loved her, and upon the recognition of his feeling he was seized with loneliness and with a sort of homesickness that he felt sure she would understand—a longing, it was, for the places that *she* would remember. Suddenly it occurred to him that the only other time he had been in Heidelberg, he had been here with his wife, two years before, and they had gone one afternoon by trolley to Schwetzingen to see the palace gardens. Virginia had always hated history and that day she had looked at a cool Louis Quatorze summerhouse, designed for witty persiflage and premeditated kisses, and had said, "It's so chichi it makes me sick." And she had meant it. How she had prided herself on despising everything that had been made before 1920, the year of her birth! Staring at the wines aglow in their fine vessels, Evan recaptured exactly the feeling he had had that day in Schwetzingen when, very abruptly, he had realized that he was only technically bound for life to this fretful iconoclast; for a short while, there beside the playing fountains, he had made her vanish and in her place there stood a quiet woman, rich in meditations and in fancies. If he had known Frau Reinmuth then, she might have been the one he thought of.

Evan watched Dr. Reinmuth as he poured the gold and garnet liquids, first one and then the other, into the glasses before his plate. The little lawyer closely attended the surge of color behind the radiant crystal and he murmured, in a soft Bavarian voice, "Lovely, lovely. Look, Liselotte, how beautiful Mrs. Andreas' *Karaffen* are!" Frau Reinmuth, wide-faced, twice his size, turned from her talk of the Salzburg Festival with Mr. Andreas and cherished both her husband and the decanters with her broad gray eyes, in whose depths love lay limitlessly. When she praised the design of the cut glass, and the etching of the silver, and the shape of the stoppers, like enormous diamonds, she managed somehow, through the timbre of her voice or its cadences or through the way she looked at him, to proclaim that she loved her husband and that the beauty of the bottles was rivaled and surpassed by the nature of this little man of hers, who, still fascinated, moved his handsome head this way and that, the better to see the prismatic green and violet beams that burst from the shelves and crannies of the glass. His movements were quick and delicately articulated, like a small animal's, and his slender fingers

touched and traced the glass as if he were playing a musical instrument that only his ears could hear. He must have been in his
middle forties, but he looked like a nervous, gifted boy not twenty
yet, he was so slight, his hair was so black and curly, his brown
face was so lineless, and there was such candor and curiosity in
his dark eyes. He seemed now to want to carry his visual and tac-
tile encounter with the decanters to a further point, to a comple-
tion, to bliss. And Evan, arrested by the man's absorption (if it
was not that of a child, it was that of an artist bent on abstracting
meanings from all the data presented to his senses), found it hard
to imagine him arguing in a court of law, where the materials, no
matter how one elevated and embellished justice, were not poetry.
Equally difficult was it to see him as he had been during the war,
in his role of interpreter for the German Army in Italy. Like
every German one met in a polite American house, Dr. Reinmuth
had been an enemy of the Third Reich; he had escaped concentration camp only because his languages were useful to the Nazis.
While Evan, for the most part, was suspicious of these self-named
martyrs who seemed always to have fetched up in gentlemanly
jobs where their lives were not in the least imperiled, he did believe in Dr. Reinmuth, and was certain that a belligerent ideology
could not enlist the tender creature so unaffectedly playing with
Mrs. Andreas' toys, so obviously well beloved by his benevolent
wife. Everyone, even Mrs. Crowell, paused a second to look from
the man to the woman and to esteem their concord.

Frau Reinmuth then returned to Mr. Andreas, but it was
plain to see that her mind was only half with him. She said, "I
envy you to hear Flagstad. Our pain is that there is no music
now," and in a lower voice she added, "I have seen August bite
his lip for sorrow when he goes past the opera house in Mannheim. It's nothing now, you know, but a ruin, like everything."
Glancing at her, Evan wondered whether she were older than her
husband or if this marriage had been entered upon late, and he
concluded that perhaps the second was true, for they were childless—the downright Mrs. McNaughton had determined that before the canapés were passed—and Frau Reinmuth looked born to
motherhood. But even more telling was the honeymoon inflection
in her voice, as if she were still marveling now to say the name
"August" as easily as she said "I" and to be able to bestow these

limnings of her dearest possession generously on the members of a dinner party. It was not that she spoke of him as if he were a child, as some women do who marry late or marry men younger than themselves, but as if he were a paragon with whom she had the remarkable honor to be associated. She, in her boundless patience, could endure being deprived of music and it was not for herself that she complained, but she could not bear to see August's grief over the hush that lay upon their singing country; she lived not only for, she lived *in*, him. She wore her yellow hair in Germanic braids that coiled around her head, sitting too low to be smart; her hands were soft and large, honestly meriting the wide wedding band on the right one. She was as completely a woman as Virginia, in spite of a kind of ravening femaleness and piquant good looks, had never been one. He shuddered to think how she must be maligning him in Nevada to the other angry petitioners, and then he tried to imagine how Frau Reinmuth would behave under similar circumstances. But it was unthinkable that she should ever be a divorcée; no matter what sort of man she married, this wifely woman would somehow, he was sure, quell all disorder. Again he felt a wave of affection for her; he fancied drinking tea with her in a little crowded drawing room at the end of one of these warm days, and he saw himself walking with both the Reinmuths up through the hills behind the Philosophenweg, proving to the world by their compassionate amity that there was no longer a state of war between their country and his.

But he was prevented from spinning out his fantasy of a friendship with the Reinmuths because Mrs. Crowell was demanding his attention. Her present servant, she told him, was an aristocrat ("as aristocratic as a German can be," she said sotto voce, "which isn't saying much") and might therefore be expected not to steal the spoons; now, having brought him up to date on her belowstairs problems, she changed the subject and drew him into the orbit of her bright-eyed, pervasive bustling. She understood that he had just come from Nuremberg, where she and the Judge had lived for two years. "Isn't it too profoundly *triste?*" she cried. "Where did they billet you, poor thing?"

"At the Grand Hotel," said Evan, recollecting the WACs with their mustaches and their soldierly patois.

"Oh, no!" protested Mrs. Crowell. "But it's simply *overrun* with awful Army children! Not children—brats. Brats, I'm sorry to say, is the only word for them. They actually roller-skate through the lobby, you know, to say nothing of the *ghastly* noise they make. I used to go to the hairdresser there and finally had to give up because of the hullabaloo."

At the mention of Nuremberg, Dr. Reinmuth had pivoted around toward them and now, speaking across Mrs. McNaughton, he said dreamily, "Once it was a lovely town. We lived there, my wife and I, all our lives until the war. I understand there is now a French orchestra in the opera house that plays calypso for your soldiers." There sounded in his voice the same note of wonder that he had used when he acclaimed the decanters that he could not own; neither could he again possess the beauties of his birthplace. And Evan Leckie, to whom the genesis of war had always been incomprehensible, looked with astonishment at these two pacific Germans and pondered how the whole hideous mistake had come about, what Eumenides had driven this pair to hardship, humiliation, and exile. Whatever else they were, however alien their values might be, these enemies were, *sub specie aeternitatis,* of incalculable worth if for no other reason than that, in an unloving world, they loved.

Mrs. Andreas, tactfully refusing Dr. Reinmuth's gambit, since she knew that the deterioration of the Nuremberg Opera House into a night club must be a painful subject to him, maneuvered her guests until the talk at the table became general. They all continued the exchange that had begun with Frau Reinmuth and Mr. Andreas on the Salzburg Festival; they went on to speak of Edinburgh, of the *Salome* that someone had heard at La Scala, of a coloratura who had delighted the Reinmuths in Weimar. Dr. Reinmuth then told the story of his having once defended a pianist who had been sued for slander by a violinist; the defendant had been accused of saying publicly that the plaintiff played Mozart as if the music had been written for the barrel organ and that the only thing missing was a monkey to take up a collection. This anecdote, coinciding with the arrival of the dessert, diverted the stream of talk, and Judge Crowell, whose interest in music was perfunctory and social, revived and took the floor. He told of a murder case he had tried the week before in Frankfurt and of a rape case on the docket in Stuttgart. Dr. Reinmuth countered with cases he was pleading; they matched their legal wits, made Latin puns, and so enjoyed their game that the others laughed, although they barely understood the meanings of the words.

Dr. Reinmuth, who was again fondling the decanters, said, "I suppose every lawyer is fond of telling the story of his first case. May I tell mine?" He besought his hostess with an endearing smile, and his wife, forever at his side, pleaded for him, "Oh, do!" and she explained, "It's such an extraordinary story of a young lawyer's first case."

He poured himself a little more Chablis and smiled and began. When he was twenty-three, in Nuremberg, just down from Bonn, with no practice at all, he had one day been called upon by the state to defend a man who had confessed to murdering an old woman and robbing her of sixty pfennig. The defense, of course, was purely a convention, and the man was immediately sentenced to death, since there was no question of his guilt or of the enormity of his crime. Some few days after the trial, Dr. Reinmuth had received an elaborate engraved invitation to the execution by guillotine, which was to be carried out in the courtyard of the Justizpalast one morning a day or so later, punctually at seven o'clock. He was instructed, in an accompanying letter, to wear a Prince Albert and a top hat.

Mrs. Andreas was shocked. "Guillotine? Did you *have* to go?"

Dr. Reinmuth smiled and bowed to her. "No, I was not required. It was, you see, my *right* to go, as the advocate of the prisoner."

Judge Crowell laughed deeply. "Your first case, eh, Reinmuth?" And Dr. Reinmuth spread out his hands in a mock gesture of deprecation.

"My fellow-spectators were three judges from the bench," he continued, "who were dressed, like myself, in Prince Alberts and cylinders. We were a little early when we got to the courtyard, so that we saw the last-minute preparations of the stage before the play began. Near the guillotine, with its great knife—that blade, my God in Heaven!—there stood a man in uniform with a drum, ready to drown out the sound if my client should yell."

The dimmest of frowns had gathered on Judge Crowell's forehead. "All this pomp and circumstance for sixty pfennigs?" he said.

"Right you are, sir," replied Dr. Reinmuth. "That is the irony of my story." He paused to eat a strawberry and to take a sip of wine. "Next we watched them test the machine to make sure it was in proper—shall I say decapitating?—condition. When they released it, the cleaver came down with such stupendous force that the earth beneath our feet vibrated and my brains buzzed like a bee.

"As the bells began to ring for seven, Herr Murderer was led out by two executioners, dressed as we were dressed. Their white gloves were spotless! It was a glorious morning in May. The flowers were out, the birds were singing, the sky had not a cloud. To have your head cut off on such a day!"

"For sixty pfennigs!" persisted the judge from Ohio. And Miss Dean, paling, stopped eating her dessert.

"Mein Herr had been confessed and anointed. You could fairly see the holy oil on his forehead as his keepers led him across the paving to the guillotine. The drummer was ready. As the fourth note of the seven struck in the church towers, they persuaded him to take the position necessary to the success of Dr. Guillotin's invention. One, he was horizontal! Two, the blade descended! Three, the head was off the carcass and the blood shot out from the neck like a volcano, a geyser, the flame from an explosion. No sight I saw in the war was worse. The last stroke of seven sounded. There had been no need for the drum."

"Great Scott!" said Mr. Andreas, and flushed.

Captain McNaughton stared at Dr. Reinmuth and said, "You chaps don't do things by halves, do you?"

Mrs. Andreas, frantic at the dangerous note that had sounded, menacing her party, put her hand lightly on the lawyer's and said, "I know that then you must have fainted."

Dr. Reinmuth tilted back his head and smiled at the ceiling. "No. No, I did not faint. You remember that this was a beautiful day in spring? And that I was a young man, all dressed up at seven in the morning?" He lowered his head and gave his smile to the whole company. "Faint! Dear lady, no! I took the tram back to Fürth and I called my sweetheart on the telephone." He gazed at his wife. "Liselotte was surprised, considering the hour. 'What are you thinking of? It's not eight o'clock,' she said. I flustered her then. I said, 'I know it's an unusual time of day to call, but I have something unusual to say. Will you marry me?' "

He clasped his hands together and exchanged with his wife a look as exuberant and shy as if they were in the first rapture of their romance, and, bewitched, she said, "Twenty years ago next May."

A silence settled on the room. Whether Evan Leckie was the more dumfounded by Dr. Reinmuth's story of a majestic penalty to fit a sordid crime or by his ostentatious hinting at his connubial delights, he did not know. Evan sought the stunned faces of his countrymen and could not tell in them, either, what feeling was the uppermost. The party suddenly was no longer a whole; it consisted of two parts, the Americans and the Germans, and while the former outnumbered them, the Germans, in a deeper sense, had triumphed. They had joyfully danced a *Totentanz,* had implied all the details of their sixty-pfennig marriage, and they were still, even now, smiling at each other as if there had never been anything untoward in their lives.

"I could take a wife then, you see," said Dr. Reinmuth, by way of a dénouement, "since I was a full-fledged lawyer. And she could not resist me in that finery, which, as a matter of fact, I had had to hire for the occasion."

Judge Crowell lighted a cigarette, and, snatching at the externals of the tale, he said, "Didn't know you fellows used the guillotine as late as that. I've never seen one except that one they've got in the antiquarian place in Edinburgh. They call it the Maiden."

Dr. Reinmuth poured the very last of the Chablis into his glass, and, turning to Mrs. Andreas, he said, "It was nectar and I've drunk it all. *Sic transit gloria mundi.*"

A Modest Proposal

The celebrated trade winds of the Caribbean had, unseasonably, ceased to blow, and over the island a horrid stillness tarried. The ships in the glassy harbor appeared becalmed, and nothing moved except the golden lizards slipping over the pink walls and scuttering through the purple bougainvillaea, whose burdened branches touched the borders of the patio. The puny cats that ate the lizards slept stupefied under the hibiscus hedges. Once, a man-o'-war bird sailed across the yellow sky; once, a bushy burro strayed up the hill through the tall, hissing guinea grass and, pausing, gazed aloft with an expression of babyish melancholy; now and then, the wood doves sang sadly in the turpentine trees behind Captain Sundstrom's house.

The Captain's guests, who had been swimming and sunning all morning at his beach below and then had eaten his protracted Danish lunch of multitudinous hors d'oeuvres and an aspic of fish and a ragout of kid and salads and pancakes, now sat on the gallery drinking gin-and-Schweppes. Their conversation dealt largely with the extraordinary weather, and the residents of the island were at pains to assure the visitors that this unwholesome, breathless pause did not presage a hurricane, for it was far too early in the year. Their host predicted that a rain would follow on the heels of the calm and fill the cisterns to the brim. At times, the tone of the talk was chauvinistic; the islanders asked the outlanders to agree with them that, unpleasant as this might be, it was nothing like the villainous summer heat of Washington or New York. Here, at any rate, one dressed in sensible décolletage—the Captain's eyes browsed over the bare shoulders of his ladies—and did not shorten one's life by keeping up the winter's fidgets in the summertime. Why people who were not obliged to live in the North did, he could not understand. It was a form of masochism, was it not, frankly, to condemn oneself needlessly to the tantrums of a capricious climate? Temperate Zone, indeed! There was no temperance north of Key West. The visitors civilly granted that their lives were not ideal, they were politely envious of the calm and leisure here, and some of them committed themselves to the extent of asking about the prices of real estate.

If the talk digressed from the weather, it went to other local matters: to the municipal politics, which were forever a bear garden; to the dear or the damnable peccadilloes of absent friends; to servant-robbers from the States; to the revenue the merchants and restaurateurs had acquired in their shops and bars when the last cruise ship was in, full to her gunwhales of spendthrift boobs. And they talked of the divorcées-to-be who littered the terraces and lounges of the hotels, idling through their six weeks' quarantine, with nothing in the world to do but bathe in the sun and the sea, and drink, and haunt the shops for tax-free bargains in French perfume. They were spoken of as invalids; they were said to be here for "the cure." Some of them did look ill and shocked, as if, at times, they could not remember why they had come.

It was made plain that the divorcées who were among the gathering today were different from the rest; *they* were not bores about the husbands they were chucking; they did not flirt with married men, or get too drunk, or try anything fancy with the natives (a noteworthy woman from Utica, some months before, had brought a station wagon with her and daily could be seen driving along the country roads with a high-school boy as black as your hat beside her); and they fitted so well into the life of the island that the islanders would like to have them settle here or, at least, come back to pay a visit. Mrs. Baumgartner, a delicious blonde whose husband had beaten her with a ski pole in the railroad station at Boise, Idaho (she told the story very amusingly but it was evident that the man had been a beast), and who meant to marry again the moment she legally could, announced that she intended to return here for her honeymoon. Captain Sundstrom reasonably proposed that she not go back to the States at all but wait here until the proper time had passed and then send for her new husband. It would be droll if the same judge who had set her free performed the ceremony. Crowing concupiscently, the Captain invited her to be his house guest until that time. A lumbering fourth-generation Dane, and now an American citizen, he had a face like a boar; the nares of his snout were as broad as a native's and his lips were as thick and as smooth. By his own profession to every woman he met, he was a gourmet and a sybarite. He liked the flavor of colonial argot and would tell her, "My bed and board are first-chop," as he slowly winked a humid blue eye. He had never married, because he had known that his would be the experience of his charming guests; it was a nuisance, wasn't it, to assign six weeks of one's life to the correction of a damn-fool mistake? Who could fail to agree that his was the perfect life, here on a hillside out of the town, with so magnificent a view that it was no trouble at all to lure the beauties to enjoy his hospitality. Mufti for the Captain today consisted solely of linen trunks with a print of crimson salamanders; below them and above them his furred flesh wrapped his mammoth bones in coils. At the beach that morning, he had endlessly regretted that there were no French bathing suits, and privily he had told Sophie Otis that he hoped that before she left, he would have the opportunity of seeing her in high-heeled shoes and black stockings.

To Mrs. Otis, who had left the rest of the party and was sitting just below the gallery on a stone bench in the garden in front of the house, this two-dimensional and too pellucid world seemed all the world; it was not possible to envisage another landscape, even when she closed her eyes and called to mind the sober countryside of Massachusetts under snow, for the tropics trespassed, overran, and spoiled the image with their heavy, heady smells and their wanton colors. She could not gain the decorous smell of pine forests when the smell of night-blooming cereus was so arrogant in her memory; it had clung and cloyed since the evening before, like a mouthful of bad candy. Nor was it possible to imagine another time than this very afternoon, and it was as if the clocks, like the winds, had been arrested, and all endeavor were ended and all passion were a *fait accompli,* for nothing could strive or love in a torpor so insentient. She found it hard to understand Mrs. Baumgartner's energy, which could perpetrate a plan so involving of the heart. She herself was nearly at the end of her exile and in another week would go, but while she had counted the days like a child before Christmas, now she could not project herself beyond the present anesthesia and felt that the exile had only just begun and that she was doomed forever to remain within the immobile upheaval of this hot, lonesome Sunday sleep, with the voices of strangers thrumming behind her and no other living thing visible or audible in the expanse of arid hills and in the reach of bright-blue sea. It was fitting, she concluded, that one come to such a place as this to repudiate struggle and to resume the earlier, easier indolence of lovelessness.

On the ground beside her lay, face down, a ruined head of Pan, knocked off its pedestal by a storm that had passed here long ago. A bay leaf was impaled on one of the horns and part of the randy, sinful grin was visible, but the eyes addressed the ground and the scattered blue blossoms from the lignum vitae tree above. Prurient and impotent, immortalized in its romantically promiscuous corruption, the shard was like the signature of the garden's owner, who now, sprawled in a long planter's chair, was telling those who had not heard of it the grisly little contretemps that had taken place the night before aboard the Danish freighter that still lay in the harbor. Twelve hours before she entered, a member of her crew, a Liberian, had fallen from the mast he was painting and had died at once, of a fractured skull. Although it was the custom of the island to bury the dead, untreated, within twenty-four hours, the health authorities, under pressure from the ship's captain, agreed, at last, to embalm the body, to be shipped back to Africa by plane.

"But then they found," said Captain Sundstrom, "that the nigger's head was such a mess that the embalming fluid wouldn't stay in, so they had to plant the bugger, after all. We haven't got enough of our own coons, we have to take care of this stray jigaboo from Liberia, what?" He appealed to little Mrs. Fairweather, a high-principled girl in her middle twenties, who had fanatically learned tolerance in college, and who now rose to his bait, as she could always be counted on to do, and all but screamed her protest at his use of the words "nigger" and "coon" and "jigaboo."

"Now, now," said the Captain, taking her small ringless hand, "you're much too pretty to preachify." She snatched away her hand and glared at him with hatred and misery; she was the most unhappy of all the divorcées, because it had been her husband's idea, and not hers, that she come here. She spent most of her time knitting Argyle socks for him, in spite of everything, the tears falling among the network of bobbins. She took the current pair out of her straw beach bag now, and her needles began to set up a quiet, desperate racket. Half pitying, half amused, the company glanced at her a moment and then began their talk again, going on to other cases of emergency burials and other cases of violent death on these high seas.

Mrs. Otis had brought the Captain's binoculars to the garden with her, and she turned away from the people on the porch to survey the hills, where nothing grew but bush and, here and there, a grove of the gray, leafless trees they called cedars, whose pink blossoms were shaped like horns and smelled like nutmeg; they did what they could, the cedar flowers, to animate the terrain, but it was little enough, although sometimes, from a distance, they looked beautifully like a shower of apple blossoms. She peered beyond the termination of the land, toward the countless islands and cays of the Atlantic, crouching like cats on the unnatural sea. They were intractably dry, and yet there was a sense everywhere of lives gathering fleshily and quietly, of an incessant, somnolent feeding, of a brutish instinct cleverer than any human thought. Some weeks before, from a high elevation on another island, through another pair of glasses, she had found the great mound of the island of Jost Van Dykes and had just made out its two settlements and its long, thin beaches, and she had found, as well, a separate house, halfway up the island's steep ascent, set in a waste as sheer as a rain catchment, where only one tree grew. And the tree was as neat and simple as a child's drawing. She had quickly put the glasses down, feeling almost faint at the thought of the terrible and absolute simplicity with which a life would have to be led in a place so wanting in shadow and in hiding places, fixed so nakedly to the old, juiceless, unloving land. Remembering that strident nightmare, she turned now to the evidences on the gallery of the prudent tricks and the solacing subterfuges of civilization; even here, as in the cities of their former days, the expatriates had managed to escape the aged, wickedly sagacious earth. See how, with optimism, gin, jokes, and lechery, they could deny even this satanic calm and heat!

Mr. Robertson, the liquor merchant, was explaining the activities of the peacetime Army here to a Coca-Cola salesman who had stopped off for a few days on the island en route from Haiti to the Argentine. Robertson, a former rumrunner and Captain Sundstrom's best friend, was as skinny as one of the island cats, and his skeleton was crooked and his flesh was cold. His eyes, through inappropriate pince-nez, mirrored no intellect at all but only a nasty appetite. He was a heliophobe and could never let the sun touch him anywhere, and so, in this country of brown skins and black ones, he always looked like a newcomer from the North and, with that fungous flesh, like an invalid who had left his hospital bed too soon. On the beach that morning, he had worn a hat with a visor and had sat under an enormous umbrella and had further fended off the sun by holding before his face a partially eviscerated copy of *Esquire*. In spite of his looks, he was a spark as ardent as the Captain, and lately, while his wife had been ailing, he had cut rather a wide swath, he claimed; all day he had giggled gratefully at his friends' charges that he had been stalking the native Negro women and the pert little French tarts from Cha Cha Town.

Rumor had it, he told the salesman, that a laboratory was presently to be set up on an outlying cay for the investigation of the possible values of biological warfare. The noxious vapors would be carried out to sea. (To kill the fancy, flashy fish weaving through the coral reefs, wondered Mrs. Otis, half listening.) Captain Sundstrom, who was connected with the project, turned again to Mrs. Fairweather, a born victim, and prefacing his sally with a long chuckle, he said, "We're hunting for a virus that will kill off the niggers but won't hurt anybody else. We call it 'coon bane.'" One of the kitchen boys had just come out onto the gallery with a fresh bucket of ice, but there was no expression at all on his long, incurious face, not even when Mrs. Fairweather, actually crying now, sobbed, "Hush!" The Coca-Cola man, in violent embarrassment, began at once to tell the company the story of an encounter he had had in Port-au-Prince with an octoroon midget from North Carolina named Sells Floto, but his heart was not in it, and it was clear that his garrulity was tolerated only out of good manners.

Mrs. Otis picked up the binoculars again and found the beach. For some time, she watched a pair of pelicans that sat on the tideless water, preposterously permanent, like buoys, until their greed came on them and they rose heavily, flapped seaward for a while, then dived, like people, with an inexpert splash, and came up with a fish to fling into their ridiculous beaks. The wide-leaved sea grapes along the ivory shingle were turning brown and yellow, a note of impossible autumn beside that bay, where the shimmer of summer was everlasting. Mrs. Otis shifted her focus to the grove of coconut palms that grew to the north of the curve of the ocean, and almost at once, as if they had been waiting for her, there appeared, at the debouchment of one of the avenues, a parade of five naked Negro children leading a little horse exactly the color of themselves. The smallest child walked at the head of the line and the tallest held the bridle. But a middle-sized one was in command, and when they had gained the beach, he broke the orderly procession and himself took the bridle and led the horse right up to Captain Sundstrom's blue cabaña. If her ears had not been aided by her eyes, Mrs. Otis thought she would not have heard the distant cries and the distant neigh, but the sounds came to her clearly and softly across the stunted trees. The children reconnoitered for a while, looking this way and that, now stepping off the distance between the cabaña and the water, now running like sandpipers toward the coconut grove and back again. Then the smallest and the tallest, helped by the others, mounted the horse; it was a lengthy process, because the helpers had to spin and prance about to relieve their excitement, and sometimes they forgot themselves altogether for an absent-minded minute and ran to peer through the cracks of the closed-up cabaña; then they returned to the business at hand with refreshed attention. When the riders were seated, one of the smaller children ran back to the grove and returned with a switch, which he handed up to the tall child. The horse, at the touch of the goad, lifted his head and whinnied and then charged into the water, spilling his cargo, only to be caught promptly and mounted by two others who had run out in his wake. They, in their turn, were thrown. Again and again, they tried and failed to ride him more than a few yards, until, at last, the middle-sized ruler managed to stick and to ride out all the way to the reef and back again. The cheers were like the cries of sea birds. The champion rested, lying flat on the sand before the cabaña, and for a while the others lay around him like the spokes of a wheel, while the horse shuddered and stomped.

On the gallery, the Captain had noticed the children. "Cheeky little beggars, muckering around on my beach, but I'll let them have it. I'm a freethinker, what?" he said; then, turning to Mrs. Fairweather, "I'm going to give you a fat little black-amoor to take back with you, to remind you of our island paradise, what?"

Mr. Robertson said, "Don't let him ride you, honey. For all his big talk, he's softer about them than you are." He leaned over to sink his fist into the Captain's thigh. "Get me?" he cried.

The Captain laughed and slapped his leg. "The whole thing's a lie, that's what it is, you outlaw!"

"It's a lie if the gospel truth's a lie," said Robertson. Mrs. Fairweather did not look up from her knitting, even though he was as close to her as if he meant to bite or kiss her. "Listen, kiddo, when I first knew him, he used to be all the time saying what he wanted most of all in the world to do was eat broiled pickaninny. All the time thinking of his stomach. So one day I said to him, 'All right, damn it, you damned well *will* one of these fine days!'"

Mrs. Baumgartner gasped, and one of the other women said, "Oh, really, Rob, you're such a fool. Everyone knows that our slogan here is 'Live and let live.'"

But Robertson wanted to tell his story and went on despite them. He said, "Well, sir, a little while after I made that historic declaration, there was a fire in Pollyberg, just below my house, and I moseyed down to have a look-see."

"Let's not talk about fires!" cried Mrs. Baumgartner. "I was in a most frightful one in Albany and had to go down a ladder in my nightie."

Captain Sundstrom whistled and blew her a noisy kiss.

"They had got it under control by the time I got there, and everyone had left," pursued the liquor merchant. "I took a look in the front door and I smelled the best goddamned smell I ever smelled in my life, just possibly barring the smell of roasting duck. 'Here's Sundstrom's dinner,' I said to myself, and, sure enough, I poked around a little and found a perfectly cooked baby—around ten and a half pounds, I'd say."

The Coca-Cola salesman, who, all along, had kept a worried eye on Mrs. Fairweather, leaped into Robertson's pause for breath and announced that he knew a man who had his shoes made of alligator wallets from Rio.

Robertson glanced at him coldly, ignored the interruption, and went on speaking directly to Mrs. Fairweather. "It was charred on the outside, naturally, but I knew it was bound to be sweet and tender inside. So I took him home and called up this soldier of fortune here and told him to come along for dinner. I heated the toddler up and put him on a platter and garnished him with parsley and one thing or another, and you never saw a tastier dish in your life."

The Coca-Cola man, turning pale, stood up and said, "What's the matter with you people here? You ought to shoot yourself for telling a story like that."

But Robertson said to Mrs. Fairweather, "And what do you think he did after all the trouble I'd gone to? Refused to eat any of it, the sentimentalist! And *he* called *me* a cannibal!"

Robertson and the Captain lay back in their chairs and laughed until they coughed, but there was not a sound from anyone else and the islanders looked uneasily from one visitor to another; when their reproachful eyes fell on their host or on his friend, their look said, "There are limits."

Suddenly, Mrs. Fairweather threw a glass on the stone floor and it exploded like a shot. Somewhere in the house, a dog let out a howl of terror at the sound, and the kitchen boy came running. He ran, cringing, sidewise like a land crab, and the Captain, seeing him, hollered, "Now, damn you, what do *you* want? Have you been eavesdropping?"

"No, mon," said the boy, flinching. There was no way of knowing by his illegible face whether he told the truth or not. He ran back faster than he had come, as if he were pursued. The

Captain stood up to make a new drink for Mrs. Fairweather, to whom speech and mobility seemed unlikely ever to return; she sat staring at the fragments of glass glinting at her feet, as if she had reached the climax of some terrible pain.

"Oh, this heat!" said Mrs. Baumgartner, and fanned herself gracefully with her straw hat.

Something had alarmed the children on the beach below, and Mrs. Otis, turning to look at them again, saw them abruptly immobilized; then, as silently and as swiftly as sharks, they led the horse away and disappeared into the palm grove, leaving no traces of themselves behind. Until she saw them go, she had not been aware that the skies were darkening, and she wondered how long ago the transformation had begun. Now, from miles away, there rolled up a thunderclap, and, as always in the tropics, the rain came abruptly, battling the trees and lashing the vines, beheading the flowers, crashing onto the tin roofs, and belaboring the jalousies of Captain Sundstrom's pretty house. Blue blossoms showered the head of Pan. Wrapping the field glasses in her sash to protect them from the rain, Mrs. Otis returned to the gallery, and when the boy brought out a towel to her—for in those few minutes she had got soaked to the skin—she observed that he wore a miraculous medal under his open shirt. She looked into his eyes and thought, Angels and ministers of grace defend you. The gaze she met humbled her, for its sagacious patience showed that he knew his amulet protected him against an improbable world. His was all the sufferance and suffering of little children. In his ambiguous tribulation, he sympathized with her, and with great dignity he received the towel, heavy with rain, when she had dried herself.

"See?" said Captain Sundstrom to his guests, with a gesture toward the storm. "We told you this heat was only an interlude." And feeling that the long drinks were beginning to pall, he set about making a shaker of martinis.

Caveat Emptor

Malcolm and Victoria agreed that if they had not discovered each other at the beginning of the fall term at the Alma Hettrick College for Girls, where they taught, they would have lost their minds or, short of that, would have gone into silent religious orders. He was twenty-three and she was twenty-two and they were both immediately out of graduate school with brand-new Master's degrees, whose coruscations they fondly imagined illumined them and dazed the Philistine. Malcolm had studied philosophy and the title of his thesis had been *A Literary Evaluation of Sören Kierkegaard and a Note on His Relation to Mediaeval Christian Dialectic.* Victoria, who had specialized in the sixteenth century, had written on *Some Late Borrowings from Provençal* fin amour *in Elizabethan Miscellanies and Songbooks.*

The altitude of their academic ideals had not begun to dwindle yet and they shivered and shook in the alien air that hovered over the pretty campus of this finishing school, whose frankly stated aim was "to turn out the wives and mothers of tomorrow." These nubile girls, all of them dumb and nearly all beautiful, knitted in class (that is how they would occupy themselves in their later lives when they attended lectures, said the dean when Malcolm complained of the clack of needles and the subordination of the concept of doubt to purling); they wrote term papers on the advisability of a long engagement and on the history of fingernail polish; they tap-danced or interpretive-danced their way to classes on walks between signs that read: *Don't hurt me. I'll be beautiful grass in the spring if you'll give me a chance.*

Pale from their ivory towers, myopic from reading footnotes in the oblique light of library stacks, Malcolm and Victoria had met on the day of their arrival in September. The heaviness and wetness of the day, smelling of mildew, had drawn them together first; both, being punctilious, had got to the Geneva S. Bigelow Memorial Library too early for the first convocation of the faculty and so, having introduced themselves, they had gone across the street to drink lemonade in a bake oven that called itself the Blue Rose and that smelled loathsomely of pork. Here, in a quarter of an hour, facing each other across a copse of catchup bottles and vinegar cruets and A-1 sauce, they found out that they had in common their advanced degrees, a dread of teaching and no experience of this kind of heat, since Malcolm came from the Rockies and Victoria came from Maine. Each divined accurately that the other was penniless and that it was this condition rather than a desire to impart what they had learned to girls that had brought them to this town, Victoria on a Greyhound bus and Malcolm in a tall, archaic Buick touring car.

At the faculty meeting that morning and at all subsequent meetings they sat side by side. Their dismay, from which they were never to recover, began with the opening address by President Harvey, a chubby, happy man who liked to have the students call him Butch—the title was optional but the girls who could not bring themselves to use it were few and far between. He began his immensely long speech with a brief account of his own life: he had been born without advantages in a one-room cabin in the Ozarks and had had, in much of his youth, the companionship only of a blind aunt and an exceptionally intelligent hound, both of whom, in their different ways, had taught him values that he would not part with for all the tea in China; from the aunt he had learned how to smile when the sledding was tough and from the dog he had learned how to relax. His transition from this affecting homily to the history of Alma Hettrick was an obscure accomplishment. He described the rise of the college from a small female seminary with twenty students to the great plant of national importance it now was. Year by year Alma Hettrick had grown with the times, adding something different here, cutting out something passé there, its goal being always that of preparing these young women for the real job of the real woman, that is, homemaking. They had dropped Elocution from the curriculum (the president smiled and his audience smiled back at him) and no longer taught how to use a fan, how to tat or how to communicate with a suitor in the language of flowers (the teachers laughed out loud and someone at the back of the room clapped his hands); nevertheless the emphasis was still on those articles of instruction particularly suited to the needs of a woman: Marriage and the Family, Child Care, Home Ec, Ballet for grace, French for elegance.

Beaming like Kriss Kringle, the president concluded his speech with a timely observation: "It may be novel but I don't think it's iconoclastic to liken education to business. We are here to sell our girls Shakespeare and French and Home Economics and Ballet. They're consumers in a manner of speaking. I don't mean that a student consumes Shakespeare in the sense that the supply of Shakespeare is decreased but that she can assimilate his work just as her body would assimilate meat or any other food. Let's each and every one of us sell ourselves to these girls and then sell our commodity, whether it's those grand old plays or how to run a sewing machine. Good luck!"

Two new programs had been added this year to help the consumer become a well-rounded woman and these were now briefly described by their directors. There was the Personality Clinic, headed by a stern-visaged Miss Firebaugh, who, with her staff, would counsel the girls on the hair styles and nail-polish shades that would highlight their best features. And there was the Voice Clinic, where, presumably, harsh neighs and twangs and whines would be wheedled into the register of a lady. This clinic was under the direction of an ebullient Mr. Sprackling, who was as pink as a rose and had a shock of orange hair and sideburns to match and a fierce exophthalmic green eye. He had the air of a surgeon about him: one saw him cleaving tongues that were tied, excising lisps, loosening glottal stops, skillfully curing girls from Oklahoma who tended to diphthongize their vowels.

At the back of the dais, where several deans and heads of departments sat, there was an arrangement of leaves and maidenhair ferns designed by the joint efforts of the Botany Club and the Flower Arrangement Hobby Group and made known as such by a large placard attached to a basket of sumac. It seemed to Victoria a setting more appropriate to a xylophonist or a bird imitator than to a college faculty. This, however, was less unusual than the housing of the general assembly, a week later, of the staff and the students: because of the greatly increased student body, they could not meet in the auditorium or in the gymnasium and they convened, instead, in a circus tent pitched on the quadrangle; the endorsement of its owner was printed boldly in red on the side: *Jim Sloat Carnival Shows.*

Malcolm and Victoria became inseparable. Under other circumstances they might not have known each other or they might have known each other in a more recreational way. But these singular circumstances produced an infrangible bond; they clung tottering together like unarmed travelers, lost from their party, in a trackless jungle inhabited by anthropophagists. Or they were like soldiers whose paths would never have crossed in civilian life but who stood shoulder to shoulder in profound fraternity in time of war. Their enemy, the entire faculty and all the students, down to the last instructor of cosmetics in the Personality Clinic, down to the last ambulatory patient in Mr. Sprackling's infirmary, was not aware of the hostilities that were being waged against him by these two or the plans that were being laid for sabotage: Victoria was thinking of requiring all her classes in Freshman English to read *Finnegans Wake* and Malcolm was considering delivering a series of twelve diatribes against Edward Bok, whose *Americanization of* he was obliged to teach in his course called "Philosophy of Life."

On the contrary, the enemy found the newcomers shy but cooperative and never dreamed that instead of being shy they were sulky and that they were obedient only because they had both hands tied behind their backs. So the enemy (in the persons of Rosemary Carriage, a great maudlin donkey of a senior; Miss Goss, secretary to the Dean of Extracurricular Activities; Mr. Borglund, who taught Marriage and the Family; and Sally-Daniel Gallagher, who ran the faculty coffee shop) observed with—depending on their ruling humor—complacence, with malice, with a vicarious thrill, that the fall term had started exactly as it should, with a love-at-first-sight romance between the two youngest teachers. These detectives and publicists who presented their data and then their exegesis in the dining rooms knew that each day after their last classes Miss Pinckney and Mr. Kirk went driving through the country in Mr. Kirk's car, that almost every night they dined at the Chicken-in-a-Basket at the edge of town, that they graded their papers together in a tavern on the highway to the city.

What the voyeurs did not know, because they were not close enough to be eavesdroppers as well, was that the exchange, over the drumsticks in the Chicken-in-a-Basket, over the beer and cheese popcorn at the Red Coach Inn, over the final cigarettes in front of Victoria's rooming house, that this exchange, which ran the gamut from gravity to helpless laughter, had nothing whatsoever to do with love. It might occasionally have to do with medieval prose or with symptoms (both of them thought they were starting ulcers), but for the most part what they talked about were the indignities that were being perpetrated against their principles by Butch Harvey's pedagogical fiddlesticks. For they were far too young and their principles were far too vernal for them to rise above their circumstance; their laughter was not very mirthful but was, really, reflexive: now and again they were whacked on the crazy bone. They did not really believe that Alma Hettrick was an actuality, although, as they often said, they couldn't possibly have made it up. Whoever heard of anything so fictitious as the production of *Lohengrin* that was currently under way with an all-girl cast, directed by an Estonian diva, Mongolian of countenance and warlike of disposition? "An Estonian diva has no provable substance," said Malcolm categorically. "Such a figment belongs to the same genus as the unicorn, the gryphon and the Loch Ness Monster."

Victoria, demure and honey-haired, and Malcolm, a black-haired, blue-eyed Scot, muscular and six-foot-four, were, said the vigilant campus, made for each other. The fact was, however, that they had assigned to each other no more of sex than the apparel. And such was the monomania of their interlocution that they had never happened to mention that they were engaged to be married to two other people to whom they wrote frequent letters, often by special delivery.

Besides their fidgets of outrage and unrest, besides their fits of ferocious giggles, Malcolm and Victoria had another mood, an extemporaneous mood of melancholy that immediate time and place determined. By the languid St. Martin River, on whose banks the bracken was turning brown and on whose sallow surface gold leaves rode, they often sat in the triste dusk of autumn, talking with rue of the waste of their lucubrations. Their woe betook them too on Sunday evenings when they were driving back to the college after spending a long and private day in a little town they had discovered early in the term. On Sunday, until the sun went down, they were in a world that was separate and far and they were serene; but when the docile Buick headed home, wrath rose and set their jaws.

Built on the crest of a kind, green hill so that its inhabitants could look far up the river and far down, this town, Georges Duval's Mill, was scarcely more credible than the Estonian diva, but unlike the other chimeras of their lives it was endearing and they loved it dearly.

The twentieth century had barely touched Georges Duval's Mill and, indeed, the nineteenth had not obliterated altogether the looks and the speech of the original settlers of the region, who had been French. There was a Gallic look in the faces of the townspeople, their cuisine was peasant French and most of them were bilingual, speaking a Cajun-like patois. Some, better educated, like the mayor and the priest, spoke as befitted their station. And there were, as well, the Parisian formalities and fillips and the niceties of syntax used by two aged maiden sisters, the Mlles Geneviève and Mathilde Papin, who once, scores of years before, had gone to school in France and who now ran L'Hôtel Dauphin and were persuaded that at some time the luckless son of Louis XVI had lived in the town.

Chickens and geese, ducks and goats and sometimes cattle and swine roved and waddled and mooed and quacked through the cobbled main street. The cats were fat and were collared with smart ribbons and bows and they sat imperiously on sunny sills, festooning themselves with their congratulatory tails. There was a public well—there was little plumbing—in the middle of a green, and here the gawky adolescents flirted, shyer than violets and bolder than brass. Through open windows came the smell of choucroute garnie and pot-au-feu. The children were verminous and out at the elbows; all the women save those over seventy were pregnant. The priest was lymphatic; the mayor was driven by cupidity and hindered by gout; the doctor was as deaf as a

post; the town crier was also the village idiot; and the teacher
was usually drunk.

It was not the quaintness of Georges Duval's Mill that attracted Malcolm and Victoria, for neither of them had a drop of
sightseer's blood. In passing, to be sure, they were pleased by the
surprising survival and supremacy of a foreign language spang
in the middle of the Middle West. And they enjoyed the rituals:
the mannered courtship by the well in which the buckets seemed
to play a part; the entourage of children that followed the priest
from the church to the rectory, led by two altar boys who carried
the chalice and the ciborium in string shopping bags; the countless alarms and excursions of indeterminate origin that would
suddenly catapult the whole populace into the street, still wearing their dinner napkins tucked into their collars, still holding a
fork or a mug. They liked all this and they liked it, too, that
there was a practicing witch at the edge of town who had been
seen in the shape of a wolf tearing sheep by the light of the full
moon.

But what made the village really precious to them, really
indispensable, was that in almost every particular they could
name it was the antithesis of Alma Hettrick. Looking at the
candles and the gaslights in L'Hôtel Dauphin (the old ladies disapproved of electricity and spoke cattily of their neighbors who
had it), seeing roosters emerge from parlors, seeing toddlers
being given vin ordinaire to drink, the teachers were oblivious
to modern times and modern education and modern girls. They
basked in backwardness.

Apparently they were the only visitors who ever came to
Georges Duval's Mill. They had not been able to find it on any
map and they were sure that none of their colleagues, especially
in the Social Studies Division, knew of it or they would have
come armed cap-a-pie with questionnaires and Kodachrome and
Binet-Simon testing equipment.

When they arrived at about noon on Sunday, Malcolm
parked his car (it had a klaxon and from the front it looked like
Barney Google) under a vast copper beech in a sylvan dingle behind the green, and then they walked through mud and over the
cobblestones to the hotel, where Mlle Mathilde, having seen
them coming, was already pouring the water into two glasses of

Pernod that stood in saucers on a round marble-topped table in one of two oriels in the dining room. The other oriel was occupied by the mayor, a widower, whose poor gouty foot was propped up on a stool and was being daily worsened by piquant sauces and rich wines. After they had drunk a good deal of Pernod and could feel that they were on the mend, Malcolm and Victoria had a subtle meal. The cook's daughter, Emma, put a white cloth on their table and a Benares vase of carnations made of crinoline and wire, a pepper mill and a salt mill and a carafe of white wine. Sometimes the soup was onion and sometimes it was leek and potato and once—and they would never forget it—it was chestnuts and cress; and then they had an omelet made with mushrooms, with delicious chanterelles that Mlle Geneviève had gathered in the summertime and had dried. With the omelet they had a salad with chervil in it, brioche, sweet butter and Brie. Their dessert was crème brûlée. And then they had coffee and with the coffee, brandy.

By now they were sleepy—the mayor was more than that, he was asleep among his chins—and they moved in a haze of contentment into the parlor, where they gradually woke up under the influences of the disciplinary horsehair sofa and the further coffee and the perky gossip of the old sisters in their nice black silk dresses trimmed with passementerie braid. While they excavated the doctor's secrets and explored the garden paths down which the grocer had led many a girl, the ladies worked at gros point, very fast. They were witty and spry and their eyes were clear but they were, as they admitted, extremely old and after a little while they excused themselves to go and take their naps. Now Victoria stretched out full length on the narrow sofa with a mass of round pillows at her shoulders and Malcolm established himself in a Morris chair. For several hours they read and smoked and drank the cool, strong coffee in the china pot. On Sundays Victoria liked to read *The Canterbury Tales*, while Malcolm, mindful of the Ph.D. he longed to get, worked away at the Whitehead-Russell *Principia Mathematica,* sometimes sighing and at other times nodding in discernment and saying quite spontaneously to himself, "Oh, I see. Oh, of course."

At half past four the innkeepers reappeared, wearing small velvet hats, for after tea they would go to benediction. They had tea and petits fours and fruit and then in the twilight they all left the hotel and shook hands and said goodbye on the steps. The ladies went quickly downhill toward the church, whose bell was ringing, and Malcolm and Victoria made their way much more slowly back to the dell and the Buick, which loomed up in the gathering dark like a moose in a rock garden. They were so heavy-hearted that they had to stop on their way home at the Red Coach and buck themselves up with whiskey at the bar.

One Sunday early in November when the first snow was flying in great melting stars against the windowpanes in L'Hôtel Dauphin and the mayor was sitting with his back to Malcolm and Victoria, toasting his swollen foot before the fire in the hearth, they fell in love. Their hearts had evidently been synchronized precisely because at the same moment they both stopped eating and met each other's astonished gaze. The hands that a moment before had been spooning up crème brûlée reached across the table and clasped; Victoria quaked from head to foot and Malcolm's mouth went dry. What had led up to it? They could not remember. They were never able to recall what they had been saying just before: had they been discussing St. Augustine as a heretic? Or had they been voicing their essential indifference to the Orient? They could not say. It was like a concussion with amnesia covering all events immediately preceding the blow.

"Vicky," murmured Malcolm. The diminutive announced his state of mind. "Why, Vicky, why, my God, Victoria!"

He clapped his free hand to his forehead and in doing so he knocked over the brass vase of artificial flowers. He is very awkward, thought Victoria, how I love him! The mayor, disturbed by the noise of the vase clattering to the floor, turned around and disapproved of them with his moist, alcoholic eyes and said fretfully, *"Quel tapage."*

"Do you know what I mean, Vicky?" said Malcolm, leaning over to pick up the scattered flowers but keeping his eyes on her. "Do you know what has happened to me . . . darling?" She nodded, scarlet.

It was difficult for them that day to follow the adventures of Mlle Mathilde's octoroon governess; they could not tell whether she had run away with a pirate or a forger and whether she had stolen a cabochon brooch or had kept a capuchin as a pet. They thought the old ladies would never leave, but at last they put their tapestry needles back into their strawberry emeries and left in a swish of silk and a zephyr of sachet, and Malcolm and Victoria began to kiss.

Of course it could not have happened like this: falling in love is not an abrupt plunge; it is a gradual descent, seldom in a straight line, rather like the floating downward of a parachute. And the expression is imperfect because while one may fall one also levitates. Nevertheless, Malcolm and Victoria enjoyed the conceit of suddenness. Forgetting all that had drawn them together, ignoring the fact that they were uncommonly attractive and intelligent (for all their schoolishness) and humorous and good-humored (for all their jeers), they pretended that at one certain moment they had been knocked galley-west by this thunderbolt out of the blue; they pretended that they had seen stars; they behaved as if there were balloons over their heads containing the word "Zowie!" And in their delirium they gave the whole credit to Georges Duval's Mill, which they personified as a matchmaker. It never in the world occurred to them that Alma Hettrick's machinations long antedated those of the town.

If they had been asked (as they might well have been if a pollster from the Alma Hettrick Social Studies Division had been around), "Which in your opinion is more important, the reading and consumption of hard books, such as *Principia Mathematica,* or the direct observation of behavior patterns in college females?" they would have replied, "Neither amounts to a hill of beans. It's love that makes the world go around."

That night they did not need to stop at the Red Coach but went directly home. A few days later a fiancée in Denver and a fiancé in Bath got airmail letters containing regretful, remorseful, ashamed, confused, but positive and unconditional goodbyes.

In the next weeks the partisans of the attachment between Miss Pinckney and Mr. Kirk were worried and the critics of it said: "I told you so. That much propinquity will willy-nilly breed contempt." For Malcolm and Victoria were seldom seen together. They quit the Chicken-in-a-Basket; Victoria ate at the Faculty Club and Malcolm ate alone in the Blue Rose. The eccentric Buick now was never parked in the cinder drive of the Red Coach and those afternoon rides were apparently a thing of the past. Miss Goss, who had mothered her three motherless sisters and had got them married off and who, through habit, was doomed to mother and marry off everyone, said in the faculty coffee shop: "What *can* have happened? They were so well-suited." Sally-Daniel Gallagher, at the cashier's desk, said: "If you ask me, it's just as well. With those kind of carrying-ons day in and day out, to say nothing of night in and night out, something is bound to happen and it wouldn't do to have it happen on campus." Ray (Marriage and the Family) Borglund, saddened but ever constructive, was moved to give an open lecture on "Snags in Courtship and How to Avoid Them."

Puzzled and disappointed, or smug and malign, the campus watched the estranged couple out of the corner of its eye.

The couple, so afflicted with delight, so feverish and crazy with bliss, had agreed at the start that they did not want their treasure to be public property. On the evening they had opened their oyster and had found therein the pearl of great price, Malcolm had said to Victoria when he took her home: "This is one commodity that's not going on the market. Let's keep this luxury item under our hats." And Victoria, fingering the leather patch on his elbow as if it were the most beloved object in the world, replied: "I don't think it has any consumer value at all."

While Alma Hettrick speculated, the Papin sisters were over-joyed that their young patrons now came to L'Hôtel Dauphin for the whole weekend. They were as sly as foxes in their departure from the college town. Victoria took a cab to the bus station and Malcolm picked her up there; and then they took a circuitous route to Georges Duval's Mill. Victoria wore dark glasses and a hat.

Alma Hettrick, however, was slyer than they were and on a Saturday morning one of its agents, Miss Peppertree of the Art Department, who was catching a bus to Chicago, saw Victoria in her thin disguise get into the Buick carrying a suitcase. She just had time to call Miss Goss before her bus left. By noon the word had spread through all the college personnel who had not gone away for the weekend. Mr. Borglund frankly did not like the sneaky looks of it at all; the word "strait-laced" could never be applied to the policy at Alma Hettrick but *propriety* was mandatory. Sally-Daniel Gallagher said "Aha!" Miss Goss said "Oh, no!" But Mr. Borglund, rallying after his initial shock, said: "We'll set things straight in a jiffy."

It took longer than a jiffy even though Mr. Borglund applied himself to the problem assiduously. On telephoning the miscreants' landladies, he learned that their lodgers always went away for the weekend but had never named their destinations. Throughout the next week, although he watched them and tried to trick them out individually with leading questions, he accomplished nothing. Both of them seemed preoccupied and a little drowsy, as if they were coming down with colds. On Saturday morning he was at the bus depot at eight o'clock, hoping that like laboratory white rats they had acquired conditioned reflexes. He parked in ambush across the street in an alley; he wore a cap, a large one, and looked a good deal like Mr. Toad. He had to wait two hours in the cold and several times he wondered how reliable Amelia Peppertree was; she was inclined to be flighty and, as a Life Drawing teacher, bohemian. All the same, at ten o'clock he was rewarded for his patience. He saw what Miss Peppertree had reported she had seen and he followed the jade and her reprobate.

He followed them over roads he had never traveled or had known existed, through country so wild and forlorn that he felt he had left his own dimension and was traversing the moon; they would go along the river for a while and then they would strike out cross-country over faint lanes through the middle of tobacco fields.

Malcolm and Victoria, half-frozen, were warming their hands around glasses of mulled claret before the fire when Ray Borglund came into the dining room of the hotel. They gasped and gaped when they saw the civic-minded Swede and sotto voce Malcolm said: "I'll kill him."

"My stars!" cried the sociologist. "Of all places to run into a couple of people I *know!* I got so cold I had to stop—I was on my way to Lakeville." Since Georges Duval's Mill was off all beaten tracks and since Lakeville was in exactly the opposite direction, he made his point very clear whether he meant to or not. He rubbed his hands gleefully and came up to the fire.

"Mind?" he said and, leaning down to sniff at Victoria's glass, he went on, "Mmm, that smells good. May I join you in a glass of it? That is, if I'm not interrupting something?"

He joined them in two glasses of hot wine and he joined them at lunch and, because they were in so ticklish a spot, they spilled all the beans about Georges Duval's Mill, cravenly giving him to understand that they were collaborating on a historical-ethnic-anthropological-ideological-linguistic study of this perfectly preserved fossil town. They did not need to go into so much detail (needn't, for example, have mentioned the witch) but out of embarrassment they did and, appalled, they watched Mr. Borglund's interest rise and inundate them. First of all, he was obviously persuaded of the asexual nature of their collusion and obviously relieved, and then he was drawn to their facts; next he was fascinated and finally he became so fanatic that he blew scalding coffee into his face.

"I don't know what's the matter with us vets at Alma Hettrick. I thought we were on our toes, but it takes you newcomers to show us what's been under our noses the whole time," he said. "Why, we never thought of this town as anything but a wide space in the road. Oh, maybe a little French still used but that's not uncommon along the river. But now I see it's a real find. Why, right here in this one area we've got material for a school-wide project. Why, good Lord, I can see how there could be a tie-in of all the divisions. Maybe not the Personality Clinic—but maybe so. Maybe they have some interesting native costumes. Maybe they still use old-time recipes for hand lotion." He went on in this fashion until the sun began to set, and when at last he left them he did so only because, as he said, he wanted to "contact President Harvey at once so that we won't waste a moment's time in setting up the Georges Duval's Mill Project."

The Papin sisters had not liked Mr. Borglund and the grouchy mayor had hated him. Malcolm and Victoria wanted to explain and apologize and enjoin the town crier to broadcast a warning that snoops were planning an invasion of these innocent precincts. But they did not know how to go about it. And they were so sick at heart at the threat to their bower that momentarily they forgot they were in love. After dinner, unable to speak, they started to read, but Malcolm suddenly threw his big book to the floor and said: "I don't know what they're talking about, this A. N. Whitehead and this Bertrand Russell." Later, they remembered that they were in love and they were happy, but the edge was off and that Sunday they stopped at the Red Coach and drank boilermakers and fell in with a Fuller Brush man who gave Victoria a free-sample whisk broom.

Now at Alma Hettrick a new attitude developed toward them. Their claque applauded the seriousness with which they had undertaken their investigations of this dodo of a town, while their detractors called them selfish and said that as members of the Alma Hettrick crowd they had no right to stake a claim on such a gold mine. The former were sorry that their earlier surmise had been wrong (that Malcolm and Victoria were in love) and glad that their second had been wrong (that they had had a quarrel) and proud that they had such trail blazers in their midst. The opposition said they were grinds and prudes and had no red blood in them.

On two successive Saturdays the Alma Hettrick station wagon and three other cars followed Malcolm's Buick to the hamlet on the hill and delegates from the faculty and from the student body swarmed through the streets and lanes, declaring and querying in restaurant French. Most of the residents were apathetic; some were amazed just as the unready must have been when the Visigoths arrived. Miss Firebaugh of the Personality Clinic went into raptures over the costumes of the Mlles Papin; she asked them to turn around slowly; she exclaimed over gussets and tucks; she took photographs of them using flash bulbs and the mayor winced and said, *"Allons donc! Quelle sottise!"* But this was the only jewel Miss Firebaugh found; the rest of the clothes in the town had come from Sears, Roebuck.

The Child Study Group, working with Marriage and the Family representatives, made gruesome discoveries: intermarriage and rampant disease had lowered the average intelligence quotient to cretinism; incest was prevalent and was not denied. The American History people came up against a blank wall: the only thing anyone knew about Georges Duval's Mill was that a miller named Georges Duval had once owned this land but they did not know when, not even roughly when, and they did not know what had become of him or of his descendants. The only information to be had about the Dauphin was the sentimental testimony of the old sisters, who simply said that he had been there—else, they inquired, why would the hotel be named for him? There were no annals, no pictorial artifacts, nothing but oral and exceedingly uninteresting legends. There were no indigenous arts and crafts. Though urged and bribed, the villagers flatly refused to sing. One idiot child did a dance on the green but the priest explained, tapping his forehead, that she was making it up as she went along and there was no tradition behind it. The Political Scientists found an unparalleled dearth of politics. The Appreciation of Art people found that in Georges Duval's Mill there was no appreciation of art. As for the deputies from the Community Health class, they wanted to report the town to Federal authorities: the lice in the children's hair were fabulous, the barnyard filth in the streets was unspeakable, there was a public drinking cup at the well and the doctor still practiced phlebotomy.

In the end, the only one who really profited was Mr. Sprackling. He hit upon an excellent formula for his students who mumbled or slurred. "We enunciate when we are not lazy," said he, a man with a nimble tongue and an alert soft palate. "There is all the difference in the world between the way you young ladies say, 'I doan know,' and the way the poorest peasant of Georges Duval's Mill says, '*Je ne sais pas.*'" What made him think the poor peasants were not lazy Malcolm and Victoria could not guess, for in point of fact they were largely loafers and spent most of their time staring at their shoes.

In short order the project was abandoned. Mr. Borglund heartily said in the men's room to Malcolm: "Well, all is not gold that glitters and one man's meat is another man's poison. It wasn't a question of missing the boat—the boat wasn't there. Say, Kirk, are you and Miss Pinckney going on with your study of this place?"

Malcolm said that they were; he said that Victoria, who was very keen on philology, was preparing a paper for *Speculum* on "The Survival of Old French Modal Auxiliaries in One Fluviatile American Town" and that he himself was working on a monograph to be called "The Periodicity of Diabolism in Georges Duval's Mill."

Mr. Borglund gave him a searching look and blinked uneasily. "That seems a little overspecialized, if you don't mind my saying so."

The news of their true, dull nature leaked out and permeated the student body. A mature Georgia peach with a provocative scolding look said to Malcolm, "Is it true that you and Miss Pinckney are all-out intellectuals?" and Malcolm, who had heretofore been intimidated by this girl's voracious flirtatiousness, said, "You bet your boots it's true, Miss Ryder."

Found out, they were pitied or despised. The waste! The waste to themselves and the waste to Alma Hettrick! Here they were, *so* good-looking, the pair of them, so young, so well equipped to put a sparkle into Freshman English and Philosophy, so well qualified for fun. And how did they spend their weekends? Grubbing away in that more than useless town, that ignorant, unsanitary, stupid town which wasn't even picturesque. And what for? For Victoria to browse about among antediluvian subjunctives and for Malcolm to concentrate on a Halloween witch.

All right: if they wanted to live in the Dark Ages, let them go ahead. But one thing was sure, their contracts would never be renewed, for Alma Hettrick was in tune with the times and that went for everyone on the staff, for every last Tom and every last Dick and every last Harry. Alma Hettrick didn't have time to fool with your reactionary and your dry-as-dust. Right now, anyhow, they were all preoccupied: *Lohengrin* was in rehearsal and the Estonian had proved to be a whiz.

Gradually Malcolm and Victoria became invisible to everyone except themselves and their aloof, accepting friends in Georges Duval's Mill.

"How I love the Dark Ages," said Victoria.

"How I love *you*," said Malcolm, and they smiled in the gloom of the shabby parlor of L'Hôtel Dauphin as, their learning forgotten, their wisdom rose to the ascendancy.

THE BOSTONIANS, AND
OTHER MANIFESTATIONS
OF THE AMERICAN SCENE

Life Is No Abyss

Lily, who was twenty, was here in this hot, bare-boned room on a luminous winter Saturday, doing poor Cousin Will's penance by proxy, for poor Cousin Will, old and fragile and unstrung, was sick in bed with bronchitis. And his housekeeper, fuming and whistling in an impersonation of his electric croup kettle, had firmly refused to let him disobey his doctor's orders. Lily was Cousin Will's ward and secretary and she loved him and was grateful to him and she had come, will willing and flesh weak, for his sake though it had meant giving up her skating date with Tucky Havemeyer, an exacting beau, who had refused point-blank to understand.

She was in the poorhouse, visiting old Cousin Isobel Carpenter, a self-appointed martyr whom Cousin Will, the worst and most ingratiating investment broker who had ever lived, had ruined. Out of some grand caprice—the Carpenters had always done everything grandly—Cousin Isobel had turned the whole of her fortune over to Cousin Will, who had put it all, she malevolently declared, into banana plantations in Winnipeg. In the pride of the absolute destitution he had brought her to, she had declined the offers of house room from him and all her other cousins, had peremptorily rolled herself to the poorhouse in her old-fashioned caned wheelchair to remain, a fixed and furious reproach to the whole family, loving every moment of her hardship, which hurt them far more than it did her. The cousins (Lily was related to no one but cousins, once and twice removed and even, in their labyrinthine crisscrossings, more distant than that—what kin Cousin Will and Cousin Isobel were to each other could only have been figured on a slide rule) came in droves on visiting days to plead with her to come away with them in their snug cars back to their big, snug houses, but she was unyielding. She was also extraordinarily clever with the authorities because, in view of all the luxury she could have had for the asking, she had no right to be here. "Will put me in the poorhouse," she said with a suicidal gloat, and having a strong strain of literal-mindedness, she was not content to use the term figuratively. She had been here eighteen months now and was, as Cousin Augusta Shephard said, as happy as the day is long. Poor Cousin Will! When he came home on Saturday after one of his visits, he could not eat his dinner but went straight up to bed with a bottle of whiskey and a triple bromide and a volume of Wilkie Collins, who was the only writer that could take his mind off Cousin Isobel. Lily, on this first visit (Cousin Will had vowed he would never expose her, in her youth and innocence, to what he always called "my problem"), had already begun to feel the malaise that glazed the old man's eyes and addled him, and she hoped that other cousins presently would come.

Cousin Isobel, after untangling the cousinly reticulum (it was a spidery family, unbosomy) and establishing to her own satisfaction that Will Hamilton's representative was the product of a man so far out on the limb of her own tree that the name "cousin" was little more than a courtesy title, now began a speech, so carefully syntactical, punctuated so accurately that Lily would not have been surprised to see her referring to a card of notes.

"The whole place is a scandal. It is a public shame. If they would give me pen and paper—don't ask me why they won't, for their regulations are quite incomprehensible to my poor brain— I would write to people in high places, where I daresay the name Judge James Carpenter has not been forgotten. I have never gone in for séances; I have never been taken in by the supernatural; if she telephoned me personally, I would not believe that Mary Baker Eddy was ringing up from her tomb in Mount Auburn Cemetery. *But* I swear I know that that good man, the august Judge, turns in his grave when his immortal soul considers where I am. He never liked Will Hamilton. Small men are shifty." Before arthritis had shortened her, Cousin Isobel had stood six foot in military heels.

Her eighty-year-old voice faltered but it persevered, climb-

ing resolutely over the surge and recession of the boogie-woogie
that came from the radio across the three-bed ward; before it, in
an engulfing Morris chair, a small woman sat beating her
temples in time to the music with forefingers as thin and bent
as the twigs that scratched the windows when the wind aroused
the trees.

"Yes, to be sure, all right, I grant, concede, accept the fact
that this is a public eleemosynary institution." Attorney for the
prosecution, she articulated each resounding syllable over the
bullfrog voices of the bass fiddles and leaned forward affirma-
tively in her wheelchair. "But are the public to be treated like
so much flotsam and jetsam? Derelict, am I? Guilty of leprosy or
vagabondage? I should like to know—and this is a question I
regularly put to the so-called doctor who deigns to visit me once
a month, to him I say, 'Just what are the torts and misdemeanors
listed on my chart for which I am being punished by having a
dinner of pap at four in the afternoon and being forbidden to
go outdoors from Thanksgiving until Patriots' Day?' This Dr.
Merrill has no answer. He bears a most remarkable resemblance
to a chore man I once had on Newberry Street."

For a moment she closed her eyes and rocked her head
slowly from side to side, thinking, perhaps, of the house on Newberry Street, a tenebrous square of brick and grilles and protuberant oriels, full of marble and chinoiserie and stalactitic
chandeliers, a house that before the Judge's death and Cousin
Isobel's Ruin had been the meeting place of Cantabrigian
luminaries and was now a residence for working girls. But the
present clearly held more interest for her than the past and she
continued, "If the food and the want of air were all, one might
endure: endurance has always been a trait prominent in the
Carpenters. But it's not alone the lack of creature comforts that
makes my father's bones waltz, it's even more the company I have
to keep. For instance, Cousin Lily Holmes (I'm beginning to
remember you a little better), it's only by the grace of God that
screams aren't coming from that bed there. Last week, three in
a row died screaming. Mad at the end, you know. The undertaker came to lay the first one out here, in front of me if you
please, and he did not see fit to pull the curtains until I told
him to in no uncertain terms. Will Hamilton may have made

ducks and drakes of my lares and penates, but I haven't lost my ginger, what?"

One yellow eye, coral-ringed and sparsely lashed, winked at Lily and then it impaled the image of the barbarous mortician as Cousin Isobel glared at the empty hospital bed where the offenders had howled and died. Above it, stuck with strips of adhesive tape to the scuffed wall, was a picture, torn from a magazine, of Franklin Roosevelt, his hand lightly resting on Fala's neck. The thought of sick old people screaming squeezed Lily's insides like an unkind hand and in her heart she called to a vision of Tucky as he wheeled round and round Jamaica Pond, "Help! Tucky, I'm drowning!"

"But depend upon it, this peace won't last," declared Miss Carpenter. "You'll see. They'll bring another lunatic to thrash about and yell, using the kind of language that I do not choose to understand. It doesn't matter to *her* . . ." She aimed a nodulous finger like a pistol at the woman by the radio. "She's blind, blind from birth. And mental. She never seemed to hear the ruckus, just went on listening to that ragtime. Tum-ti-tum, tum-ti-*ta*. I say the whole of it cries to heaven for vengeance."

She described an uneven arc with her trembling hand to include the room and the larger ward beyond it and the other rusty buildings of the quadrangle visible through tall, uncurtained windows. She caught sight of two old men moving along the walk painfully as if they trod on broken glass and her head jerked alertly forward. "My dear Cousin Lily, the discrimination that goes on here beggars description," she said. "Pray tell why should those old codgers who can barely creep be allowed outdoor privileges when I, who can go like the wind in this contraption, must be confined till April?"

She wheeled herself rapidly forward to demonstrate her skill and then wheeled back. Triumphantly she gave her visitor a long, commanding look and Lily monosyllabically applauded her and murmured her regret and her perplexity that Cousin Isobel was not allowed the same freedom as the old (and, Miss Carpenter's look implied, badly born) men.

Just then, providentially for Lily, Cousin Augusta Shephard came into the ward like a garden on wings. Her mink was permanently imbued with Fleurs de Rocaille and she was beauti-

ful, intelligent, fortunate in her husband (if no one else at all
had come, Reno could have made a comfortable living on
boarding Lily's family) and was by far the happiest of all the
cousins. Now she kissed Lily and inquired for Cousin Will, but
before Lily could answer, Cousin Isobel said, "He sent me
word—oral word, would not even set his hand to paper—that he
had the sniffles."

"The doctor said . . ." Lily began possessively.

"The doctor said!" mocked Cousin Isobel. "Will Hamilton
said, 'I cannot face the music.' Men of slight stature have slight
character."

"Dry up, Izzy," said Cousin Augusta cheerfully and began
undoing the paper around a bunch of freesias. "Have you been
bending Lily's ear? Complaining when all you have to do is say
'knife' to be whisked off to the lap of luxury and pampered
within an inch of your life?"

"Fork!" said Cousin Isobel spitefully, but she smiled a
little, for she admired Cousin Augusta's forthright teasing.

"Pretty Lily! She ought to be out with her best beau this
afternoon. How you do try us! Roger said for me to tell you, 'For
God's sake, dear, enough is enough. It's high time to cut the
comedy.' We've done the whole third floor over for you in the
most heavenly moss green and plum."

"You always did have taste, Augusta," said Cousin Isobel,
pleased. "Will hired a decorator who did *his* third floor over in
off-white and rose, which certainly never was my style. However,
though I thank you kindly, ma'am, I won't come. Will Hamilton
put me in the poorhouse."

Cousin Augusta began, with gentle ragging, to cajole. She
spoke of the kitchen they had installed so that Cousin Isobel
could have her meals alone if she preferred to be conventual; she
said it was simply a question of dialing a number to have at
Cousin Isobel's beck and call an educated Swedish woman who
was equally adept at cooking and massage; Easter was coming . . .
would Cousin Isobel not *please* get out of the trenches before
then?

Midway through the futile wheedling (for Cousin Isobel
was clearly bent on prolonging her tantrum for some time to
come and she stuck out her tongue at each goody dangled before

it, said she mistrusted Swedes and that Easter had had no meaning since the year one) an attendant came in to give the old
woman a pill and in the interruption Cousin Augusta leaned
over to whisper to Lily, "Darling, you shouldn't be here! Darling, promise you won't be traumatized." Lily did not know the
word but she nodded reassuringly to her cousin, whose pellucid
blue eyes were grave. She suddenly felt much younger than she
was and her whisper was a whimper when she said, "May I go
when you do?" Cousin Augusta nodded and then turned back
to Cousin Isobel, saying, "Why must you be so medieval?"

"I want you to know, Augusta . . ." Cousin Isobel's whole
twisted carcass canted over the side of her chair as she began a
low and sibilant monologue, her hand almost completely covering her mouth so that Lily could hear nothing of what she said.

Now that the heavy, mottled, whiskered face was turned
away and she was mercifully excluded from this part of the visit,
Lily looked out the window and tried to think her own thoughts,
of how she would make it up to Tucky Havemeyer, with whom
she was in love to the point of torment. The things he had said
on the telephone! At first he had pleaded and then he had
abused, "You're soft. Or else you're lying. An old sick cousin is
the corniest excuse I ever heard of. Besides, I know all your
cousins and they're no more sick than my aunt's cat."

It was amazing how adroitly Cousin Isobel had kept her
being in the poorhouse a secret; she was believed to be abroad,
sunning in a nursing home in Switzerland, and, caught in her
passion for masochism and intrigue, had made Cousin Will
hire someone to dispatch letters and picture postal cards for her
from Vevey. Lily was in no position to let the family cat out of its
bag; if she did convince Tucky that she had broken their engagement out of necessity and not whim, and told him why, he
would as likely as not end up by despising her whole clan. For
Tucky was high-minded, rather socialist and rather poor, and
undoubtedly his whole heart would go out to this mischievous
old poseur.

In her imagination she argued with Tucky but she lost, and
hopelessly she tried to become engrossed in the bustle of some
sparrows to whom one of the old men had thrown what looked

to be part of a graham cracker. But she could not pay attention. She was embarrassed half to death.

She was embarrassed remembering Cousin Isobel before she came here, remembering the North Shore summer house and the lawns that had sloped down to the sumptuous sea, remembering the figure of her father, who had died at the age of a hundred and three, the Judge, Cousin Jamie, a learned, tart-tongued wisp, six and a half feet high in a Palm Beach suit, who delighted, while he excoriated them, the people who came to pay him homage as he held court on August afternoons beneath a huge umbrella. The house had been superbly elegant and Cousin Augusta had said of the Judge and of Cousin Isobel, "They're probably the greatest swells you'll ever know, Lily, so have yourself a good look." They had been, indeed, so much sweller, so much richer, so much more imperious than anyone else that no compromise had ever been possible for them: they never went in for repairs but always for replacement. After the Judge's death, Cousin Isobel had invited Cousin Will "to play a game of exchequers" with her—she knew better; at the time everyone told her she was out of her mind; his harum-scarum business methods were axiomatic and no other member of the family would have touched the doorknob of his brokerage office with a ten-foot pole although they all adored him. And he had madly and instantly thrown her whole fortune to the four winds. The Judge, a little queer when he had reached the hundred mark, had left no part of it in trust. And thus Cousin Isobel, penniless and untrained, was not equipped to modify her way of life at all: she could not and she would not substitute, she could only and she would only lose. Her descent to threadbare penury had been lightning-paced, so fast that it had had in itself a kind of theatrical splendor. When he heard that she was down to her last sou, Cousin Roger Shephard, troubled as he was, nevertheless had been unable to suppress a smile as he said, "No half measures for *them.*"

Eighteen months, a year and a half now, she had been living in the poorhouse, growing progressively more helpless with arthritis and progressively more cunning in the tortures she contrived for poor Uncle Will. She refused, sarcastically, to eat the edibles he sent her, saying that he had ruined her but he was not going to poison her; she wrote diabolical replies to his letters, threw away the flowers he sent her and his presents of books and magazines and seedless grapes. Someone had said, "The only thing that will dislodge her will be the promise that she can eat poor Will Hamilton alive."

Cousin Augusta, still captive to the whispered diatribe, had closed her eyes and Lily knew that she was suffering, as Cousin Isobel made everybody suffer, a mixture of pity and rage. But after the visit Cousin Augusta would be free to return to the absorbing gaiety of her life, to a charming cocktail party, probably, or to drinks at the Ritz bar with one of the innumerable men she claimed she loved and meant to marry the moment Roger was in his grave. But Lily could only go back to an empty evening and the smell of benzoin in the house and the memory of *this!* This ghastly place! She looked around, resentful and appalled.

It would have been hard to find a place barer than this three-bed ward or one that smelled more dismally, of institutional soup, of sodden mops and iodoform and sweating plaster walls. A steadfast winter sunlight further warmed the overheated room and searched its disheartening appointments of three thin beds, furnished with flat pillows and graying counterpanes, three metal commodes whose paint was chipped and whose delinquent doors sagged open, showing, in the blind woman's, nothing, in Cousin Isobel's, a red, heart-shaped candy box and a pile of cotton handkerchiefs. On top of it there was a listing heap of miscellany, a box of Kleenex and a copy of *McCall's* (sheer fraud! Cousin Isobel never read anything but Pliny and Gibbon), a packet of Christmas cards tied with a string, a distempered batik scarf and, crowning the whole, a lifelike armadillo basket containing a bottle of hand lotion from the five-and-ten, a box of cough drops and a frayed, brown photograph, bound in passe partout, of Miss Carpenter and the Judge, taken sixty years before as they sat in an imposing brougham drawn up before a house swaddled to its chimneys in wistaria. In addition to this array, each item of which had the look of having been salvaged from a wastepaper basket or borrowed from a family pensioner of low rank, there was Cousin Augusta's offering of freesias, crushed into a water glass, their fragrance angelically struggling against the rude smells. Confronting Lily, in one of the window-sills, there was an African violet whose limp leaves languished over the sides of a white pot; not quite dead but in its mortal coma, it looked as if it had been struck down by a virulent and rapid disease and yet, such was the quality of the soil it had been planted in, that robust green weeds were sprouting up among its purulent, disintegrating stems.

Lily hunted cautiously for some sign of vitality or of joy upon this melancholy scene. It was not to be found within the faces or the effects of the two inmates, but the attendants appeared healthy and lively, almost impertinent—impertinence in such a place was macabre; it was like a songbird singing in a cage in a prison. The matron at her desk beside the door was chewing gum and reading a book that made her laugh; and at a long counter against the far wall of Cousin Isobel's ward, beyond the blind woman, several girls in bright blue, dirty uniforms were folding hospital gowns and unironed sheets and were good-humoredly arguing over what was included in the term "cake," which all of them, it appeared, had given up for Lent. The liberal camp maintained that layer cake and éclairs and the like were all they must deny themselves, but two purists, who were older than the others and thinner, said that it was their intention, personally, to abstain as well from corn-meal muffins and raisin bread.

Beyond this hearty band and beyond the laughing matron, Lily could see into the large ward, where every bed—and there were four long rows of them—was occupied by an ancient, twisted woman; the humps of their withered bodies under the seersucker coverlets looked truncated and deformed like amputated limbs or mounds of broken bones, and the wintry faces that stared from the stingy pillows had lost particularity: among them it would have been impossible to determine which was primarily bleak or mean or brave or imbecile, for age and humiliation had blurred the predominant humor and had all but erased the countenance. A few of the women had visitors and the tops of their commodes were littered with purses and hats and gloves; those who were alone glared greedily at their luckier neighbors and, like crones in a comic strip, cupped their ears to eavesdrop. A constant, female babble came from the room, and though they were immobile, the bedridden seemed to bustle and flit; they gave the impression of housewives hurriedly setting things to rights as they saw unexpected callers coming up the drive; the impression came solely from their voices, in which there was neither resonance nor modulation; they chirped like crickets, dry and shrill.

"Why will they not allow me to have my own clothes?" said Cousin Isobel as, shifting in her chair, she briefly took her hand away from her mouth. Cousin Augusta shot back her eyelids to full attention, and Cousin Isobel once again muzzled herself.

Half the size that Lily remembered her to have been (according to a legend, Cousin Isobel, as a tall and stalwart and facetious girl, had been the founder of a society called The Amazonic Sisterhood of Langdon Shore, whose members had been whizzes with the Indian club), she wore a printed cotton dress, bound at the round neck and kimono sleeves with bias tape; tan cotton stockings wrapped her shrunken legs like puttees sizes too big and fell in folds over the tops of her men's high shoes. But around her scaly neck she wore a string of artificial pearls and pinned askew near her shoulder was a brooch of fire opals, surely bought for next to nothing in a curio shop on Revere Beach and surely never bought by Miss Carpenter. A hair net caged her shingled white hair, which she had worn, when it was thick, in a shining chignon. What a show-off she was! How wicked was her squalor! Her fingernails were filthy and Lily knew that her hair would have a rancid smell. She is mad, thought Lily, why can't they see that and commit her to a mental sanitarium?

Oblivious to Lily's inspection, Cousin Isobel went on with her hushed and dogged philippic and Lily was about to turn away again when suddenly her mind registered the nature of the print of her cousin's dress: it was a freize of children rolling hoops, repeated endlessly, round and round the narrow, brittle torso. Aghast at this unwitting humor, she quickly averted her eyes, but her mood was bitter now and instead of watching the sparrows as they fussed and hopped, causing the easily pleased old men to cheer, she turned to see how the blind woman was dressed.

Similarly, she wore this jocose goods, five-year-olds on a play-

ing field of daisy-scattered blue, and around her shoulders had
been thrown a tousled pillowcase that fitted in the back like a
cowl. Out of the careless hole that made the neck of the dress,
the woman's neck rose long and limber and blue-white, a neck of
pre-Raphaelite dimensions that oscillated gently with an un-
tutored, noble grace, its perfect rhythm inspired by but in no
way related to the deep-throated piano which, in a distant radio
station, played "Hold 'em Hootie." The woman, Lily realized,
was not old. Her hair was gray but it was cut short in a youthful
style; a demure bang lay on her forehead; and her skin, though here
and there it was flecked with blemishes that probably came from
some dietary outrage, was smooth and delicately pink. She had a
small, straight nose and a firm chin, and though Lily saw only
her profile, she was sure that the smile on the lips was broad and
genuine. But still, the hands uninterruptedly thumping the
temples—in a rhythm independent both of the piano and of the
waving neck—were old; heavily veined, dappled with liver spots,
they looked ice-cold and nearly mortified and the fingertips were
needle-sharp.

The boogie-woogie record ended and a drawling voice with
bogus Southern diphthongs and blotted consonants joshed the
unseen audience. "What' y'all doin' settin' by the raddio when
y'all oughta be washin' the dishes? Wa-el, since you're daid set on
loafin', le's take a look into the old ma-el bag and see who'm
wantum whatum." The pleasant Irish Catholics laughed and a
plump, red-haired girl said, "Those disc jockeys! They're so
informal, you know what I mean? It's sort of cute the way they
act, telling you they've got a hangover or something."

"Dog mah cats, wha' in the worl' is this?" said the voice and
Lily imagined a bored and puffy-faced young man scratching his
head and strangling a yawn as he laboriously ad-libbed. "Hyear's
somebody from way down yonder in Braintree that asks me to
play 'Bluebird of Happiness' boogie style. Honey-chile, Miz
Edna Murphy of 109 Van Buren Street, there just ain't no sich
animal. But I'll tell you what, I'm gonna play it ole style for ole
times' sake."

In the brief backstage silence as the new record was being
readied, the blind woman was seized with a surprising and
irrelevant animation; her hands left her forehead and she

clapped them silently and spastically and then she held them, palms together, under her chin like a child saying bedtime prayers, but even in this attitude they were not still; they jerked and crooked and wriggled in a dreadful excitement and Lily became aware that the woman was simultaneously stamping her feet. Though Lily could not see them, since her bed impeded her view, she could hear them, ploddingly and erratically marking time on the linoleum-covered floor; the movement of the columnar neck also grew more pronounced and abruptly the small cropped head began to rotate quickly on its beautiful stem. All these calisthenics were performed at a different pace; she was like someone successfully patting her stomach and rubbing her head at the same time and the effect was dizzying.

At the very moment that the music began again, the blind woman completed the half circle with her head and faced Lily fully. The dead, wide-open eyes lay in deep violet craters; the skeleton was obvious under the nacreous skin, and to complete this imitation of a death's-head, the mouth, thin-lipped and altogether toothless, was open in a permanent, unfeeling grin. For perhaps half a minute, she was motionless, seeming to stare at Lily, and then, with the chin-up non-sequitur of the song,

> Just remember this,
> Life is no abyss,
> Somewhere you'll find the bluebird of happiness

she was momentarily galvanized again. She clasped her hands together on her shallow breast in an onrush of delight and she sighed, embedding in her inspiration a little cry. Her head then resumed its former position, her forefingers returned to the edges of her piquant bangs, and Lily Holmes, stricken and sickened and stunned, closed her eyes.

The generic face had seemed to be no more than a clever armature to support the promontories, apertures and embellishments because neither knowledge nor experience was written on it; its only signature was that of absolute and monstrous poverty. It was a parody, the scaffolding of ageless bone; it was an illustration, a paradigm of total, lifelong want. Because there had been no progress in the life (unless the fleet stirrings of the

déjà vu could be called progress), there could be no retrogression,
so that this woman could not say—if, indeed, she could speak at
all—as Cousin Isobel could, "Once I was that and now I am this.
Once I dwelt in marble halls and now I live in quarters that the
least of my serfs would have scorned," and take from the contrast
a certain satisfaction, galling as it might be. To descend, however ignobly, was, nevertheless, to participate. In speaking of
Cousin Isobel's tribulations, it was possible to use verbs: she had
lost her money, she had been ruined, she had plunged from the
highest heights to the lowest depths. But to the woman who had
been born without the most important sense and, as Cousin
Isobel had implied, been born witless, only adjectives were ap-
plicable: she was blind, alone, animal. In that hideous grin and
that convulsive dance and that moan of bliss, she had demonstrated something sheer and inhuman and unnamable, and by
the very virtue of its limitation, her joy in the puling song was
rhapsodic and superlative. There had been no mistaking it: the
look on the thinly covered skull had been one of white-hot
transport, but what emotions had generated it? Hope? Gratitude
for the heartening assurance that life was no abyss? A desire for
love? Could there be in that travailing length of blue flesh and
devious bone a longing, like Lily's own longing to be with
Tucky? If there was, it was too terrible to contemplate. She felt
a painful woe rising through the center of her being, inundating
her lungs and lashing the tears to her eyes. Help, Tucky! But
she knew that nothing he could ever do could efface her memory
of that empty ecstasy.

Cousin Isobel altered her position and in the process removed her hand from her mouth; in concluding tones, she said,
"Never learned to read Braille because, as I understand it, there
was a marked deficiency in gray matter. I meant to inquire of
this same well-informed social worker where the radio came
from, for not a soul has come to see her in the eighteen months
we have shared this cubbyhole. It simply materalized one
day last fall. In one way it was a blessing because until it came
she had nothing to do but sit and make peculiar noises. She did
something with her back teeth that sounded like a hornet."

"I know," said Cousin Augusta with a sigh. "It's pitiful."

"Yes, pitiful," said Cousin Isobel. "I say it's pitiful, but I also say, is it right for me to be imprisoned with an incontinent cretin and her radio, playing that confounded rubbish from matins until vespers? I say damn."

She now looked straight ahead and gave a lecture on the food, which was, she said, without a doubt the very worst in Christendom. She was certain that an East German was in charge of the kitchen.

"Will Hamilton put me in the poorhouse," her quarrelsome voice went on. "This building is known as 'the death house,' but I have given Will to understand that my ghost is all I have left to give up and I'm not parting with it yet. I say damn and double damn." She fell silent, preparing a new deviltry, and she twisted a narrow silver ring on her finger as she gazed with a contemptuous smile out the window at the pampered old men who had now been joined by a fat, lame woman who pointed to the sparrows with her cane and roared with laughter.

"For the last time, Isobel," said Cousin Augusta, "at least for the last time this afternoon, *will* you come live with Roger and me?"

"Why, Gusta," said Cousin Isobel with hateful waggishness, "what would Will say? After all the trouble he went to with his old-rose and off-white? *He* offered me a Finn who would belabor me with birch twigs."

"Poor Will!" cried Cousin Augusta and raised her eyes to heaven. *"Poor* Will!"

Cousin Isobel, ignoring her, wheeled her patrician head slowly around to give Lily a penetrating look. "I hope your father left your money in trust, because if he didn't, Will Hamilton will ruin you. I liked your father," she said and factually she added, "His name was Matthew Holmes."

Lily could think of no rejoinder to this, but there was no need of one, for Cousin Isobel ground on, "I liked Matt Holmes. He was a first-rate sailor, as Judge Carpenter many times remarked. I'm sorry that he's dead. He would still be young, which is more than you can say for most people. Most people are dead by now. Eva Tuckerman's funeral was Thursday. Did a Kingsolving officiate?"

"Yes," said Cousin Augusta. "It was a lovely funeral. Your flowers, cabled from Vevey, were much admired."

"I shall be buried in potter's field," exulted Cousin Isobel. "You didn't answer my question, Cousin Lily. Did your father leave your wherewithal in trust?"

"My father left nothing," said Lily, and this, substantially, was true. A trifling sum, to cover Christmas shopping and hair-dressing, would come to her in the next year, but she was now wholly dependent on Cousin Will, who gave her, in addition to a pretty suite of rooms and three agreeable meals a day, a small salary for typing the letters in which he was forever trying to extricate himself from some financial bear-garden.

"Nothing!" howled Cousin Isobel. "What do you mean by 'nothing'?"

"No money," said Lily and felt an inexplicable warm rush of pride.

"Stop joking," said Cousin Isobel sharply. "I've never heard of such a thing. Is she telling the truth, Augusta?"

Cousin Augusta, embarrassed, nodded and said, "You remember that Matt and Laura put everything into that flying school of theirs in Arizona and it all went smash after they were . . . you know, dear, after the accident. It didn't leave Lily much, but damn it, Izzy, Lily knows how to make do."

Old Cousin Isobel looked from one cousin to the other like a planning rat. "Are you edging up to a sermon on imponderabilia?" she demanded. "It's the prerogative of an antique to speak what's on its mind and I want to warn you that in this place we inmates do not speak in terms of 'spiritual wealth.'" Now she reached out her hand to take between her fingers a pinch of Cousin Augusta's broadcloth sleeve and she said, "Excellent cloth. You had that sent from England at a king's ransom. Roger Shephard is beautifully rich."

"He's rich," said Cousin Augusta, "and he's got a heart of gold. He wants you, *I* want you, everybody wants you to come to us. Roger made me bring you something today to tempt you to rejoin the world," and out of her purse she brought a photograph of two young women in ball gowns and two young men in swallow-tails.

"That's me," said Cousin Isobel, smiling, "and this is Susie Holmes. There's Don Tucker standing behind me, and this, of course, is Stevie Holmes. Will you look at those trains and those pompadours? What made us think we needed ostrich-feather fans two feet wide? And tiaras no less! Mine, I recall, was emeralds." She gazed in fascination at the picture, holding it close to her nose, then moving it away, exclaiming derisively, as pleased as Punch.

The girl attendants had finished with the last of the sheets and gowns and they quit the room, except for one who was pretty and petite and amiably cross-eyed. She came to pull the window shade against the sun, which, beginning to set, was blinding now, and she said, "Time's up, ladies. It's suppertime, Miss Carpenter."

"Suppertime! It's barely time for tea."

"Shall it be the silver service, Moddom?" asked the girl pertly. "Or shall Moddom want the Spode?" But this was a joke, for the girl patted Cousin Isobel affectionately on the shoulder and said, "What you got there, honey? A picture postal?"

"Bernice, this is a picture of me dressed for the Charity Ball. Just look at me."

"The Charity Ball! Oh, Miss Carpenter, you're a caution! Sometimes she puts me in stitches with her sarcastic sayings." The girl appealed genially to Cousin Augusta and to Lily and then, marveling, she studied the photograph. "Tell me about them all, hey, Miss Carpenter? You were kidding, weren't you, about it being you and you going to the Charity Ball?"

"I tell you, Bernice, that's *me* arrayed in all my glory. My visitors will bear witness. Have you observed, ladies, the costume I wear to my daily Charity Ball? Do you like these rambuctious babies playing on the ground? They upset Will. Will seems to have lost his sense of humor."

"The ground is too damp for arthritis patients to go out of doors."

Uttered like a slogan, the words hung over the voices and the radio. It was the blind woman who had spoken, briskly and loud, and Lily, turning, saw that her profile, as shallow as a bas-relief, was pulled upward in a vicious sneer. An attendant was sitting on the arm of the Morris chair, trying to feed her cereal with a wooden spoon, but the woman's flailing hands continually thwarted the service and the attendant muttered and sighed and impatiently cried out, "Oh, come *on*, it's not roach poison."

"Don't mind Viola," said Bernice to the visitors. "Viola hates to eat."

"Who wouldn't?" demanded Miss Carpenter, grimacing as her own tray was brought to her. This afternoon she was to eat a bowl of cream-of-wheat and a salad of shredded carrot and raisins; for dessert she was to have a wedge of pound cake smudged here and there with dark and glutinous jam. Lily wondered what she would do after the tray had gone back to the kitchen and when the winter night set in and she looked to see whether there were a suitable bedside lamp by which to read the copy of *McCall's*. But there were no lamps at all in the room except one small, bare bulb in the center of the ceiling, and as she stared, dismayed, at this, Cousin Isobel read her mind and said, "The nights here are more than twice as long as the days. Tell me, if you can, a Chinese torture worse than mine: that radio goes on till ten o'clock in the dark. And I can do nothing but sit in this chair or lie on that bed and sew a fine seam. Sew! With these hands rendered totally useless by arthritis deformans, for which there is no known cure? Don't make me laugh!"

"You could have cortisone," said Cousin Augusta wearily, "if you only *would*."

Bernice was urging her food on Cousin Isobel. "Take your nourishment like a good girl, hon," she said kindly. "Here's a lovely oyster stew for you. What's in a name? Just use your imagination, hon, and pretend it's an oyster stew."

"Yum," said Cousin Isobel sourly.

It was clear that the food was far more than physical sustenance for her. As she began to spoon up the cereal, her eyes lighted with rage and Lily thought she would probably not have traded the white mush for all the succulent oysters in the world. Her wrath animated and rejuvenated her; she fed avidly.

"Miss Carpenter, why didn't you ever get married if that was really you in the picture?" asked Bernice. "A pretty young girl like you?"

"I was too good to get married," said the old woman, winking evilly. "I was too good and too rich."

"Only the good die young," announced the blind woman.

"That's all *you* know, Viola," retorted Miss Carpenter and, facing Viola, lectured her, "You do not know the meaning of half the things you say. You cannot think, you can only imitate like a monkey. You might be an interesting case if one happened to be interested in that sort of thing. I am not."

"'Just remember this, life is no abyss,'" screamed Viola over a tinkling cascade of Hawaiian ukuleles, and with amorous despair she put her brittle hands on her small, adolescent breasts.

"Go away, dears," said Cousin Isobel. "Poor little Lily will be here to stay soon enough."

"Now that's the limit!" cried Cousin Augusta. She was really angry and her cheeks flamed as she swirled herself into her coat and drew Lily to her feet. "You leave this child alone! Money *isn't* everything!"

"The lack of money is everything," said Cousin Isobel, smirking, indomitable. "The lack of money is the eternal punishment."

"Don't lie! You love it here! It's not your punishment, it's poor Will Hamilton's."

"And why not, may I ask?" Never had wickedness been more serene. Lily, whose physical demonstrations were limited to the patterned motions of dancing and skating and giving and receiving kisses, wanted to slap Cousin Isobel's face and pull her short hair and pinch her twisted fingers. Such passion as she had never known before in all her life, greater even than the grief she had known when her parents died violently in a plane crash, rose like a second person inside her and in this manifestation she towered above her cousin and she accused, "You are a vulture! You haven't got a drop of love in you! Viola has!" And not wishing to at all, she burst into tears.

For a moment Cousin Isobel was taken aback, but only for a moment, and then she said, "Viola has nothing. Viola is the embodiment of what Will Hamilton has brought me to." Her eyes grew vague, she gestured her cousins away like a distracted dowager queen, and Cousin Augusta led Lily weeping from the room. They went out through the large ward, and in spite of her tears, Lily smiled back at the senile bed patients who smiled patronizingly at her. One of them quaveringly said, "I'm glad *I* don't have to go out on a nasty day like this," and she burrowed into her harsh gray blankets.

The abyss of winter twilight opened like a huge mouth before them and a crude wind scraped their cheeks. Cousin Augusta, hurrying along, scolded like a mother bird, "Will shouldn't have let you come. He must be very low, poor Will, to have let you come."

"I *wanted* to come," sobbed Lily. "I mean, I wanted to do it for Cousin Will."

"You're a loyal little girl. You're a good girl. I know, I know positively in my bones that you had to give up something to come here today. You did, didn't you, darling?"

Now they were in the soft, sweet depths of Cousin Augusta's Cadillac and Lily, putting her head on her relative's shoulder, allowed her tears to peter out before she tried to speak. She said, "I was only going skating on Jamaica Pond. But we had a row. Tucky Havemeyer and I, I mean. He didn't believe I was going to see a sick cousin."

Cousin Augusta took her hand, and looking straight ahead at her chauffeur's neck, she said, "Sweet Lily. I feel awful. I don't know whether to drink champagne with gold leaf floating in it or go sell pencils in the Common. It's an abyss any way you look at it."

Because she was young, and optimistic, and did not, in her heart of hearts, believe that all was over and done for her and Tucky Havemeyer, Lily, in direct proportion to Cousin Augusta's collapse, began to be restored. She watched the draggled purlieus of the city replace the open countryside and for no reason at all rejoiced to see the ugly, nervous neon advertising beer and drugs and double-decker sandwiches and all the other palliatives and excesses available in this non-abysmal life. Adult—though still she teetered—and consoling, she said to Cousin Augusta, "Do you know what I'd do if I were you or Cousin Roger or Cousin Will? I'd send her to an insane asylum. One for the criminally insane."

"But, Lily!" Cousin Augusta turned to face her, wide-eyed. "But, Lily, don't you understand that we all love Cousin Isobel?"

Until the car dropped Lily at Cousin Will's door, they said

not another word. Cousin Augusta was too horrified to speak and Lily was too baffled. Love Cousin Isobel! How was it possible to love what was so intransigently unloving? She felt outside her family and betrayed by her own betrayal of convention, which, through some oversight, she had never learned. Did this mean that poor Cousin Will, too, loved Cousin Isobel, who was killing him, murdering him as surely as if she had her hands on his throat? If they did love her, then Lily did not love them. In deep repugnance she withdrew from the woman beside her, in anger watched the distance lessen between herself and her guardian, who was in love with his destruction, and turned, without reward or comfort, to the thought of Tucky Havemeyer. There's only one person who has love, she thought, and that's Viola, who can't take anything and can't give anything. The rest of them are flirts.

Lily grappled with her paradox and, clutched in its Laocoön embrace, felt ancient. And when the car drew into Brimmer Street and she saw her blond, scowling, hunter-capped and booted boy ringing the bell at the Hamilton house, she bridled at her pleasure, repudiated her hypocritical family blood, cast one last intellectual look at Viola in her state of grace, and catapulted from the car to cry, "Oh, Tucky! Isn't this well timed?"

The Hope Chest

Miss Bellamy was old and cold and she lay quaking under an eiderdown which her mother had given her when she was a girl of seventeen. It had been for her hope chest. Though damask tablecloths and Irish linen tea napkins, Florentine bureau runners and China silk blanket covers, point-lace doilies and hemstitched hand towels had gone into that long carved cherry chest (her father had brought it all the way from Sicily and, presenting it to her, had said, "Nothing is too good for my Rhoda girl"), she had never married. The chest now stood at the foot of her bed, and the maid put the tea napkins on her breakfast tray.

It was just before Belle knocked on her door in the gray dawn of winter with the tray that Miss Bellamy quaked so much, as if nothing on earth could ever warm her up again. This unkind light made her remember how old she was and how, in a few minutes when Belle came in, she would be cantankerous; no matter how hard she tried, she could never be pleasant to a servant, black or white, a failing for which her father had once rebuked her, declaring that she behaved like a parvenu. He had scolded her thus when he finally had to admit to himself the fact that she would never marry. There had not, in the history of Boston society, been a greater fiasco than Rhoda Bellamy's debut. It had, indeed, been a miscarriage so sensational that she had forced her parents to move north, into Maine, where her mother soon had died and where she and her father dwelt together in their angry disappointment. *Well, Papa, the laugh's on you. Here I am, thirty-five years old, and in the eighteen years since I came out, I have had no beau but my dear papa. No, I will not go to the concert at Bowdoin College. No, I do not want to join you in a glass of claret. I shall return to my bedroom and read Mrs. Gaskell, thanking you every time I turn a page for giving me so expensive a copy of* Cranford.

This was the Christmas morning of her eighty-second year and she steadfastly held her eyes closed, resisting the daylight. She had been like that as a child, she had loved sleep better than eating or playing. She was not sure whether she had had a dream just now or whether there was something she had meant to remember or to think about that was troubling her aged mind like a rat in a wall. At last, vexed and murmuring, she opened her eyes and what did she see hanging upon the wall (very probably staining the hand-blocked French paper with a design of pastoral sweethearts) but a scraggly Christmas wreath to which had been wired three pine cones, one gilded, one silvered, one painted scarlet. At first she was half out of her mind with exasperation and she reached out her hand for her stick to rap tyrannically for Belle. How *dare* she desecrate this, of all rooms, which, as any fool should know, was not to be changed in any way! But memory stayed her hand: it all came back.

Yesterday, when she was sitting on the lounge in the drawing room, making spills out of last year's Christmas wrappings and sipping hot milk, she heard a timid knocking at the door. She had no intention of answering it, although Belle had gone out to shop and the by-the-day girl had gone home. But she said to herself, "Who is it? Who are they that they can't knock out loud like a Christian? If they want something, why don't they try the doorknob? They'll find it locked, but if they had any gumption, they'd try." She slowly made a spill.

It went on, this gentle, disheartened knocking. Was it a squirrel, she wondered, playing with a nut somewhere? *If there is a destructive squirrel in my house, I shall give Belle her walking papers at once.* She did not find the creatures cunning as some people did: they were as wicked as any other rodent and the tail, so greatly admired in some quarters, was by no means a disguise that could not be seen through: essentially they were rats. Perhaps it was not a squirrel but was a loose branch blowing in the wind: *I shall speak severely to Homer. If he calls himself my yard-man, he can attend to these details.* Perhaps it was a dog of the neighborhood, foolishly thumping his tail against the door. *People*

*should keep their dogs at home, tied up if necessary. If they are
not kept at home, they come rummaging in my refuse containers
and defiling my lawn and littering the garden with things I do
not like to know exist.* Aloud in the long drawing room, she said,
knowing that she smiled cleverly in her lean lips and in her small
eyes, "If you want to come in, knock loud enough so that I shall
hear you. Call out your name, confound you. Do you think I receive just anyone?"

She slopped her milk and it made a row of buttons down the
front of her challis guimpe. Outraged, she threw the spill she
was making into the fire and then she hobbled to the door, saying
under her breath, "Whoever you are, I will frighten the living
daylights out of you. If you are an animal, I will beat you with
my stick; if you are a human being, I will scare you out of ten
years' growth. I will say the worst thing you have ever had said
to you in your life."

In the winter she had a green baize door and a storm door
sandwiching the regular door to keep out any possible draft. She
pulled open the green baize one and unlocked the wooden one
with a long iron key and she opened it the merest bit, pushing it
with the silver ferrule of her blackthorn stick. Through the glass
of the storm door, she saw a child standing there in the snow,
holding a spruce wreath in his hands. He had come across the
lawn, making his own path, deliberately to spoil the looks of the
clean, unmarked snow, when he could *much more easily* have
walked in Belle's footprints.

He opened the storm door without asking leave and he said,
"Will you buy this?"

She prided herself on never having been tricked by anyone.
She investigated first and bought afterward. She, Rhoda Bellamy,
would be the last to be taken in by a child, and she did not, of
course, answer his question. She pushed the door open a little
farther and said, "Who are you? What is your name?"

His teeth, she saw, were short and crooked and a nasty yellow
color. She supposed he came from one of those indigent families
who clustered together, squalidly and odoriferously, on the banks
of the Sheepscot. He was not decently shy and he spoke up immediately: "My name is Ernest Leonard McCammon. Will you buy
this wreath?"

The spinster said, "Well, Ernest Leonard, you may wipe your feet on my *Welcome* mat and step into the entry, but I am not promising to buy your wreath. We'll see about that later on."

(The sycamores before Miss Bellamy's windows creaked in the cold: *Where is my breakfast? Where is Belle? Why did I invite Ernest Leonard McCammon to cross my threshold in his snowy galoshes, puddling the Tabriz Father bought half price in Belgrade?* She creaked, too, like a tree, and a feather from the eiderdown walked on her ear like a summer fly.)

The child stood before her, small and ambitious, bundled to his ears in a blue plaid mackintosh which was patched with leather at the elbows. He wore blue jeans and in his mittenless hands he carried now, besides the wreath, the purple stocking cap he had taken off before he came through the door. He bore a faint, unpleasant smell of mud. *I will eat you, little boy, because once upon a time I, too, had pink cheeks and a fair skin and clear eyes. And don't you deny it.*

Ernest Leonard McCammon looked at the Adam hall chair, looked at the portrait of Mr. Bellamy, looked at the priceless Florentine coffer, looked at the luster pitchers in which stood cattails ten years old; she had had a man come down from Portland one year to oil the books and at the same time had had him shellac the cattails, although he protested a little, declaring that this was not in his line. No workman ever got anywhere protesting with her. She had simply said, "I don't know what you're talking about, sir. My father picked these cattails by the Jordan." This did not happen to be true, as her father had been dead for twenty years and she had gathered them herself in her own meadow beside the local river.

The rag-tag-and-bobtail boy looked at her father's treasures as if he had seen such things every day of his life. *Do you know who I am, you smelly scrap? Does the name Bellamy mean anything to you, you wool-bound baggage?*

(How the wind was blowing! Where was Belle? Where was her breakfast? Where was her stick? Where was her wrapper? Why did no one come to wish her a merry Christmas?)

He said, "Miss Bellamy, will you buy my wreath?"

"What do you want for it, McCammon?"

"A quarter."

"A quarter! Twenty-five cents for a bit of evergreen you more than likely stole off one of my trees!"

His pink cheeks paled under her shrewd gaze and his blue eyes clouded. "I never stole 'um off your tree, Miss Bellamy. I went to the woods, I did, and I got 'um there off nobody's tree."

She said, not giving in, "Perhaps so, perhaps not. All the same, a quarter is too much."

"But I painted the pine cones, Miss Bellamy! I had to buy the gold and the silver. Daddy gave me the red."

"And who is this Daddy?"

"The chimney cleaner. We are the ones with the mule. Maybe you have seen our house with the mule in the yard? My daddy's name is Robert John McCammon."

I will blow your brains out with the bellows Father brought from Dresden. I will lay your slender little body on Cousin Anne's andirons that came from the Trianon, and burn you up like a paper spill.

"Come, come, Ernest Leonard," she said, "I don't care what your daddy's middle name is and I have certainly not seen your mule. I will give you fifteen cents for your wreath."

"No, ma'am," he said. "If you don't buy it, some other lady will."

"Some *other* lady? What do you mean, McCammon?"

"Well, Mrs. Wagner would buy it or Mrs. Saunders or Mrs. Hugh Morris, I reckon. Anyways, somebody."

"I will give you fifteen cents for the wreath alone. You can take off the pine cones."

"No, ma'am. That would spoil it."

She fixed him with a severe aristocratic eye, determined now to resolve this impasse to her own liking and not to his. She said slowly, "If I decided to buy your wreath and paid you the absurd king's ransom of twenty-five cents, would you do a favor for me?"

"Yes, Miss Bellamy."

(Belle! Belle! Where is my breakfast? Come before I die of loneliness. Come before the sycamores break at the top and crush the roof over my head!)

"Do you promise, Ernest Leonard?"

"I promise, Miss Bellamy," he said and moved a step away from her.

She took a twenty-five-cent piece out of the purse she carried strapped to her belt and, bending down, took the wreath, which she placed on the coffer. Now Ernest Leonard clutched the stocking cap in both hands. His aplomb had left him; she could tell that he wanted to run away.

"You must give me a kiss, Master McCammon," she said and, leaning heavily upon her stick, stooped toward that small face with pursed lips, coral-colored. They touched her bone-dry cheek and then the boy was gone, and through the door he had left open in his headlong flight there came a blast of cold December. But for a moment she did not move and stared at a clot of snow upon the rug. *I told you, Ernest Leonard, to wipe your feet carefully on my Welcome mat.*

Belle's big country feet were on the stairs. Miss Bellamy trembled for her knock. *Wait a minute, Belle, I have not yet thought out what I am going to say to you.* Had she left any stray spruce needles on the coffer? Had any fallen as she climbed the stairs, breathless with recollection? Belle was at the door. She knocked and entered with the tray.

"Explain that monstrosity," said Miss Bellamy, pointing to the Christmas wreath she had hung last night at the stroke of midnight. *Merry Christmas, Papa dear. Oh, how cunning of you to hang up mistletoe! What girl in the world would want more than a beau like you? Can I have my presents now? It's one past midnight, Papa! Oh, Papa, darling, you have given me a brass fender for my fireplace! Oh, Papa, a medallioned sewing drum! An emerald ring! A purple velvet peignoir! I wish you a very merry Christmas, Papa.*

"Don't pretend you know nothing about it, my good woman. Why did you do it, Belle? Have you no respect for other people's property? Do you think I can have my bedroom repapered every week or so merely for the sake of your vulgar whims?"

Kind, stupid Belle shook out the napkin and she said, as she sprinkled a little salt on the lightly boiled egg, "I'm sorry, Miss Rhoda, that I never seem to do what's right. I thought you'd like the wreath."

The old lady cackled hideously and screamed, "You goose! You namby-pamby! I hung it there myself!"

The maid, unruffled, smiled and said, "Merry Christmas, Miss Rhoda." When she had gone, the spinster closed her eyes against Ernest Leonard's painted pine cones, but she nursed her hurt like a baby at a milkless breast, with tearless eyes.

Polite Conversation

"It is so good in you to come to tea," said Mrs. Wainright-Lowe as she plucked one last weed beside a petunia that grew out of a crack in the flagstoned terrace. "I have seen so little of you lately."

"I know," said Mrs. Heath, casting about for a new excuse for her unneighborliness, but the effort, on this New England summer afternoon, was too great, and she said only, "It is good in you to let me come," and she wondered how it had been possible to fall so quickly into this habit of saying "in you" instead of "of you." It was but one of the many concessions she had made to the culture of her hostess during the year she had known her, the greatest of all being her frequent attendance at this prolonged alfresco meal. Mrs. Wainright-Lowe, small and brown, like a larger rendering of the nuthatch that nervously regarded her from a shrub of Japanese quince, made a purling sound of understanding or of deprecation—it was not possible to tell which—and felt the belly of the teapot to test its warmth.

One of the Wainright-Lowe daughters, the only one at home today, came through the kitchen door to the terrace bearing a tea cozy appliquéd with Scotties. She had turned on the phonograph, and the first movement of the "Jupiter" soon burst surprisingly upon them, with a blast that sent the nuthatch whirring off to the pine woods. So displeasing was the tone of all the music one heard in this house that one imagined the family often attacked the records with steel wool or pumice stone, or that they used them as properties in the rambunctious charades it was the nightly custom of this high-spirited brood to play.

Mrs. Wainright-Lowe said, "The music is intended to distract your attention from the barn," and she pointed toward the lopped-off elm branches that the tree men had been accumulating

for some days past and that were piled now in lavish disorder in
the doorway of the barn, the scene of weekly square-dancing parties. The Heaths were bidden to the dances every Saturday by
one or by all of the eleven Wainright-Lowe children, not one of
whom had ever, under any circumstances, taken no for an answer.
For the eleven Wainright-Lowes were seldom idle when they came
home from school and college, or from jobs at schools and colleges
(they revered education and, even when married, even when pregnant, took graduate courses in political science and Eastern philosophy), to spend the summer with their mother. Their notions
of entertainment were on a scale so grand that it was necessary
for them to recruit far and wide throughout the county in order
to fill the large house and the larger barn with tireless merry-
makers. Day after day and night after night, the buildings bulged
and burst with nonalcoholic jollifications, with laughing, singing,
whistling, with the imitations of birds and beasts, with the spasms
of accordions and the yammer of fiddles playing jigs, with the
shooting of bottles and the chopping of trees and the repairing of
boats and the ringing of old cowbells bought at auctions for next
to nothing. The Heaths, who were writers and did not look on
the summertime as all beer and skittles, accepted all the invitations but did not appear at any of these shindigs. Indeed, they seldom stirred farther than the lake behind their house, or the general store, and the gentry (and especially the Wainright-Lowes),
who had done so much to make them feel "at home" in the town,
did not know whether they were abnormal or stuck-up.

It was quiet today; all the children but Eva had gone to the
seashore to fly some kites belonging to a house guest and to dig
for clams, to swim, to sail, to consume cases of Moxie and pounds
of frankfurters, and, in general, to occupy themselves every moment of the radiant day. Eva had not gone with them because,
through some unheard-of phenomenon, she was tired.

She put the cozy on the teapot beside her mother and said
to Mrs. Heath, "But where is Tommy?"

Margaret Heath told them that her husband was working,
and Mrs. Wainright-Lowe, giving her a swift appraisal out of eyes
that did not believe her for a minute, said, "He works *all* the
time, Eva. That's the first thing you must learn about Tommy
Heath." Her voice and her manner implied much more, and she

smiled with mild, motherly derision as she bent her attention to a tin of foie gras. Margaret bristled at this devious criticism of her husband (she could never be sure exactly what the implication was, but it was clear that the Wainright-Lowes looked on writing as something that could be taken or left alone), even though, half an hour before, she had all but exhausted herself in a polemic addressed to him on why he should go across the road with her to tea at the Bishop's widow's house. Her arguments had been unspeakable; she had sounded like Mrs. Wainright-Lowe herself—had spoken of their need to become a part of the citizenry, had said they would soon be hated by everyone if they did not occasionally accept an invitation; he had irrefutably replied that he would not go today or any other day, because he was an eccentric.

There was an abundant tea. There were lettuce sandwiches and cheese sandwiches, peanut-butter sandwiches and tomato sandwiches, crackers spread with pâté. There was a cake, and there were brownies, and there was a plate of candy made by Eva Wainright-Lowe. And the hostess said sweetly, with ineffable forgiveness, "We had expected Tommy, you see. I had told Eva that he eats like a proper man. I simply cannot bear men who have poor appetites, can you?"

"No," said Tommy's wife, although she had never pondered this question before and could not feel that she had an opinion on it at all; she had not, until this moment, ever considered her husband's feeding habits, and she wondered, quite unemotionally, if she gave him enough to eat. She supposed that the departed Bishop had been very much up to snuff in this particular, for in an august portrait in the library he looked a thorough trencherman about the jowls and the satisfied eyes.

"Perhaps Tommy would change his mind?" said Eva, a large girl, eagerly. "If I went and yodeled under his window, do you think he might succumb?"

The odious image made Margaret's "Oh, no!" come out like a petition. She said, "He must get this off in the mail tomorrow." She hoped they would not ask what "this" was, but they did, and she said, "His proofs," although the last of the proofs had gone off days before.

"His proofs?" said Mrs. Wainright-Lowe. "What are those? Are those the suggestions the publishers have made to him?"

"Well, no, Mrs. Wainright-Lowe," she said, aimlessly displeased, as she had always been since she had known these pious people, at their failure to understand that her husband was not receiving a favor from his publishers but that it was the other way around. And she explained what proofs were.

"Ah, then," said Mrs. Wainright-Lowe craftily, "then after this he *will* be free to come to tea."

Eva said, "Oh, to be a writer!"

Her mother said, "Eva has written some very clever things herself, you know, Margaret. Such a cunning poem it was you wrote on Bishop Masterman's Christmas present when we were in Toledo, Eva!"

"Oh, sweetie," said Eva, "don't tell Margaret about *that!* My goodness, Tommy and Margaret are *real* writers!"

Happily—because, clearly, Mrs. Wainright-Lowe was on the very point of telling Margaret about it—the record ended, and Eva galloped across the terrace to the house, hollering good-humoredly, "That's the trouble with a Vic."

"I wish you would get her to show you some of her writing, Margaret," Eva's mother said. "You've no idea how much my children *respect* you Heaths. On every postal card, Martin sends his love to you and Tommy." She referred to her boarding-school son, an indefatigable youth who, during his vacations, liked to lurk in the shrubbery of the Heaths' yard, waiting until he heard the sound of a typewriter; then he would pounce, hammering madly on the door and entering to cry, "I heard the typewriter, so I knew you were at home! May I come and bother you for half an hour or so?" And bother he did, but who could refuse the red-cheeked, fair-haired lad when he was so exuberant, so full to overflowing with long school-pranks and headmaster anecdotes, through the narration of which he gulped with a glee that was a kind of seizure, sometimes sending his voice wailing into the octaves of his infancy?

Eva, returning, said, "He's in St. Louis now. He says St. Louis isn't what it's cracked up to be."

Mrs. Wainright-Lowe seemed to be eyeing Margaret narrowly, for what dark purpose she could not guess. She said, "You can't think what a delight it is for Martin to have a young man in the neighborhood. He has so many sisters. When he comes back, I hope he and Tommy will often go sailing and fishing together." She paused, and Margaret, sighing for her husband, who was thus to be beset, blew her tea into her face. But the incident went unnoticed, and Mrs. Wainright-Lowe continued, "And skiing at the Christmas holiday and all sorts of things!"

They talked graciously of Martin's three-week tour with a band of schoolfellows, and of Mrs. Wainright-Lowe's snapdragons, and of the wickedly ribald postmaster, who made everyone— not only women—blush, and of the plumber, who had recently adopted the pubescent daughter of a murderer father and a diabetic mother. Midway through tea, they were joined by Sister Evelyn, an Anglican nun of the neighborhood, who, belonging to some order of surpassing liberality, spent long furloughs away from her convent with her truculently unwell mother in an ancestral dwelling here at the top of the hill. She liked to read the Office of the Day with Mrs. Wainright-Lowe in the dead Bishop's study. This evening, she came across the broad and brilliant lawn gently, like a gull, her habit drifting on the early-evening breeze. She came straight to Margaret and shook her hand, an unusual gesture for her and a painful one for Margaret, who had, the day before, dislocated her thumb while she was stacking firewood. Sister Evelyn said, "I hope you are better." Margaret recalled no recent illness, so she said, "Oh, thank you, yes, it's much better. I had it X-rayed and nothing is broken."

The nun looked puzzled, and then she said, "Oh, I was speaking of your being ill on the day of Cousin Peggy's swimming party," and Margaret said "Yes," and was unable to say more. "I thought you must be very low," continued the truth-lover, giving her a straight look, "since you had not come to pick the lettuce."

Although the Heaths had quite adequate lettuce of their own, and although Margaret knew that Sister Evelyn and her mother wanted them to pick theirs only so that it would not go to seed and be a mess all over their kitchen garden, she said docilely, "If I may, I will come tomorrow."

"Do," said the nun. "Come in the late afternoon and have a

cup of tea. Mama will be so pleased. She was saying only the other day she did wish the young Heaths would feel more free to call."

It struck Margaret that the word "free" in this sense was the antonym of "free" in all others, for to enter Mrs. Yeoman's house was to consign oneself to a period of imprisonment, to be turned to stone by the hostess's self-supporting and infuriated monologue on the way the times had changed.

Mrs. Wainright-Lowe, with the sure insinuations of a lifelong habit of self-defeat, said, "It is a rare thing to get the Heaths to drink a cup of tea. And almost never does one get both of them together. Now and again, Margaret will come, and once in a blue moon Tommy will."

"Perhaps they don't like tea," said Sister Evelyn.

"Perhaps they don't like the institution of tea," said Eva, going again across the terrace to attend to the phonograph. Everyone laughed at the implausibility of this last suggestion, and Margaret laughed the hardest of all.

Sister Evelyn had brought a slip of pink paper with her, and when Eva, who taught school in Salt Lake and perfectly adored the West, even though she was still a dude, came back and poured herself another cup of tea, the nun said to her, "Now, here are the names of the teachers. I found them out from Audrey. There is a Mrs. Robertson, a Mrs. Pinkham, and someone who was née Kendricks but Audrey didn't know who she had married."

"Audrey is slipping!" cried Eva with a kind of guttural, barroom laugh.

"Isn't she, just?" said Sister Evelyn. "Well, anyhow, we can start out on this. I think we should ask them all to the first meeting, don't you?"

Mrs. Wainright-Lowe, tucking an overlapping bit of lettuce into her sandwich, explained to Margaret, "We are starting some young people's activities in the village. You and Tommy need not think you can get out of helping us! You evaded us in the winter, but we forgave you, since it was your first year here. But now we have you!"

Margaret vividly recalled the scenes of January, when she and Tommy had been made to feel irresponsible and stonehearted because they would not give up their Saturdays to direct the games of sullen children who wholly hated this Christian intrusion upon their privacy. She said hopefully, "Are the activities to be under the auspices of your church?"

"I suppose that, technically, they are, aren't they, Sister?"

And the Sister, glancing at Mrs. Wainright-Lowe's lettuce and thinking, no doubt, of Margaret's negligence in other quarters, said, "I should think so, certainly. We appear to be the only enterprising group in the county."

"Then, in that case," said Margaret, looking at no one lest her relief show too plainly, "we can't, you know. It's the same as it was last winter. The priest we wrote to said we could not possibly have anything to do with a movement outside our church."

"It's not a movement," said Eva, again with that peculiar, beerhouse laugh.

"I think it's too tiresome," said her mother peckishly. "We are all Catholics, whether we are Romans or Anglicans."

Sister said, with a laugh, with a look of disdain for the Romans on her aristocratic, wimple-bound face, "I don't think Rome would quite accept that dictum, my dear," and Mrs. Wainright-Lowe, pouting, said, "Well, I don't care. I think it's tiresome to deprive these underprivileged youngsters of the writing instruction Margaret and Tommy could give them."

The ladies went on with their plans, and presently it was forgotten that Margaret and Tommy had not "fallen in" with the life that centered around Mrs. Wainright-Lowe's house. Margaret envied Tommy, alone in his study; she looked across the road at their house and at the broad, heart-shaped leaves of the Dutchman's pipe that encroached upon his windows, and she knew that he was as happy as a lark there, lying on his couch reading either the memoirs of Saint-Simon or the New English Dictionary, while she, poor martyr, listened to these hell-for-leather crusaders scheming and facetiously arguing.

Mrs. Wainright-Lowe finally included her and said, "You don't think we're asking too much of the teachers, do you? If you were a teacher, wouldn't your interest in your pupils carry through the summer?"

"Well, I doubt if it would," replied Margaret, astonished at her forthrightness, and then she mellowed it: "But, of course, I'm not a teacher."

"By the way," said Sister Evelyn to Mrs. Wainright-Lowe, "has your *Atlantic* come?"

"Why, no, has yours?" said Mrs. Wainright-Lowe, full of zeal, for upon the *Atlantic* hung these gentlewomen's hopes and fears.

"It came this morning, and I do hope yours will arrive soon, because there is a most interesting article in it by Sir Evanston Marks. It is one of a series of lectures he gave at McGill. He suggests that education is, after all, nothing more than character-building."

"That's just what the Bishop always said," cried the Bishop's loyal widow, spilling her tea in her excitement.

"Besides being ever so original in his ideas, Sir Evanston *does* know his Scripture. He begins with a verse from Jeremiah and scatters bits of the Psalms throughout, and ends up with a passage from Our Lord."

"That is the trouble with us these days," said Mrs. Wainright-Lowe. "We do not read the Bible. Sakes! When I was a child, we read a chapter every night, and we read all sorts of other people, like Newman. Who reads Newman now? Or anyone *like* Newman?"

"That makes me think of *A Tree Grows in Brooklyn*," said Eva, laughing in her private saloon. "Because, don't you remember, it says they read a chapter of the Bible and a page of Shakespeare every night, so that when they went to school, they knew more than anyone else? Did you read the book, Margaret?"

"No," said Margaret.

"Wasn't that girl terribly young to write a novel?" said Mrs. Wainright-Lowe, who had sent over a cake the week before, on Margaret's thirtieth birthday, and seemed, in her rapt glare, to be counting the wrinkles in her neighbor's face. "Wasn't she only twenty-four?"

"I'm sure I don't know," said Margaret coldly, and Sister Evelyn, who had no idea what they were talking about, said, "My soul! That *is* young!"

Mrs. Wainright-Lowe said, "Later, I believe the book was made into a movie. I heard the author on 'Town Meeting of the Air' and did not think she was very quick. Do you ever listen to 'Town Meeting,' Sister?"

"Is that one of those breakfast clubs?"

"Not exactly," said Mrs. Wainright-Lowe. "It's in the evening, but it's the same idea."

"Oh, it isn't at all," cried Eva, and started to explain, but Sister went on, "Our children at the orphanage adored those breakfast clubs. They had guests, you see. They would introduce someone and say, 'Here's Jim, just back from Tokyo,' and then everyone would begin to tease Jim. The children loved them, I think, because there was so much laughing. Do you listen to them, Margaret?"

Wonders followed wonders today. Margaret said, as courteously as she could, that she did not; then, feeling that perhaps she had gone too far in her apathy to this conversation, she said, "But I did hear an amusing thing on the radio the other day when I was trying to get the news. I tuned in to a children's quiz program—"

"Oh, the 'Quiz Kids'!" shouted Eva.

"No, no, it wasn't that," said Margaret, already bored with her contribution. "It was something else entirely. Anyhow, the announcer asked one child what he wanted to be when he grew up, and he said, 'A dry cleaner.' "

They all smiled, but it was not their sort of thing. Sister Evelyn said, "That reminds me of the child who told me he wanted to be a mortician, just like his Uncle George, whom he admired."

"A mortician!" gasped Mrs. Wainright-Lowe. "Sakes!"

"And I was afraid he had learned some of the tricks of his Uncle George's business before he came to us," said the nun, "although he did not seem to be a morbid child."

"Oh, well," said Eva, "kids will be kids."

Sister Evelyn patted her knee, for Eva's love of children was well known. "You ought to know." And Eva gurgled like a stomach.

After a moment's silence, it was announced that the gardener's mother, who had died at noon the day before, was ninety. Mrs. Wainright-Lowe said, "Bishop Masterman spoke once of going to a party for a woman who was a hundred and eight years old, and she remembered that in her childhood General Washington and his staff had often stopped at her father's house on the upper Hudson. All the women of the neighborhood came to help cook for the General. It makes one feel it is just a step from our times to those, doesn't it?"

"It does," said Sister Evelyn. "The sheriff was telling me a similar story the other day. About some old lady in Saco who had memories of the same kind. George Washington, or something of that sort."

"Yes, yes," said Mrs. Wainright-Lowe, sighing to think of the proximity of history. "Bishop Masterman was so clever when he taught children. I remember, on this same occasion, he explained to mine that although the Year One seemed a long time ago, it would only be back twenty lifetimes. Twenty men, that is, living to be a hundred and overlapping one another would be all that would be necessary to go back to the Year One."

"That's awfully good," said Eva, "but I don't remember his telling *me* that."

"You have a good forgetter," said her mother.

"But I do remember that house he took us to see in England. Do you remember the cobblestone court, and how the chapel entry was right under a cherry tree?"

"Such a lovely house!" said Mrs. Wainright-Lowe. "The best sitting room was on the third floor."

"They were always on the second or third floor," said Sister Evelyn. "Even in my mother's day, there was always a 'best' parlor on the second floor. And the ballroom, of course, at the top of the house."

Now Mrs. Wainright-Lowe turned directly to Margaret and said, "I forgot to ask you, what did your architect friend say about your house? Sister, Margaret has an architect friend who is spending the summer in West Bath, and we are both so keen to have him advise us about our kitchens."

Margaret said, "I'm afraid he's not really interested in old houses."

A veil of disapproval came down over the widowed eyes, and she said evenly, "Oh. He's from New York, isn't he?"

"New York," said Sister Evelyn, stating a regrettable fact.

"Yes," said Margaret, and, probing the ugly, public wound, she added, "As a matter of fact, he was born there."

The lacuna hovered like a leaf about to fall. The teacups

somehow did not reach their saucers but stayed still in midair. Mrs. Heath's manners and her friend's character would get their due at future teas.

Suddenly, Mrs. Wainright-Lowe sat up straight, in an inexplicable little tantrum, and said, "I think Tommy is gravely mistaken if he thinks one can live by art alone. But I daresay he would call *me* bourgeois for posing that question!"

Eva popped a pâté cracker into her big mouth and said, "Oh, dry up, Mother! Did you knit that sweater yourself, Margaret?"

"No, my mother-in-law did."

Sister Evelyn said, "Mama was so disappointed that your mother-in-law did not come to call when she visited you."

"We didn't like to disturb her, since we knew she'd been ill, and we knew what a time you were having getting servants." This was not exactly true. Margaret's mother-in-law, after hearing the Heaths' description of their neighbor, had said, "I think it's lovely to have her next door, and I'm sure it must be relaxing for you and Tommy to go there to tea after a hard day's work. But don't let's go."

Sister Evelyn, riding the crest of this earthly life, said severely, "She might at least have come to see the woodwork in the library."

Mrs. Wainright-Lowe said, "What *is* your servant situation these days, Sister?"

"The handmaiden arrived from Rockland yesterday. But she will not sleep in. She is staying with her aunt in the village, and the aunt delivers her a little before seven and comes to fetch her a little after seven."

"Who is the aunt?" asked Mrs. Wainright-Lowe.

Sister Evelyn laughed. "It's very intricate. Her name is Annie Bedlow, and she was—I found out all this from Audrey—Annie Cashman before she was married, and her mother, Nellie Cashman, used to live in Arthur Rutherford's house, on the Pond Road, the house that now belongs to the Misses Archer. And these Misses Archer are first cousins, once removed, to Annie Cashman Bedlow, and our child—Betty Temple, her name is—will divide her time between her aunt and these cousins, who are her second cousins. Second?" she asked herself. "Yes, that's right, second cousins."

"Whoop-de-doo!" cried Eva, lying down flat on her back on the lawn. "I vote you get A for recitation, Sister."

The sun was beginning to set. Margaret fixed her eye on Sister Evelyn's broad cuff, and when the nun raised her hand with the teacup, she saw with relief that the hands of the big, efficient watch stood at half past six. She returned her cup to the tray and said, "I must go get dinner."

"You've just had tea," said Mrs. Wainright-Lowe.

"But Tommy hasn't."

"Not because he wasn't *asked* to have it. I do declare, I shall have His Lordship here tomorrow at tea and I shan't take no for an answer. You tell him that for me, Margaret—I shan't take no for an answer. With his thingumbobs off in the mail, he'll have no excuse."

"None," said Sister Evelyn firmly.

"Won't you take some roses to adorn his dinner table?" said the invincible widow.

And Margaret was obliged to wait while Eva went to fetch the shears, while Mrs. Wainright-Lowe, obsessed, donned her thornproof gloves and meticulously and maliciously selected the handsomest of all her flowers, handling each as if it were an inestimably precious chalice, full of hemlock, and, giving them to Margaret, she said, "Thank you for coming. It was so good in you to come to tea."

At that moment, a car came racing down the road, burgeoning with Wainright-Lowes home from the beach, and against this racket Sister Evelyn, who would wait just a moment before she, too, left, said, with a dim, tea-party smile, "And tomorrow, while Tommy is here, you will come and visit with Mama, won't you? So glad you are going to be in residence the year around."

A Country Love Story

An antique sleigh stood in the yard, snow after snow banked up against its eroded runners. Here and there upon the bleached and splintery seat were wisps of horsehair and scraps of the black leather that had once upholstered it. It bore, with all its jovial curves, an air not so much of desuetude as of slowed-down dash, as if weary horses, unable to go another step, had at last stopped here. The sleigh had come with the house. The former owner, a gifted businesswoman from Castine who bought old houses and sold them again with all their pitfalls still intact, had said when she was showing them the place, "A picturesque detail, I think," and, waving it away, had turned to the well, which, with enthusiasm and at considerable length, she said had never gone dry. Actually, May and Daniel had found the detail more distracting than picturesque, so nearly kin was it to outdoor arts and crafts, and when the woman, as they departed in her car, gestured toward it again and said, "Paint that up a bit with something cheery and it will really add no end to your yard," simultaneous shudders coursed them. They had planned to remove the sleigh before they did anything else.

But partly because there were more important things to be done, and partly because they did not know where to put it (a sleigh could not, in the usual sense of the words, be thrown away), and partly because it seemed defiantly a part of the yard, as entitled to be there permanently as the trees, they did nothing about it. Throughout the summer, they saw birds briefly pause on its rakish front and saw the fresh rains wash its runners; in the autumn they watched the golden leaves fill the seat and nestle dryly down; and now, with the snow, they watched this new accumulation.

The sleigh was visible from the windows of the big, bright kitchen where they ate all their meals and, sometimes too bemused with country solitude to talk, they gazed out at it, forgetting their food in speculating on its history. It could have been driven cavalierly by the scion of some sea captain's family, or it could have been used soberly to haul the household's Unitarians to church or to take the womenfolk around the countryside on errands of good will. They did not speak of what its office might have been, and the fact of their silence was often nettlesome to May, for she felt they were silent too much of the time; a little morosely, she thought, If something as absurd and as provocative as this at which we look together—and which is, even though we didn't want it, our own property—cannot bring us to talk, what can? But she did not disturb Daniel in his private musings; she held her tongue, and out of the corner of her eye she watched him watch the winter cloak the sleigh, and, as if she were computing a difficult sum in her head, she tried to puzzle out what it was that had stilled tongues that earlier, before Daniel's illness, had found the days too short to communicate all they were eager to say.

It had been Daniel's doctor's idea, not theirs, that had brought them to the solemn hinterland to stay after all the summer gentry had departed in their beach wagons. The Northern sun, the pristine air, the rural walks and soundless nights, said Dr. Tellenbach, perhaps pining for his native Switzerland, would do more for the "Professor's" convalescent lung than all the doctors and clinics in the world. Privately he had added to May that after so long a season in the sanitarium (Daniel had been there a year), where everything was tuned to a low pitch, it would be difficult and it might be shattering for "the boy" (not now the "Professor," although Daniel, nearly fifty, was his wife's senior by twenty years and Dr. Tellenbach's by ten) to go back at once to the excitements and the intrigues of the university, to what, with finicking humor, the Doctor called "the omnium-gatherum of the schoolmaster's life." The rigors of a country winter would be as nothing, he insisted, when compared to the strain of feuds and cocktail parties. All professors wanted to write books, didn't they? Surely Daniel, a historian with all the material in the world at his fingertips, must have something up his sleeve that could be the *raison d'être* for this year away? May said she supposed he had, she was not sure. She could hear the reluctance in her voice as she escaped the Doctor's eyes and gazed through his windows at the mountains behind the sanitarium. In the dragging months Daniel had been gone, she had taken solace in imagining the time when they *would* return to just that pandemonium the Doctor so deplored, and because it had been pandemonium on the smallest and most discreet scale, she smiled through her disappointment at the little man's Swiss innocence and explained that they had always lived quietly, seldom dining out or entertaining more than twice a week.

"Twice a week!" He was appalled.

"But I'm afraid," she had protested, "that he would find a second year of inactivity intolerable. He does intend to write a book, but he means to write it in England, and we can't go to England now."

"England!" Dr. Tellenbach threw up his hands. "Good *air* is my recommendation for your husband. Good air and little talk."

She said, "It's talk he needs, I should think, after all this time of communing only with himself except when I came to visit."

He had looked at her with exaggerated patience, and then, courtly but authoritative, he said, "I hope you will not think I importune when I tell you that I am very well acquainted with your husband, and, as his physician, I order this retreat. *He* quite agrees."

Stung to see that there was a greater degree of understanding between Daniel and Dr. Tellenbach than between Daniel and herself, May had objected further, citing an occasion when her husband had put his head in his hands and mourned, "I hear talk of nothing but sputum cups and X-rays. Aren't people interested in the state of the world any more?"

But Dr. Tellenbach had been adamant, and at the end, when she had risen to go, he said, "You are bound to find him changed a little. A long illness removes a thoughtful man from his fellow beings. It is like living with an exacting mistress who is not content with half a man's attention but must claim it all." She had thought his figure of speech absurd and disdained to ask him what he meant.

Actually, when the time came for them to move into the new

house and she found no alterations in her husband but found, on the other hand, much pleasure in their country life, she began to forgive Dr. Tellenbach. In the beginning, it was like a second honeymoon, for they had moved to a part of the North where they had never been and they explored it together, sharing its charming sights and sounds. Moreover, they had never owned a house before but had always lived in city apartments, and though the house they bought was old and derelict, its lines and doors and window lights were beautiful, and they were possessed by it. All through the summer, they reiterated, "To think that we own all of this! That it actually belongs to us!" And they wandered from room to room marveling at their windows, from none of which was it possible to see an ugly sight. They looked to the south upon a river, to the north upon a lake; to the west of them were pine woods where the wind forever sighed, voicing a vain entreaty; and to the east a rich man's long meadow that ran down a hill to his old, magisterial house. It was true, even in those bewitched days, that there were times on the lake, when May was gathering water lilies as Daniel slowly rowed, that she had seen on his face a look of abstraction and she had known that he was worlds away, in his memories, perhaps, of his illness and the sanitarium (of which he would never speak) or in the thought of the book he was going to write as soon, he said, as the winter set in and there was nothing to do but work. Momentarily the look frightened her and she remembered the Doctor's words, but then, immediately herself again in the security of married love, she caught at another water lily and pulled at its long stem. Companionably, they gardened, taking special pride in the nicotiana that sent its nighttime fragrance into their bedroom. Together, and with fascination, they consulted carpenters, plasterers, and chimney sweeps. In the blue evenings they read at ease, hearing no sound but that of the night birds—the loons on the lake and the owls in the tops of trees. When the days began to cool and shorten, a cricket came to bless their house, nightly singing behind the kitchen stove. They got two fat and idle tabby cats, who lay insensible beside the fireplace and only stirred themselves to purr perfunctorily.

Because they had not moved in until July and by that time the workmen of the region were already engaged, most of the major repairs of the house were to be postponed until the spring, and in October, when May and Daniel had done all they could by themselves and Daniel had begun his own work, May suddenly found herself without occupation. Whole days might pass when she did nothing more than cook three meals and walk a little in the autumn mist and pet the cats and wait for Daniel to come down from his upstairs study to talk to her. She began to think with longing of the crowded days in Boston before Daniel was sick, and even in the year past, when he had been away and she had gone to concerts and recitals and had done good deeds for crippled children and had endlessly shopped for presents to lighten the tedium of her husband's unwilling exile. And, longing, she was remorseful, as if by desiring another she betrayed this life, and, remorseful, she hid away in sleep. Sometimes she slept for hours in the daytime, imitating the cats, and when at last she got up, she had to push away the dense sleep as if it were a door.

One day at lunch, she asked Daniel to take a long walk with her that afternoon to a farm where the owner smoked his own sausages.

"You never go outdoors," she said, "and Dr. Tellenbach said you must. Besides, it's a lovely day."

"I can't," he said. "I'd like to, but I can't. I'm busy. You go alone."

Overtaken by a gust of loneliness, she cried, "Oh, Daniel, I have nothing to *do!*"

A moment's silence fell, and then he said, "I'm sorry to put you through this, my dear, but you must surely admit that it's not my fault I got sick."

In her shame, her rapid, overdone apologies, her insistence that nothing mattered in the world except his health and peace of mind, she made everything worse, and at last he said shortly to her, "Stop being a child, May. Let's just leave each other alone."

This outbreak, the very first in their marriage of five years, was the beginning of a series. Hardly a day passed that they did not bicker over something; they might dispute a question of fact, argue a matter of taste, catch each other out in an inaccuracy, and every quarrel ended with Daniel's saying to her, "Why don't you leave me alone?" Once he said, "I've been sick and now I'm busy and I'm no longer young enough to shift the focus of my mind each time it suits your whim." Afterward, there were always apologies, and then Daniel went back to his study and did not open the door of it again until the next meal. Finally, it seemed to her that love, the very center of their being, was choked off, overgrown, invisible. And silent with hostility or voluble with trivial reproach, they tried to dig it out impulsively and could not—could only maul it in its unkempt grave. Daniel, in his withdrawal from her and from the house, was preoccupied with his research, of which he never spoke except to say that it would bore her, and most of the time, so it appeared to May, he did not worry over what was happening to them. She felt the cold old house somehow enveloping her as if it were their common enemy, maliciously bent on bringing them to disaster. Sunken in faithlessness, they stared, at mealtimes, atrophied within the present hour, at the irrelevant and whimsical sleigh that stood abandoned in the mammoth winter.

May found herself thinking, If we redeemed it and painted it, our house would have something in common with Henry Ford's Wayside Inn. And I might make this very observation to him and he might greet it with disdain and we might once again be able to talk to each other. Perhaps we could talk of Williamsburg and how we disapproved of it. Her mind went toiling on. Williamsburg was part of our honeymoon trip; somewhere our feet were entangled in suckers as we stood kissing under a willow tree. Soon she found that she did not care for this line of thought, nor did she care what his response to it might be. In her imagined conversations with Daniel, she never spoke of the sleigh. To the thin, ill scholar whose scholarship and illness had usurped her place, she had gradually taken a weighty but unviolent dislike.

The discovery of this came, not surprising her, on Christmas Day. The knowledge sank like a plummet, and at the same time she was thinking about the sleigh, connecting it with the smell of the barn on damp days, and she thought perhaps it had been drawn by the very animals who had been stabled there and had pervaded the timbers with their odor. There must have been much life within this house once—but long ago. The earth immediately behind the barn was said by everyone to be extremely rich because of the horses, although there had been none there for over fifty years. Thinking of this soil, which earlier she had eagerly sifted through her fingers, May now realized that she had no wish for the spring to come, no wish to plant a garden, and, branching out at random, she found she had no wish to see the sea again, or children, or favorite pictures, or even her own face on a happy day. For a minute or two, she was almost enraptured in this state of no desire, but then, purged swiftly of her cynicism, she knew it to be false, knew that actually she did have a desire —the desire for a desire. And now she felt that she was stationary in a whirlpool, and at the very moment she conceived the notion a bit of wind brought to the seat of the sleigh the final leaf from the elm tree that stood beside it. It crossed her mind that she might consider the wood of the sleigh in its juxtaposition to the living tree and to the horses, who, although they were long since dead, reminded her of their passionate, sweating, running life every time she went to the barn for firewood.

They sat this morning in the kitchen full of sun, and, speaking not to him but to the sleigh, to icicles, to the dark, motionless pine woods, she said, "I wonder if on a day like this they used to take the pastor home after lunch." Daniel gazed abstractedly at the bright-silver drifts beside the well and said nothing. Presently a wagon went past hauled by two oxen with bells on their yoke. This was the hour they always passed, taking to an unknown destination an aged man in a fur hat and an aged woman in a shawl. May and Daniel listened.

Suddenly, with impromptu anger, Daniel said, "What did you just say?"

"Nothing," she said. And then, after a pause, "It would be lovely at Jamaica Pond today."

He wheeled on her and pounded the table with his fist. "I did not ask for this!" The color rose feverishly to his thin cheeks and his breath was agitated. "You are trying to make me sick again. It was wonderful, wasn't it, for you while I was gone?"

"Oh, no, no! Oh, no, Daniel, it was hell!"

"Then, by the same token, this must be heaven." He smiled, the professor catching out a student in a fallacy.

"Heaven." She said the word bitterly.

"Then why do you stay here?" he cried.

It was a cheap impasse, desolate, true, unfair. She did not answer him.

After a while he said, "I almost believe there's something you haven't told me."

She began to cry at once, blubbering across the table at him. "You have said that before. What am I to say? What have I done?"

He looked at her, impervious to her tears, without mercy and yet without contempt. "I don't know. But you've done something."

It was as if she were looking through someone else's scrambled closets and bureau drawers for an object that had not been named to her, but nowhere could she find her gross offense.

Domestically she asked him if he would have more coffee and he peremptorily refused and demanded, "Will you tell me why it is you must badger me? Is it a compulsion? Can't you control it? Are you going mad?"

From that day onward, May felt a certain stirring of life within her solitude, and now and again, looking up from a book to see if the damper on the stove was right, to listen to a rat renovating its house-within-a-house, to watch the belled oxen pass, she nursed her wound, hugged it, repeated his awful words exactly as he had said them, reproduced the way his wasted lips had looked and his bright, farsighted eyes. She could not read for long at any time, nor could she sew. She cared little now for planning changes in her house; she had meant to sand the painted floors to uncover the wood of the wide boards and she had imagined how the long, paneled windows of the drawing room would look when yellow velvet curtains hung there in the spring. Now, schooled by silence and indifference, she was immune to disrepair and to the damage done by the wind and snow, and she looked, as Daniel did, without dislike upon the old and nasty wallpaper and upon the shabby kitchen floor. One day, she knew that the sleigh would stay where it was so long as they stayed there. From every thought, she returned to her deep, bleeding injury. He had asked her if she were going mad.

She repaid him in the dark afternoons while he was closeted away in his study, hardly making a sound save when he added wood to his fire or paced a little, deep in thought. She sat at the kitchen table looking at the sleigh, and she gave Daniel insult for his injury by imagining a lover. She did not imagine his face, but she imagined his clothing, which would be costly and in the best of taste, and his manner, which would be urbane and anticipatory of her least whim, and his clever speech, and his adept courtship that would begin the moment he looked at the sleigh and said, "I must get rid of that for you at once." She might be a widow, she might be divorced, she might be committing adultery. Certainly there was no need to specify in an affair so securely legal. There was no need, that is, up to a point, and then the point came when she took in the fact that she not only believed in this lover but loved him and depended wholly on his companionship. She complained to him of Daniel and he consoled her; she told him stories of her girlhood, when she had gaily gone to parties, squired by boys her own age; she dazzled him sometimes with the wise comments she made on the books she read. It came to be true that if she so much as looked at the sleigh, she was weakened, failing with starvation.

Often, about her daily tasks of cooking food and washing dishes and tending the fires and shopping in the general store of the village, she thought she should watch her step, that it was this sort of thing that *did* make one go mad; for a while, then, she went back to Daniel's question, sharpening its razor edge. But she could not corral her alien thoughts and she trembled as she bought split peas, fearful that the old men loafing by the stove could see the incubus of her sins beside her. She could not avert such thoughts when they rushed upon her sometimes at tea with one of the old religious ladies of the neighborhood, so that, in the middle of a conversation about a deaconess in Bath, she retired from them, seeking her lover, who came, faceless, with his arms outstretched, even as she sat up straight in a Boston rocker, even as she accepted another cup of tea. She lingered over the cake plates and the simple talk, postponing her return to her own house and to Daniel, whom she continually betrayed.

It was not long after she recognized her love that she began to wake up even before the dawn and to be all day quick to everything, observant of all the signs of age and eccentricity in her husband, and she compared him in every particular—to his humiliation, in her eyes—with the man whom now it seemed to her she had always loved at fever pitch.

Once when Daniel, in a rare mood, kissed her, she drew back involuntarily and he said gently, "I wish I knew what you had done, poor dear." He looked as if for written words in her face.

"You said you knew," she said, terrified.

"I do."

"Then why do you wish you knew?" Her baffled voice was high and frantic. "You don't talk sense!"

"I do," he said sedately. "I talk sense always. It is you who are oblique." Her eyes stole like a sneak to the sleigh. "But I wish I knew your motive," he said impartially.

For a minute, she felt that they were two maniacs answering each other questions that had not been asked, never touching the matter at hand because they did not know what the matter was. But in the next moment, when he turned back to her spontaneously and clasped her head between his hands and said, like a tolerant father, "I forgive you, darling, because you don't know how you persecute me. No one knows except the sufferer what this sickness is," she knew again, helplessly, that they were not harmonious even in their aberrations.

These days of winter came and went, and on each of them, after breakfast and as the oxen passed, he accused her of her concealed misdeed. She could no longer truthfully deny that she was guilty, for she was in love, and she heard the subterfuge in her own voice and felt the guilty fever in her veins. Daniel knew it, too, and watched her. When she was alone, she felt her lover's presence protecting her—when she walked past the stiff spiraea, with icy cobwebs hung between its twigs, down to the lake, where the black, unmeasured water was hidden beneath a lid of ice; when she walked, instead, to the salt river to see the tar-paper shacks where the men caught smelt through the ice; when she walked in the dead dusk up the hill from the store, catching her breath the moment she saw the sleigh. But sometimes this splendid being mocked her when, freezing with fear of the consequences of her sin, she ran up the stairs to Daniel's room and burrowed her head in his shoulder and cried, "Come downstairs! I'm lonely, please come down!" But he would never come, and at last, bitterly, calmed by his calmly inquisitive regard, she went back alone and stood at the kitchen window, coyly half hidden behind the curtains.

For months she lived with her daily dishonor, rattled, ashamed, stubbornly clinging to her secret. But she grew more and more afraid when, oftener and oftener, Daniel said, "Why do you lie to me? What does this mood of yours mean?" and she could no longer sleep. In the raw nights, she lay straight beside him as he slept, and she stared at the ceiling, as bright as the snow it reflected, and tried not to think of the sleigh out there under the elm tree but could think only of it and of the man, her lover, who was connected with it somehow. She said to herself, as she listened to his breathing, "If I confessed to Daniel, he would understand that I was lonely and he would comfort me, saying, 'I am here, May. I shall never let you be lonely again.'" At these times, she was so separated from the world, so far removed from his touch and his voice, so solitary, that she would have sued a stranger for companionship. Daniel slept deeply, having no guilt to make him toss. He slept, indeed, so well that he never even heard the ditcher on snowy nights rising with a groan over the hill, flinging the snow from the road and warning of its approach by lights that first flashed red, then blue. As it passed their house, the hurled snow swashed like flames. All night she heard the squirrels adding up their nuts in the walls and heard the spirit of the house creaking and softly clicking upon the stairs and in the attics.

In early spring, when the whippoorwills begged in the cat-tails and the marsh reeds, and the northern lights patinated the lake and the tidal river, and the stars were large, and the huge vine of Dutchman's-pipe had started to leaf out, May went to bed late. Each night she sat on the back steps waiting, hearing the snuffling of a dog as it hightailed it for home, the single cry of a loon. Night after night, she waited for the advent of her rebirth while upstairs Daniel, who had spoken tolerantly of her vigils, slept, keeping his knowledge of her to himself. "A symptom," he had said, scowling in concentration, as he remarked upon her new habit. "Let it run its course. Perhaps when this is over, you will know the reason why you torture me with these obsessions and will stop. You know, you may really have a slight disorder of the mind. It would be nothing to be ashamed of; you could go to a sanitarium."

One night, looking out the window, she clearly saw her lover sitting in the sleigh. His hand was over his eyes and his chin was covered by a red silk scarf. He wore no hat and his hair was fair. He was tall and his long legs stretched indolently along the floorboard. He was younger than she had imagined him to be and he seemed rather frail, for there was a delicate pallor on his high, intelligent forehead and there was an invalid's languor in his whole attitude. He wore a white blazer and gray flannels and there was a yellow rosebud in his lapel. Young as he was, he did not, even so, seem to belong to her generation; rather, he seemed to be the reincarnation of someone's uncle as he had been fifty years before. May did not move until he vanished, and then, even though she knew now that she was truly bedeviled, the only emotion she had was bashfulness, mingled with doubt; she was not sure, that is, that he loved her.

That night, she slept a while. She lay near to Daniel, who was smiling in the moonlight. She could tell that the sleep she would have tonight would be as heavy as a coma, and she was aware of the moment she was overtaken.

She was in a canoe in a meadow of water lilies and her lover was tranquilly taking the shell off a hard-boiled egg. "How intimate," he said, "to eat an egg with you." She was nervous lest the canoe tip over, but at the same time she was charmed by his wit and by the way he lightly touched her shoulder with the varnished paddle.

"May? May? I love you, May."

"Oh!" enchanted, she heard her voice replying. "Oh, I love you, too!"

"The winter is over, May. You must forgive the hallucinations of a sick man."

She woke to see Daniel's fair, pale head bending toward her. "He is old! He is ill!" she thought, but through her tears, to deceive him one last time, she cried, "Oh, thank God, Daniel!"

He was feeling cold and wakeful and he asked her to make him a cup of tea; before she left the room, he kissed her hands and arms and said, "If I am ever sick again, don't leave me, May."

Downstairs, in the kitchen, cold with shadows and with the

obtrusion of dawn, she was belabored by a chill. "What time is it?" she said aloud, although she did not care. She remembered, not for any reason, a day when she and Daniel had stood in the yard last October wondering whether they should cover the chimneys that would not be used and he decided that they should not, but he had said, "I hope no birds get trapped." She had replied, "I thought they all left at about this time for the South," and he had answered, with an unintelligible reproach in his voice, "The starlings stay." And she remembered, again for no reason, a day when, in pride and excitement, she had burst into the house crying, "I saw an ermine. It was terribly poised and let me watch it quite a while." He had said categorically, "There are no ermines here."

She had not protested; she had sighed as she sighed now and turned to the window. The sleigh was livid in this light and no one was in it; nor had anyone been in it for many years. But at that moment the blacksmith's cat came guardedly across the dewy field and climbed into it, as if by careful plan, and curled up on the seat. May prodded the clinkers in the stove and started to the barn for kindling. But she thought of the cold and the damp and the smell of the horses, and she did not go but stood there, holding the poker and leaning upon it as if it were an umbrella. There was no place warm to go. "What time is it?" she whimpered, heartbroken, and moved the poker, stroking the lion foot of the fireless stove.

She knew now that no change would come, and that she would never see her lover again. Confounded utterly, like an orphan in solitary confinement, she went outdoors and got into the sleigh. The blacksmith's imperturbable cat stretched and rearranged his position, and May sat beside him with her hands locked tightly in her lap, rapidly wondering over and over again how she would live the rest of her life.

The Bleeding Heart

Every morning and on alternate afternoons, Rose Fabrizio, a Mexican girl from the West, worked at a discreet girls' boarding school as secretary to the headmistress, a Miss Talmadge, who had a sweet voice. It was sweet even when she was dictating a warm comeuppance to the laundry about its mistreatment of the school's counterpanes and bureau runners; and sweet when she was explaining the value of physical education to a recalcitrant pupil who declared that she loathed volleyball. Every day when she arrived shortly after Rose had unlocked the office and uncovered her typewriter, Miss Talmadge cried "Good morning" twice and then she said with a lilt, "How is our Westerner? Acclimated? Finding the charm of New England both within and without?" She then stepped briskly into her own office and made a great clatter with the files, rudely flung up the window no matter what the thermometer said and set to work like a whirlwind. At first Rose, who was twenty-one and uncommonly sensitive, bridled at this greeting, which she believed to be subtly derisive, but now after two months she knew that there was no feeling behind it at all; Miss Talmadge inquired, in the same sweet rapid way, quite indifferent to the answers, about the parlormaid's fiancé and the French teacher's needlepoint and the riding master's brother's greenhouse. But even now, this reminder of her origin (vague as it must be in Miss Talmadge's mind, for if she imagined anything at all, she probably imagined cigar-store Indians and clumps of sage) sometimes brought on a subcutaneous prickle and distracted Rose from her shorthand so that on occasion she had fetched up with sentences that could not possibly be parsed.

Except in the vocal presence of Miss Talmadge, she *was*

acclimated and she *did* find New England charming, although she was not quite sure that she had found it so both within and without, having no idea what the headmistress meant. She rejoiced in the abundance of imposing trees, in the pure style of the houses and the churches, in the venerable graveyards and in the unobtrusive shops. One was not conscious of any of the working parts of the town, not of the railroad or of the filling stations or of the water towers and the light-plants. Her own town, out West, had next to no trees and those were puny and half bald. The main street there was a row of dirty doorways which led into the dirtier interiors of pool halls, drugstores where even the soda-fountain bar had a flaccid look, and small restaurants and beer parlors and hotels whose windows were decorated sometimes with sweet-potato vines growing out of jam cans painted red, and sometimes with a prospector's pick-ax and some spurious gold ore, and sometimes with nothing more than the concupiscent but pessimistic legend that ladies were invited or that there were booths for them. The people here in this dignified New England town, shabby as they might be, wore hats and gloves at all hours and on all days and they appeared moral, self-controlled, well-bathed, and literate. The population of her own town was largely Mexican and was therefore, by turns, criminally quarrelsome or grossly stupefied so that when they were not beating one another up they stared into dusty space or lounged in various comatose attitudes against the stock properties of the main street: the telephone poles and fire hydrants and hitching posts. They were swarthy and they tended, on the whole, to be fat and to wear bright, juvenile colors. Repudiating all that, she greatly admired the pallor of the people here and their dun dress and their accent so that the merest soda-jerk sounded as if he had gone to Harvard.

In this atmosphere of good breeding and adulthood, Rose was happy half the time and altogether miserable the rest of it, miserable, that is, with envy of the people who had been born here of upright gentlefolk and had been reared in mannerly calm. And Rose, although she was full-grown and had a Bachelor of Arts degree (to be sure, she had not gone to Radcliffe and her education had been a shabby, uninteresting affair), longed to be adopted by a New Englander. Sometimes this longing coupled with her loneliness—it was not to its detriment that the town was unfriendly but quite the contrary—fretted her so that she could neither read nor play Canfield and she sat idle and unhappy in her bed-sitting room where the wind came down the chimney like a failing voice and now and then caused the long-handled bed-warmer to stir on its hook, chiming against the bricks.

She had selected the very person she wished to become her foster-father, a man about sixty whom she saw on Tuesday and Thursday and Saturday afternoons in the town library, an incongruously modern building dedicated to the memory of Samuel Sewell. Here Rose read books on psychology in a western room where the sun came amply through the windows; in this room, besides herself, there always sat a thoughtful gentleman, wearing a lemon-yellow ascot and a sober dark blue suit. The ascot alone would have set him down as a person of prominence, for no one unimportant, she reasoned, could afford to be so boldly eccentric. She did not know what he read through the scholarly Oxford glasses which perfectly fitted on his stately nose and were anchored to his lapel by a black ribbon ending in a silver button. The books were big, she knew that much, and their bindings were a usual maroon. He did not take any notes (as she did voluminously, having been so recently graduated) and he read quite slowly. He did not move all afternoon save that at half past three he went outside and stood on the steps to smoke a cigarette; she could see him clearly through the window beside which she sat reading of Pavlov's submissive dog. Either he stood still, leaning against a half pillar of the half-Ionic façade with his eyes closed and his lips moving a little, or he took a turn around the little triangular yard, holding his hatless white head at a dignified backward angle. Occasionally he paused under a tree and there, ankle deep in fallen leaves from the wine-glass elm, he was lost impressively in speculation. She thought he might be a mathematician or a novelist. Often when he returned, bringing with him a final remnant of the autumn air, he looked over at Rose across the tables and gave her an amiable, perfunctory nod as if he were her busy employer passing through the office of his underlings. Once he said something to her but in so low a voice and with so noncommittal an expression on his face that she did not understand and only smiled.

Despite a heritage of headlong impulse and her practice of setting forth before the signal was given, Rose made no move to further her acquaintance with the man and, indeed, she took pains never to see him out of his context. She always left the library before he did so that she would be tempted neither to find out what he was reading, since this would give a clue to his profession, nor to discover the direction he took to go home. Earlier in the fall, before she was aware that her library habits coincided with his and before she wanted to be adopted by him, she had enjoyed walking through the woods and over the hills and beside the river. On Sundays she had always gone to the largest and the oldest cemetery and there, upon a crest of rocks which overlooked the thin, ungarnished headstones, she had thoroughly read the literary supplement of *The New York Times* and had absently considered the hedge of barberry that flourished every which way beside a brook. She had liked to imagine the furnishings of the houses she could just see opposite and to wonder what scions of *Mayflower* families lived in them and were about to order tea. But now on Sunday she stayed in her room, long as the day seemed, for it would in no way serve her purpose, she thought sensibly, to be caught spying on the library man if he should come some time to pay his respects to someone's bones, those of his wife, perhaps, or a beloved daughter dead in early womanhood.

And before this, she had gone to dinner once or twice a week to an inn a mile out of the town on a byroad. This inn had the mark of Henry Ford upon it and so had the diners who disputed facts to do with the American Revolution and who exclaimed over the hasty-pudding. The landlord, a lethargic man from Bangor, sat in a chimney corner smoking an authentic pipe and the cook was said to be descended from King Philip on the maternal side. Rose did not think it probable that the man in the yellow ascot would ever come to a place like this since the atmosphere of his own dining room would be, if anything, even more bona fide. But she did not wish to run any risk, for, just as she did not want to know what books he read (he might be proved by them to be in his second childhood) and did not want to see him laying flowers upon his daughter's grave (for it might not be a daughter at all but only some old aunt by marriage), so she did not want to see him eating lest she discover that he followed an idiosyncratic diet and therefore had a constitutional disease.

All this abstention and the restiveness that accompanied it made her days and evenings monotonous and she became very much aware of the drawbacks of her room, which until now she had found—at least by comparison with the room at home which she shared with two younger sisters, both of whom walked in their sleep and one of whom gnashed her teeth—ideal. She lived on the ground floor of a double house that stood on a corner and was shaped like a wedge so that the front doors were on different streets. Her room, at Number 8 Patriot Road, was flush with what she thought must be the parlor at Number 6 Faneuil Lane and through the wood and plaster she sometimes heard throttled voices, heavy footsteps, and the indignant squawk of a mistuned radio. But she never heard a sound in Number 8. She was the only lodger on the first floor, but upstairs there were several meek and apparitional figures whom she met in the mildewed hall as she went to and from the bathroom. The landlady lived across the entryway from Rose and was visible only on Wednesday evening when she came to collect the rent and present the clean towels. Generally this transaction was performed as a dumb show and without smiles. The telephone seldom rang and the door-bell never. Besides this rather sepulchral air, the house was chilly and the lamps in Rose's room were poor.

Her feeling toward the silence of Number 8 and the sounds, low and distorted as they were, of Number 6, passed through several stages between the middle of October and the Thanks-giving holiday. At first the quiet of her own house pleased her because she could read with such concentration, and the noises of 6 irritated her when they were loud enough to intrude upon her page, yet not quite loud enough to be properly identified. Then she was disturbed and next annoyed by the silence and felt that it was unnatural, while she was grateful for the indica-tions through the wall that there was life just yonder. And, again, she would be strained and unsettled, waiting for the noises and unable to make use of the interstices of silence between them. She never saw the tenants of the other house, but she had an idea what sort they might be, for frequently there was an electric car in front, looking like a large, abandoned toy. The driver of it, she was certain, would be a brisk old lady with no nonsense about her, and she came to believe, groundlessly, that there were two such old ladies, sisters, perhaps, or friends since boarding-school days at Lausanne. One must be either rather fat or else somewhat lame and wear special shoes, for nothing else could account for the heavy tread Rose sometimes heard. Once, on a Sunday afternoon, out of a clear blue sky she wondered if the man in the yellow ascot ever called at Number 6 and she snubbed the thought, snubbed the peculiarly awful possibility that he might be there at this very moment.

On Thanksgiving Day, she went to the inn outside the town for midday dinner. The library man was there and the moment she saw him, dressed as usual, she knew that she had secretly expected him, for she was not at all surprised. He was sitting at a table near the fireplace, engaged in conversation with the landlord and simultaneously reading the menu. A bright fire burned in the hearth and his fresh skin shone in the light like a leaf turned golden and it appeared to have a leaf's smooth texture. He sat very straight in his chair and while he waited for the soup he closed his eyes and calmly smiled as he listened to the landlord, who was apparently telling a long joke. He looked as if he might be sitting for his portrait and, indeed, he would have been a distinguished subject for a painter who did accurate "likenesses" of college presidents and notable physicians, for his face had admirable qualities of mellowness and deep, pacific wisdom and irony and casualness. He was in no hurry. He waited for his dinner with his eyes closed, not having to be occupied with looking round the room at the other diners and at the Currier and Ives prints on the walls and all the antique furniture which one might buy if one were able. Rose's own young and impatient mind immediately pranced away from him and dwelt, in quick succession, upon the brindle cat who was balancing for no earthly reason on the newel post; upon the lemon tree in the bay window, fed like an animal to produce fruit of a dreadful size; two quiet brown-eyed children who sat silent at a table with two thin old women, holding their hands between courses in an attitude of prayer. Fleetly it struck her that these two might be her neighbors and at that very moment, as if she had been di-

rected by a voice, she looked out the window at the far driveway
and saw the electric car, its square top grizzled with frost. It
must be that the children were with their aged great-aunts for
the day and she thought it must be a doubtful pleasure to them
all since the four mute mouths bore an illegible expression.

Rose did not look at her foster-father save when her eyes fell
on him by accident. Once she caught him looking at her over a
piled fork and in his surprise he let some of the stuffing fall off.
Every inch of her skin felt roasted and her hands shook so that
for a moment she dared not try to lift her water glass although
her mouth was dry. And later when his salad came she looked
again and he distinctly winked at her as he tossed the cloves of
tomato and the water cress. It was not a plain-spoken wink at all
and it made her nervous. She hurried through her meal in order
that she might leave before he did because, besides the ambiguous gambit of his eye, she was inadmissibly afraid that *he,* not
the old ladies, might enter the electric car. She grappled hard
with her suspicions about him and imperatively pointed out to
herself that this stately aristocrat lived in a handsome house and
that he had naturally given his housekeeper and his cook the
day off and, because the air was fine and sharp, had liked to walk
a mile to his dinner. She could not help feeling that it was
strange he had not been invited anywhere, for surely a man of
his position, whatever it was, would have friends in the town.
Perhaps he despised the sentimental fanfare of holidays. Next
year, after his adoption of her was a legal fact, she imagined that
on Thanksgiving, Christmas, and Easter they would dine alone
and afterward would play backgammon. Yet already she was
visited with a nettlesome problem: should she play badly so that
he would have the pleasure of winning or cleverly so that he
would praise her? She rather hoped that he did not have a violin
or any whimsical hobbies like collecting Revolutionary artifacts
or taking bird-walks.

Rose did not wait for her dessert and on her way out she
glanced quickly at the coats hung on the pegs in the hall. She
recognized his immediately; it was black with a beaver lining,
and although it was quite worn, it still was very rich and service-
able. His derby was there too and a tartan muffler. Fearing the
road along which, at any moment, the electric car might pass,

she struck into the woods and walked home along the pale, thick river. She found a nickel and a fresh-water mussel shell and she came upon a beached canoe, withering in the dry fall. She passed behind the girls' school and glanced at the windows of the dormitory with their starched dimity curtains. The little girls had all gone home to their fathers for the holiday. She was very lonely here beside the river and she began to walk fast, counting her footsteps to forestall her melancholy, but then she slowed down again as she realized that she would be just as lonely in her room. Until now she had been content with seeing the man in the library and had even been a little proud in a queer way that he had a life quite secret, quite independent of the alternate afternoons in the reading room and that what she did at other times was equally unimaginable to him. But now beside the woeful river, she was almost frightened to think of him just as she had almost been frightened as a child when everyone had left the church after the last mass and she had wondered what happened then, whether the plaster saints came to life and if God emerged, full-bodied, from the wafers in the ciborium.

Rose did not know, until she was actually within her room again, shadowy with dusk and musty with the old upholstery of the buckling wicker chairs, that there had been another reason why she had not liked to come back: now she was face to face with the knowledge that she had seen the driver of the electric car, who was, therefore, one of the authors of the noises in the other house. The car had got there before she did. The very moment she stepped across her threshold onto the distempered carpet with its muddy oak leaves, the sounds came, feebly ill-natured, straight to her anticipating ears. There were no new sounds, no children's voices.

All that afternoon, while she was thinking of the man as he sat in his own library (the Samuel Sewell was closed today) in one of the white clapboard houses in the side streets of the town, the dulled hubbub went on beyond the wall. At first she paid little heed; she was thinking of the chintz wing chair he might be sitting in with his feet on a brass fender before a fire. And at first the sounds were unobtrusive. But toward dark they became more insistent and she grew fully conscious of them. Although she could not hear words nor could she tell what sort of movements were being made, she was entirely alert, straining to read this trifling mystery. After a little, she was able to separate some of the noises and she heard a door open and close and a telephone ring and a clock strike and outside, in the street, she heard a boy irrelevantly cry, "Richard?" and she heard something bump over an uncarpeted floor. But above—or rather beneath, for it was little more than a jerky hum—the other sounds, there was a voice complaining, directly on the other side of the wall; it was a venomous and senile whimper which went on and on. It seemed to be uttering short curses with just time for a breath in between the tenth, perhaps, and the eleventh. Presently there was another opening and closing of the door and a second voice, a man's voice, spoke. There was, as well, a rattle of metal and now Rose constructed a picture: someone was ill and someone else was bringing a tray to the sickbed. But the important fact was that she must revise her general notion of the household: it included a man. Yet why could it not be a doctor, summoned hastily because one of the old ladies had eaten unwisely at the inn? She regretted that she had not scrutinized her neighbors more closely to see if they bore any marks of frailty in the color of the skin or the look about the nose. She sighed and went to the window to pull down the shade, for it had grown dark, and once again the electric car served her, for here it came, a silent, absurd box, round the corner and on its way toward the Mill Dam. "They have gone for the prescription," she said happily, and she saw a peaked spinster lying in a bed, another peaked one operating the simple machinery of the car. And she assured herself that the driver must, indeed must, be one of the children's great-aunts, for no man in his right mind would be seen in such a thing in this day and age.

When she had pulled the bottle-green blinds and turned on her two lamps, no brighter than candle flames, she was momentarily disgusted with herself for spending so much time conjecturing on unseen and unknown people. She was as bad as her mother, who could search a whole evening through for the inner meanings of a neighbor's greeting when they had not been on speaking terms for weeks or the impertinence of a salesgirl in the five-and-ten. So she tried to forget about the other house and to go back to the man in the yellow ascot but he was suddenly gone altogether and instead of him she could only see her real father, Joseph Fabrizio, who would be having a holiday today like everyone else and who, stupid and cynical, would be shambling about the house out West where even the hopvines at the windows were limp and unclean. Her father wore a black coat-sweater from J. C. Penney's and a spotty gray cap and Army store pants and miner's shoes studded with cleats that tore up the linoleum and made a brash racket. The putrefied smell of sugar beets clung to him constantly even after a bath, which he took only once in a month of Sundays. She did not know one good thing about her father except when she was very small she had been delighted to hear him sing "Juanita" and "Valencia" in a tenor voice for which he was admired by two or three people in the town; and one time when he must have been as drunk as a monkey, he brought her a box of Cheese-bits and a copy of *Sweetheart Stories* when she had the pinkeye. Although as far back as she could remember, she had been driven to get away, far away, and never go home again, she was often resentful that he never wrote to her and that he had not been at all sorry when she had gone away. As a matter of fact, he had not even seen her off on the bus and her mother did not know where he was. Her mother said, looking vaguely up and down the street and nodding to several acquaintances, "Well, I'll tell him goodbye for you," and handed her a lunch in a Honey Kist bread wrapper. The simple and humiliating fact was that he cared so little that he had clean forgotten.

The memories of her father, each one of which was uglier than the one before, made her so cross and jumpy that she knew she must quiet herself and she sat down to read *Self Reliance* which she had always found very soothing because it was so sedately dull. But she could pay attention to it even less than usual and the pattern of sounds next door presently was repeated: the telephone, the opening and closing of the door, the sound of china and silver on a tray. She was irritated and when she returned to Emerson, exhorting him to lull her, the voice would give her no peace but went on in its protracted peeve, hovering like a gnat over every word on the page. Finally she grew really angry and she knocked sharply on the wall. There was an immediate silence and then a most terrible and much louder sound: it was a laugh! And such a laugh as she had never heard in her life, for it was as thin as a needle and, unlike the speech, it did not quaver. For a moment she was afraid and she stepped away as if there were real danger, and then she was even angrier than before and her thoughts went quickly down this ladder of unreason, "If my father had not been a low person and if he had loved me, I would not have grown up in poverty and I would not have hated him so much that I had to go away from home to the first job that came along, this mean one that pays so little that I must live in a dark, depressing room where the walls are so thin that the sound of sickness comes through and for no reason at all I am laughed at by a cruel person who does not even know me." And she envisaged her father as he had probably been that day she had boarded the orange bus; fat and foul-tongued, he would have been shooting Cowboy at the pool hall, where they had spittoons since most of the patrons, including (God damn him) her father, chewed tobacco.

It was no longer possible for Rose to stay in her room in the evenings because of the busy personalities so near, and after dinner she went back to the Samuel Sewell. The overhead light was poor and made her eyes smart and she missed not sitting in her wrapper and her slippers. She was impatient with the spinster's prolonged illness and she saw no reason why she was not taken to the hospital. Sometimes they went on for years that way, just clinging to the ragged edge of nothing, getting more and more querulous and bothersome. Miss Talmadge noticed that Rose was distraught and when she asked and Rose said that she was dissatisfied with her room, Miss Talmadge objected with vehement sweetness, "But it is a quaint room! It is a lovely, lovely, lovely room!" and began instantly to dictate a stunning letter to the parent of a pupil who, in a tantrum over nothing at all, had deliberately broken a hockey stick belonging to the school.

One morning just before the Christmas holiday, Miss Talmadge asked, in her pink voice, if Rose would run an errand for her in the afternoon. The girls of the fourth form wished to send a potted plant to someone who was ill, a former matron. Rose was not surprised at all when she heard that the address was

Number 6 Fanueil Lane. So important was this illness with which she lived that it did not occur to her that there was another invalid in the town and Miss Talmadge, never dreaming that the retired matron was the reason she did not like her room, said, with pointless cheer, "It will be so handy for you."

She accepted the commission with the greatest reluctance, not only because she wanted the occupants of the other house to remain anonymous but because, as well, she had a horror of being near old people and she remembered a time when the fifth grade had gone to sing Christmas carols at the old people's home. There had been a smell of senility in the long room with its glaring linoleum and Mission benches where the old people sat fiddling with their neckties or with pieces of holly purloined from the dining-room decorations. The last song was "We Three Kings" and by this time Rose was so sick that she only moved her lips, not making any sound. When it was over and they stood for a moment, dumb and immobile, until the teacher came to herd them away, a terribly, terribly old man rose to his feet and cried, "Damned brats! Clear them damned brats out p.d.q." He had bicycle clips on his eleemosynary plus-fours.

She had never actually passed the other house and she was surprised to find that its façade was altogether different from that of Number 8 Patriot Road. The paint was a darker shade of red and instead of two bay windows it had only one, just to the right of the off-center door. In the windows at Number 8, the landlady kept ferns and cactuses, but there was nothing at all alive in those of Number 6 and there were no curtains. There was only a solitary tuberculosis seal from the year before pasted in the lowest middle pane. Instead of a neat brass letter slot, there was a raveling raffia basket which hung on a hammock hook to hold the mail and there was no knocker but a bell instead, the kind you rang by turning an embossed iron handle. She turned it and heard a tinkle and instantly a voice very near her cried thinly, "Just a minute!" Rose could not tell where it came from but she waited in discomfort, feeling that she was being looked at from some vantage point no more than a foot away. Still, no one came. It was snowing and the big soft flakes dissolved in beautiful splashes on the glazed green paper that wrapped the bleeding heart. She rang again, and again, immediately, the voice encouragingly said, "Just a minute!" It was a high and genderless voice and was, she thought, the same one that had laughed at her when she had knocked on the wall. She was despondent here in the twilight snowstorm and her fingers clutching the pot were growing numb. The voice broke its promise for the second time; several minutes passed and nothing happened. She would try once more and if still no one came she would leave the plant on the doorstep even though it might freeze. Each moment she hated her role more, no matter what its outcome was to be. It would be worse than ever now to hear the sounds through the wall if she had the misfortune actually to see the interior of the house (how dreadful if she had to go into the sickroom itself!) and it would be almost as bad if the door was never opened and whoever it was that bade her wait a minute saw her leave and enter Number 8. Her comings and goings would thereafter be observed; or, even if they weren't, she would think they were and now, besides the sounds, she would be rattled by hypothetical eyes spying upon her.

She was about to ring for the last time when out of the corner of her eye she saw the electric car coming cautiously down the gentle slope of the street. Now there was no escaping. The great-aunt driving the car and the bodiless procrastinator behind the door would catch her there with the bleeding heart and make her explain herself. "Just a minute!" The voice, speaking this time of its own accord and not in answer to the bell, startled her and the plant slipped in her hands. The car disappeared in a driveway behind the house and in a little while a distant door opened and closed and Rose firmly rang the bell. This time the voice laughed mockingly up and down an untrue scale and she was in no doubt at all that it was the same one that had sneered at her knock.

The mysterious house behind the black door was seized with spasms. Someone screamed, "Tea!" and a stove was madly shaken down. Heavy footsteps crossed a room and a man's voice roared, "What? What do you say?" "Tea! Toast!" the screamed reply rang clear and the "s" in the toast was prolonged with hatred. "Give a person a chance to turn around, Mother!" said the man and the laughing voice near Rose chuckled high in its throat and mimicked itself, "Just a minute!" and then mimicked the deep voice of the man, "Just a minute!" She would have set the present down and run for dear life, but she was too late, for a light came dimly on in the front hall and feet approached the door.

"Well!" said the man in the yellow ascot with the same comforting smile he gave her in the library when he came in from smoking. He held the door wide open so that she saw a tall spooky staircase and a room to the right where chairs were arranged in a circle as if for a funeral or a clergyman's tea. Rose took a step forward and held out the bleeding heart to him, unable to say a word.

"Well!" he said again. "What's this? A posy for my poor sick mother?" He, for his part, was not in the least discomfited by this meeting. It was clear that he recognized her but he was not surprised; it was almost as if he had expected her all along. Now that she was up close, she saw that the ascot was made of diapered foulard but she saw, as well, that it was not clean and had the uncleanliness that accumulates over a period of weeks. She wondered if it hid something repulsive like a goiter or a birthmark or if it were some sort of fascist insignia and he was cat's-paw to a band of crooks.

"Yes," she said, as bashful as a child. "It is a plant from the school."

From the left came the scream again, beside itself with rage, "Tea! Toast! Me!" The man, as if to himself, said, "Bring my tea and toast to me," and then smiling and looking directly at Rose with active brown eyes, he explained, "My mother has lost her verbs and adjectives. In fact, she has lost all parts of speech except her nouns and pronouns, a very interesting phenomenon. Come in, please," and he put his hand under her elbow with gallant pressure. There was nothing she could do and she stepped inside the vestibule, which had a sweet smell like the taste of Neccos.

"Where shall I put it?" Rose asked.

"Oh, we'll take it right in to Mother, don't you think? What kind is it? A geranium, I hope."

"A bleeding heart."

"Oh," he said, scowling. "Well, we'll have to make the best of it." He tucked her arm in his and bent down toward her.

"She likes either geraniums or cut flowers. She has forgotten the names of all the others."

Now that she was so close to him she discovered that it was he who smelled of Neccos and that actually the hall smelled of ordure. There was a rustling like that of stiff silk and the man said, "Excuse me just a minute," and right beside them but still invisible the voice malevolently aped him. He shut the door and there she saw a parrot in a cage on a marble-topped bureau. It regarded her with wicked eyes like a patient maniac.

"I'll bet Waldo here had you buffaloed, didn't he?" said the man with a laugh as he opened the cage and the parrot stepped out on to his wrist with a haughty mutter. "He's a great old bird."

"Hours!" shrieked the voice of the invalid and the man translated for the smug bird, "You have been gone for hours."

Rose, while she could not claim to be really surprised herself, could not adjust herself to the man's unhesitating acceptance of the situation as if they had planned it together some days before. He indicated that she was to precede him down the corridor as if this were the most natural thing in the world, and they went, all three of them, down the slightly veering hall where ghostly pictures hung, and on the way the man said, like a guide, "As you see, we live very simply, Mother and I. The room to your right is the parlor, which we seldom use in winter. Perhaps you observed the portrait on the far wall of that room? An illustrious ancestor. Upstairs there are four bedrooms besides yours truly's. Linen closet, of course, and ample attic space." They paused at a door and he said, secretly as if the parrot were eavesdropping, "I have seen you in the library, you know, Rose." He said her name in a way that the greenest schoolgirl could not have misconstrued and she trembled from head to foot and had to grasp the plant tightly or it would have fallen. His breathing was a little heavy and the parrot, eyeing Rose in the twilight of the hall, gave forth a glottal giggle full of wisdom.

All the low furniture in the invalid woman's room was painted white except for the narrow bed, which was blackish-brown and looked like a catafalque. The bones of the flagging body on it jutted up under a royal purple counterpane. At first only the head and shoulders of the ancient woman showed, but when the small red eyes, witlessly mean with age, saw the parrot, she drew forth a huge piebald hand and her tongue labored on her lip as she said, "Him me."

"Quite like a child," said her son tolerantly as he handed over the parrot, which settled down on her wrist. "The young lady here, Miss Rose, has brought you a plant, Mother. She says it's from the school."

The old woman's fingernails were painted a morbid red and one of the fingers stroked the parrot's stout yellow talons. Although the woman did not look at her, she said, "Roses. Gratitude."

"No, Mother, not roses. I said this young lady's name was Miss Rose. She has brought a bleeding heart." He added in an exasperated aside, "Not that it matters a hoot in hell what kind of any old thing it is."

The invalid covered Rose with an ambiguous glance and said, "I her."

"I her," repeated her son. "I don't know what she means." He began to take the paper off the plant and growled, "I surely hope she likes it. She surely should. Very thoughtful of the school, to my way of thinking."

"I her," repeated the old woman in a louder voice and the man flushed. Obviously this could signify anything: "I hate her," "I want her to go," or "I have never seen her before." It was a cul-de-sac that could not very well be ignored because she said it over and over and presently Waldo joined with his one sentence and they chanted antiphonally, "I her," "Just a minute," "I her," "Just a minute." While these two obscene creatures on the bed were making a spectacle of themselves, the man was clumsily trying to get the string off the flowerpot and nudging Rose every now and again although he did not need to. There was an awful odor in the room, both medicinal and decayed, and everything looked soiled and moist. The shape of the room and the situation of the furniture were the same as in Rose's room as if in a planned parody.

The man got the knot untied and slipped the paper off and his mother said to the parrot, "Silence," and to her son, "I her bell."

"Of course!" cried the man with relief. "I heard her ring

the bell?" And the woman nodded her head up and down with a delighted smile on the thin crescent of her mouth.

He put the bleeding heart on the low white table beside the bed where a Bible lay, conventional and new, and some sticky bottles of medicine and some revolting gobbets of cotton. The other old hand with veins as thick as pencils came staggering out of the bed to pluck a blossom from the plant which it held out for the parrot. The fingernails were the same color as the little flower which disappeared in Waldo's greedy bill.

"Roses. Waldo."

"Yes, Mother," said the man soothingly, "Roses for Waldo." On the wall over the bed hung a sampler that said, "LOOK UP-WARD NOT DOWN."

Rose finally found her voice and she said urgently, "I must go." But the man detained her with a soft pat on her arm. "But you haven't had your tea. You must have tea with Mother." Mother was plucking the flowers and feeding them to Waldo very rapidly for one of her years and debility. After each gobble, Waldo ducked his head with villainous coquetry.

"I'm sorry," said Rose, "but I really must go."

He was looking with some consternation at his mother. "I say, you don't think a bleeding heart is toxic, do you? I wouldn't like anything to happen to Waldo."

"I don't know," she said miserably, and to the woman on the bed she said, "Goodbye. I am glad to have met you," although this was a double lie, for she was not glad and there had been no proper meeting.

"Oh, you must have tea!" cried the man and he fingered his yellow ascot nervously as if he could not bear to have her leave. "You must! It isn't often that Mother and I have such a pretty guest." She shivered and buttoned the top button of her coat. "It will only take a minute," he wheedled. "It's on the tray and I just plug in the electric kettle thing and we're all set." He gave himself a private smile and said, "All set and rarin' to go."

She was about to be very firm and cutting if necessary to this tiresome old child by whom she had been so foolishly taken in at the library, but she thought of Miss Talmadge and was afraid if she were discourteous there might be trouble. It could not last long and he could not do anything improper to her in front of his mother and the parrot whose sagacious gaze missed nothing. So she gave in and he drew a rocking chair to the center of the room and beside it he put a bench. "The tray goes here," he said, "and you can pour." And then he left the room, walking out backwards to unnerve her all the more.

The ten minutes he was gone were for Rose a bizarre and separate experience. The old woman and the parrot clucked at one another over the sinister meal of bleeding hearts and but for this there was silence in the darkening room. She was forced to accept the reality of the afternoon, that the man in the yellow ascot lived here and that he drove the electric car and that in no particular did he resemble her image of her foster-father. And it was quite possible to accept it now, but she was apprehensive of the evening to come and the next afternoon when she would meet him again in the Samuel Sewell. There were only two flowers left on the plant and for some reason she hoped that tea would be here before they were gone. She glanced toward the bed; the headboard was just opposite her desk and she knew that she could never again write there with the picture in her mind of the old woman feeding the evil bird. A good deal in her quiet life would be changed. She doubted if she would ever go again to the library on the customary afternoons, for example. She would be free, it is true, to walk once again in the parts of the town and the country she had enjoyed before but this gain was offset by the knowledge that there was no mystery left: she knew exactly where the man lived and, moreover, to her regret, she knew *how* he lived.

The next to the last blossom was gone and then the last was gone and the feeding hand retired under the covers. The old woman looked at Waldo and at Rose and said, "You him." She pretended neither to hear nor to see but stared at the sampler, which had a border of pine cones. A foot surreptitiously moved under the counterpane and Waldo walked off his mistress' hand so that Rose, nauseated, saw that he had not eaten the bleeding hearts at all, but had only mauled them and then had dropped them onto the bed, where they lay in a heap like bloody matter. The command was repeated but she heard her host coming back and she got up to open the door for him. She said, "I think your mother wanted me to take the parrot."

"Oh, did she?" he asked with interest. "That shows she likes you. Yes, sir, that shows you've made a big hit with Mother."

"But I don't like birds," she said.

"Really? How extraordinary! I had a very charming Brazilian oriole to whom I was much attached. Waldo killed her, I never was just sure how."

On the tray were a plate of English muffins and a jar of peanut butter and one of marmalade and a store-bought pound cake and a dish of pickled peaches. There were a can of evaporated milk and a tin of bouillon cubes. This last he picked up, mouthing the words, "This is what she thinks is tea. Isn't allowed tea. A stimulant." Waldo laughed.

It took a long time to prepare the meal. A good deal of furniture had to be moved before the kettle could be plugged in; then he had to go back to the kitchen for spoons which he had forgotten and then for some plates for the pickled peaches. Then he stopped everything when he saw the mess Waldo had made with the flowers and for a moment Rose thought he was going to lose his temper. "Pest!" he said sharply and gave Waldo a baleful look. When everything was ready, the old woman said "Radio," so the lamp had to be unplugged and the radio plugged in and candles had to be lit. The kettle made the radio splutter and creak and Waldo, the everlasting Mr. Fixit, stared at the box and said patiently, "Just a minute." But at last everything was ready and Rose began to pour the tea while the man spread peanut butter on the English muffins. The old woman sucked the bouillon and gave a sip to Waldo now and then.

"I wish she wouldn't do that," said the man, preoccupied with the muffins. "It gives him an intestinal condition."

Rose said politely, "How old is Waldo?"

"Forty-eight," he said. "Quite a character. He used to say some other things. 'I think you're rather foolish' was one and 'Go by-by, Aunt Louisa' was another, but he's lost everything but 'Just a minute.' "

"It is remarkable," said Rose, referring to the habit in this household of mislaying language.

"Yes," he mused, giving her a muffin in his hand. "Yes, Waldo's quite a character. He keeps Mother company. If it weren't for Waldo, I'd never get to have my little afternoons off at the library."

Because there was something in his voice that was not altogether trustworthy, she said, "What does he eat?"

"A special food for parrots," he said. "Called 'Polly's Perfect Preparation.' But he likes fruit too. The trouble with fruit, though, is that it gives him that intestinal condition I alluded to."

Mother finished her bouillon with a hoarse swallow and said, "Time toast."

"Right you are, Mother. Time for toast," and handed her a muffin with marmalade. Returning, he said *sotto voce,* "Time for toast and tea for two, what? Do you often eat at the inn?"

"Oh, no, almost never. Do you?"

"No. Thanksgiving, Christmas, Easter, Patriots' Day, that's all. Not that the cuisine is not to my liking. But I am rather tied here to my poor sick mother. That is to say, I generally dine *en famille.*" A note of woe came into his voice: *"En famille* with Waldo."

She could not think of any comment to make on this very sad state of affairs and so she said, "What delicious peanut butter." In point of fact, it was dry and tasteless and the muffin was cold and rubbery. As for the tea, *it* could not be described. She promised herself that she would eat the whole muffin and drink the whole cup of tea and then she would go even if it meant being rude.

"Is it delicious peanut butter? Oh, thank you," he said joyfully and from the bed the old woman clamored, "Gratitude!"

The man asked her how she liked Miss Talmadge and if she were ever homesick for the West and if she did not find her room at Number 8 rather chilly when the wind came off the river. He said he imagined she found the fare at the Minute Man café pretty much the same old thing from day to day: swordfish, canned peas, boiled potatoes. It was a little cold for sitting in the cemetery on Sunday afternoon nowadays, wasn't it?

"Lonesome, aren't you, little lady?" he said and Waldo warned from the footboard of the bed, "Just a minute."

She drank the last of the sour tea and returned the cup to

the tray. She drew on her gloves and stood up. "Thank you so much for the tea," she said. "It was most kind of you."

The old woman beckoned to her and said, "Time."

"Yes, I know. It's time for me to go." She tried to smile warmly.

"No, no," cried her son anxiously, "she means there's plenty of time."

But Rose would not be detained any longer and she moved toward the door. He was immediately beside her, following her down the hall as long and as dark as a tunnel. Halfway down Waldo came bustling after them and walked between them, laughing busily. The man held Rose's elbow tightly as if by the pressure of his fingers he could communicate the desperate state of his loneliness. "You can't imagine how awful it is," he confided urgently. "Today you only saw her company manners, but you should hear the things she says to me when we're alone." His voice was full of tears. "Rose! Rose, we're near neighbors. Strictly speaking we live in the same house, Rose. Won't you come again?"

"I'll try," she said without any pity at all.

"When?"

"I don't know."

"Tomorrow? Oh, no, tomorrow we meet in the library, don't we? What do you read there?"

She was remote and academic. "I am doing some research work."

"That's wonderful. I knew you were cultured. I went to Harvard. I daresay you've heard of that little old college down Cambridge way?"

He was such a terrible mixture of unattractive qualities that she did not know how his face managed to be so aristocratically handsome. They were at the door now and she put her hand out toward the knob, but he was ahead of her. "Permit me, Rose," he said. "Please greet Miss Talmadge for my mother and me, but don't tell her what happened to the bleeding heart." He grasped her hand in both of his and squeezed it warmly and looking deep into her eyes he whispered, "The Samuel Sewell tomorrow."

She ran down the steps and he called after her, "Rose! My name is Mr. Benson!"

She heard him close the door and at the corner she paused in the snowfall, senseless with misery. She could *not* sleep another night in that room but she had nowhere to go. Tears for her homeless self went down her cheeks with the snowflakes and she let a little sound escape her, the murmur of an unhappy child. And then, because there was nothing else to do, she opened the front door of Number 8 and went into her room. She turned the radio on very loud and got a program of jazz played on an organ and, deafened to any other possible sound, she began to play solitaire, violently slapping the cards down on the table. In this futile tantrum with the cards, she bent a corner of the Queen of Hearts and this reminded her of her father's custom of spending whole winter evenings cleaning a deck of cards with a jackknife. A jackknife which he used, as well, to slice off a plug of chewing tobacco, to trim his fingernails and, in the spring, to dig embedded woodticks out of his skin.

When she came back from her dinner of swordfish at the Minute Man, she found a note on the rug just inside the door which said:

My dear Rose,

If you would care to go to the picture show tonight in Acton, I am at your disposal and wish you would telephone me. My name is in the book. I could come to your door or you could come to mine. Mrs. Morton Ripley is coming to call on Mother. I do not know when another opportunity will offer so hope you will not refuse.

Awaiting your communication via telephone,

I am,

Lucius Benson

There was no sound from the room beyond the wall but the silence was an uneasy one and she shuddered thinking of what might be going on in there. Waldo and his mistress were capable of any sort of monstrous tableau if the demonstration this afternoon with the bleeding heart had not been unusual. She thought of going to the priest to ask for his advice or to the policeman for his protection. In any case, she could not stay here and after a minute of debate she let herself out quietly and went down the street and into the Mill Dam on her way to the library. But she had only just got to the square of lawn in front of it when the electric car eased up alongside her and Mr. Benson leaned across and opened the door.

"Here, here," he gaily cried. "This is no way to treat your Dutch uncle. Climb in! Hop right in, Rosie O'Grady, and off we'll go to the picture show."

"Mr. Benson," she began, giving his derby a hard look, "I can't go to the movies with you tonight."

"Nonsense," he said. "Stuff and nonsense. Hop in, dear, we'll be in time for the newsreel. Good gracious, Rosie, what are you afraid of? Do you mean to say that you're afraid of a harmless old codger, old enough to be your father?"

"No, Mr. Benson," she said, "I'm not afraid of you." And it was true, she was not afraid, she was only displeased. "But I won't go to the movies."

"Just think of me as your father," he said. "Why don't you call me that as a matter of fact? I mean, not 'Father' but one of the more familiar things like 'Daddy'?"

It was not at all likely, she thought, that this was taking place. It was much too improbable that she was talking under an arc lamp in a snowfall to an elderly roué in an electric car who had invited her to call him Daddy.

"If you won't come with me," he said rather testily, "then I will come into the library and read."

She was at the end of her tether. No longer scared, certainly not respectful of his age, no longer polite for Miss Talmadge's sake, she burst out, "Oh, go to grass," and she scuffled up the snowy path.

"Let me tell you about my Brazilian oriole," he called desperately through the quiet storm. "Waldo killed it out of pure spite! I preferred it to Waldo and Waldo killed it out of spite!"

Rose went on up the path.

"Rose!"

She heard him come running after her but she was not afraid, for the library was brightly lighted. She stopped when he was abreast of her and stamped her foot. "Go away, Mr. Benson," she said.

His head fell forward dejectedly and his beaver-lined coat

which was not buttoned hung loosely on him as if he had suddenly shriveled. He was a die-hard. "Oh, Rose," he said, "I assure you I mean no harm." He touched the yellow ascot with the palm of his hand and said, "The most unsightly wen you ever saw. All I am asking is a little pity." He began to undo the scarf as she mounted the steps. When she was within the storm doors, she looked back and saw him standing there in the snow with his neck bare and his arms spread out, his palms upward in supplication. He had flung his head back and his derby had fallen to the ground; he wore the yellow ascot on his left arm like a maniple. Just behind him, the electric car cast an absolutely square shadow on the white ground.

The Lippia Lawn

Although its roots are clever, the trailing arbutus at Deer Lick had been wrenched out by the hogs. Only a few bruised and muddied blossoms still clung to the disordered stems. The old man and I, baskets over our arms, had come looking for good specimens to transplant. It had been a long walk, and Mr. Oliphant was fatigued. Oppressed also with his disappointment, he lowered himself carefully to the ground and sighed.

"They're carnivorous, you know," he said, speaking of the hogs. "They're looking for worms." Everywhere about us, the cloven hoofprints had bitten into the soil, and it was easy to imagine the sow and her retinue lumbering to this place on their preposterously shapely legs, huffing and puffing with incessant appetite. Mr. Oliphant, a man who loved nature in an immense yet ungenerous way, complained as he lay there, shading his eyes against the sunlight that was finely sifted through the hemlock above us. "In town the chickens come to spoil my jonquils, and here the hogs tear up the arbutus. But what good would it do to beg the mountain people to keep their stock at home?"

He was such a spirited and able man that he never seemed old until he commenced to fret, and then, when his deliberate voice became sibilant, I saw how white his hair was and how the flesh of his brown face had been twilled into hundreds of tiny pleats. His large hands, stained with the grime of garden earth, simultaneously became the uncertain, misshapen hands of an aged person. I stopped listening to him and plucked a cluster of trampled blossoms from among the leaves, hoping that my idle twirling of it would make him think I was following what he said. The unvarying tone of his voice made time seem absolute, and absolute, too, became my contemplation of the flower. Once I realized that he had paused. I found myself wanting him to continue, for I was distracted by the ragged petals which, in their revolutions between my fingers, assumed many shapes.

He had only stopped to choose a word, and, having found it, resumed his tirade. I ceased the flower's rotations, and abruptly my rambling daydreams were arrested as the arbutus began to resemble something I had seen before. Although I knew that Mr. Oliphant, a devout horticulturalist, could help me name its cousin, I hesitated to interrupt him lest I interrupt also my own tranquillity. The tenuous memory wove in and out of my thoughts, always tantalizingly just ahead of me. Like the butterfly whose yellow wings are camouflaged to look like sunlight, the flower I could not remember masqueraded as arbutus whenever I had almost discovered it in its native habitat. As I pursued it in the places where I had lived, a voice came back to me. It was not so elusive. Its unique timbre and its accent established it in a particular time, and with only a little research, I found its owner, Fräulein Ströck, my landlady in Heidelberg. She gave me German lessons in exchange for English, and afterward she served me coffee. Of a once fine set, all that remained was the tall pot of white china scattered with pink flowers and minute heart-shaped leaves. I must have complimented her on it, for I recalled her strenuous, elevated reply in English: "No, it makes me very sorry that I do not know the name of the bloom."

Slowly, like a shadow, the past seeped back. A wise scout was reconnoitering for me and at last led me to a place where I never would have looked. The arbutus was larger, pinker, but was something like the lippia that had grown on the lawn when I was a child in California. It was as thick and close to the ground as clover, and it looked like a head of cropped and decorated hair. Under an umbrella tree, I used to sit waiting for the school bus bringing my sisters and my brothers and pretend that the lawn was the ocean at Redondo Beach, and that I could see them coming through the breakers after a long swim. Once, as I ran toward them, the springy earth cool to my feet, I was stung on the ankle by a bee at work in the brilliant sunlight.

Because I was only five years old when we went away, I have never been able to remember much about our ranch. Whenever I think of California, my impressions are confused and ramified with later ones apprehended in Santa Fe, Denver, Chicago, Toledo, and New Orleans. Only a few of my early memories are pure. I can still summon up the taste of oxalis, but whether I ate the stem or the leaf, I cannot say. I remember the day my grandmother came from Santa Barbara, bringing me a pink tatted handbag to carry to Sunday School, but beyond that, all I can reconstruct of my grandmother is her blackthorn walking stick which had belonged to my grandfather, an Irishman. Now and again a random recollection will swim vaguely across my mind, a wisp too ephemeral to detain: a dairy in Covina where we bought Schmierkäse from a German who frightened me by saying that the Bolsheviks would get me because bright red ribbons streamed from my sailor hat; a Mexican's house with a dried mud floor where a girl named Fuchsia made drawn-work doilies and where my brother and I went one Sunday afternoon, instructed by our mother, to say, "Muchas gracias, señorita," for she had sent us a lemon pie. Sometimes I think of a dream I often had of a thousand new pennies heaped up beneath a fig tree. The more I picked up, the more there were, and I cried with impatience because the skirt of my dress was not big enough to hold them all. Sometimes I can see a green glass pig which my brother kept in the china closet, forbidding anyone to touch it. Or suddenly I am standing beside Hana, the Japanese washerwoman, as she lifts the lid of a trunk: the smell of camphor balls is strong as she holds up my mother's pin-striped hobble skirt.

But I remember nothing of the house. From photographs and conversation, I know that my father's den was hung with serapes from Tía Juana and that the floor was covered with deerskins. I know that at the back of the house the grove stretched for eighty acres and that within a south field of chrysanthemums there was a frog pond. But I cannot recall how the fruit looks on an English walnut tree, and the feel and color of those chrysanthemums are spurious, come from later ones I bought or gathered. I can accomplish only a partial reconstruction even of the umbrella tree.

That day in the woods of the Cumberland plateau, the lippia returned unaltered. Tender, fragrant, lavender and white, it extended across a flat and limitless terrain upon which the tree and I, the only altitudes, cast our brief shadows.

"The ground was carpeted with it," said Mr. Oliphant. "Literally carpeted with it, before the mountaineers started digging it up to send off to New York. There used to be a place in the gorge where it grew right out of the rock, but I suppose that's gone too."

He grumbled on as monotonously as the waterfall to our right, reviewing the mountaineers' past offenses and those they would perpetrate in the future. He said it would be his bad luck to come after they had stripped the laurel thicket. They had no respect for nature, he declared, no desire to conserve the beauty of the woods. Why, they were as ruthless as the Visigoths and it was unimaginable to Mr. Oliphant that they should devastate their native soil. "It is my native soil too!" he cried passionately. "They have no right to hurt my share of it!"

He came from city stock, but he had been born here in the mountains. Off and on for seventy years, with an occasional winter in Florida or France, he had lived alone in the flimsy yellow house in the summer resort where he had been born. From September until late May nearly every year, his was the only chimney in the grounds that regularly sent up a tendril of smoke. The village and houses of the mountain people were a mile away, and sometimes, for as long as a week, the only face he saw was his own reflected in the mirror as he shaved. This winter I had shared the settlement of empty cottages with him, but my house was so far from his that even on a clear day he could not hear my radio. Occasionally, he rambled up my front walk, bringing a packet of *tilleul* which he brewed himself on my electric plate.

Mr. Oliphant was not pitiful as friendless old bachelors often are. His innumerable interests and projects kept him perpetually busy. I had encountered him first in the autumn in the woods, where he was gathering mushrooms to dry for winter use. I joined him in the hunt and, as we scrambled over fallen trees and under low branches, he gave me a receipt for making mead and told me how he canned peas in long-necked wine bottles. A few weeks later he summoned me formally through the mail to dine with him. It was late in September and already so cold that we ate beside the fireplace in his cluttered sitting room. He painted in oils and water-colors for his own amusement, and canvases were stacked against every wall, and the room smelled of turpentine and the wood fire. He pointed out his pleasant, untalented pic-

tures of grape hyacinth and wild azalea, and a wavering, ectoplas-
mic landscape in fog. A gourmet of sorts, he had such reverence
for the broiled beefsteak mushrooms, the curried veal and the
avocado salad and the home-made sauterne, that we ate in silence.
Afterward, he addressed a fluent monologue to me on the repairs
he planned for his flagstone walk, his summer house, his roofs and
floors. And finally, he took me to his conservatory, as fragrant and
luxuriant as a jungle, where all through the winter he nursed his
plants. Just as I left the house, he gave me a tin of mingled herbs
which he had taken from his glass-windowed cabinet, allowing
the smell of basil and thyme to hover in the air a moment.

All winter I saw him roving through the grounds collecting
kindling after a wind or an ice storm. Or I saw him, armed with
shears and a basket, going to the woods for holly. On fine days, if
I called on him, usually I found him working in the pit, fitted
with a glass door, where he kept his hydrangeas through the cold
months. Early in February he informed me that he had begun
negotiating with the mountaineers for fertilizer and that his seed
catalogues had arrived. In March, he heard the first flock of wild
geese honking over his house, and knowing by this sign that
spring was here to stay, he began to get up earlier in the mornings, making use of every hour of daylight to work in his garden.

Nevertheless, people often asked Mr. Oliphant how he put in
his time. A look of bewilderment would invade his face and his
lips would curve in a tentative smile like that of a child who does
not know for a moment whether to laugh or cry. Once he had replied, "Why, I don't know. Seems like there never *is* enough
time."

His character was not arresting, and his continual murmuring, which amounted to a persecution mania, was tedious. He had
done nothing noteworthy in his life; his religion was of the scant-
iest and most sentimental. He was not charming, and his information, beyond flowers and food and weather, was banal. But I
admired him, for there was something deep about him, a subtle
vitality that resided in his fingertips and his eyes which enabled
him to make anything flourish in the sour mountain soil and to
detect to the hour the coming of frost or rain or wind. I had
wondered why he chose to live in a place so inimical to gardening,

and he had replied, "If I moved, I'd lose all the years I've spent learning my land."

He was saying, "You might make out that I had no room to talk the way I dig up flowers myself to put in my garden. But I maintain there's a world of difference between transplanting something and uprooting it to send off to New York City. I don't know what gets into people to make them take and tear things up."

I had been silent for so long that I felt obliged to speak, and I said, "Mr. Oliphant, this trailing arbutus reminds me of a flower I used to know as a child. Have you ever seen lippia?"

"Lippia? No'm, I've never heard of it." He allowed his eyes to rest on my face for the briefest moment as though a sudden curiosity about me had stirred in him. But he immediately looked away. "I reckon a hundred and fifty years ago my kin were coming here for salt."

On our walk, he had told me that the deer, the Indians and the pioneers had been drawn here by the excrescences of salt in the gorge, from which the name, Deer Lick, had been taken. To our right, the chasm dropped a hundred feet. At the head of it, to our left, the waterfall, almost as high, crashed down, furious and swollen with heavy spring rains. We were on a triangular promontory halfway between the walls. Mr. Oliphant had said that here had been found the thighbone of a prehistoric animal that had been big enough to be used as a tent pole. Colossal, aged hemlocks crowded the wild slopes.

I would have asked the old man about his pioneer ancestors, but he had already reverted to the arbutus. "Hard as it is to get it to grow, I just had the feeling this spring I'd succeed. If I was younger, I'd look for that other patch I was telling you about."

His voice was so senile that, although I knew he was as nimble almost as I, I got to my feet and said, "If you'll tell me the way, I'll try to find it for you, Mr. Oliphant."

"That's mighty obliging of you," he said with a smile. "You follow the path through the laurel and go a little beyond a big flat rock. You start going down there, and that arbutus used to grow under a ledge just beyond the first hemlock."

I took the knife and trowel he offered me and set out. Long thorny vines clutched at my dress and stockings and the laurel branches whipped my face. The path was obscure and, though it was only March, the brush was green enough for midsummer. But the autumn leaves, blackened by the winter's wetness, were still deep. I found the flat rock, surrounded by blueberry bushes on which the last year's fruit was dry and rusty. From here, the roar of the waterfall was thunderous, and from here I could see far down into the lower chasm. A straight wall of gray and pinkish rock rose sheer to the cloudless sky, and against it were patterned the blue-green feathers of the hemlocks.

After the rock, the going was difficult, and twice I slipped on the wet leaves and only kept my balance by seizing old roots and rocks. Mr. Oliphant's directions had been precise. I stooped under the low-hanging branch of the first hemlock and, when I straightened up again, I saw the arbutus growing in a shelf, shadowed by a roof of violet stone. The fragile flowers, nudging clean dark leaves, were refined, like something painted on china.

When I knelt down to uproot the plant, though, I found I was dealing with nothing frail. Its long, tough sinews branched under the ground far in every direction, grasping the earth so tightly that when I tugged at the main root, no more than the subsidiary tentacles came loose, and with them came great clods of black earth, leaving triangular gouges in the ground. The root did not go deep; instead, it crept just under the surface, but it was so long that my fingertips could not even guess where it ended, and the vine was confused with fern and low weeds, making it impossible to trace the stubborn filament so as to dig around it with the knife and trowel. I pulled again. It was as though the root was instinct with will. There was something so monstrous in its determination to remain where it grew that sweat, not from exertion but from alarm, streamed from my face, and the broken leaves were pasted to my wet fingers. Something prevented me from cutting it, not only my fear that this was the incorrect procedure, but a sort of inexplicable revulsion at the thought that the knife might not cleave through.

My labor was barely visible when I stood up. I knew that when I told Mr. Oliphant it was gone, I should be obliged to hear his droning tantrum all the way home. But I neither could nor would carry back to him that violent artery and its deceptively dainty flowers.

It was a little cooler now, and the sun was beginning to go down. Narrowing my eyes to shut out from their corners the chasm and the trees, I had a last look at the trailing arbutus and saw that it hardly resembled the lippia at all, or rather, that the lippia had faded away so completely that its name was all I could remember. As though I were being watched, as though some alert ear were cocked to the slightest noise I should make, swiftly, as quietly as possible, I ascended the path. When I had passed the rock, I ran through the blueberries. Halfway through the laurel thicket I stopped and rested, then went slowly so that Mr. Oliphant would not see I was out of breath.

He was lying where I had left him. His wiry old legs in blue jeans were set on the needle-littered ground, bent at the knee, with the long feet in sneakers resting firmly in the pockets he had scooped out for them. Although his eyes were closed, his face wore an attentive look as if all his other senses were still active. As I stepped forward into the clearing, he at once sprang up, not at the sound of my footfall but at the low grunting of a lubberly black boar that came trotting along the path, its snout close to the ground. Mr. Oliphant flung up his arms and screamed imprecations at the creature that came on, oblivious. He reached down and picked up a stone, hurled it, and the hog, clipped on the shoulder, turned and ran squealing, its coiled tail bobbing.

The rout, though it was complete, did not satisfy the old man, and for some minutes he gesticulated and cried out, seemed actually to dance with rage. My gaze descended to his feet. They had not moved from the holds prepared for them, as if they shared the zealous intelligence of their master and of the trailing arbutus and of all beings that resist upheaval and defy invasion. Flushed and shaking, he cried out to me, "It's a crime, I tell you! When I was a boy this place was Eden!"

With quick, juvenile blue eyes he glanced around, and I knew that in that moment he was seeing the place as it had been when he first came here, sixty years ago. I envied him the clarity of his vision. I envied him his past when, pacified for a moment, he said gently, "Anyhow, a man can call the old things to mind."

He turned and led the way down the path. In the silence that had fallen upon us, his words repeated themselves to my disquieted mind, like a phrase of music once admired and now detested.

The Interior Castle

Pansy Vanneman, injured in an automobile accident, often woke up before dawn when the night noises of the hospital still came, in hushed hurry, through her half-open door. By day, when the nurses talked audibly with the internes, laughed without inhibition, and took no pains to soften their footsteps on the resounding composition floors, the routine of the hospital seemed as bland and commonplace as that of a bank or a factory. But in the dark hours, the whispering and the quickly stilled clatter of glasses and basins, the moans of patients whose morphine was wearing off, the soft squeak of a stretcher as it rolled past on its way from the emergency ward—these suggested agony and death. Thus, on the first morning, Pansy had faltered to consciousness long before daylight and had found herself in a ward from every bed of which, it seemed to her, came the bewildered protest of someone about to die. A caged light burned on the floor beside the bed next to hers. Her neighbor was dying and a priest was administering Extreme Unction. He was stout and elderly and he suffered from asthma so that the struggle of his breathing, so close to her, was the basic pattern and all the other sounds were superimposed upon it. Two middle-aged men in overcoats knelt on the floor beside the high bed. In a foreign tongue, the half-gone woman babbled against the hissing and sighing of the Latin prayers. She played with her rosary as if it were a toy: she tried, and failed, to put it into her mouth.

Pansy felt horror, but she felt no pity. An hour or so later, when the white ceiling lights were turned on and everything— faces, counterpanes, and the hands that groped upon them—was transformed into a uniform gray sordor, the woman was wheeled away in her bed to die somewhere else, in privacy. Pansy did not quite take this in, although she stared for a long time at the new, empty bed that had replaced the other.

The next morning, when she again woke up before the light, this time in a private room, she recalled the woman with such sorrow that she might have been a friend. Simultaneously, she mourned the driver of the taxicab in which she had been injured, for he had died at about noon the day before. She had been told this as she lay on a stretcher in the corridor, waiting to be taken to the X-ray room; an interne, passing by, had paused and smiled down at her and had said, "Your cab driver is dead. You were lucky."

Six weeks after the accident, she woke one morning just as daylight was showing on the windows as a murky smear. It was a minute or two before she realized why she was so reluctant to be awake, why her uneasiness amounted almost to alarm. Then she remembered that her nose was to be operated on today. She lay straight and motionless under the seersucker counterpane. Her blood-red eyes in her darned face stared through the window and saw a frozen river and leafless elm trees and a grizzled esplanade where dogs danced on the ends of leashes, their bundled-up owners stumbling after them, half blind with sleepiness and cold. Warm as the hospital room was, it did not prevent Pansy from knowing, as keenly as though she were one of the walkers, how very cold it was outside. Each twig of a nearby tree was stark. Cold red brick buildings nudged the low-lying sky which was pale and inert like a punctured sac.

In six weeks, the scene had varied little: there was promise in the skies neither of sun nor of snow; no red sunsets marked these days. The trees could neither die nor leaf out again. Pansy could not remember another season in her life so constant, when the very minutes themselves were suffused with the winter pallor as they dropped from the moon-faced clock in the corridor. In the same way, her room accomplished no alterations from day to day. On the glass-topped bureau stood two potted plants telegraphed by faraway well-wishers. They did not fade, and if a leaf turned brown and fell, it soon was replaced; so did the blossoms renew themselves. The roots, like the skies and like the bare trees, seemed zealously determined to maintain a status quo. The bed-side table, covered every day with a clean white towel, though the one removed was always immaculate, was furnished sparsely with a water glass, a bent drinking tube, a sweating pitcher, and a stack of paper handkerchiefs. There were a few letters in the drawer, a hairbrush, a pencil, and some postal cards on which, from time to time, she wrote brief messages to relatives and friends: "Dr. Nash says that my reflexes are shipshape (*sic*) and Dr. Rivers says the frontal fracture has all but healed and that the occipital is coming along nicely. Dr. Nicholas, the nose doctor, promises to operate as soon as Dr. Rivers gives him the go-ahead sign (*sic*)."

The bed itself was never rumpled. Once fretful and now convalescent, Miss Vanneman might have been expected to toss or to turn the pillows or to unmoor the counterpane; but hour after hour and day after day she lay at full length and would not even suffer the nurses to raise the headpiece of the adjustable bed. So perfect and stubborn was her body's immobility that it was as if the room and the landscape, mortified by the ice, were extensions of herself. Her resolute quiescence and her disinclination to talk, the one seeming somehow to proceed from the other, resembled, so the nurses said, a final coma. And they observed, in pitying indignation, that she might as *well* be dead for all the interest she took in life. Among themselves they scolded her for what they thought a moral weakness: an automobile accident, no matter how serious, was not reason enough for anyone to give up the will to live or to be happy. She had not—to come down bluntly to the facts—had the decency to be grateful that it was the driver of the cab and not she who had died. (And how dreadfully the man had died!) She was twenty-five years old and she came from a distant city. These were really the only facts known about her. Evidently she had not been here long, for she had no visitors, a lack which was at first sadly moving to the nurses but which became to them a source of unreasonable annoyance: had anyone the right to live so one-dimensionally? It was impossible to laugh at her, for she said nothing absurd; her demands could not be complained of because they did not exist; she could not be hated for a sharp tongue nor for a supercilious one; she could not be admired for bravery or for wit or for interest in her fellow creatures. She was believed to be a frightful snob.

Pansy, for her part, took a secret and mischievous pleasure

in the bewilderment of her attendants and the more they courted her with offers of magazines, crossword puzzles, and a radio that she could rent from the hospital, the farther she retired from them into herself and into the world which she had created in her long hours here and which no one could ever penetrate nor imagine. Sometimes she did not even answer the nurses' questions; as they rubbed her back with alcohol and steadily discoursed, she was as remote from them as if she were miles away. She did not think that she lived on a higher plane than that of the nurses and the doctors but that she lived on a different one and that at this particular time—this time of exploration and habituation— she had no extra strength to spend on making herself known to them. All she had been before and all the memories she might have brought out to disturb the monotony of, say, the morning bath, and all that the past meant to the future when she would leave the hospital, were of no present consequence to her. Not even in her thoughts did she employ more than a minimum of memory. And when she did remember, it was in flat pictures, rigorously independent of one another: she saw her thin, poetic mother who grew thinner and more poetic in her canvas deck chair at Saranac reading *Lalla Rookh*. She saw herself in an inappropriate pink hat drinking iced tea in a garden so oppressive with the smell of phlox that the tea itself tasted of it. She recalled an afternoon in autumn in Vermont when she had heard three dogs' voices in the north woods and she could tell, by the characteristic minor key struck three times at intervals, like bells from several churches, that they had treed something: the eastern sky was pink and the trees on the horizon looked like some eccentric vascular system meticulously drawn on colored paper.

What Pansy thought of all the time was her own brain. Not only the brain as the seat of consciousness, but the physical organ itself which she envisaged, romantically, now as a jewel, now as a flower, now as a light in a glass, now as an envelope of rosy vellum containing other envelopes, one within the other, diminishing infinitely. It was always pink and always fragile, always deeply interior and invaluable. She believed that she had reached the innermost chamber of knowledge and that perhaps her knowledge was the same as the saint's achievement of pure love. It was only convention, she thought, that made one say "sacred heart" and not "sacred brain."

Often, but never articulately, the color pink troubled her and the picture of herself in the wrong hat hung steadfastly before her mind's eye. None of the other girls had worn hats, and since autumn had come early that year, they were dressed in green and rusty brown and dark yellow. Poor Pansy wore a white eyelet frock with a lacing of black ribbon around the square neck. When she came through the arch, overhung with bittersweet, and saw that they had not yet heard her, she almost turned back, but Mr. Oliver was there and she was in love with him. She was in love with him though he was ten years older than she and had never shown any interest in her beyond asking her once, quite fatuously but in an intimate voice, if the yodeling of the little boy who peddled clams did not make her wish to visit Switzerland. Actually, there was more to this question than met the eye, for some days later Pansy learned that Mr. Oliver, who was immensely rich, kept an apartment in Geneva. In the garden that day, he spoke to her only once. He said, "My dear, you look exactly like something out of Katherine Mansfield," and immediately turned and within her hearing asked Beatrice Sherburne to dine with him that night at the Country Club. Afterward, Pansy went down to the sea and threw the beautiful hat onto the full tide and saw it vanish in the wake of a trawler. Thereafter, when she heard the clam boy coming down the road, she locked the door and when the knocking had stopped and her mother called down from her chaise longue, "Who was it, dearie?" she replied, "A salesman."

It was only the fact that the hat had been pink that worried her. The rest of the memory was trivial, for she knew that she could never again love anything as ecstatically as she loved the spirit of Pansy Vanneman, enclosed within her head.

But her study was not without distraction, and she fought two adversaries: pain and Dr. Nicholas. Against Dr. Nicholas, she defended herself valorously and in fear; but pain, the pain, that is, that was independent of his instruments, she sometimes forced upon herself adventurously like a child scaring himself in a grave-yard.

Dr. Nicholas greatly admired her crushed and splintered nose which he daily probed and peered at, exclaiming that he had never seen anything like it. His shapely hands ached for their knives; he was impatient with the skull-fracture man's cautious delay. He spoke of "our" nose and said "we" would be a new person when we could breathe again. His own nose was magnificent. Not even his own brilliant surgery could have improved upon it nor could a first-rate sculptor have duplicated its direct downward line which permitted only the least curvature inward toward the end; or the delicately rounded lateral declivities; or the thin-walled, perfectly matched nostrils.

Miss Vanneman did not doubt his humaneness or his talent —he was a celebrated man—but she questioned whether he had imagination. Immediately beyond the prongs of his speculum lay her treasure whose price he, no more than the nurses, could estimate. She believed he could not destroy it, but she feared that he might maim it: might leave a scratch on one of the brilliant facets of the jewel, bruise a petal of the flower, smudge the glass where the light burned, blot the envelopes, and that then she would die or would go mad. While she did not question that in either eventuality her brain would after a time redeem its original impeccability, she did not quite yet wish to enter upon either kind of eternity, for she was not certain that she could carry with her her knowledge as well as its receptacle.

Blunderer that he was, Dr. Nicholas was an honorable enemy, not like the demon, pain, which skulked in a thousand guises within her head, and which often she recklessly willed to attack her and then drove back in terror. After the rout, sweat streamed from her face and soaked the neck of the coarse hospital shirt. To be sure, it came usually of its own accord, running like a wild fire through all the convolutions to fill with flame the small sockets and ravines and then, at last, to withdraw, leaving behind a throbbing and an echo. On these occasions, she was as helpless as a tree in a wind. But at the other times when, by closing her eyes and rolling up the eyeballs in such a way that she fancied she looked directly on the place where her brain was, the pain woke sluggishly and came toward her at a snail's pace. Then, bit by bit, it gained speed. Sometimes it faltered back, subsided altogether, and then it rushed like a tidal wave driven by a hurricane, lashing and roaring until she lifted her hands from the counterpane, crushed her broken teeth into her swollen lip, stared in panic at the soothing walls with her ruby eyes, stretched out her legs until she felt their bones must snap. Each cove, each narrow inlet, every living bay was flooded and the frail brain, a little hat-shaped boat, was washed from its mooring and set adrift. The skull was as vast as the world and the brain was as small as a seashell.

Then came calm weather and the safe journey home. She kept vigil for a while, though, and did not close her eyes, but gazing serenely at the trees, conceived of the pain as the guardian of her treasure who would not let her see it; that was why she was handled so savagely whenever she turned her eyes inward. Once this watch was interrupted: by chance she looked into the corridor and saw a shaggy mop slink past the door, followed by a senile porter. A pair of ancient eyes, as rheumy as an old dog's, stared uncritically in at her and a toothless mouth formed a brutish word. She was so surprised that she immediately closed her eyes to shut out the shape of the word and the pain dug up the unmapped regions of her head with mattocks, ludicrously huge. It was the familiar pain, but this time, even as she endured it, she observed with detachment that its effect upon her was less than that of its contents, the by-products, for example, of temporal confusion and the bizarre misapplication of the style of one sensation to another. At the moment, for example, although her brain reiterated to her that *it* was being assailed, she was stroking her right wrist with her left hand as though to assuage the ache, long since dispelled, of the sprain in the joint. Some minutes after she had opened her eyes and left off soothing her wrist, she lay rigid, experiencing the sequel to the pain, an ideal terror. For, as before on several occasions, she was overwhelmed with the knowledge that the pain had been consummated in the vessel of her mind and for the moment the vessel was unbeautiful: she thought, quailing, of those plastic folds as palpable as the fingers of locked hands containing in their very cells, their fissures, their repulsive hemispheres, the mind, the soul, the inscrutable intelligence.

The porter, then, like the pink hat and like her mother and the hounds' voices, loitered with her.

Dr. Nicholas came at nine o'clock to prepare her for the operation. With him came an entourage of white-frocked acolytes, and one of them wheeled in a wagon on which lay knives and scissors and pincers, cans of swabs and gauze. In the midst of these was a bowl of liquid whose rich purple color made it seem strange like the brew of an alchemist.

"All set?" the surgeon asked her, smiling. "A little nervous, what? I don't blame you. I've often said I'd rather break a leg than have a submucous resection." Pansy thought for a moment he was going to touch his nose. His approach to her was roundabout. He moved through the yellow light shed by the globe in the ceiling which gave his forehead a liquid gloss; he paused by the bureau and touched a blossom of the cyclamen; he looked out the window and said, to no one and to all, "I couldn't start my car this morning. Came in a cab." Then he came forward. As he came, he removed a speculum from the pocket of his short-sleeved coat and like a cat, inquiring of the nature of a surface with its paws, he put out his hand toward her and drew it back, gently murmuring, "You must not be afraid, my dear. There is no danger, you know. Do you think for a minute I would operate if there were?"

Dr. Nicholas, young, brilliant, and handsome, was an aristocrat, a husband, a father, a clubman, a Christian, a kind counselor, and a trustee of his preparatory school. Like many of the medical profession, even those whose specialty was centered on the organ of the basest sense, he interested himself in the psychology of his patients: in several instances, for example, he had found that severe attacks of sinusitis were coincident with emotional crises. Miss Vanneman more than ordinarily captured his fancy since her skull had been fractured and her behavior throughout had been so extraordinary that he felt he was observing at first hand some of the results of shock, that incommensurable element, which frequently were too subtle to see. There was, for example, the matter of her complete passivity during a lumbar puncture, reports of which were written down in her history and were enlarged upon for him by Dr. Rivers' interne who had been in charge. Except for a tremor in her throat and a deepening of pallor, there were no signs at all that she was aware of what was happening to her. She made no sound, did not close her eyes nor clench her fists. She had had several punctures; her only reaction had been to the very first one, the morning after she had been brought in. When the interne explained to her that he was going to drain off cerebrospinal fluid which was pressing against her brain, she exclaimed, "My God!" but it was not an exclamation of fear. The young man had been unable to name what it was he had heard in her voice; he could only say that it had not been fear as he had observed it in other patients.

Dr. Nicholas wondered about her. There was no way of guessing whether she had always had a nature of so tolerant and undemanding a complexion. It gave him a melancholy pleasure to think that before her accident she had been high-spirited and loquacious; he was moved to think that perhaps she had been a beauty and that when she had first seen her face in the looking glass she had lost all joy in herself. It was very difficult to tell what the face had been, for it was so bruised and swollen, so hacked-up and lopsided. The black stitches the length of the nose, across the saddle, across the cheekbone, showed that there would be unsightly scars. He had ventured once to give her the name of a plastic surgeon but she had only replied with a vague, refusing smile. He had hoisted a manly shoulder and said, "You're the doctor."

Much as he pondered, coming to no conclusions, about what went on inside that pitiable skull, he was, of course, far more interested in the nose, deranged so badly that it would require his topmost skill to restore its functions to it. He would be obliged not only to make a submucous resection, a simple run-of-the-mill operation, but to remove the vomer, always a delicate task but further complicated in this case by the proximity of the bone to the frontal fracture line which conceivably was not entirely closed. If it were not and he operated too soon and if a cold germ then found its way into the opening, his patient would be carried off by meningitis in the twinkling of an eye. He wondered if she knew in what potential danger she lay; he desired to assure her that he had brought his craft to its nearest perfection and that she had nothing to fear of him, but feeling that she was perhaps both ignorant and unimaginative and that such consolation would create a fear rather than dispel one, he held his tongue and came nearer to the bed.

Watching him, Pansy could already feel the prongs of his pliers opening her nostrils for the insertion of his fine probers. The pain he caused her with his instruments was of a different kind from that she felt unaided: it was a naked, clean, and vivid pain that made her faint and ill and made her wish to die. Once she had fainted as he ruthlessly explored and after she was brought around, he continued until he had finished his investigation. The memory of this outrage had afterward several times made her cry.

This morning she looked at him and listened to him with hatred. Fixing her eyes upon the middle of his high, protuberant brow, she imagined the clutter behind it and she despised its obtuse imperfection. In his bland unawareness, this nobody, this nose-bigot, was about to play with fire and she wished him ill.

He said, "I can't blame you. No, I expect you're not looking forward to our little party. But you'll be glad to be able to breathe again."

He stationed his lieutenants. The interne stood opposite him on the left side of the bed. The surgical nurse wheeled the wagon within easy reach of his hands and stood beside it. Another nurse stood at the foot of the bed. A third drew the shades at the windows and attached a blinding light that shone down on the patient hotly, and then she left the room, softly closing the door. Pansy stared at the silver ribbon tied in a great bow round the green crepe paper of one of the flowerpots. It made her realize for the first time that one of the days she had lain here had been Christmas, but she had no time to consider this strange and thrilling fact, for Dr. Nicholas was genially explaining his anesthetic. He would soak packs of gauze in the purple fluid, a cocaine solution, and he would place them then in her nostrils, leaving them there for an hour. He warned her that the packing would be disagreeable (he did not say "painful") but that it would be well worth a few minutes of discomfort not to be in the least sick after the operation. He asked her if she were ready and when she nodded her head, he adjusted the mirror on his forehead and began.

At the first touch of his speculum, Pansy's fingers mechanically bent to the palms of her hands and she stiffened. He said, "A pack, Miss Kennedy," and Pansy closed her eyes. There was a rush of plunging pain as he drove the sodden gobbet of gauze high up into her nose and something bitter burned in her throat so that she retched. The doctor paused a moment and the surgical nurse wiped Pansy's mouth. He returned to her with another pack, pushing it with his bodkin doggedly until it lodged against the first. Stop! Stop! cried all her nerves, wailing along the surface of her skin. The coats that covered them were torn off and they shuddered like naked people screaming, Stop! Stop! But Dr. Nicholas did not hear. Time and again he came back with a fresh pack and did not pause at all until one nostril was finished. She opened her eyes and saw him wipe the sweat off his forehead and saw the dark interne bending over her, fascinated. Miss Kennedy bathed her temples in ice water and Dr. Nicholas said, "There. It won't be much longer. I'll tell them to send you some coffee, though I'm afraid you won't be able to taste it. Ever drink coffee with chicory in it? I have no use for it."

She snatched at his irrelevancy and, though she had never tasted chicory, she said severely, "I love it."

Dr. Nicholas chuckled. "De gustibus. Ready? A pack, Miss Kennedy."

The second nostril was harder to pack since the other side was now distended and this passage was anyhow much narrower, as narrow, he had once remarked, as that in the nose of an infant. In such pain as passed all language and even the farthest fetched analogies, she turned her eyes inward, thinking that under the obscuring cloak of the surgeon's pain she could see her brain without the knowledge of its keeper. But Dr. Nicholas and his aides would give her no peace. They surrounded her with their murmuring and their foot-shuffling and the rustling of their starched uniforms, and her eyelids continually flew back in embarrassment and mistrust. She was claimed entirely by this present, meaningless pain and suddenly and sharply she forgot what she had meant to do. She was aware of nothing but her ascent to the summit of something; what it was she did not know, whether it was a tower or a peak or Jacob's ladder. Now she was an abstract word, now she was a theorem of geometry, now she was a kite flying, a top spinning, a prism flashing, a kaleidoscope turning.

But none of the others in the room could see inside and when the surgeon was finished, the nurse at the foot of the bed said, "Now you must take a look in the mirror. It's simply too comical." And they all laughed intimately like old, fast friends. She smiled politely and looked at her reflection: over the gruesomely fattened snout, her scarlet eyes stared in fixed reproach upon her upturned lips, gray with bruises. But even in its smile of betrayal, the mouth itself was puzzled: it reminded her that something had been left behind, but she could not recall what it was. She was hollowed out and was as dry as a white bone.

They strapped her ankles to the operating table and put leather nooses round her wrists. Over her head was a mirror with a thousand facets in which she saw a thousand travesties of her face. At her right side was the table, shrouded in white, where lay the glittering blades of the many knives, thrusting out fitful rays of light. All the cloth was frosty; everything was white or silver and as cold as snow. Dr. Nicholas, a tall snowman with silver eyes and silver fingernails, came into the room soundlessly, for he walked on layers and layers of snow that deadened his footsteps; behind him came the interne, a smaller snowman, less impressively proportioned. At the foot of the table, a snow figure put her frozen hands upon Pansy's helpless feet. The doctor plucked the packs from the cold, numb nose. His laugh was like a cry on a bitter, still night: "I will show you now," he called across the expanse of snow, "that you can feel nothing." The pincers bit at nothing, snapped at the air and cracked a nerveless icicle. Pansy called back and heard her own voice echo: "I feel nothing."

Here the walls were gray, not tan. Suddenly the face of the nurse at the foot of the table broke apart and Pansy first thought it was in grief. But it was a smile and she said, "Did you enjoy your coffee?" Down the gray corridors of the maze, the words rippled, ran like mice, birds, broken beads: Did you enjoy your coffee? your coffee? your coffee? Similarly once in another room that also had gray walls, the same voice had said, "Shall I give her some whisky?" She was overcome with gratitude that this young woman (how pretty she was with her white hair and her white face and her china-blue eyes!) had been with her that first night and was with her now.

In the great stillness of the winter, the operation began. The knives carved snow. Pansy was happy. She had been given a hypnotic just before they came to fetch her and she would have gone to sleep had she not enjoyed so much this trickery of Dr. Nicholas' whom now she tenderly loved.

There was a clock in the operating room and from time to time she looked at it. An hour passed. The snowman's face was melting; drops of water hung from his fine nose, but his silver eyes were as bright as ever. Her love was returned, she knew: he loved her nose exactly as she loved his knives. She looked at her face in the domed mirror and saw how the blood had streaked her lily-white cheeks and had stained her shroud. She returned to the private song: Did you enjoy your coffee? your coffee?

At the half-hour, a murmur, anguine and slumbrous, came to her and only when she had repeated the words twice did they engrave their meaning upon her. Dr. Nicholas said, "Stand back now, nurse. I'm at this girl's brain and I don't want my elbow jogged." Instantly Pansy was alive. Her strapped ankles arched angrily; her wrists strained against their bracelets. She jerked her head and she felt the pain flare; she had made the knife slip.

"Be still!" cried the surgeon. "Be quiet, please!"

He had made her remember what it was she had lost when he had rammed his gauze into her nose: she bustled like a housewife to shut the door. She thought, I must hurry before the robbers come. It would be like the time Mother left the cellar door open and the robber came and took, of all things, the terrarium.

Dr. Nicholas was whispering to her. He said, in the voice of a lover, "If you can stand it five minutes more, I can perform the second operation now and you won't have to go through this again. What do you say?"

She did not reply. It took her several seconds to remember why it was her mother had set such store by the terrarium and then it came to her that the bishop's widow had brought her an herb from Palestine to put in it.

The interne said, "You don't want to have your nose packed again, do you?"

The surgical nurse said, "She's a good patient, isn't she, sir?"

"Never had a better," replied Dr. Nicholas. "But don't call me 'sir.' You must be a Canadian to call me 'sir.' "

The nurse at the foot of the bed said, "I'll order some more coffee for you."

"How about it, Miss Vanneman?" said the doctor. "Shall I go ahead?"

She debated. Once she had finally fled the hospital and fled Dr. Nicholas, nothing could compel her to come back. Still, she knew that the time would come when she could no longer live in seclusion, she must go into the world again and must be equipped to live in it; she banally acknowledged that she must be able to breathe. And finally, though the world to which she would return remained unreal, she gave the surgeon her permission.

He had now to penetrate regions that were not anesthetized and this he told her frankly, but he said that there was no danger at all. He apologized for the slip of the tongue he had made: in point of fact, he had not been near her brain, it was only a figure of speech. He began. The knives ground and carved and curried and scoured the wounds they made; the scissors clipped hard gristle and the scalpels chipped off bone. It was as if a tangle of tiny nerves were being cut dexterously, one by one; the pain writhed spirally and came to her who was a pink bird and sat on the top of a cone. The pain was a pyramid made of a diamond; it was an intense light; it was the hottest fire, the coldest chill, the highest peak, the fastest force, the furthest reach, the newest time. It possessed nothing of her but its one infinitesimal scene: beyond the screen as thin as gossamer, the brain trembled for its life, hearing the knives hunting like wolves outside, sniffing and snapping. Mercy! Mercy! cried the scalped nerves.

At last, miraculously, she turned her eyes inward tranquilly. Dr. Nicholas had said, "The worst is over. I am going to work on the floor of your nose," and at his signal she closed her eyes and this time and this time alone she saw her brain lying in a shell-pink satin case. It was a pink pearl, no bigger than a needle's eye, but it was so beautiful and so pure that its smallness made no difference. Anyhow, as she watched, it grew. It grew larger and larger until it was an enormous bubble that contained the surgeon and the whole room within its rosy luster. In a long-ago summer, she had often been absorbed by the spectacle of flocks of yellow birds that visited a cedar tree and she remembered that everything that summer had been some shade of yellow. One year of childhood, her mother had frequently taken her to have tea with an aged schoolmistress upon whose mantelpiece there was a herd of ivory elephants; that had been the white year. There was a green spring when early in April she had seen a grass snake on a boulder, but the very summer that followed was violet, for vetch took her mother's garden. She saw a swatch of blue tulle lying in a raffia basket on the front porch of Uncle Marion's brown house. Never before had the world been pink, whatever else it had been. Or had it been, one other time? She could not be sure and she did not care. Of one thing she was certain: never had the world enclosed her before and never had the quiet been so smooth.

For only a moment the busybodies left her to her ecstasy and then, impatient and gossiping, they forced their way inside, slashed at her resisting trance with questions and congratulations, with statements of fact and jokes. "Later," she said to them dumbly. "Later on, perhaps. I am busy now." But their voices would not go away. They touched her, too, washing her face with cloths so cold they stung, stroking her wrists with firm, antiseptic fingers. The surgeon, squeezing her arm with avuncular pride, said, "Good girl," as if she were a bright dog that had retrieved a bone. Her silent mind abused him: "You are a thief," it said, "you are heartless and you should be put to death." But he was leaving, adjusting his coat with an air of vainglory, and the interne, abject with admiration, followed him from the operating room, smiling like a silly boy.

Shortly after they took her back to her room, the weather changed, not for the better. Momentarily the sun emerged from its concealing murk, but in a few minutes the snow came with a wind that promised a blizzard. There was great pain, but since it could not serve her, she rejected it and she lay as if in a hammock in a pause of bitterness. She closed her eyes, shutting herself up within her treasureless head.

COWBOYS AND INDIANS,
AND MAGIC MOUNTAINS

The Healthiest Girl in Town

In 1924, when I was eight years old, my father died and my mother and I moved from Ohio to a high Western town, which, because of its salubrious sun and its astringent air, was inhabited principally by tuberculars who had come there from the East and the South in the hope of cure, or at least of a little prolongation of their static, cautious lives. And those of the town who were not invalids, or the wives, husbands, or children of invalids, were, even so, involved in this general state of things and conversant with its lore. Some of them ran boarding houses for the ambulatory invalids ("the walkers," as we called them) and many were in the employ of the sanitarium which was the *raison d'être* of the community, while others were hired privately as cooks, chauffeurs, or secretaries by people who preferred to rent houses rather than submit to the regulations of an institutional life. My mother was a practical nurse and had come there because there were enough people to need her services and therefore to keep a roof over our heads and shoes on our feet.

My contemporaries took for granted all the sickness and dying that surrounded us—most of them had had a first-hand acquaintance with it—but I did not get used to these people who carried the badge of their doom in their pink cheeks as a blind man carries his white stick in his hand. I continued to be fearful and fascinated each time I met a walker in the streets or on the mountain trails and each time some friend's father, half gone in the lungs, watched me from where he sat in enforced ease on the veranda as other girls and I played pom-pom-pulla-way in his front yard. Once Dotty MacKensie's father, who was soon to die, laughed when I, showing off, turned a cartwheel, and he cried, "Well done, Jessie!" and was taken thereupon with the last awful cough that finally was to undo and kill him. I did not trust their specious look of health and their look of immoderate cleanliness. At the same time, I was unduly drawn to them in the knowledge that a mystery encased them delicately; their death was an interior integument that seemed to lie just under their sun-tanned skin. They spoke softly and their manners were courteous and kind, as if they must live hushed and on tiptoe, lest the bacilli awaken and muster for the kill. Occasionally, my mother was summoned in the middle of the night to attend someone in his final hemorrhage; at times, these climactic spasms were so violent, she had once told me, that blood splattered the ceiling, a hideous thought and one that wickedly beguiled me. I would lie awake in the cold house long after she had left and would try to imagine such an explosion in myself, until finally I could all but see the girandole of my bright blood mount through the air. Alone in the malevolent midnight darkness, I was possessed with the facts of dying and of death, and I would often turn, heartless and bewitched, to the memory of my father, killed by gangrene, who had lain for weeks in his hospital bed, wasted and hot-eyed and delirious, until, one day as I watched, the poisonous tide deluged him and, as limp as a drowned man, he died. The process had been so snail-paced and then the end of it so fleet that in my surprise I had been unable to cry out and had stood for several minutes, blissful with terror, until my mother came back into the room with a doctor and a nurse. I had longed to discuss with her what I had seen, but her grief— she had loved him deeply—inhibited me, and not until we had come West did I ask her any questions about death, and when I did, I appeared to be asking about her patients, although it was really about my father.

The richer of the tuberculars, especially those who had left their families behind, were billeted in the sanitarium, an aggregate of Swiss chalets that crested the western of our twin hills. If they were not bedridden, they lived much as they might have done at a resort, playing a great deal of bridge, mah-jongg, and cowboy pool, learning to typewrite, photographing our declamatory mountain range. Often in the early evening, from the main lodge there came piano music, neither passionate nor complicated, and once, as I was passing by, I heard a flute, sweet and single in the dusk. On walks, the patients slowly ranged the mesas, gathering pasque-flowers in the spring and Mariposa lilies in the summer, and in the winter, when the snow was on the ground, they brought back kinnikinnick, red-berried and bronze-leaved. These pastimes were a meager fare and they were bored, but they were sustained by their stubborn conviction that this way of life was only temporary. Faithfully, winter and summer, spring and fall, they went abroad each day at noon to get the high sun, and because the sanitarium was near my school, I used to see them at the lunch recess, whole phalanxes of them, indulging sometimes in temperate horseplay and always in the interchange of cynical witticisms that banded them together in an esoteric fellowship. In the winter—and our winters were so long and cruel that the sick compared this region to Siberia and their residence there to exile—their eyes and noses alone were visible through their caparisons of sweaters, mufflers, greatcoats, but their sanguine, muted voices came out clearly in the thin air. Like all committed people, whether they are committed to school or to jail, to war or to disease, there was among them a good-natured camaraderie that arose out of a need to vary the tedium of a life circumscribed by rules. I would hear them maligning and imitating the doctors and the nurses, and laying plans to outwit them in matters to do with rest periods and cigarettes, exactly as my schoolmates and I planned to perpetrate mischief in geography class or study hall. I heard them banteringly compare X-rays and temperatures, speak, in a tone half humorous and half apprehensive, of a confederate who had been suspended temporarily (it was hoped) from the fraternity by a sudden onslaught of fever. They were urbane, resigned, and tart. Once, I recall, I met two chattering walkers on a path in the foothills and I heard one of them say, "All the same, it's not the bore a nervous breakdown is. We're not locked in, at any rate," and his companion amiably answered, "Oh, but we are. They've locked us into these ratty mountains. They've 'arrested' us, as they say."

This colony was tragic, but all the same I found it rather grand, for most of the sanitarium patients had the solaces of money and of education (I was sure they all had degrees from Eastern universities) and could hire cars to go driving in the mountains and could buy books in quantity at Miss Marshall's snobbish shop, the Book End, where they could also drink tea in an Old Englishy atmosphere in the back room. I did not feel sorry for them as I did for the indigent tuberculars, who lived in a settlement of low, mean cottages on the outskirts of the town. Here I saw sputum cups on windowsills and here I heard, from every side, the prolonged and patient coughing, its dull tone unvarying except when a little respite came and its servant sighed or groaned or said, "Oh, God Almighty," as if he were unspeakably tired of this and of everything else in the world. There were different textures and velocities to the coughing, but whether it was dry or brassy or bubbling, there was in it always that undertone of monotony.

It was neither the rich nor the poor that my mother nursed but those in between, who rented solid houses and lived—or tried to live—as they had in Virginia or in Connecticut. Whole families had uprooted themselves for the sake of one member; mothers had come out of devotion to a favorite son. There were isolated individuals as well, men with valets and motorcars and dogs (I thought that the bandy-legged basset belonging to the very rich Mr. Woodham, of Baltimore, was named Lousy Cur, because that was how I always heard Mr. Woodham's man address him), and women who were invariably called grass widows whether they were spinsters or divorcées or had left a loving husband and family behind. Grass widows, walkers, lungers— what a calm argot it was! Many of them were not so much ill as bored and restive—lonely and homesick for the friends and relatives and for the landscapes they had left behind. Ma was a valiant, pretty woman and she was engaged more, really, as a companion than as a nurse. She read aloud to her charges or played Russian bank with them or took them for slow walks. Above all, she listened to their jeremiads, half doleful, half ironic, and tried, with kindly derision, to steer them away from their doldrums. It was this attitude of "You're not alone, everyone is in the same boat" that kept them from, as Ma said, "going mental." A few times, solitary gentlemen fell in love with her, and once she accepted a proposal—from a Mr. Millard, a cheerful banker from Providence, but he died a week before they were to be married. I was relieved, for I had not liked to think of living with a stepfather riddled with bugs.

Soon after Mr. Millard died, Ma went to work for a family named Butler, who had come West from Massachusetts, resentfully but in resignation, bringing their lares in crates and barrels, leaving behind only the Reverend Mr. Butler, who, feeling that he could never duplicate his enlightened congregation, remained in Newton to propagate the Low Church faith. Mrs. Butler, a stout, stern woman who had an advanced degree from Radcliffe, had been promised that here her life, threatened twice by hemorrhages, would be extended to its normal span and that the "tendency" demonstrated by all three of her children would perhaps be permanently checked. Besides the mother and the children, there was a grandmother, not tubercular but senile and helplessly arthritic, and it was for her that Ma had been hired. It was the hardest job she had had, because the old woman, in constant pain, was spiteful and peckish, and several times she reduced my intrepid mother to tears. But this was also the best-paid job she had had, and we were better dressed and better fed than we had been since we left Ohio. We ate butter now instead of margarine and there was even money enough for me to take dancing lessons.

Two of the Butler children, Laura and Ada, were in my grade at school. There was a year's difference between them but the elder, Laura, had been retarded by a six-month session in a hospital. They were the same size and they looked almost exactly alike; they dressed alike, in dark-blue serge jumpers and pale-blue flannelette guimpes and low black boots. They were sickly and abnormally small, and their spectacles pinched their Roman noses. All of us pitied them on their first day at school, because they were so frightened that they would not sit in separate seats, and when Miss Farley asked one of them to sing a scale, she laid her head down on her desk and cried. But we did not waste our sympathy on them long, because after their first show of vulnerability we found them to be haughty and acidulous, and they let it be known that they were not accustomed to going to a public school and associating with just anyone. Nancy Hildreth, whose father was a junkman, excited their especial scorn, and though I had always hated Nancy before, I took her side against them

and one day helped her write a poison-pen letter full of vitupera-
tive fabrication and threats. We promised that if they did not
leave town at once, we would burn their house down. In the
end, the letter was too dangerous to send, but its composition
had given us great pleasure.

After about a month, Laura and Ada, to my bewilderment
and discomfort, began to seek me out at recess, acknowledging in
their highhanded way that they knew my mother. They did not
use the word "servant" in speaking of her but their tone patronized her and their faint smiles put her in her place. At first, I
rebuffed them, for they were too timid to play as I played; they
would never pump up in the swings but would only sit on the
seats, dangling their feet in their *outré* boots, trying to pretend
that they were not afraid but were superior to our lively games.
They would not go near the parallel bars or the teeter-totter,
and when the rest of us played crack-the-whip, they cowered,
aghast, against the storm doors of the grammar school. But when
I complained to Ma of how they tagged after me and tried to
make me play their boring guessing games, she asked me, for her
sake, to be nice to them, since our livelihood depended on their
mother, a possessive woman who would ferociously defend her
young. It was hardly fair of Ma to say to me, "Just remember,
it's Laura and Ada who give you your dancing lessons," but all
the same, because she looked so worried and, even more, because
I could not bear to think of not going to my lessons, I obeyed
her, and the next day grudgingly agreed to play twenty questions
while, out of the corner of my eye, I enviously watched the other
children organizing a relay race.

Not long after I had made this filial compromise, Laura and
Ada began asking me to come home with them after school, and
though my friends glared at me as we left the playground together, I never dared refuse. Anyhow, the Butlers' house enchanted me.

It smelled of witch hazel. As soon as we entered the cool and
formal vestibule, where a gilded convex mirror hung above a
polished console table on which there stood a silver tray for
calling cards, the old-fashioned and vaguely medicinal fragrance
came to meet me, and I envisaged cut-glass bottles filled with it

on the marble tops of bureaus in the bedrooms I had never seen.
It made me think of one particular autumn afternoon, in the
Ohio woods, when my father and I went for a walk in a clean,
soft mist and he cut me a witch-hazel wand, with which I
touched a young orange salamander orphaned in the road. As
palpable and constant as the smell in the house was the hush of
an impending death; somewhere, hidden away in such isolation
that I could not even guess where she was, whether upstairs or in
a room behind the parlor, lay the grandmother, gradually growing feebler, slowly petering out as my mother spooned up medicine for her and rubbed her ancient back with alcohol. There
was hardly a sound in that tomb-still house save for the girls'
voices and mine, or the footsteps of their older brother, Lawrence, moving about in his chemical laboratory in the basement.

Again, as vivid as the fragrance and the portentous quiet
was the sense of oldness in this house, coming partly from the
well-kept antique furniture, the precious Oriental rugs, the
Hitchcock settles that formed an inglenook beside the hearth,
the quaint photographs hung in deep ovals of rich-brown wood
(there was a square piano, and a grandfather clock that told the
time as if it knelled a death), but coming even more from the
Boston accents and the adult vocabularies and the wise, small
eyes of my two playmates. I did not think of them as children
my own age but rather as dwarfed grownups, and when I walked
along between them, towering over their heads, my own stature
seemed eccentric, and in my self-consciousness I would stub my
toe or list against one of the little girls (who did not fail to call
me awkward). Probably they had never been children; if they
had, it had only been for a short time and they had long since
cast off the customs and the culture of that season of life. They
would not stoop to paper dolls, to pig Latin, to riddles, to practical jokes on the telephone, and in their aloofness from all that
concerned me and my fellows they made me feel loutish, noisy,
and, above all, stupid.

At other houses, visitors were entertained outside in good
weather. In the spring and fall, my friends and I roller-skated or
stood on our heads and only looked in at the back door to ask for
graham crackers or peanut-butter sandwiches; in the winter we
coasted down the hills and occasionally made snow ice cream in

some tolerant mother's kitchen. If rain or wind quarantined us, we rowdily played jacks with a golf ball or danced to the music of a Victrola. Whatever we did, we were abandoned to our present pleasure.

But at the Butlers' house the only divertissements were Authors and I Spy, and it was only once in a blue moon that we played those. Usually we sat primly, Laura and Ada and I, in the parlor in three wing chairs, and conversed—it is essential to use that stilted word—of books and of our teachers. The Butler girls were dauntlessly opinionated and called the tune to me, who supinely took it up; I would not defend a teacher I had theretofore admired if they ridiculed her; I listened meekly when they said that *Rebecca of Sunnybrook Farm* was silly. Sometimes they told me their dreams, every one of which was a nightmare worse than the one before; they dreamed of alligators and gargantuan cats, of snakes, ogres, and quicksand. I would never tell my vague and harmless dreams, feeling that they would arouse the Butlers' disdain, and once, after they had asked me to and I had refused, Ada said, "It's obvious Jessie doesn't have any dreams, Laura. Didn't Father say that people who sleep soundly have inferior intellects?"

Those long words! They angered and they charmed me, and I listened, wide-eyed, trying to remember them to use them myself—"obvious," "intellect," "logical," "literally." On one of my first visits, Ada, picking up a faded daguerreotype of a bearded man, said, "This is my great-grandfather, Mr. Hartford, whom my brother intends to emulate. Great-grandfather Hartford was a celebrated corporation lawyer." My astonishment at her language must have shown in my face, for she laughed rather unkindly, and, in shocking vernacular, she added, "That is, Larry will be a lawyer *if* he doesn't turn into a lunger first." The Butlers, like the patients at the sanitarium, had their intramural jokes.

Laura and Ada told me anecdotes of Lawrence, who went to high school and was at the head of his class and contributed regularly to the *Scholastic* magazine. They adored him and looked on every word of his as oracular. He was a youth of many parts, dedicated equally to the Muses (he was writing an epic on Governor Bradford, from whom the family was obliquely descended) and to the study of chemistry, and often, commingled with the witch hazel, there was a faint odor of hydrogen sulfide wafted up through the hot-air registers from his basement laboratory. "Lawrence is a genius," said Laura once, stating a fact. "Think of a genius having to live *here* all his life! But, of course, he's stoical."

They told me, also, of incidents in the brilliant university career of their mother, who wore her Phi Beta Kappa key as a lavaliere. They spoke of her having studied under Professor Kittredge, as if this were equivalent to having been presented at court. The formidable bluestocking, Mrs. Butler, seldom came into the parlor, for usually she was out shopping or doctoring or was upstairs writing a play based on the life of Carlyle. But when she did make one of her rare appearances, she took no cognizance of me, although it seemed to me that her discerning eyes, small, like her daughters', and monkey-brown, like theirs, discovered my innermost and frivolous thoughts and read them all with disapproval. She would come in only to remind the girls that that night they must write their weekly letters to their father or to remark indignantly that it was difficult to shop when one was nudged and elbowed by barbarians. For Mrs. Butler had an orthodox aversion to the West, and although almost no one was native to our town, she looked down her pointed nose at the entire population, as if it consisted of nothing but rubes.

After we had talked for half an hour, Laura would go out of the room and come back after a while with a tole tray on which stood a china cocoa set and a plate of Huntley & Palmers sweet biscuits, ordered from S. S. Pierce. We would drink in sips and eat in nibbles and continue our solemn discourse. Often, during this unsatisfying meal (the cookies were dry and the cocoa was never sweet enough for me), the talk became medical, and these sophisticated valetudinarians, nine and ten years old, informed me of extraordinary facts relating to the ills that beset the human flesh and especially those rare and serious ones that victimized them. They took such pride in being hostesses to infirmity that I was ashamed of never having suffered from anything graver than pinkeye, and so light a case of that that Ma had cured it in a day with boric acid. The Butlers, besides being prey to every known respiratory disorder, had other troubles:

Laura had brittle bones that could be fractured by the slightest blow, and Ada had a rheumatic heart, a cross she would bear, she said, until the day she died. They had had quinsy, pleurisy, appendicitis; they were anemic, myopic, asthmatic; and they were subject to hives. They started off the morning by eating yeast cakes, and throughout the day popped pellets and capsules into their mouths; at recess, I would see them at the drinking fountain, gorging on pills. Their brother was a little less frail, but he, too, was often ill. The atmosphere of the house was that of a nursing home, and Ma told me that the whole family lived on invalid fare, on custards and broths and arrowroot pudding. The medicine chest, she said, looked like a pharmacy.

I never stayed long at the Butlers' house, for Laura and Ada had to go upstairs to rest. I stayed only until Lawrence came up from the basement, and as I closed the storm door, I saw, through the side lights, the three of them, weak, intellectual, and Lilliputian, carefully climbing the stairs in single file on their way up to their bedrooms, where they would lie motionless until their dinner of soft white food.

I had had friends before Laura and Ada whose lives were far more overcast by tuberculosis than theirs—children born in the same month and the same year as myself who had already spat out blood, children whose mothers had died in the dead of night, whose fathers would never rise from their beds again. But never before had I been made to feel that my health was a disgrace. Now, under the clever tuition of the Butlers, I began to look upon myself as a pariah and to be ashamed not only of myself but of my mother, who was crassly impervious to disease, although she exposed herself to it constantly. I felt left out, not only in the Butlers' house but in this town of consumptive confederates. I began to have fantasies in which both Ma and I contracted mortal illnesses; in my daydreams, Laura and Ada ate crow, admitting that they had never had anything half so bad and praising my bravery. Whenever I sneezed, my heart leapt for joy, and each time my mother told me she was tired or that her head ached, I hoped for her collapse, anxious for even a vicarious distinction. I stood before the open window after a hot bath in the hope of getting pneumonia. Whenever I was alone in the house, I looked at the pictures in a book of Ma's called *Diagnostics of Internal Medicine* and studied representations of infantile spinal paralysis, of sporadic cretinism, of unilateral atrophy of the tongue. Such was my depravity that when I considered the photograph of a naked, obscenely fat woman who was suffering, so the caption read, from "adiposis dolorosa," I thought I could endure even that disfigurement to best the Butlers.

Because my mother valued health above all else (she was not a prig about it, she was only levelheaded), I knew that these of mine were vicious thoughts and deeds, but I could not help myself, for while I hated the sisters deeply and with integrity, I yearned for their approbation. I wanted most desperately to be a part of this ailing citizenry, to be able casually to say, "I can't come to your house this afternoon. I have to have an X-ray." If I had known about such things when I was nine, I might have been able to see the reasons for my misery, but at nine one has not yet taken in so much as the meaning of the words "happy" and "unhappy," and I knew only that I was beyond the pale, bovine in the midst of nymphs. Epidemics of scarlet fever and diphtheria passed me by. Other children were bitten by rabid dogs and their names were printed in the paper, but the only dogs I met greeted me affably and trotted along beside me if the notion took them to. My classmates broke their collarbones and had their tonsils taken out. But nothing happened to me that Unguentine or iodine would not cure, and all the while the Butlers' pallor seemed to me to deepen and their malicious egotism to grow and spread.

I do not think that Laura and Ada despised me more than they did anyone else, but I was the only one they could force to come home with them. "Who wants to be healthy if being healthy means being a cow?" said Ada one day, looking at me as I reached for a third insipid cooky. I withdrew my hand and blushed so hotly in my humiliation that Laura screamed with laughter and cried, "The friendly cow all red and white, we give her biscuits with all our might."

Oh, I hated them! I ground my anklebones together, I clenched my fists, I set my jaw, but I could not talk back—not here in this elegiac house where my poor ma was probably simultaneously being insulted by the querulous octogenarian. I could do no more than change the subject, and so I did, but my choice was infelicitous, for, without thinking and with a kind of self-defeating desperation which I saw to be calamitous even before the words were finished, I asked Laura and Ada if they did not like the tumbling we were having in gym, and Ada, horrified, appealed to her sister (she rarely spoke directly to me but through Laura, as if she spoke a separate language that must be translated)—"Oh, tell her that we don't *tumble*"—and her sister went on, "While the rest of you tumble, we write essays." Who could scale this Parnassus? On the flatlands of Philistia, I held my tongue, and I endured, for the sake of learning how to execute a *tour jeté* in Miss Jorene Roy's dance salon.

And then, one day, at the height of my tribulation, Ada, quite by accident, provided me with the means to petrify them for an hour with curiosity and awe. It was nearing Christmas, and the parlor was pranked out with holly wreaths in the windows and a tree in the bay window and early greeting cards lined up in military ranks on the mantel. The girls had been uncommonly animated lately, for their father was coming from Boston to spend two weeks with his brood. I would have the privilege, as would everyone else in town, of hearing him deliver a sermon as the guest preacher at St. John's; the girls' implication was that his erudition was so great that not a soul in this benighted place would understand a word he said. That day, in the dark room—a beautiful, obscuring snow was falling and the heavy branches of the cedar trees leaned against the windows—I envied them this tribal holiday, envied them their peopled house, and pitied myself for being a fatherless and only child. I thought I would have given anything at this moment for a brother, even for Lawrence Butler, with his peaked, mean face and the supercilious way he had of greeting me by saying, "How *do* you do?" Ada, as if she had read my melancholy thoughts and wished to twist the knife, said complacently, "What a shame she doesn't have a father, isn't it, Laura? Laura, ask her what her father died of."

My brilliant answer sprang instantly to my lips without rehearsal or embellishment. "Leprosy," I said, and watched the

Bostonians freeze in their attitude as if they were playing Statues. I had learned of leprosy some weeks before from the older sister of a friend, who had held me spellbound. The belief that was soon to be current among my friends and me when the movie *Ben Hur* was to enthrall us all was that lepers slowly vanished, through the rotting away of their fingers and toes, and then of their hands and feet, and then of their arms and legs, and that all exterior appointments, as ears and noses, hair and eyes, fell off like decayed vegetables finally falling from the vine. If this had been my first impression of leprosy, I doubt whether I would, even in this emergency, have thus dispatched my father to his grave, but at the time, thanks to the quixotic older sister, who had got her information in some byway trod by no one but herself, I was under the impression that leprosy was a kind of sleeping sickness brought on by the bite of a lion. This intelligence I passed on to Laura and Ada, glib crocodile tears gathering in the corners of my eyes, and never dreamed, as I pursued my monologue, that they had a Biblical acquaintance with leprosy and that what rooted them to the spot was the revelation that I was the daughter of an unclean man.

Before I could finish my story or make the most of its picturesque details, Laura gasped, "He was unclean!"

"Unclean?" I was incensed. "He was *not* unclean! He washed himself exactly like a cat!" I screamed.

"She said he was asleep for thirty months," said Ada. "Ask her how he could wash in his sleep."

"Well, he did, anyway," I said, flummoxed at being caught out. "I don't know how, but he did. He didn't have fleas, if that's what you mean."

"Unclean," repeated Ada, savoring the word. "Tell her to stay where she is until we get out of the room and tell her never to come back to this house again."

"She never will," said Laura. "She'll be sent to the Fiji Islands or someplace. Lepers can't run around loose."

"Oh, Laura, do you think she has it? Do you think we'll get it?" moaned Ada. "Where is Mother? We must tell her *now!*"

"Be careful, Ada," said Laura. "Go out of the room backwards and keep your eye on her, and if she starts to move, scream. We'll be all right as long as she doesn't touch us."

"Poor Grandmother!" wailed Ada. "Did you think of Grandmother being *touched* all this time by that unclean woman?" She backed to the door, her eyes fixed on me, who could not have moved for anything.

"It's awful!" said Laura, following her sidewise, like a crab. "Of all days for Mother to be at the osteopath! Still, Larry will have an idea."

"Yes," said Ada from the doorway. "Probably Lawrence will send for the Black Maria."

My many selves, all bedlamites, clamored in my faint, sick heart. I wished to tell them on the spot that the whole thing had been a lie. I wished to say it had been a joke. "I was only kidding," I would say. But how heartless that would make me! To jest about my dead father, whom I had loved. Still, I must say something, must in some way exonerate myself and my mother and him. But when I opened my mouth to speak, a throttled sound came out, as surprising to my ears as to theirs, and before I had a chance to find my voice, the girls, appalled, had shut the door. I heard them slowly mount the stairs—even in their alarm they were protective of themselves—and I waited, frozen, for the sound of their avenging brother's footsteps up the stairs from the basement that entered into the front hall. When, at last, mobility returned to me, I slipped out of the parlor and made my way down the corridor to the back of the house, fearful of meeting him in the vestibule. I think I had half expected to encounter my mother in these precincts, but the passage I walked along was doorless until I came to the kitchen, a still, enormous room where there was a soft, sporadic hissing from the banked coal fire in the hooded Glenwood range. Against the varnished wainscoting stood ladder-back chairs, demanding perfect posture of their occupants, and on the trestle table there was a fruit bowl full of wholesome prunes. I knew without looking that there would be nothing good to eat in the cupboards—no brown sugar, no mayonnaise, nothing but those corky cookies. Within the pantry was a deer mouse hunched in death in a trap, and the only ray of light coming through the curtained window made an aura around its freckled fur. I bent to look more closely at the pathetic corpse, and as I did so, I heard, from directly overhead, the sound of Laura and Ada Butler giggling. *At what?* It was a high, aquatic giggle that came in antiphonal wavelets, and then one of the girls began to cough. I fled, mystified, and let myself out into the snow that whirlingly embraced me as I ran blindly home. A block from home, I began wildly to call my cat. "Kitty, kitty, kitty, *kitty!*" I shrieked, to drown out the remembered sound of my terrible lies, and Mr. Woodham's valet, passing me with Lousy Cur on a leash, said, "Whoa, there! Hold on! Where's the fire?" Pretending, with great effort, that I was the same person I had been an hour ago, I stopped and forced myself to grin and to stoop down and lightly pat the sad-eyed dog, and when this amenity was done, I continued on the double-quick.

Mine was a desperate dilemma, for I must either stick to my story and force my mother to confirm it, with the inevitable loss of her job and our probable deportation to the Fiji Islands, or grovel before the girls and admit that I had told a lie. I had told many lies before but I had never told one that involved the far future as well as the near. The consequences of telling my mother that, for example, I had been at the public library when in fact I had been prowling on the dump, hunting for colored bottles, were not serious. I might smart under her disapproval and disappointment (I was not forbidden to go to the dump and the needlessness of the lie made her feel, I suppose, that my character, in general, was devious) but I recovered as soon as her reproach was over. But this one, involving everyone—my father, whom I had, it seemed, maligned (although the concept of uncleanness still puzzled me); my mother, whose job and, indeed, whose whole life I had jeopardized; myself, who could never face the world again and must either wear the mark of the beast forever or spend the rest of my days under a banana tree—this lie was calamity. I thought of stowing away on the interurban to the city, there to lose myself forever in the dark alleys under the viaducts or in the Greek Revival comfort stations at the zoo. I thought of setting fire to the Butlers' house, as Nancy Hildreth and I had threatened to do, and burning them all to death. I thought, more immediately, of shaving off my hair by way of expiation.

When I got to the house, I scooped up Bow, the cat, from the rocking chair where she was sleeping, and went to my bedroom. Without taking off my coat, or even my galoshes, I lay down on my bed, my head beneath two pillows, the outraged and struggling cat clutched in my arms. But before I had time to collect my wits to formulate a plan of action (my disappearance in the city had its attractions), the telephone screamed its two hysterical notes, one short, one long, and I catapulted down the stairs to answer it. Bow trotted after me, resumed her place in the rocking chair, and went instantly to sleep.

It was Laura Butler, who, in a muffled voice, as if she did not want to be overheard by someone nearby, said, "Larry has arranged everything. He knows how we can cure you, and no one will ever know. So you come here tomorrow afternoon on the dot of three o'clock."

The next day was Saturday, and at three o'clock on Saturdays I went to Miss Roy's, and so dear to my heart was dancing class that even in this crisis I protested. "Can't I come at four instead?"

"Why should you come at four?" asked Laura imperiously.

"Because I'm the prince in 'The Cameo Girl.'"

"The *what* in the *what?*"

"I mean I go to dancing class at three," I said. "You know? My fancy-dancing class?"

"Dancing will do you very little good, my dear girl, if your legs fall off," Laura said severely.

"If my legs fall off?" I cried. "What has that got to do with it?"

"Larry says that your legs will undoubtedly fall off if you don't come here at three o'clock tomorrow." There was a slight pause; I felt she was conferring with someone, and she said, "By the bye, your mother doesn't have to have the cure, because she was too old to get leprosy, but of course if you don't have the cure, she'll have to go to the Fiji Islands with you. Larry says that's the law."

"Laura?" My voice explored the tiny tunnel of space between our telephones. Shall I tell her now, I thought. "Laura?" I asked again.

"You know it's Laura," she said, so briskly, so contemptuously that on the instant I was stubborn.

"I can't come," I said.

Aside—to Ada or to Lawrence, I presumed—she said, "We may have to take steps after all. Larry says—"

"Wait!" I cried. "Hey, Laura, are you still there? Laura, listen, let me come right now!" For I was thinking of the *entrechat* I had almost perfected, and more than anything else in the world I wanted Miss Roy to tell me, in her jazzy way, that it was "a lulu." But I knew that until my mind lay at rest, I could not dance a single step.

I could hear whispers at the other end, and finally Laura said, "Very well, although it will inconvenience us," and then she warned, "If you are late, my mother will come home. I suppose you don't want *her* to know?"

I sighed deeply into the telephone and heard the other receiver being returned to its hook. Immediately the bell rang again, and Laura said, "Come in ten minutes. We have to get things ready."

The stillness of the house unnerved me as I waited those ten minutes, and, perversely, I frightened myself still more by speaking aloud and hearing my voice come hollowly back to me. "What are they going to do to me, Bow? What *things* have they got to get ready?"

It occurred to me to kill myself. I heard the interurban going out and thought again of skipping town. *Cure* me. What did that mean? I picked up Bow and carried her to the window with me and stood there with her face against mine, watching the storm. She was tense, watching Lousy Cur as he trotted home. "Shall I take the cure, Bow?" I said, and she growled deep in her gentle white belly. "Does that mean yes, Bowcat? Or shall I tell them it was a lie?" She growled again, for Lousy Cur was opposite our house, and, as if he sensed her being there, he paused, one foot uplifted, and gazed with interest at our front door. "Which?" I asked her, and in answer she writhed with a howl from my arms, furious at this double invasion of her privacy. She forgot us both and abruptly took a bath.

My hands were so damp that I could hardly peel my mittens off when I got to the Butlers' front door, and there was a severe pain in my stomach that made me think I had probably got cancer in punishment for my sin (not, as I might have hoped earlier, as a reward for my virtue). Planless still, my parched lips mouthed my alternative opening speeches: "It was a lie" and "I am ready for the cure." The door opened the moment I rang the bell, and Laura and Ada stood waiting for me in the vestibule, ceremonious in odd brown flannel wrappers with peaked hoods attached at the back of the neck. Gnomelike and leering, they ushered me into the parlor, where they had set up a card table and had covered it with a white cloth. On it stood a group of odd-shaped bottles, which, they explained to me, Larry, the chemist, had lent to them. Did they mean to burn me with acids? To sprinkle me with lye? There was also a covered willowware tureen on the table, and an open Bible.

"Ask her if she believes in God," said Ada.

"Yes," I said quickly, although I was by no means sure. "Listen, Laura—" What if I said the joke was on them? What if I said I'd planned this hoodwink for weeks? The worst they could do was get angry. But I knew I could not convince them, and I floundered, stuttering, beginning, stopping dead.

"The prisoner at the dock wishes to speak," said Ada. "Hear ye! Hear ye!"

"Yes?" said Laura, preoccupied. She had lifted the lid of the tureen and to her sister said, "Do you think the insides of one bird will do?"

Ada, looking into the dish, grimaced. "It will simply have to. There's only one to be had. Larry said it would be all right."

"Do you mind asking him again, just to make sure?"

"I wouldn't dream of disturbing him," said Ada. "He's in his laboratory, boiling his spittle. He can make it turn purple and he can make it turn green."

It made me even more uneasy to know that Lawrence was in the house, and again I started to speak. "Laura, listen to me—" But Laura had picked up the Bible now, and she read, " 'Two birds alive and clean, and cedar wood' "—she held up a beaker half full of cedar berries—" 'and scarlet, and hyssop.' " And her sister pointed to two test tubes, which appeared to be filled, one with red ink and the other with blue.

"Laura—"

"One moment. Be quiet, please." She continued to read, " 'And the priest shall command that one of the birds be killed in an earthen vessel over running water.' " She opened the tureen again and poured out water from a cream pitcher while Ada murmured doubtfully, "Of course, it's already dead."

"A very good thing it is that she believes in God, or the cure would never work," said Laura and went on reading. " 'As for the living bird, he shall take it, and the cedar wood, and the scarlet, and the hyssop, and shall dip them and the living bird in the blood of the bird that was killed over the running water.' " With this, she put into the bowl the picture of an eagle, which she had probably cut out of a magazine, and she poured in the red ink, the blue ink, and the cedar berries. Then, bearing the vessel in both hands, she came to where I stood and allowed me to look into a dreadful mess of ink and feathers and the entrails of the chicken that they were doubtless going to have that night for dinner. She dipped her fingers into the stew, and though she shuddered and made a face, she persevered, and before my nose she dangled a bit of dripping innards.

This was enough for me. I would not be touched by those slithering, opalescent intestines, and I shrank back and I cried out, "Will you listen to me? I told a lie!"

Laura's look roasted and froze me, sent me to jail, to hell; it drew and quartered me. "A lie!" she exclaimed, as if I had confessed to murder. Ada turned to her sister with a pout and said crossly, "I *told* you it would never work."

Laura continued to look hard at me, but at last her face relaxed and, patronizing, like a minister, speciously kind, like a schoolteacher, she said, "Now, what's all this about a lie?"

"He didn't die of leprosy," I said. I looked at my feet and moved them slightly, so that the toes of my shoes pointed to the hearts of two roses in the carpet.

"Why did you say that he did?"

"Because—"

"It's more important, I should think," said Ada sulkily, "to find out what he *did* die of. It's quite possible that he died of something worse."

"Why did you say that he did?" said Laura, ignoring her.

"Because it was a joke."

"A joke? I thought you said you had told a lie. There is a

world of difference between the two, Jessie. Well, which was it, a joke or a lie?"

"A joke!" I cried, almost in tears.

"Do you hear that, Laura?" said Ada. "She tells a *joke* about the deceased."

"I mean it was a lie," I said. I was on the verge of a fearful sobbing. "A lie, and I am sorry." The smell of witch hazel was inordinately dense. In the silence, I heard the click of a ball on the Christmas tree. Suddenly, my ignorance of where my mother was in this unhealthy house terrified me, and I loudly said, "How is your grandmother today?"

"Stick to the subject," said Laura.

But Ada was glad to tell me. "Grandmother is not well at all today. She had a bilious attack this morning. So did I."

She smiled smugly at me, and I, magically emboldened by my distaste, moved to the door, and as I went, I said, "*I* am never sick. I have never been sick in my life."

"Lucky you," gloated Ada.

"What did he die of?" persisted Laura.

"He got shot out hunting, if you want to know," I told them. "My father was as tall as this room. The district nurse told Ma that I am the healthiest girl in town. Also I have the best teeth."

Across those small, old faces there flickered a ray of curiosity to know, perhaps, how the other half lived, and for just that split second I pitied them. My mind cleared and I realized that all this torment had been for nothing. If the Butlers had tried to blacken my name for telling a lie, no one would have believed them, for they had no friends, and, by the same token, if they had noised it about that my father had died of leprosy, I could have said *they* were telling lies. Now I was exalted and hungry and clean, and when I had put on my coat and opened the door, I cried exuberantly, "So long, kids, see you in church!"—a flippancy I would not have dared utter in that house two hours before. By way of reply, Ada coughed pitifully, professionally.

Until the grandmother died, in April, and Ma took another job, I went two or three afternoons a week to the Butlers' house, and over our light collation, as Laura and Ada called it, we talked steadily and solely of the girls' grave illnesses. But as I left, I always said, with snide solicitude, "Take care of yourselves." They were unshakable; they had the final word: "We will. We have to, you know." My vanity, however, was now quite equal to theirs. Feeling myself to be immortal and knowing myself to be the healthiest girl in town, I invariably cut an affronting caper on the Butlers' lawn and ran off fast, letting the good mountain air plunge deep into my sterling lungs.

The Tea Time of Stouthearted Ladies

"As I tell Kitty, this summer job of hers is really more a vacation with pay than work. What wouldn't *I* give to be up there in the mountains away from the hurly-burly of this town! They have a lake right there below the main lodge where the girls can cool off after they serve lunch. And quite often they can have the horses to trot off here, there, and the other place—go down to Brophy, for instance, and have a Coke. They can help themselves to the books in the lounge, play the Victrola, sit in the sun and get a good tan. They go to the square dances and dance with the dudes as if they were dudes themselves, and if there's a home movie they're invited to come and view. Mrs. Bell and Miss Skeen are very democratic along those lines and when they first hired Kitty, when she was just fourteen, they told me they didn't look on their employees as servants but as a part of the family."

"Not my idea of work," agreed Mrs. Ewing, and made a hybrid sound, half deprecating giggle, half longing sigh. "Some different from *our* summers, what with those scorching days in August and no let-up in the way of a breeze. Oh, I'm by no means partial to summer on the plains. And all those pesky grasshoppers spitting tobacco juice through the screens onto your clean glass curtains, to say nothing of the fuss-budget old school-marms—give me a dude any day of the week sooner than Miss Prunes and Prisms from Glenwood Springs still plugging away at her M.A. after fifteen years. Kitty's in luck all right."

Lucky Kitty Winstanley, home from her last class for the day at Nevilles College, stood in the middle of her small, shadowy bedroom, her arms still full of books, and listened to the voices in the kitchen below her. She visualized her mother and the turnip-shaped, bearded neighbor as they lingered in the bright hollow of the dying May afternoon. Their ration of icebox cookies eaten, their pale, scalding coffee drunk, they would be sitting in the breakfast nook, facing each other through spotless, rimless spectacles. Their tumid hands mutilated by work would be clasped loosely on the tulip-patterned oilcloth and their swollen feet would be demurely crossed as they glibly evaluated the silver lining of the cloud beneath which they and their families lived, gasping for every breath. It was out of habit, not curiosity, that Kitty listened; she knew all their themes by heart and all of them embarrassed her. She listened with revulsion, with boredom, pity, outrage, and she moved stealthily so that they would not know she had come home.

Each afternoon, in one house or another along this broad, graveled street, there was such an imitation tea party in such a fiercely clean kitchen as Mrs. Winstanley's when two women or more established themselves in speckless cotton dresses in the breakfast nooks for a snack and a confab. United in their profession, that of running boarding houses for college students, and united more deeply but less admissibly in hardship and fatigue and in eternal worry over "making ends meet," they behaved, at this hour of day that lay tranquilly between the toasted peanut-butter sandwiches of lunch and the Swedish meatballs of dinner, like urban ladies of leisure gossiping after a matinee. Formal, fearful of intimacy lest the full confrontation with reality shatter them to smithereens, they did not use each other's first names, asked no leading questions; it was surprising that they did not wear gloves and hats. They did not refer, even by indirection, to personal matters, not to the monotonous terror of debt that kept them wakeful at night despite the weariness that was their incessant condition, or to the aching disappointment to which they daily rose, or to their hopeless, helpless contempt for their unemployed husbands who spent their days in the public park, clustering to curse the national dilemma or scattering to brood alone upon their individual despair.

Valorously, the landladies kept their chins up, rationalized; they "saw the funny side of things," they never said die. One would not guess, to listen to their light palaver, that they had been reduced to tears that same morning by the dunning of the grocer and the coal man and had seen themselves flung into debtors' prison for life. To hear their interchange of news and commentary on their lodgers, one might have thought they were the hostesses of prolonged, frolicsome houseparties. The cancer was invisible, deep in their broken, bleeding hearts.

They sat at the social hour of four to five in the kitchens because their parlors were either rented out or were used as a common room by the lodgers, but even in this circumstance they contrived to find expansive consolation. Often Mrs. Winstanley, sitting at attention on the stark bench, had said, "I can relax so much better in a kitchen." Did she think, her daughter wondered, that the repetition of this humbug was one day going to make it true? She sometimes went on from there to say, "When I was a girl back home in Missouri, we used to call our kitchen 'the snuggery,' and we used it more than any other room in the house." As she complacently glanced around, her manner invited her caller to believe that she saw a Boston rocker and braided rugs, copper spiders hanging on whitewashed walls, a fireplace with a Dutch oven and cherry settles in the inglenooks, and a mantel crowded with pewter tankards and historic guns. In fact, the caller looked on a room all skin and bones: a coal-oil range with gaunt Queen Anne legs, a Hoosier cabinet ready to shudder into pieces, a linoleum rug worn down to gummy blackness save in the places that were inaccessible to feet and still showed forth its pattern of glossy bruises—a room, in short, in which there was nothing to recommend itself to the eye except the marmalade cat and the sunshine on the windowsill in which he slept.

But the neighbor conspiratorially played the game with her hostess, gladly breathed in these palliative fibs without which the ladies would have spent their days in tears. In one way or another, they had all "come down in the world," but they had descended from a stratum so middling, so snobbish, and so uncertain of itself that it had looked on penury as a disgrace and to have joked about it would have been as alien to their upright natures as it would have been to say aloud the name of a venereal disease. They had come to Adams, this college town in the Rocky Mountains, from the South and the Midwest and New England, most of them driven there by tuberculosis in one member of the family, and now that the depression had slid to its nadir and there were no jobs for their husbands, they had taken up this hard, respectable work.

They bore their shame by refusing to acknowledge its existence: except in the bitter caverns of the night when they reproached their husbands in unflagging whispers, too soft for the boarders to hear but not too soft for their own sons and daughters. For years, Kitty had heard these static diatribes coming up through the hot-air register from her parents' bedroom off the kitchen; sometimes they lasted until the coyotes howled at sunup in the foothills. Rarely did her ruined father answer back; all the charges were true, brutally unfair as they were, and he had nothing to say for himself. He was a builder, but no one was building houses these days; he had only one lung and so he could not work in the mines. The oppressive facts of the depression and of his illness testified to his innocence, but his misery, so long drawn out and so unrelieved, had confused him until he was persuaded that he was jobless because he was no good at his work and he believed his wife when she, cruel out of fear, told him that if he had a little more gumption they would not have to live this way, hand to mouth, one jump ahead of the sheriff. Kitty hated her father's unmanliness (once she had seen him cry when a small roof-repairing job that he had counted on was given to someone else, and she had wanted to die for disgust) and she equally hated her mother for her injustice; and she hated herself for hating in them what they could not help.

In the daytime, the woe and bile were buried, and to her lodgers Mrs. Winstanley was a cheery, cherry-cheeked little red hen who was not too strict about quiet hours (their portable phonographs and radios drove Kitty nightly to the library) or about late dates.

With her friends, she liked to talk of her lodgers and of theirs: of their academic failures and successes ("I wasn't a bit surprised when Dolores got a con in psych," Kitty once heard Mrs. Ewing say, using the patois as self-confidently as if it were her own. "She told me herself that she hadn't cracked a book all term," and Mrs. Winstanley, au courant and really interested, replied, "But won't those A's in oral interp and business English bring her average up?"); they talked of the girls' love affairs, their plans for holidays, their clothes, their double dates. Gravely and with selfless affection, they told each other facts and sometimes mildly looked for overtones and meanings. Once, Kitty heard her mother say, "Helen went to the Phi Delt tea dance on Thursday with the boy in Mrs. McInerney's single front, but she didn't have a good time at all. She said afterward she was sorry that she had turned down an invitation to go to the show at the Tivoli, even though everyone said it was punk. Of course, I didn't ask any questions, but between you and me and the gatepost I think she was simply cutting off her nose to spite her face by going to the dance instead of keeping her regular date with her steady. Jerry Williams, that is, that big tall engineer with the Studebaker."

They liked to speculate on the sort of homes their students came from; someone's mother's diabetes, someone's younger brother's practical jokes, someone else's widowed father's trip to Mexico were matters that mattered to them. They counted it an equal—and often thrilling—trade if one landlady, offering to her interlocutor the information that one of her girls or boys had been elected to Phi Beta Kappa, got in return the news that Helen or Joyce or Marie had been "pinned" with his Chi Psi pin by a prominent member of the football team.

It was not often that they discussed their own sons and daughters who were working their way through college, but when they did their applause was warm. They were, said the landladies, a happy-go-lucky bunch of kids (though serious in their studies) despite the fact that they did not belong to fraternities and sororities (and were known, therefore, as Barbarians) and could not have exactly the clothes they wanted ("But they keep warm!" the ladies cried. "And when you come right down to it, what else are clothes for?") and had to think twice about spending a nickel on a Coca-Cola. They mouthed their sweet clichés like caramels: "Anything you work hard for means so much more than something just handed to you on a silver platter." "Our children's characters will be all the better for their having gone to the School of Hard Knocks." "For these youngsters of ours, Mrs. Ewing, the depression is a blessing in disguise."

With this honorable, aggressive, friendly mendacity, they armed themselves against the twilight return of their gray-faced husbands from the park and of their edgy children, exhausted from classes and study and part-time jobs and perpetually starved for status (they loathed the School of Hard Knocks, they hated being Barbarians) and clothes (a good deal of the time they were *not* warm) and fun. The husbands ate early, fed like dogs in the kitchen, and then, like dogs, they disappeared. Kitty's father spent his evenings in the furnace room where, under a weak light, he whittled napkin rings. But the landladies' sons and daughters, at the end of the day, became maids or footmen to the students whom they had earlier sat next to in Latin class or worked with on an experiment in chemistry. Kitty Winstanley, setting a plate of lamb stew in front of Miss Shirley Rogers, rejoiced that the girl had flubbed her translation in French and had got a scathing jeer from the instructor, but it was cold comfort because this did not detract at all from the professional set of Miss Rogers' fine blond hair or the chic of her flannel skirt and her English sweater on which, over her heart, was pinned the insignia of her current fiancé. Sometimes in the kitchen, as Kitty brought out dirty dishes or refilled the platter of meat, her mother whispered angrily, "Don't look so down in the mouth! They'll go eat some place where they can find a cheerful smile and then what will we do?" Blackmailed, Kitty set her lips in a murderous grin.

A little work never hurt anyone, the landladies assured each other, and if it was not Mrs. Winstanley yearning to trade places with Kitty in the debonair life she led as waitress and chambermaid at the Caribou Ranch, it was Mrs. Ewing, similarly self-hypnotized, enumerating the advantages that accrued to her asthmatic son in nightly setting up pins in a bowling alley. What a lark she made of it! And what a solemn opportunity. It was a liberal education in itself, according to his mother, for Harry Ewing to mingle until one in the morning with coal miners and fraternity boys, a contrast of class and privilege she found profoundly instructive. A cricket match on the playing fields of Eton would not seem to offer more in the demonstration of sportsmanship than a bowling tournament between the Betas and the ATOs at the Pay Dirt Entertainment Hall. And, again, a stranger might have thought that Harry was only slumming when Mrs. Ewing spoke, with a sociologist's objectivity, of the low mentality and lower morality of the men from the mines and the scandalous girls they brought with them on Ladies' Night. She never touched upon the sleep that Harry lost or on those occasions when a doctor had to be summoned on the double to give the pin boy an injection of adrenalin. "I do believe Harry's outgrowing his asthma," she said once, although that very morning Kitty had seen him across the hall in modern European history buffeted suddenly by an attack so debilitating that he had had to be led out by a monitor.

Kitty sat down at her study table and opened her Renaisrance survey book to Donne, shutting her ears against the voices of the heroines below. But she was distracted and disconsolate, and the *Divine Poems* fled from her eyes before her mind could detain them. She turned to stare out of her narrow window at the sweet peas that her father's green thumb had coaxed to espalier the wall of the garage. Somewhere in the neighborhood, a music student was phrenetically practicing a polonaise, making villainous mistakes, and somewhere nearer a phonograph was playing "I Wonder Who's Kissing Her Now," the singer's tribulation throbbing luxuriously in the light spring air. Beyond the garage, over the tops of the mongrel houses and through the feathery branches of mountain ash trees, Kitty could see the red rock terraces of the foothills and the mass of the range beyond where, in a high, wild, emerald and azure and bloodstone park, she would spend her summer.

She would not spend it exactly as her mother imagined. She thought of that lake Mrs. Winstanley so much admired, sight unseen, where the girls could swim after lunch if they were not repelled by the mud puppies that abounded in the icy water; and then she thought of the lambent green pool in the main lodge for the exclusive use of the dudes. She thought of the one spooked and spavined old cow pony the kitchen help could ride if they wanted to go where he contrarily wanted to take them, up in the hot sage where the rattlers were or through thick copses of scratchy chokecherry or over sterile, stubbly fields pitted with gopher holes into which he maliciously stumbled when there was no need; and then she saw in her mind's eye the lively blooded bays and palominos that the dudes rode, never failing, as they mounted, to make some stale, soft-boiled joke about

Western saddles. It was true, just as her mother said, that the help was asked to the square dances, only "asked" was not the right word; they had to go to show the Easterners the steps, and there could not have been any dances at all if Wylie, the horse-wrangler, had not been there to call the turns. And it was hardly like going to Paris to go down to Brophy, all but a ghost town, where the only buildings that were not boarded up were a drug-store, a grocery, the post office, a filling station, and a barber-shop that was open on Tuesday and Saturday when an itinerant barber came to town. A handful of backward people, most of them named Brophy, lived in battered cabins in the shadows of the ore dumps of extinguished gold mines. In the wintertime, the story was, they often killed each other because they had nothing else to do.

The help at the Caribou blundered out of bed at five o'clock before the sun came up to begin a day that did not end until after nine at night, a day filled, besides work, with the fussy complaints about their cabins and their food from the older guests, pinches and propositions from the randy younger ones (who were not that young). There was ceaseless bickering among the staff who, xenophobic, despised the dudes and, misanthropic, despised each other. The kitchen was ruled by a fat red cook and a thin yellow pantry girl who did not speak to each other although they glared verbosely across the room, the cook from under the lowering hood of her enormous stove, the pantry girl over the counter of her bailiwick, where the smell of rancid butter was everlasting.

Every morning, as the girls and the wranglers drowsed through their breakfast of flapjacks and side meat, Miss Skeen appeared in the outer doorway of the kitchen, a homicidal Ger-man shepherd at her side (his name was Thor and he lived up to it; he had bitten many ankles and had abraded countless others), and boomed through the screen, "Howdy, pardners!" Miss Skeen, a tall and manly woman, combined in her costume the cork helmet of the pukka sahib, the tweed jacket of the Cotswold squire, the close-fitting Levi's and the French-heeled boots of the wry American cowboy, and the silver and turquoise jewelry of the colorful Southwestern aborigine. Her hair was short, her face was made of crags, she spoke in a Long Island basso profundo.

While Miss Skeen gave the men their orders for the day, her partner, Mrs. Bell, entered the kitchen to chirp admonitions to the female servants. Mrs. Bell was stout, small-mouthed, doggishly dewlapped, and she wore the khaki uniform of a Red Cross ambulance driver; her contribution to the Great War still gave her great satisfaction, and her memories of France, which were extensive and fresh, were ever on the tip of her tongue. Quite often she lapsed from Western into Army lingo, called the dining room "the mess hall," asked a guest how he liked his billet, spoke of the wranglers as "noncoms." Her awful greeting was, "Cheerio, boys and girls! Everybody get out of the right side of bed this morning, I hope, I hope?"

The five waitress-chambermaids lived a mile from the main lodge down in a pine-darkened gulch in what had once been a chicken coop and what now Mrs. Bell archly called "the girls' dorm." The door still latched on the outside and the ceilings were so low that no one taller than a child could stand up straight in any of the three small rooms. There was an outhouse, vile and distant; they were so plagued by trade rats that they had to keep everything they could in tin boxes if they did not want to find their money or their letters stolen and replaced by twigs or bluejay feathers. At that altitude it was freezing cold at night, and the laundry stove in which they burned pine knots could not be regulated, so that they had the choice of shivering or being roasted alive. They had a little time off in the afternoon, but, as often as not, Mrs. Bell would dream up some task for them that she tried to make out was a game: they would have to go gather columbines for the tables in the dining room or look for puffballs to put in the pot roast. It was exhausting work; sometimes, after a thronged weekend or a holiday, Kitty's arms ached so much from carrying burdened trays that she could not sleep, and through the long night listened anxiously to the animals gliding and rustling like footpads through the trees.

But, all the same, each spring for the past four years Kitty had been wild with impatience to get to the Caribou, to get away from home, from the spectacle of her eaten father and from her mother's bright-eyed lies, from all the maniacal respectability with which the landladies strait-jacketed the life of the town. The chicken coop was filthy and alarming, but it was not this genteel, hygienic house in which she was forced to live a double life. At the Caribou, she was a servant and she enjoyed a servant's prerogative of keeping her distance; for instance, to the rich and lascivious dude, Mr. Kopf, a painter, she had been respectful but very firm in refusing to pose for him (he wanted to paint her as Hebe), had said, in a way that left no room for argument, "I have to rest in my time off, sir." But, at home, what could she do if a boarder, valuable to her mother for the rent she paid, asked for help with a translation or the loan of lecture notes? She could not put the girl, her contemporary and classmate, in her place by calling her "ma'am," she could do nothing but supinely deliver the lecture notes together with the dumplings or lend a hand with *De Amicitia* after she had taken to the various rooms the underwear and blouses her mother had washed and ironed.

At the Caribou, there was no one she knew in any other context. Her fellow waitresses were local mountain girls, so chastely green that they were not really sure what a college was and certainly did not care. They never read, but it did not embarrass them that Kitty did. At Christmas she exchanged cards with them but they did not exist for her, or she for them, before the first of June or after Labor Day. And the dudes whose bathtubs she scoured and whose dietary idiosyncrasies she catered to came from a milieu so rich and foreign and Eastern that she could not even imagine it and therefore did not envy it.

Friendless, silent, long and exasperating, the summers, indeed, were no holiday. But she lived them in pride and without woe and with a physical intelligence that she did not exercise in the winter; there in the mountains, she observed the world acutely and with love—at dusk, the saddle horses grazing in the meadow were joined by deer seeking the salt lick; by day the firmament was cloudless and blinding and across the blue of it chicken hawks and eagles soared and banked in perpetual reconnaissance; by night the stars were near, and the mountains on the moon, when it was full, seemed to have actual altitude. On these wonders, Kitty mused, absorbed.

The voices downstairs invaded her trance. She began to calculate in pencil on the margin to the left of "If poisonous minerals . . ." how many more hours there were to come before she got into the rattletrap mail coach that would take her, coughing spastically in its decrepitude, up the rivered canyons and over the quiet passes to her asylum. Her arithmetic did not deafen her. She heard:

"I grant you that the hours are long and the pay is low," her mother said, "but the Caribou attracts big spenders from the East and the tips more than make up for the poor wages. I don't mean your flashy tourists and I don't mean your snobby new rich but simply your settled, well-to-do people, mostly middle-aged and older. Mrs. Bell and Miss Skeen are cultured—went to boarding school in Switzerland as I understand it—and they are ladies and, as a result, they are particular about their clientele—absolutely will not tolerate anything in the least out-of-the-way. For one thing, they don't allow drinking on the premises, and anyone who breaks the rule is given his walking papers without any further ado, I don't care if his name is Astor or John Doe. And with all the beer-drinking and what-not going on down here when those fast boys come flocking to town from heaven knows where in those convertible roadsters with the cut-outs open and those horns that play a tune, it's a comfort to me to know that my daughter is out of the way of loose living."

"Oh, I agree," said Mrs. Ewing, and Kitty could imagine her nodding her head spiritedly and shaking loose the bone hairpins that held her gray braids in place. "I happen to know that the drinking that goes on in this town is decidedly on the upgrade. In these bowling alleys and so on, they spike the three point two with grain alcohol. And that's the very least of it. There are many, many ether addicts in the frat houses. Oh, I'm telling you, there are plenty of statistics that would make your hair stand on end. D.T.s and so on among the young."

For a few minutes then the ladies lowered their voices and Kitty could not hear what they said, but she knew the bypath they were joyfully ambling down; they were expounding the theory that beer-drinking led to dope and dope to free love and free love to hydrocephalic, albino, club-footed bastard babies or else to death by abortion.

The fact was that both Mrs. Bell and Miss Skeen were lushes, and they fooled nobody with their high and mighty tee-total rule and their aura of Sen-Sen. The rule was at first a puzzle and a bore to the dudes, but then it became a source of surreptitious fun: outwitting the old girls became as much a part of the routine as fishing or hunting for arrowheads. For the last two years, Kitty Winstanley had acted as middleman between the guests and the bootlegger, Ratty Carmichael. There was local option in the state, but in Meade County where the Caribou lay there was nothing legal to drink but three point two. In an obscure, dry gully back of the cow pasture, Kitty kept her trysts with Ratty (his eyes were feral and his twitching nose was criminal) and gave him handfuls of money and orders for bottles of atrocious brown booze and demijohns of Dago Red. These he delivered at dinnertime when Miss Skeen and Mrs. Bell were in their cabin, The Bonanza, oblivious to everything but their own elation, for which excellent Canadian whisky, bought honorably in Denver, was responsible. Kitty had no taste for this assignment of hers—she was not an adventurous girl—but she was generously tipped by the dudes for running their shady errands and for that reason she put up with the risks of it—being fired, being caught by the revenue officers and charged with collusion.

She smiled, finishing her multiplication. In 283 more hours, immediately after her last examination in final week, she would be putting her suitcase into the mail truck parked behind the post office. And a good many of those hours would be blessedly spent in sleep. Then she'd be gone from this charmless town on the singed plains where the cottonwoods were dusty and the lawns were straw. She'd be gone from the French dolls and baby pillows in the lodgers' rooms. And, in being gone, she would give her mother a golden opportunity to brag to the summer roomers: "Kitty has the time of her life," she could hear her mother say to some wispy, downtrodden schoolteacher waif, "up there where the ozone is as good as a drink, as they say."

Now the light was paling on the summit snows. Kitty heard her father's soft-footed, apologetic tread on the back porch and heard Mrs. Ewing brightly say, "Well, I must toddle along now and thanks a million for the treat. My turn next time."

The music student was at work on *The Well-Tempered Clavichord* and the phonograph was playing "The Object of My Affection" as fast as merry-go-round music. And down in the kitchen, as she clattered and banged her pots and pans, Mother Pollyana began to sing "The Stein Song."

The Mountain Day

When I woke up that morning, in the fallow light before the sunrise, and remembered that the night before I had got engaged to Rod Stephansson, I could feel my blue eyes growing bluer; I could feel them becoming the color of the harebells that were blooming now in August all through the pasture beneath my window, and I thought, Will Rod notice this change and how will he speak of it? For weeks, like a leaf turning constantly to the sun for its sustenance, so my whole existence had leaned toward Rod's recognition and approval of me, as if without them I would fade and wither. When I was alone and he was miles away from me, not thinking of me at all, probably, as he catalogued botanical specimens at the Science Lodge, I nevertheless caused his eyes to take in the way I brushed my hair or mounted my horse or paddled my little brother Davy across our lake and back in the canoe. And going further, I would project us into the autumn, when our Western holiday would be over and he would come down from Harvard for a weekend in New York. I would, in my daydreams, receive him in a dozen different dresses and a dozen different countenances: now I was shy, now I was *soignée,* now unassailably cool and pure; sometimes I was talking in sparkling repartee on the telephone when he arrived, and sometimes I was listening to phonograph records; depending on my costume and my coiffure, the music was Honegger or Louis Armstrong or plainsong. Often, in the self-conceit of my love, I was so intent upon his image of me that I could not, for a moment, summon up an image of *him.* How was that possible! The mountain sun had turned him amber and had lightened his leonine hair; he was tall and lithe and sculptured and violet-eyed, and the bones of his intelligent face were molded perfectly. My sister Camilla, two years older than I and engaged to be married to a brilliant but distinctly batrachian Yale man, had, on first seeing Rod, said, "If he's really going to be a doctor, the girl that marries him is in for trouble. What a practice he's going to have among women! Brother!"

I think I got this pressing need for high opinion from my father, who was a rich man of intellect and education but one of no vocation. Our life was sumptuous and orderly, and we lived it, in the winter, in New York and, in the summer, in the mountains of Colorado. The Grayson fortune, three generations old, founded on such tangibles as cattle, land, and cargo vessels, was now a complex of financial abstractions, the manipulation of which my father had turned over to bankers and brokers, since money, as a science, did not interest him. He had zeals and specialties, but I think he spent his whole life worrying about what people thought of him; a man of leisure had become an anachronism. One time, when he came to visit me at college and I had been telling him about a close friend of mine who was going on to study law after she finished at Bryn Mawr, he said, "D'you know, Judy, if I hadn't been rich, I'd have been a bum." He was not ashamed of his millions—they were no fault of his—but he *was* ashamed that his life was not consecrated; he had no fixed orbit. And, in a different way, this unease of his had come down to me, his middle child.

But I wasn't thinking of Daddy that morning—it was only years later that I was able to arrive at this analysis—and when I thought of Camilla's reaction to Rod, I went back to the first time I had met him and reviewed all the stages of growth that had culminated the night before in his asking me to marry him. I lay straight and still and smiling, my eyes wide open, hearing the pristine song of the first meadow larks on the fence posts, and hearing the famished, self-pitying coyotes wailing up in the sage.

One day late in June, soon after our arrival in Colorado, Daddy and Mother and Camilla and I had ridden our horses over to the Science Lodge to have lunch with a friend of Daddy's— Dr. Menzies, a geophysicist from Columbia, who taught there in the summers. It was an annual expedition, like the trip to the glacier, and the regatta at Grand Lake, and opening night at Central City; Daddy was a ritualist—each year, for example, he had the same four seats at Carnegie Hall for the Boston Symphony— and whether we liked it or not, we participated in his ceremonies.

It had always bored Camilla and me terribly to go to the Science Lodge. The place was a dismal aggregate of log cabins, some of which were laboratories and lecture rooms and others Spartan living quarters for the faculty and for the dozen or so students —solemn, silent, myopic youths, who, we decided, must be even more solemn in the winter, at college, since coming to the Lodge to study high-altitude vegetation and the mineralogy of moraines was their notion of a holiday; the boys we knew bicycled through France or fooled around on boats off Martha's Vineyard. Everyone, staff and students and guests, sat at one long table in the mess hall and ate fried beefsteak, dehydrated potatoes, canned peas, and canned Kadota figs, and drank sallow coffee with canned milk. Daddy and Dr. Menzies would fervently discuss some such thing as the wisdoms and the follies of foundations. Mother, who was a beauty and had no intellectual class consciousness, would try to talk about flower arrangement with the ecologists and the systematic botanists, who blushed and addressed their eyes to their food. And Camilla and I would flounder through the maneuvers of "Do you know So-and-So at Dartmouth?" or "Have you been up to Troublesome Falls yet?," and, for our pains, got monosyllabic replies, usually in the negative. Not one time, until this summer, had she and I found any of these young men worthy of comment; they were, indeed, so much of a kind and so stunningly dull that in our private language we had a generic term, "a Science Lodge type," to designate nonentities we got stuck with at parties.

And then, this year, sitting directly across the table from me was Rod Stephansson, so sudden, somehow, so surprising, that I averted my eyes, as if his radiance would blind me. He was as serious as the other boys, but he was not solemn, and he and Mother, in a conversation about Boston, which she knew from visits to our aunts and cousins there and he knew because he went to Harvard, so charmed each other that long before we had reached the Nabiscos and the viscous figs, she had invited him to our house for Sunday supper. He was sophisticated and funny and acute, but he was gentle, too, and mannerly. His smile, in which the responsive eyes played the leading role, made me giddy, but I wanted, nevertheless, to remain within its sphere.

As soon as lunch was over, the scientists and their apprentices bolted for their microscopes and samples of pyrites—all except Dr.

Menzies and Rod, who came with us to the hitching post where we had left the horses. As we sauntered through the red dust under the amazing alpine sky, I was breathless, filled with trepidation that I was going to do something clumsy and cause this paragon, who had not once looked in my direction, to despise me. So emphatic had been his immediate effect on me that, as if I had already committed the blunder and excited his disdain, I angrily shrugged my shoulders and said to myself, "Oh, to hell with him! He's nothing but a Science Lodge grind." But something quite else happened; when I had mounted Chiquita, my squatty little pinto cow pony, Rod took a blue bandanna handkerchief out of his pocket and, as if this were the most natural thing in the world, began to wipe the red dust off my boot and the edge of my jodhpurs, and when he was through—in my heady reveries later on I was to find it significant that he cleaned only *one* boot, so that my horse concealed him from the rest of the party—he looked up and gave me that inebriating smile and, in a secret voice, for my ears only, he said, "You'll be there on Sunday, won't you? You won't go off to Denver, or anything like that?" It never occurred to me to give him a flirtatious reply; I realized, with awe and with self-consciousness, that Rod had outgrown boyhood and the games of boyhood.

On the five-mile ride home, I was glad that Camilla and Daddy questioned Mother about him, because my voice would have come out as a croak or a squeak. Mother said he had told her that he was of Norwegian descent and came from Buffalo, and that he was going into his second year at Harvard Medical School. His family for generations had been landscape gardeners and horticulturists, and he had come out to the Science Lodge because, through his father, he had become interested in plant pathology ("He's very keen on viruses," said Mother), and Dr. Miles Houghton, eminent in the field, was on the staff this year. It was then that Camilla expressed her pity for the girl who married him, but Mother said, "I don't think he's in the least like that. His looks wouldn't mean a blessed thing if he weren't so awfully bright and nice. I think his character is very well put together."

It was a storybook summertime romance, woven in the mountain sun and mountain moonlight, beginning that first Sunday

when he came to supper and delighted everyone. All my senses
were heightened, as if I had been inoculated with some powerful,
sybaritic drug: the aspen leaves were more brilliant than they had
ever been before, the upland snow was purer, the pinewoods were
more redolent, and the gentle winds in them were more melliflu-
ous; the berries I ate for breakfast came from the bushes of Eden.
In love with Rod, I seemed to love my parents more than ever,
and Camilla and Davy, and my grandmother, who summered in
a house across the lake from us; I adored the horses and the dogs
and the barn cats and the wary deer that sometimes came at dusk
down to the salt lick after the cows had been taken in.

Rod had never been West before, and because I had been
coming here in the summer ever since my infancy, I was his cicerone, and took him to beaver dams and hidden waterfalls and
natural castles of red rock, and to isolated, unmarked tombstones
where God knew what murdered prospectors or starved babies
were buried. We sifted the fool's gold of the cold streams through
our fingers and we ate sweet piñon nuts; we rowed and rode and
climbed and fished, and played doubles with Daddy and Camilla.
No other young man—not even Camilla's Fritzie Lloyd, whom
Daddy liked enormously—had ever evoked from Daddy so much
esteem, and once he said, "He plays at everything so well and
handsomely, *besides* having medicine and virtue."

Rod rose at dawn to study ergot and potato blight, but in
midafternoon he walked over to our house, in long, easy strides.
When he got to the foot of the broad steps that led up to the
veranda, he was not out of breath or hot or exhausted. I, trembling inwardly and greeting him with a falsely cool "Hey, Rod,"
would think, If I tell him I have been reading *War and Peace,*
will he respect me?

For it was his respect, I suppose, that I wanted as much as I
wanted his love. I wanted him to honor my judgments and my
abilities as much as I honored his, but through some fortunate
poise, inherited from my mother to counterbalance the doubt I
had got from Daddy, I was not compelled to compete with him,
as I often had to compete, to my grief, with boys whose unsure-
ness of themselves made me arrogant. I must complement, not
equal, Rod. Actually, I was not so uneasy with him as I sound;
in his presence I was simply and naturally happy, and it was only

when we were apart that I tried on different attitudes and opinions in search of the one he would like in me the best.

When August came and the holiday began to wane, I grew restive. In two weeks more, Rod would go back to Buffalo and I would go back to New York with my family, and soon after that we would be separated—we who had been inseparable since June —by a million light-years, he in Cambridge and I at Bryn Mawr. The night before, I had thought that if he did not speak in some way of the future, I would get sick. But I had set my sights so low that the most I had hoped for was an invitation to the Yale-Harvard game, and instead of that he had asked me to marry him! Is there anything on earth more unearthly than to be in love at eighteen? It is like an abundant spring garden. My heart was the Orient, and the sun rose from it; I could have picked the stars from the sky.

The evening had started out badly. Fritzie Lloyd had come on from St. Louis for a week's visit, and at dinner he and Daddy had had an argument about Truman's foreign policy that had unsettled everyone. My father was, except in one particular, the very mildest of men: politically, he was a mad dog, and someone who disagreed with him became, temporarily, his mortal enemy. As I have said, he was very fond of Fritzie and highly approved of him for Camilla, but that night, over the Nesselrode, when Fritzie suggested, at considerable length, that the British attitude toward Communist China was more realistic than ours, Daddy protested so violently that you would have thought he might at any moment go and get a gun and shoot to kill. Everyone, and Fritzie most of all, was frightened by his fuming, stuttering rage, and after dinner Mother, to get us out of the house and calm Daddy down with a game of cribbage, proposed that Camilla and Fritzie and Rod and I take the station wagon and go somewhere to dance.

The only place within miles was a squalid, dusty honky-tonk in Puma, patronized by subhuman ne'er-do-wells and old wattled trollops who glared hostilely at us when we went in; at the bar an ugly customer, very drunk, spat on the floor as we walked by, and with feral hatred said, "Goddam yearling dudes!" The reek of beer and green moonshine and nasty perfume, together with my grief that the summer was almost gone, harried me and made me hot and weak, and I was silent. Fritzie was morose and kept saying things like "I *know* which way the land lies with your old man, so why do I have to make him sore? Damn it, I like him so, what makes me pick the one thing that's going to make him take a scunner to me?" And Camilla kept stroking the back of his hand and consoling him, telling him that of *course* he didn't have to go back to Missouri the next day, and that while she knew it had been an awful experience, she was awfully proud of his sticking to his guns, and he must stop fretting, because Daddy honestly was probably dying of remorse this minute and was the *original* hatchet-burier. Rod and I danced once—speechless, except at the very end of the jukebox record, when he said, his lips in my hair, "I wish when we went out it would be snowing." Snowing! He wanted the winter to come? I gasped and whispered back, "Oh, no! I love the summer," and he replied, "I know, but I love the snow. I love the Public Garden in the snow. The swan-boat pond, those trees . . ." And he drifted off into a musing reverie that excluded me. Soon after that, we went back home, in melancholy silence.

Mother and Daddy had gone to see Grandmother, and Camilla and Fritzie, cheered by Daddy's absence, went into the house to drink Jack Daniels, which they had just discovered, and which they talked about as if their drinks of it, on the rocks, were the insignia of a particularly lofty secret society. Rod wanted to go out on the lake, and as I was helping him put the red canoe into the water, my mood of sorrow left, and I was abruptly dreadfully excited and felt that all my nerves were pulsing.

At its widest, Daddy's lake was just under a mile, and it was so deep in places that whenever I took Davy out on it, I put him in a Mae West. It was a wonderful lake—limpid, blue, shaped like a heart. Daddy stocked it each year, and the rainbow trout that came from it were so beautiful they looked like idealized paintings of trout. Not far from the pier at Grandmother's house, there was a dense meadow of water lilies, and in the shallows near the shores tall cattails grew. But there were some horrid inhabitants of that lovely water, too—huge turtles and hellbenders, about which Davy sometimes had screaming nightmares. Rod and I paddled smoothly and languidly across to Grandmother's shore, and when we turned back, he said, "Let's sprint." The speed, our harmony, our skill, the spicy smell of the serviceberry bushes blooming along the bank, the stars, the lost, lorn, glamorous admonitions of far-off owls—these, and my love for Rod, required of me some articulation, for I could not bear the pressure and the tension of my experience. I might have screamed, I might have cried, but instead I began uncontrollably to laugh. It was my nervous system, not my mind at all, that initiated this uproarious giggling, which was immediately communicated to Rod. The lake had an echo, and we could hear our gagging, pealing ha-ha's coming back to us from all sides, but we managed, crippled as we were—aching, undone—to continue at the speed we had set and, still laughing, get the canoe to shore and up into the reeds and grass. We were spent. There had been no joke and I was a burst balloon. Now, in me, there was nothing but dejection, like a burden on my bones, and I lay down on the grass with my arms straight at my sides, as if I were lying in my casket.

And it was then, in the vast mountain hush, after our meaningless, visceral bout of mirth, that Rod asked me to marry him. Oh, the originality of my sensation! The uniqueness of this circumstance!

We heard Camilla and Fritzie talking on the veranda, and after a while we went up to join them, and to tell them that we were engaged They seemed immeasurably old to me, for they had been through this delirious distemper so long ago, and they seemed kind and staid, as if they were our aunt and uncle, when, soothingly, they said that in this case we must have champagne.

Now, the next morning, the household was sleeping late, for it was Sunday, and there wasn't a sound except for the birds and an occasional moo or whinny; the sun had risen, and the derelict coyotes had slunk away, still hungry and pessimistic. While I was bewitched with my treasures—my memories were as new and crisp and astonishing as Christmas presents—I grew restless and could not wait for everyone to get up. I wanted to talk to Camilla and Mother, I wanted to hug Davy, I wanted to rush across the lake in the outboard to embrace my acerb, Dresden-doll grandmother and tell her what had happened to me; she would quiz me and tease me and insult me for being so young, and in the end she would rummage through the bottle-green velvet reticule she al-ways carried and give me something antique and precious—a tiny perfume flask or a set of German-silver buttons.

Rod was coming over at eleven, and he and Fritzie and Camilla and I were going up to the glacier. We would ride as far as the ruin of the Bonanza silver mine, and go the rest of the way on foot and have our lunch on the summit of McFarland's Peak, above the mammoth slope of ice. But that was eleven and it was only six! Is he awake, I thought. Is he trying to imagine what I'm doing? With his eyes following me, I got up and put on my pink quilted peignoir and went to the window to see what sort of day we would have for our excursion. It was going to be perfect; it was what my father called "a mountain day." The air was so clear and rarefied it seemed to be an element superior to anything terrestrial —an unnamable essence that had somehow made its way to our valley and our range from another hemisphere. The violent violet peaks stood out against a sky of cruel, infuriated blue, and the snows at timberline shone like sun-struck mirrors. There was no wind; the field of harebells was motionless; the dark-blue lake was calm, and the red canoe, bottom up in the reeds, gleamed in the pure light like a bright, immaculate wound.

I dressed at last, changing a dozen times, trying first slacks, then Levi's, then khaki frontier pants, then jodhpurs, next a red shirt, a blue pullover, a black turtleneck, a striped apache jersey; I did my hair in a ponytail, in a pompadour, in pigtails, and finally I brushed it out straight and let it hang loose to my shoulders.

As soon as I decently could, I went across to Grandmother's and had breakfast with her and told her about Rod. She was pleased; she said that Rod was an Adonis and that she saw no point in marrying if one couldn't marry a handsome man. She opened up that vast, obsolete bag of hers and gave me a gold pin in the shape of two clasped hands.

My grandmother's house was, in these wildwoods of Colo-rado, a remarkable incongruity, for while she loved the West—she and my grandfather, who died when I was six, had started coming out here when my father, their son, was a baby, suffering from asthma—she despised roughing it. She could not bear crudity or imperfection, and she constantly implored Mother and Daddy to get rid of our cowhide rugs and our flawed, bubbly Mexican glass-ware and our redwood furniture. Her own house, though its ex-terior was the same as ours—rambling and made of logs—was fur-nished much as her apartment in New York was; the Oriental rugs were second-best and some of the tapestry chair-seat covers were machine-made, but the total effect, nonetheless, was that of an oasis of civilization in a barbaric waste. Each year she brought her maids with her, and for the past two or three summers they had been two red-haired Irish girls, Mary and Eileen, who looked down their pretty noses at Mother's servants—local mountain girls who wore ankle socks and cardigans when they served dinner.

Grandmother was not a snob. It was simply that her nature demanded continuity. Her maids today were going to Mass in Peaceful Glen, twenty miles away, and were to be driven there by Bandy, our horse-wrangler and general handyman. Mass was cele-brated at the Glen only once a month, by an itinerant priest, who toured continually through the mountains and the plains to the sparse and widely separated settlements of Catholics. Like all such Sundays, it was a red-letter day for Mary and Eileen, and I could hear them in the kitchen, chattering as excitedly as girls going to a dance. Grandmother, a benign and understanding mistress, al-ways gave them the day off after breakfast until it was time for them to prepare her tea, and she came to our house for lunch. After church, if the weather was good, the girls had a picnic be-side the lake—an endearing, old-fashioned picnic, with a table-cloth and a wicker hamper. They were planning one for today, Mary said when she came in to clear away the breakfast things.

Grandmother told her that I was going to marry Rod. "That Viking lad," said Grandmother, and Mary, transfigured with hap-piness for anyone else's happiness, said, with her habitual lavish sentimentality, "It's as if it was my own wedding day. Oh, Miss Judy! May every saint and angel bless you!"

The rest of the morning somehow passed. Daddy had com-pletely forgotten his wrath of the evening before and was talking baseball with Fritzie on the veranda while Mother and Camilla and I sat in Mother's bedroom and talked about engagements and marriage, and about Rod. Mother said, "What good girls I have, to pick out such extremely agreeable young men!" Finally, the last drop of the coffee in the pot on Mother's breakfast tray was gone, and she got up and went to the window and exclaimed, "What a day, what a day! How I envy you pretty girls going off up to McFarland's with your beaux! Do you realize how *important* love is at this time of your lives?" She was ragging us, of course, as Grandmother always did, but she partly meant what she said, for there was the faintest note of the disappointment of maturity in her voice. "What a mushy woman you are!" said Camilla affectionately, and Mother said, "And what a cold, critical woman you are! Now run, the pair of you, and have the grandest skylark ever."

Camilla and Fritzie rode ahead and carried on an enthusiastic conversation. Fritzie was studying architecture at Yale, and Camilla was studying art at Vassar, and they were both extremely ardent and in the know; they were, besides, after nearly a year of being engaged, so comfortable with each other that their relationship was no longer an *idée fixe*. But Rod and I were shy and strained, and, I suppose, in a sense we were wretched. These early stages of love are an egg-treading performance, and one is stiff and scared; the day after betrothal is made up almost equally of hell and heaven. He told me at length and feelingly, as if he were talking about the death of beloved kinsmen, how blight had all but obliterated the chestnut trees in the Northeast; so earnestly did I seek to maintain our concord of the night before that I nearly moaned to hear his facts, and languished with the roots of those afflicted trees, and turned my face away from the disease spores disseminated by the wind, and with my whole heart hoped that the attempt to cross the American species of chestnut with the blight-resistant Asiatic would be successful. After this, a leaden silence fell. But gradually, as we ascended the faint trail through Indian paintbrush and columbines, and the air began to make us drunk, we were infected by the glory and the grace of the day and we relaxed a little. I had, indeed, been so rigidly controlled that I had got cramps in the calves of both legs. Finally, ready to cry out with pain, I told Rod, who at once became my doctor and my protector. We dismounted in a field of volunteer timothy, and he massaged my legs until the knots were gone; the gesture, in itself utilitarian, served to return us to our rapture of the night before, and we were able to meet each other's eyes.

And now, much happier, we spurred our horses and came abreast of Camilla and Fritzie, and all the rest of the way to the mine the four of us had a general, factual conversation about New York restaurants, and Broadway musicals we had seen. To the unspoken relief of both Camilla and me, Rod and Fritzie obviously liked each other, and when they were hobbling the horses, we stood aside, praising them. Camilla said, "Rod really is a pet," and I said, "Fritzie grows on one. Last night when Daddy was being such a pain in the neck, I decided he was made of *steel*."

We had our lunch at the top of the world, sitting on saddle blankets spread out upon waxy yellow glacier lilies, which grew beside a snowdrift that some exotic bacteria had made the color of raspberry sherbet. We had cold fried chicken and tomato sandwiches and melon balls and lemony iced tea; it was unquestionably the best meal I had ever eaten in my life. I suddenly remembered Mary and Eileen and their picnic; they would be sitting among the wildflowers, eating dainty nasturtium sandwiches and telling each other spooky ghost stories in their delicious Dublin voices, and I thought, Everyone is happy today; this is the happiest day in the history of the world.

We dozed a little, all four of us, and drowsily watched an eagle banking and wheeling overhead as he scanned the earth for a jack rabbit for his lunch. We remained in this golden somnolence until a sharp wind riffled our hair and warned us that not long from now the sun would start going down. We gathered some of the lilies to decorate our bridles, and then we went slowly back to the horses, all of us quiet from our tranquil cat naps and our fulfillment and our unshakable faith in our future lives.

In Colorado, almost every afternoon in the summertime the Devil briefly beat his wife; the skies never darken but there is a short, prodigal fall of crystal rain. When it came today, we made for shelter in a stand of spruce, and when it was over, in only a few minutes, and we emerged, we found a vivid rainbow arched over the eastern sky. The pot of gold must be in the middle of our lake, I thought, exactly where my paroxysmal laughter had begun last night.

"This is too much," said Fritzie. "This is overdoing things. It's a cheap Chamber of Commerce trick."

"I know," said Camilla. "This is the most embarrassing, show-off place in the world. It's like advertisements for summer resorts. Strictly corn."

By the time we came in sight of the clearing where Grandmother's house stood, the shadows were beginning to lengthen and the air was turning cold. Camilla, shivering, said, "Let's stop at Grandmother's for tea. If we play our cards right, she'll give us rum in it."

"I want Jack Daniels," said Fritzie. "I feel so good I want to get loaded."

"You can't get loaded in my well-bred grandmother's drawing room," said Camilla. "She loathes oafs. But she won't mind if you get *comfy* with booze."

I was hesitant. "Grandmother won't like us to be dressed this way for tea," I said, but Camilla overrode my finicking objection, and we followed her lead, going the rest of the way at a lope and enthusiastically agreeing that we were hungry and that we wanted the indoor amenities of a hearth fire and soft sofas. After we had dismounted, leaving the horses free to crop the grass, and were walking up the path to the house, I heard, from our house, across the broad expanse of water, the sound of the phonograph playing Daddy's favorite Mozart quintet; every stimulus that my senses received intensified the enraptured condition of my heart, which was palpitating now in anticipation of Grandmother's regal greeting to Rod.

Tousled and dusty, we tramped through the foyer, where stood a venerable grandfather clock and two ponderous Spanish chairs, and into the long, generous drawing room, where vases of columbines were everywhere. But there was no fire burning and the tea table had not been laid, and Grandmother, dressed in Sunday-afternoon taffeta, with a fichu at her throat, was pacing up and down, Grandfather's thin gold pocket watch in her hand. She turned to us with a look of consternation and appeal, and, forgetting, in her engrossing worry, to be a hostess, she said, "Did you come round the lake? Did you see Mary and Eileen? They were due back long ago!"

"No, we didn't come that way," said Camilla. "We've come down from the glacier. Don't you suppose they're just off looking for puffballs? They so love the nasty things."

Grandmother shook her head. "They're the most punctilious servants I've ever had. They wouldn't go roaming off without letting me know. I was taking a nap, but all the same they would have left a note."

"Maybe they went to sleep after their picnic," I said. "We did."

"Oh, I don't think they'd do a thing like that," said Grandmother. "Still . . ."

"Bandy brought them home all right?" I said, and when Grandmother nodded, Rod said, "Then they can't be far."

"We'll go and see if they went to sleep," said Camilla. "We'll find them, darling, never you fear. They've got to make us an enormous tea, because we're absolutely ravenous."

"We'll find them," echoed Rod reassuringly, and Fritzie said, "Don't worry, Mrs. Grayson. We'll be back with your girls in a minute."

"Good children," said Grandmother, and smiled at us, but then she looked fearfully out the window, where vermilion had begun to tinge the western sky. "Hurry, my dears, it'll soon be dark."

My grandmother's anxiety had not really infected us, partly because, being fearless ourselves, we were not afraid for anyone else, and partly because we were unwilling to relinquish our earlier carefree mood, and we started our walk around the lake in a spirit of sport, affectionately making fun of Grandmother for sending us out as a posse, as if the West were still wild and her maids had been scalped by Indians or were being held as hostages by road agents. We took the trail around the lake that was the longest way to our house, for Camilla and I knew that it was on this side, on a favorite plot of grass, that the girls always had their picnic; we had often seen them there. After they had come back from Mass, they would take off their perky, beflowered, beribboned hats and their white cotton gloves and their good shoes, but they would keep on their Sunday-best dresses for their light and ladylike collation. To Camilla and me, whenever we spied on them, they looked like an illustration in an old-fashioned romantic novel.

As we walked along, in single file, we discussed the many places they might be, safe and innocent, if we did not—as we were sure we would—find them snoozing in the dying day. Perhaps, all unknown to Grandmother, they had beaux, who had flattered and cajoled them into being late; perhaps they were bird watchers and could not tear themselves away from some fascinating rite of magpies; perhaps they had strolled over to the dude camp nearby and were watching an amateur rodeo; perhaps a dozen things. Punctilious as Grandmother said they were, they were bound to lapse at least once in a blue moon.

Presently, halfway around the lake, we came to that favorite plot of grass, where, sure enough, the Irish girls had spread out their picnic. Its corners neatly held down with rocks, the table-cloth with a pattern of tulips was neatly set for two with blue willowware plates and kitchen silver and jelly glasses; in the middle of the tablecloth there was a Dundee marmalade jar filled with Mariposa lilies. But the embossed-paper napkins had not been unfolded, the glasses had not been filled from the thermos, and the hamper had not been opened.

Perplexed and at last alarmed, we stood silent and unmoving for a minute, pointlessly scanning the immediate neighborhood, as if the maids were going to materialize before our eyes. It was Rod who spoke first.

"It does look queer," he said. "If they'd gone for a swim, they'd have come back by now. They'd have been starved after fasting for so long."

"Anyhow, they don't know how to swim," I said. "Neither one of them. Not a stroke."

"Then the lake's out, thank God," said Fritzie. "Or— They never use the boats, I suppose?"

Camilla and I exchanged a look of horror. Mary and Eileen were forbidden to use the canoe, but, out of their ignorance, they could not, would not, believe in the perils of the lake, and over and over again someone would catch them paddling, grotesquely maladroit, through the shallow water under the willow trees that lined the shore on this side.

"Oh, God!" cried Camilla, and she and I, with the boys at our heels, plunged down through the bushes that hid the water from us here, stumbling over the rocks and the willow suckers. When we got to the lake's edge, we saw the canoe immediately, away to our right, riding upside down in the mild wind over a deep spot in the lake, not far from shore.

"Where do you keep the outboard?" asked Rod. His voice, though it was urgent, was controlled.

"There's one at Grandmother's," I said. "That's nearest."

"Then come on!" he said.

As Grandmother and Camilla and I stood by the dock watching the boys get into the outboard, it occurred to me suddenly that there was just possibly a chance that the poor, dear, clumsy girls had let the canoe go adrift after their guilty outing in it, and that—first debating for a while, dreading the scolding Daddy would give them for their carelessness—they had decided to go to our house to get help. Galvanized by this wild, ingenious hope, I ran off, saying nothing to the others, and this time I took the shorter path, on the other side of the lake. As I ran, I could hear the bee-buzz of the outboard and, faintly, from our house, the promise of peace of Bach's "Sheep May Safely Graze." Daddy seemed to be having a Roman holiday this afternoon, with all the music he fancied most. And as I ran, my mouth dry and my heart hurting, through the wavering, leafy patterns of sun and shade, my obsessed and egocentric mind began, in this crisis, to seek Rod's admiration, and I thought, What will he think of this practical, intelligent, well-thought-out act of mine? Dear God, let Mary and Eileen be there! Let nothing have happened to them but Daddy's dressing down! Just then I tripped and twisted my ankle, and the pain was so sharp that it took my breath away, and, pausing for a moment in my surprise and shock, I was seized with a passion of self-loathing for wanting the girls to be alive chiefly because their being so would set me up in Rod's eyes. I began to cry for the fair-skinned, green-eyed Dublin girls, and then I faltered on.

"Sheep May Safely Graze" still floated out serenely from our house, and a peaceful tower of smoke rose from our chimney. I prayed that in a minute I was going to see Mary and Eileen. But, instead, I saw Mother standing at our dock, and Daddy and Bandy starting out in our boat. The living-room windows of our house commanded a comprehensive view of the lake, as did Grandmother's, directly opposite, and Mother told me later that she had

seen Rod and Fritzie in the outboard by chance as she was water-
ing the terrarium she kept on the sill; she had gazed at them idly
for some time before she sensed that something was wrong and
called my father. He had gone immediately down to the shore
and shouted at the boys, who shouted back what they were doing.

"Have they—" I began, out of breath.

"They've found them, yes," said Mother. Out on the lake, I
could see Rod and Fritzie diving from the boat. "Come, Judy,
we must go and break the news to your grandmother. They're
going to bring the bod— They're going to come back to this
shore."

"Where's Davy?" I said. "Davy mustn't see!"

"Davy's all right. Luella will keep him busy. Come now."
And Mother and I started out briskly, our eyes on the ground,
not looking again, lest we see the boys bring two pitiful burdens
to the surface of the water.

When we got to Grandmother's, we found Camilla and
Grandmother in the drawing room. Even before the boys had
sighted the bodies, Camilla had gone back there, to comfort
Grandmother and to take her inside and persuade her not to look
at the lake. We found them both in front of the fire, which
Camilla had lit, Grandmother huddled in a big chair, looking
terribly old and enervated. None of us could think of a word to
say; we kept warming our hands at the fire and listening to the
loud ticking of the grandfather clock. An age went by before we
finally heard both outboards coming to this shore.

When the three men came into this silent room, their faces
were stricken and sickened. My father went to his mother and
put his arm around her shoulder, and she looked up at him im-
ploringly and said, "How ever shall I tell their poor families? Ah,
Samuel, we should have destroyed that canoe." My father bent
down and whispered something in her ear, and she got up, weakly,
and went with him into the next room. Daddy had taken her away
to tell her, as gently as he could, what Fritzie told us now. Mary
and Eileen could not have been in the water for more than a few
hours, but in that time the hellbenders and the ravenous turtles
had eaten their lovely faces and their work-swollen hands; no one,
certainly no kinsman, must see them.

A heavy hush and torpor fell on all of us after we had heard this new piece of frightful intelligence. I wanted to busy myself—to turn on the lamps and dispel the murk of twilight, to straighten a stalk of yucca that was leaning gracelessly out of a vase, to prod the logs and make the sparks scintillate and snap. But my flesh was leaden, and I sat still. Once, I looked at my mother, sagging in her chair as inertly as the rest of us, and I thought, with a rush of sympathy, that living did not insulate one against shock. What must my gentle, humane grandmother be going through there in the library! How was she going to write to the girls' distant families of their death? And how, without going into the ghastly details, could she enjoin them not to open the coffins?

After a long time, Grandmother came back into the room and, mistress of her house again (though the bright unshed tears in her eyes and the quivering of her thin old hands showed that she was not yet mistress of herself), flicked the master light switch and went to draw the curtains, saying, as she did so, "By this time of day, I have had enough of the wonders of Colorado." Strengthened by her example, I got up now and attended to the listing yucca. There was a general stir in the room, and our voices were restored to us. Fritzie asked Camilla if she thought our horses would be all right, and she assured him that by this time they would have gone back to the barn and one of the men would have unsaddled them; Mother, going to the fireplace, asked Rod to help her return to its proper place one of the andirons that had shifted. My grandmother came at last to the windows that gave on the lake, and she pulled the curtains shut quickly; she shuddered and for a moment stood still, confronting the blank expanse of wine-red velours. As if she were alone, as if she were speaking to herself or to God, she murmured, "I won't come here again with innocents."

She turned around then and said to my mother, "Samuel and I have agreed that under the circumstances someone should personally explain to the girls' families what happened—Samuel will go to Ireland at once."

My mother said only, "He'll have no trouble booking at this time of year," and my grandmother nodded, closing the subject of the sudden voyage.

My father came into the room carrying a tray of drinks, and Grandmother said, "It's cold; there's autumn in the air. Samuel and I decided that we all needed something to warm us on the inside."

It was the first time I had ever been given a real drink, and as Daddy handed me the glass, I thought, Is he being absentminded or does this mean I'm accepted as grown up? I didn't know which it was—the symbol of the whiskey, or my family's love for me and my love for them and my recognition of my security (I was thinking simultaneously of Mary's family and Eileen's, still ignorant of the crumbling of *their* solidarity as they lived through an ordinary day in Dublin), or whether it was my grandmother's moral majesty, which I saw for the first time and wanted to emulate. Whatever it was, I found myself just then standing firmly on my own, and I was able to see everyone clearly —even myself. Earlier, in my blinding cocoon, when I had thought so constantly about Rod's respect for me, I had lost, in a sense, my respect for myself, but now, at last, I was able to think of *him* and not of his opinion of *me*. Bedraggled, my hair all wild, beggar's-lice on my sweater and my trousers, I did not care at all how I looked. I cared only, looking at the green pallor of his face, that he had suffered. I wanted him to be as happy as he had been before we had started our search for the girls, and I thought, Love, real love, is just that: it is wanting the beloved to be happy. The simplicity of the equation surprised me, but only for a moment and then it was incorporated into me as naturally as if it had been there all along.

The Darkening Moon

There was not a star in the sky, scarcely a sound in the air except for the soft gabbling of the creek. The little girl, when she had shut the kitchen door behind her and so shut in the yellow light, stood for a moment in the yard, taking her breath in sharply as though to suck in the mysterious element that had abruptly transformed day into dark. She was alone beneath the black firmament and between the blacker mountains that loomed up to the right and to the left of her like the blurred figures of fantastic beasts. She stepped forward, round the corner of the house where her brother's horse was tied. Before her lay the town with its long, glittering serpentine line of lights leading down from the mine, the double line marking the main street, and the helter-skelter porch lights of the miners' cabins. She heard the children tumbling out screen doors, calling, "One, two, three, four, five, six, Red Light!" before they had swallowed the last mouthful of their suppers. And the jukeboxes at The Silver Slipper and Uncle Joe's commenced to play conflicting tunes.

Ella was glad that tonight she was going to take a ride on Squaw, who, impatiently stamping one foot, gave voice to a muted whinny as if to show that she, too, was ready for adventure. Ella slipped the loose knot of the reins and turned the mare to mount. As she threw her leg over the saddle, her brother Fred opened the front door and called, "Wait a shake, sister." Without turning, he reached back to the table in the center of the room. His bare arm, against the glare of the lamp, was enormously magnified and knotted like the branch of a tree. He came out, leaving the door open, hesitated on the porch, and closed it just as their mother's voice came from the back of the house, "Fred! You see that stuff is tied on good and tell her not to waste

no time." Ella was taking ten pounds of elk steak, tied on behind her saddle under a tarp, Fred's payment to Mr. Temple
for the use of his gun sight and hackamore on the hunting trip he had just made. Her mother, who never knew a
moment's peace when game was in the house, was afraid that
the warden, Mr. Flint, would come by before Ella was out of the
yard.

As Fred slipped the hackamore over the pommel, his sister
laughed, "Golly, she's a big crybaby."

"Well! If it ain't Grandma!" he replied, and although she
could not see his face for the shadows, she knew by the tone of
his voice that there was a long grin on his face under the scanty
blond mustache and a spiteful glint in his narrow blue eyes.
Suddenly, she was spoiling for a fight. Instead of riding through
the gate which he had opened for her, she lingered in the yard,
waiting for an excuse to start a quarrel. But when he spoke
again, it was in a different voice, the one he used when he remembered that their father's death, a year ago, had made him
the head of the house.

"You shove. What do you think the Temples pay you for?"
He reproduced their father's inflections so well that had she not
seen his tow head, hung like a ball of mist in the darkness, she
would have thought the speaker was red-haired and gray-eyed.
He had perfected the imitation only in the last month: at first,
his voice would break and his peremptory tone would then be
merely absurd. The sound of his voice did not inspire her to
obey now. Rather, it made her turn her head as though from
some intolerable sight and slowly relax the reins, though she still
held her feet quiet in the stirrups.

Fred slapped Squaw on the rump and the mare leaped forward violently, flinging back her head. "Looky here, when I say
shove, I mean shove."

Ella did not reply, but she spurred sharply and galloped
through the gate. Her brother's voice pursued her, "If you run
my horse on the highway, I'll beat the living hell out of you."
As she went up the steep gravel road that led to the highway, the
wind whistling in her ears, she knew that he was waiting in the
yard, listening to see what change in the sound of the hoofs

there would be when she turned off onto the macadam. As soon as he could hear nothing more, he would turn toward the house next door and, making a megaphone of his hands, would bellow, "Harold! Oh, Harold!" Fred and Harold Bowman, who was only a senior in high school, went to Uncle Joe's about this time every night. She had heard them make the engagement this afternoon as they squatted on their haunches on either side of the fence, boasting at cross-purposes. "Yessir," Fred had been saying, "I got me a six-point buck in the flattops and it took some huntin' to get him." "Uh-huh," said his friend, "I know where there's a beaver must weigh sixty pounds."

As soon as the town was behind her, her skin stopped tingling and she gave herself up to enjoying the ride. Sometimes she dreaded this trip down to the Temple ranch to keep the children. When there was a moon or when snow had fallen, the glowing bluffs on the right side of the highway, just out of town, alarmed Squaw and she would wheel and rear, trying to throw her rider. Once, on the way home, after a heavy snow, Ella had been tossed as lightly as though she had been a pillow to the side of the road just as the big one o'clock Sante Fe Trailways went past. The bus, with its popeyes on a blunt snout, had swerved and missed her and sped on. She had had to walk the rest of the way, a mile and a half, numb with cold.

Tonight she had no trouble with the horse until she left the highway and took the Snake River road. At John Perkins' head gate, the beavers were at work in their lodge, and at the sound of them tamping the mud with their tails or dropping a stone from their forepaws, Squaw shied and it was all Ella could do to keep her from pivoting round toward home. Farther on, Squaw was startled when, coming round a bend in the narrow road, they were confronted by a grove of sarvis berry bushes, phosphorescent in the darkness. And then, when they had reached the crest of the first hill, a splash of something in the river made her rise on her hind legs, a trembling column of terror. But these antics did not disquiet Ella, for the road was only dirt and was infrequently traveled so that a fall would not amount to much. For the last mile, up and down five low hills, the horse behaved herself and Ella slowed her to an easy trot, for, although she was late, she wanted to postpone as long as possible the moment when she would go into the house.

So long as she was outdoors, she was not afraid at night. Her father had taught her that, long ago, when she was only a little girl of five and he had taken her and Fred fishing one night when the grayling were spawning. They had left her alone at the riverbank for half an hour while they went upstream through brush that would have cut her bare legs. Before they left, her father had said, "There ain't nothing to harm you, sister. The animals is all there is and they won't be looking you up." She had never been frightened by the coyotes lamenting in the sage or the bobcats howling in the woods. But if she heard them when she was alone in the Temples' house, she fancied them closing in, sobbing and whining for fresh meat, peering through the windows at her with their sulphur-colored eyes. Nor did the owls dismay her if she heard them while she was riding, but when their smug prophecies of doom were sifted through distance and closed windows, she trembled, for they seemed to speak directly to her, to say, "Look out! Look out!" Even the rats, frolicking through the walls, and even the old collie making his rounds hinted at danger. Afraid to move lest by moving she make a noise that would obscure another noise, like a footstep in the yard, she would sit motionless all evening in a big pink wing chair, staring at the wall opposite her where hung an oil painting of Mr. Temple's prize bull, Beau Mischief. By midnight, she would be wringing wet with sweat, although it was cold and she had let the fire go out. And yet, as soon as she had mounted for the ride back, her fear changed its focus and she was not anxious to get home, but only to get Squaw safely past the bluff.

One night, her foot had gone to sleep, and though it hurt enough to make her sick, she was too frightened to stamp it or even to change its position. Early in the evening, she had heard a cowbell tinkling nearby the house. None of Mr. Temple's stock wore bells. She knew she should chase away the intruder, but before she had risen to her feet, it occurred to her that perhaps it was a gypsy with a tambourine, or it might be a cow with her owner, one of those half-crazy men from Oklahoma who came to Colorado to get away from the dust and went around the country with all they owned in the world slung over their backs, sometimes leading an emaciated animal. Long after the bell had stopped, she continued to hear its echo, and dared look nowhere but at the copper ring in Beau Mischief's nose, for a straying glance might discover a sly and bitter face in the deep shadows of the open dining-room door.

She had reached the Temples' lane. In the wide hollow, the farmhouse was so brilliantly illuminated that it seemed twice its natural size. There were lamps only on the lower floor, but over the windows of the upper story there was cast a smoky shimmer of reflected light. Two pointed chimneys at opposite ends of the roof were clearly outlined, like a bear's wide-set ears. Mr. Temple always said that if you left your house well-lighted there was less danger of being robbed, but Ella took little stock in the argument, for she reasoned that a dark house, on a dark night, was hard to see.

The children were already asleep when Ella came in, and the Temples were putting on their coats. Mr. Temple thanked her for the meat and said, "Ella, there's a cow down to the corral that's crying for her calf I butchered today. She'll carry on all night, I reckon, but don't you pay her no mind."

"Pshaw, Milton. Ella's not afraid, are you, Ella? A big girl going on twelve."

"No, ma'am, I'm not afraid," Ella said, but she clasped her hands nervously and looked down at the scuffed toes of her moccasins.

"Well, I guess a person that'll pack ten pounds of San Quentin bacon behind her saddle ain't going to be rattled by a dairy cow." Mr. Temple laughed. His wife, to urge him on, put her plump, smooth hand on his massive shoulder and, as she did so, the light caught her diamond ring, which shot forth swift filaments of green and purple. Mr. Temple, in his store clothes, would have looked like a city man if it had not been for his sunburned face and his bowlegs. But Mrs. Temple, in spite of her permanent wave and her high-heeled shoes and her georgette redingote, would always look like a farmer's wife.

Mr. Temple asked Ella if she would like to put Squaw in

the east pasture by the house with the team and the boys' ponies since Squaw was clever at getting loose from a hitching post. When they started, she followed the car up the lane and turned in at the gate by the slough. The six dark forms in the field, standing in an almost perfect semicircle, did not move as the newcomer trotted toward them, but when she had taken her place, all, with one accord, lowered their massive heads and began rhythmically to crop the invisible grass.

The Temples waited until she got back to the house and shouted, "All right!" She watched the car go over the hill and listened until its diminishing snore was absorbed. In the silence that followed, the mourning cow moaned deeply; an owl gave forth one loitering, melancholy note. As she turned the door-knob, she heard, close by, a splash in the river, the second one tonight, and thought that it was either a trout leaping or an aspen sapling falling after the beavers had gnawed it down. But as she closed the door and stepped onto the shining hardwood floor, it seemed to her that the tone of the disturbed water had not been true and therefore had not been made by an animal. She stopped short, wondering what it was.

Was it one of the Negroes from the mine fishing? Often, when they did not go to The Silver Slipper on a Saturday night after they had been paid, they went to the river, taking their liquor with them. You could see them starting out about five in the afternoon. A battered, protesting old Dodge sedan would be full of black figures, so many that, although there appeared to be seven or eight in the driver's seat, no one seemed to be in charge, and the car would careen in every direction like a chicken with its head cut off. Later on, from the highway, their fires would be visible along the banks, and on a clear night, rich, imploring songs would wind through the weeping-willow trees. Ella knew what she would do if one of them came to the house. She would say, "Mr. Temple's asleep, but I'll call him," and then she would go to the back bedroom and take a .22 out of the gun cabinet and, pointing it at the man's heart, she would say, "Mr. Temple says for you to clear out."

In three long, stealthy steps she crossed the room and slipped so far back into the pink chair that her feet did not touch the floor, and then began counting by ones, calculating that when she had reached a hundred, five minutes would have passed. The clock was in the kitchen, but she had not the courage to go through the dining room, across the creaking floor of the pantry, into the spacious kitchen, where not even bright daylight dispelled the gloomy shadows cast by large cabinets and by the many chaps hanging along one wall. Mrs. Temple, knowing that she always spent the evening in the pink chair, had put some jigsaw puzzles, *Good Housekeeping*, and the Montgomery Ward midsummer sale catalogue on a little table beside it, but Ella disliked the rustle the leaves made. She preferred to count. Sometimes, if she felt that she had gone too fast through the last decade, she made herself go back the way a teacher made a child start at the beginning again if he made a mistake in something he had memorized. It didn't pay to think it was nine o'clock when it was only a quarter to.

When she was in the eighties of her ninth hundred, so that she knew it must be around nine-thirty, she was suddenly frozen to the bone by the abrupt trotting of a horse, so near that it seemed to be halfway past the slough. Immediately, she heard another horse then another and another until it sounded like a dozen, trotting abreast. At first she thought they were on the road and would presently turn into the lane. But she did not hear the hoofs on the bridge over the slough and the sound did not come any closer. Yet it did not recede, and directly the pace speeded up to a gallop and then to a full run, and one of the creatures neighed crazily. At once, as if this had been a signal, there was a dead silence. In a moment came the epilogue: the cow's heartbreaking moo. Ella tried to go on with her counting, but she could not remember if she had left off at eighty-five or sixty-five and no sooner did she get her bearings than the horses began again: first just one trotting, then two, and so on until they had all joined in the race. The lunatic neigh was repeated; once more there was a pause, but this time it lasted only a second or two and was followed by a different sound, that of hoofs stamping on the soft sod.

"Squaw!" Ella cried the name aloud and sprang to her feet. For she knew now that Mr. Temple's Steamboat was kicking her horse. He was a big, mean, ball-faced black, sixteen hands high, and if he took a dislike to another horse, went crazy mad.

He had once attacked a fine, blooded palomino that belonged
to a dude from Boston who was boarding with the Temples.
Steamboat had backed him up against a barbed-wire fence, and
there had been a ten-inch tear in the creamy withers, and for
months tufts of the white tail had stuck like feathers to the barbs.

She ran out of the house and down the lane, calling, but
uselessly, for the little mare never knew her name. As she
stumbled across the fields, pitted with gopher holes, she could
just make out the four team horses running after her paint, and
when she was halfway there, she saw the largest of them get
Squaw cornered by the branding corral and start to kick, while
the others stood at attention, watching respectfully. She edged
along the board fence and, when she was face to face with Steamboat, flapped her arms and shouted, "Whoosh!" And the big
black horse, as though he had had nothing to do with the
rumpus, turned disdainfully and gave his tail an impudent flick.

As she led Squaw back to the hitching post, she looked up
into the sky and, to her amazement, saw that there was a full
moon overhead. It was as large as a harvest moon, as pale as lard.
There had been no moon when she rode down, nor even moon
sign. It was as though it had not risen, but had been slid along
to cover a round hole in the sky, the way a plate with a picture
on it was sometimes put over the place in a wall where a stove-
pipe had been.

"Ah, hell," she thought. "She'll try to buck me sure, bright
as that is."

It could not have taken her more than two or three minutes
to tie the horse, but when she looked up again, it seemed to her
that the moon was a little smaller than it had been. It was not
hidden behind a cloud, for no cloud she had ever seen could cut
so clean a line. It looked as though Fred's curved butcher knife
had been laid over the top part; around the curve was a narrow
rim of red, not bright and barely luminous, but a rusty, burnt-
out color. The immense moon had little light. The team and
ponies were invisible; a faint sheen lay on the south pasture but
only as far as the first irrigation ditch, and the river bridge, ten
yards away, was only a black square.

The timothy had been cut two weeks before and the smell

came strong and sweet. She heard the animals in the woods telling her where they were and, surveying the line of trees along the
river, she saw there were no fires tonight. She gave the horse a
last caress with the tips of her fingers and started back to the
house. At the porch, she looked over her shoulder at the moon.
At least an eighth of it was gone! The red rim glowed now and
the circumference of the rest of the orb had shrunk. Her sharp
eyes sought clouds to explain the phenomenon; they found
nothing but the moon in the black vault.

The numbers twisted in her head. She seemed unable to get
past the sixties and kept repeating herself: sixty-nine, sixty-two,
sixty. It was odd, but the cow did not moo again. Usually they
were inconsolable all the first night. And the owls were still. The
rats traveled so lightly that they sounded more like moth millers
flapping against the walls. She began counting again; she would
get to fifty and then strain her ears for sounds. Once, she thought
she heard a bobcat, but it was only the loose door to the bunk-
house wailing in a gust of wind. Another time, the distant drone
of a truck on the highway made her think for a second that the
cow had tuned up again. She counted another fifty, slipping
backward, going forward two at a time, and listened. But everything was quiet. At the end of each five hundred, she went on
tiptoe to the front window and knelt down, fitting her hands to
her temples like blinders to look out at the moon. Each time she
looked, a little more had dwindled away and the red girdle
gleamed brighter. Her mouth was dry and she sucked the sides
of her cheeks to moisten her throat with saliva.

Perhaps the owls and the coyotes and the beavers were still
busy, quieter than usual for their own reasons. She would be
able to hear them if she went outside. She could lean up against
one of the porch pillars and, when she heard the car, could slip
back into the house and no one would be any the wiser. And yet,
when she tried to get up, her legs were wooden and she was so
cold that a shiver went the length of her. The four Coleman
lamps, placed at regular intervals about the long room, no
longer seemed so garish; they cast a warm, saffron glow over the
curly cowhide rugs and the serapes on the davenports. For the
first time, she reflected that it was an elegant room. She had

never before noticed the tasseled velvet runner on the library table.

Crouching on the top step, her head resting against the banister, she did not allow herself to look up into the sky for a few minutes, but instead gazed directly in front of her, making out the contours of the horse across the yard. It was motionless between the two tall leaning posts and seemed unnaturally large. At last, she admitted to herself that there were no sounds out here either. A deep silence had settled down over the sage-covered hills to the left, over the east pasture where the horses were, over the timothy and the fields beyond it. She would have been glad to hear the cow again, or the measly whine of a mosquito, or to hear . . . even a footstep! But there was nothing.

At last she looked at the sky. Less than a sixth of the moon was left, and beyond that one livid slice of light, the heavens stretched blacker than a mine shaft. As she watched, it seemed to her that the darkness, bit by bit, encroached upon the last thin rind.

Were all the creatures waiting, like her, for the final disappearance of the moon and the disaster that would follow it? Was the owl in its treetop staring upward with its yellow, impassive spectacles? Were the ravenous eyes of the quivering coyotes fixed on the moon? Perhaps the beavers had stopped in their housebuilding to keep a horrified vigil, and the cow was upturning her velvety gaze to the mortal moon. Ella could not tell precisely when the last scrap of the moon had been covered over. In a moment, even the red ring was gone, and then there was no evidence of any kind that in the sky there had hung that great white disk.

She whimpered without volition and instantly an owl in the cottonwood grove warned her, "Look out! Look out!" Holding her hands clasped over her rowdy heart, she leaped across the porch, through the door, and into the living room. One of the lamps was going out. The mantel spit forth a final spark and upon the wall above it was thrown an oblong shadow where before had been the pale green kalsomine. All the other lamps seemed mellower than usual, and she knew that any moment they, too, would use the last drop of their fuel. As though to fend off the sight of this second catastrophe, she lifted her arm, and, as she did so, saw that, just as Fred's had been, its size was doubled and its joints were caricatured.

A second lamp went out, and at once a grove of shadows shot up beside the bookshelves. They looked like cattails and made her think of the place in the river where they had gone to catch the grayling. The water had been cold and once she had slipped and fallen in up to her waist. The fish were so thick that they swarmed slimily over her and she had nearly gagged at the smell. "Bring me them on the bank there," her father had said and she had had to pick up the fat slithering blobs in her bare hands. Her father, reaching out to take them, had smeared her wrist with fish's blood which dripped in gouts from his fingertips as if it were his own. Even if he were still alive and asked her, she would not go there again! The memory for some reason, though it was only a memory of a time long ago, made her start to cry. She bent her head and crossed her arms on her chest and allowed the tears to stream down her face. She could not drive away the horror of the reptilian odor, nor could she summon her father's good-natured face. When she tried and said to herself the word "Daddy," the fruitless effort made her sob aloud and her lips lifted in the grin that accompanies the misery of weeping.

After one sob that made her rock with pain, she heard a car slowing at the water gap, picking up speed, going up the hill, and coming down it. It turned into the lane before she had wiped her eyes. So that they would not see her swollen face, she ran out and stood beside the gate.

"Why, Ella!" cried Mrs. Temple getting out of the car.

"I come out to get my horse," she said. "Your Steamboat was kicking at her and I thought I better get her out. I was just going in the house."

"Well, that ornery old bench," said Mr. Temple. "I'll straighten him out. I thought maybe my cow spooked you."

"No, sir. She never scared me. She never bellowed only once or twice."

"You're shaking, Ella," said Mrs. Temple and took her by the elbow. So that she would not see the tears, Ella turned her face away. Mrs. Temple was saying, "Maybe we oughtn't to make a little girl stay here all by her lonesome."

"Why, Opal! You're the one always says Ella don't get scared."

"I know, Milton. But it's a funny thing. Works backward with some people, you might say. Some way, as you get older . . . I don't know. I'm just thinking the way I used to be. Until I was fifteen, wasn't a living thing could give me a turn. And then, later on. . . ."

She turned away meditatively. Mr. Temple said, "Well, Ella, would you like me to take you home in the car?"

"No, sir," she replied. "I can make it."

He untied Squaw and held her steady for Ella to mount. When she had her seat, he handed her a fifty-cent piece. As she put it in the money pocket of her Levi's, Mrs. Temple called from the gate, "Oh, Ella, did you see the eclipse? The earth's shadow passed right over the moon . . . we heard about it on the radio."

"Go on, Opal," said Mr. Temple. "Ella wasn't stargazing. She was too busy looking at the pretties in the catalogue."

Ella moistened her lips with the tip of her tongue. She said, "I seen it."

"It'll come out again, you know, Ella," cried Mrs. Temple. "It'll be a full moon again by the time you get to the highway!"

Ella did not answer, for Squaw, eager to be off now that her nose was pointed toward home, pranced and whinnied so that her flanks rippled like a hard, fast pulse, and at the touch of the lines on her neck, she bounded forward at a gallop. Steamboat's long head was hung over the fence and they passed so close to him that Ella could see how his lip was hooked up, showing his grass-stained teeth. For a moment, it looked as though Squaw were going straight into the sage-covered hill and that both of them would be flattened against the boulders at the base. But the horse was no lunatic. She took the turn without slackening her pace and up and down the hills, between the scrub oak and the sarvis berry, she skimmed the air, while her dry-mouthed rider sat in the saddle with her eyes closed, certain of the animal's sagacity. A world slipped past her blinded eyes as she traversed a road she would not recognize again, beneath the full, unfaithful moon.

Bad Characters

Up until I learned my lesson in a very bitter way, I never had more than one friend at a time, and my friendships, though ardent, were short. When they ended and I was sent packing in unforgetting indignation, it was always my fault; I would swear vilely in front of a girl I knew to be pious and prim (by the time I was eight, the most grandiloquent gangster could have added nothing to my vocabulary—I had an awful tongue), or I would call a Tenderfoot Scout a sissy or make fun of athletics to the daughter of the high-school coach. These outbursts came without plan; I would simply one day, in the middle of a game of Russian bank or a hike or a conversation, be possessed with a passion to be by myself, and my lips instantly and without warning would accommodate me. My friend was never more surprised than I was when this irrevocable slander, this terrible, talented invective, came boiling out of my mouth.

Afterward, when I had got the solitude I had wanted, I was dismayed, for I did not like it. Then I would sadly finish the game of cards as if someone were still across the table from me; I would sit down on the mesa and through a glaze of tears would watch my friend departing with outraged strides; mournfully, I would talk to myself. Because I had already alienated everyone I knew, I then had nowhere to turn, so a famine set in and I would have no companion but Muff, the cat, who loathed all human beings except, significantly, me—truly. She bit and scratched the hands that fed her, she arched her back like a Halloween cat if someone kindly tried to pet her, she hissed, laid her ears flat to her skull, growled, fluffed up her tail into a great bush and flailed it like a bullwhack. But she purred for me, she patted me with her paws, keeping her claws in their velvet scabbards. She was not only an ill-natured cat, she was also badly dressed. She was a calico, and the distribution of her colors was a mess; she looked as if she had been left out in the rain and her paint had run. She had a Roman nose as the result of some early injury, her tail was skinny, she had a perfectly venomous look in her eye. My family said—my family discriminated against me—that I was much closer kin to Muff than I was to any of them. To tease me into a tantrum, my brother Jack and my sister Stella often called me Kitty instead of Emily. Little Tess did not dare, because she knew I'd chloroform her if she did. Jack, the meanest boy I have ever known in my life, called me Polecat and talked about my mania for fish, which, it so happened, I despised. The name would have been far more appropriate for *him,* since he trapped skunks up in the foothills— we lived in Adams, Colorado—and quite often, because he was careless and foolhardy, his clothes had to be buried, and even when that was done, he sometimes was sent home from school on the complaint of girls sitting next to him.

Along about Christmastime when I was eleven, I was making a snowman with Virgil Meade in his back yard, and all of a sudden, just as we had got around to the right arm, I had to be alone. So I called him a son of a sea cook, said it was common knowledge that his mother had bedbugs and that his father, a dentist and the deputy marshal, was a bootlegger on the side. For a moment, Virgil was too aghast to speak—a little earlier we had agreed to marry someday and become millionaires—and then, with a bellow of fury, he knocked me down and washed my face in snow. I saw stars, and black balls bounced before my eyes. When finally he let me up, we were both crying, and he hollered that if I didn't get off his property that instant, his father would arrest me and send me to Canon City. I trudged slowly home, half frozen, critically sick at heart. So it was old Muff again for me for quite some time. Old Muff, that is, until I met Lottie Jump, although "met" is a euphemism for the way I first encountered her.

I saw Lottie for the first time one afternoon in our own kitchen, stealing a chocolate cake. Stella and Jack had not come home from school yet—not having my difficult disposition, they were popular, and they were at their friends' houses, pulling taffy, I suppose, making popcorn balls, playing casino, having fun—and my mother had taken Tess with her to visit a friend in one of the T.B. sanitariums. I was alone in the house, and making a funny-looking Christmas card, although I had no one to send it to. When I heard someone in the kitchen, I thought it was Mother home early, and I went out to ask her why the green pine tree I had pasted on a square of red paper looked as if it were falling down. And there, instead of Mother and my baby sister, was this pale, conspicuous child in the act of lifting the glass cover from the devil's-food my mother had taken out of the oven an hour before and set on the plant shelf by the window. The child had her back to me, and when she heard my footfall, she wheeled with an amazing look of fear and hatred on her pinched and pasty face. Simultaneously, she put the cover over the cake again, and then she stood motionless as if she were under a spell.

I was scared, for I was not sure what was happening, and anyhow it gives you a turn to find a stranger in the kitchen in the middle of the afternoon, even if the stranger is only a skinny child in a moldy coat and sopping-wet basketball shoes. Between us there was a lengthy silence, but there was a great deal of noise in the room: the alarm clock ticked smugly; the teakettle simmered patiently on the back of the stove; Muff, cross at having been waked up, thumped her tail against the side of the flower box in the window where she had been sleeping—contrary to orders—among the geraniums. This went on, it seemed to me, for hours and hours while that tall, sickly girl and I confronted each other. When, after a long time, she did open her mouth, it was to tell a prodigious lie. "I came to see if you'd like to play with me," she said. I think she sighed and stole a sidelong and regretful glance at the cake.

Beggars cannot be choosers, and I had been missing Virgil so sorely, as well as all those other dear friends forever lost to me, that in spite of her flagrance (she had never clapped eyes on me before, she had had no way of knowing there was a creature of my age in the house—she had come in like a hobo to steal my mother's cake), I was flattered and consoled. I asked her name and, learning it, believed my ears no better than my eyes: Lottie Jump. What on earth! What on earth—you surely will agree with me—and yet when I told her mine, Emily Vanderpool, she laughed until she coughed and gasped. "Beg pardon," she said. "Names like them always hit my funny bone. There was this towhead boy in school named Delbert Saxonfield." I saw no connection and I was insulted (what's so funny about Vanderpool, I'd like to know), but Lottie Jump was, technically, my guest and I *was* lonesome, so I asked her, since she had spoken of playing with me, if she knew how to play Andy-I-Over. She said "Naw." It turned out that she did not know how to play any games at all; she couldn't do anything and didn't want to do anything; her only recreation and her only gift was, and always had been, stealing. But this I did not know at the time.

As it happened, it was too cold and snowy to play outdoors that day anyhow, and after I had run through my list of indoor games and Lottie had shaken her head at all of them (when I spoke of Parcheesi, she went "Ugh!" and pretended to be sick), she suggested that we look through my mother's bureau drawers. This did not strike me as strange at all, for it was one of my favorite things to do, and I led the way to Mother's bedroom without a moment's hesitation. I loved the smell of the lavender she kept in gauze bags among her chamois gloves and linen handkerchiefs and filmy scarves; there was a pink fascinator knitted of something as fine as spider's thread, and it made me go quite soft—I wasn't soft as a rule, I was as hard as nails and I gave my mother a rough time—to think of her wearing it around her head as she waltzed on the ice in the bygone days. We examined stockings, nightgowns, camisoles, strings of beads, and mosaic pins, keepsake buttons from dresses worn on memorial occasions, tortoiseshell combs, and a transformation made from Aunt Joey's hair when she had racily had it bobbed. Lottie admired particularly a blue cloisonné perfume flask with ferns and peacocks on it. "Hey," she said, "this sure is cute. I like thing-daddies like this here." But very abruptly she got bored and said, "Let's talk instead. In the front room." I agreed, a little perplexed this time, because I had been about to show her a re-markable powder box that played "The Blue Danube." We went into the parlor, where Lottie looked at her image in the pier glass for quite a while and with great absorption, as if she had never seen herself before. Then she moved over to the window seat and knelt on it, looking out at the front walk. She kept her hands in the pockets of her thin dark-red coat; once she took out one of her dirty paws to rub her nose for a minute and I saw a bulge in that pocket, like a bunch of jackstones. I know now that it wasn't jackstones, it was my mother's perfume flask; I thought at the time her hands were cold and that that was why she kept them put away, for I had noticed that she had no mittens.

Lottie did most of the talking, and while she talked, she never once looked at me but kept her eyes fixed on the approach to our house. She told me that her family had come to Adams a month before from Muskogee, Oklahoma, where her father, before he got tuberculosis, had been a brakeman on the Frisco. Now they lived down by Arapahoe Creek, on the west side of town, in one of the cottages of a wretched settlement made up of people so poor and so sick—for in nearly every ramshackle house someone was coughing himself to death—that each time I went past I blushed with guilt because my shoes were sound and my coat was warm and I was well. I wished that Lottie had not told me where she lived, but she was not aware of any pathos in her family's situation, and, indeed, it was with a certain boastfulness that she told me her mother was the short-order cook at the Comanche Café (she pronounced this word in one syllable), which I knew was the dirtiest, darkest, smelliest place in town, patronized by coal miners who never washed their faces and sometimes had such dangerous fights after drinking dago red that the sheriff had to come. Laughing, Lottie told me that her mother was half Indian, and, laughing even harder, she said that her brother didn't have any brains and had never been to school. She herself was eleven years old, but she was only in the third grade, because teachers had always had it in for her—making her go to the blackboard and all like that when she was tired. She hated school—she went to Ashton, on North Hill, and that was why I had never seen her, for I went to Carlyle Hill—and she especially hated the teacher, Miss Cudahy, who had a head shaped like a pine cone and who had killed several people with her ruler. Lottie loved the movies ("Not them Western ones or the ones with apes in," she said. "Ones about hugging and kissing. I love it when they die in that big old soft bed with the curtains up top, and he comes in and says 'Don't leave me, Marguerite de la Mar'."), and she loved to ride in cars. She loved Mr. Goodbars, and if there was one thing she despised worse than another it was tapioca. ("Pa calls it fish eyes. He calls floating island horse spit. He's a big piece of cheese. I hate him.") She did not like cats (Muff was now sitting on the mantelpiece, glaring like an owl); she kind of liked snakes—except cottonmouths and rattlers—because she found them kind of funny; she had once seen a goat eat a tin can. She said that one of these days she would take me downtown—it was a slowpoke town, she said, a one-horse burg (I had never heard such gaudy, cynical talk and was trying to memorize it all)—if I would get some money for the trolley fare; she hated to walk, and I ought to be proud that she had walked all the way from Arapahoe Creek today for the sole solitary purpose of seeing me.

Seeing our freshly baked dessert in the window was a more likely story, but I did not care, for I was deeply impressed by this bold, sassy girl from Oklahoma and greatly admired the poise with which she aired her prejudices. Lottie Jump was certainly nothing to look at. She was tall and made of skin and bones; she was evilly ugly, and her clothes were a disgrace, not just ill-fitting and old and ragged but dirty, unmentionably so; clearly she did not wash much or brush her teeth, which were notched like a saw, and small and brown (it crossed my mind that perhaps she chewed tobacco); her long, lank hair looked as if it might have nits. But she had personality. She made me think of one of those self-contained dogs whose home is where his hand-out is and who travels alone but, if it suits him to, will become the leader of a pack. She was aloof, never looking at me, but amiable in the way she kept calling me "kid." I liked her enormously, and presently I told her so.

At this, she turned around and smiled at me. Her smile was the smile of a jack-o'-lantern—high, wide, and handsome. When it was over, no trace of it remained. "Well, that's keen, kid, and I like you, too," she said in her downright Muskogee accent. She gave me a long, appraising look. Her eyes were the color of mud. "Listen, kid, how much do you like me?"

"I like you loads, Lottie," I said. "Better than anybody else, and I'm not kidding."

"You want to be pals?"

"Do I!" I cried. So *there*, Virgil Meade, you big fat hoot-nanny, I thought.

"All right, kid, we'll be pals." And she held out her hand for me to shake. I had to go and get it, for she did not alter her position on the window seat. It was a dry, cold hand, and the grip was severe, with more a feeling of bones in it than friendli-ness.

Lottie turned and scanned our path and scanned the side-walk beyond, and then she said, in a lower voice, "Do you know how to lift?"

"Lift?" I wondered if she meant to lift *her*. I was sure I could do it, since she was so skinny, but I couldn't imagine why she would want me to.

"Shoplift, I mean. Like in the five-and-dime."

I did not know the term, and Lottie scowled at my stupidity.

"*Steal*, for crying in the beer!" she said impatiently. This she said so loudly that Muff jumped down from the mantel and left the room in contempt.

I was thrilled to death and shocked to pieces. "Stealing is a sin," I said. "You get put in jail for it."

"Ish ka bibble! I should worry if it's a sin or not," said Lottie, with a shrug. "And they'll never put a smart old whatsis like *me* in jail. It's fun, stealing is—it's a picnic. I'll teach you if you want to learn, kid." Shamelessly she winked at me and grinned again. (That grin! She could have taken it off her face and put it on the table.) And she added, "If you don't, we can't be pals, because lifting is the only kind of playing I like. I hate those dumb games like Statues. Kick-the-Can—phooey!"

I was torn between agitation (I went to Sunday School and knew already about morality; Judge Bay, a crabby old man who loved to punish sinners, was a friend of my father's and once had given Jack a lecture on the criminal mind when he came to call and found Jack looking up an answer in his arithmetic book) and excitement over the daring invitation to misconduct myself in so perilous a way. My life, on reflection, looked deadly prim; all I'd ever done to vary the monotony of it was to swear. I knew that Lottie Jump meant what she said—that I could have her friendship only on her terms (plainly, she had gone it alone for a long time and could go it alone for the rest of her life)—

and although I trembled like an aspen and my heart went pita-pat, I said, "I want to be pals with you, Lottie."

"All right, Vanderpool," said Lottie, and got off the window seat. "I wouldn't go braggin' about it if I was you. I wouldn't go telling my ma and pa and the next-door neighbor that you and Lottie Jump are going down to the five-and-dime next Saturday aft and lift us some nice rings and garters and things like that. I mean it, kid." And she drew the back of her forefinger across her throat and made a dire face.

"I won't. I promise I won't. My *gosh*, why would I?"

"That's the ticket," said Lottie, with a grin. "I'll meet you at the trolley shelter at two o'clock. You have the money. For both down and up. I ain't going to climb up that ornery hill after I've had my fun."

"Yes, Lottie," I said. Where was I going to get twenty cents? I was going to have to start stealing before she even taught me how. Lottie was facing the center of the room, but she had eyes in the back of her head, and she whirled around back to the window; my mother and Tess were turning in our front path.

"Back way," I whispered, and in a moment Lottie was gone; the swinging door that usually squeaked did not make a sound as she vanished through it. I listened and I never heard the back door open and close. Nor did I hear her, in a split second, lift the glass cover and remove that cake designed to feed six people.

I was restless and snappish between Wednesday afternoon and Saturday. When Mother found the cake was gone, she scolded me for not keeping my ears cocked. She assumed, natu-rally, that a tramp had taken it, for she knew I hadn't eaten it; I never ate anything if I could help it (except for raw potatoes, which I loved) and had been known as a problem feeder from the beginning of my life. At first it occurred to me to have a tantrum and bring her around to my point of view: my tantrums scared the living daylights out of her because my veins stood out and I turned blue and couldn't get my breath. But I rejected this for a more sensible plan. I said, "It just so happens I didn't hear anything. But if I had, I suppose you wish I had gone out in the kitchen and let the robber cut me up into a million little tiny pieces with his sword. You wouldn't even bury me. You'd just put me on the dump. *I* know who's wanted in this family and who isn't." Tears of sorrow, not of anger, came in powerful tides and I groped blindly to the bedroom I shared with Stella, where I lay on my bed and shook with big, silent *weltschmerzlich* sobs. Mother followed me immediately, and so did Tess, and both of them comforted me and told me how much they loved me. I said they didn't; they said they did. Presently, I got a headache, as I always did when I cried, so I got to have an aspirin and a cold cloth on my head, and when Jack and Stella came home, they had to be quiet. I heard Jack say, "Emily Vanderpool is the biggest polecat in the U.S.A. Whyn't she go in the kitchen and say, 'Hands up'? He woulda lit out." And Mother said, "Sh-h-h! You don't want your sister to be sick, do you?" Muff, not realizing that Lottie had replaced her, came in and curled up at my thigh, purring lustily; I found myself glad that she had left the room before Lottie Jump made her proposition to me, and in gratitude I stroked her unattractive head.

Other things happened. Mother discovered the loss of her perfume flask and talked about nothing else at meals for two whole days. Luckily, it did not occur to her that it had been stolen—she simply thought she had mislaid it—but her monomania got on my father's nerves and he lashed out at her and at the rest of us. And because I was the cause of it all and my conscience was after me with red-hot pokers, I finally *had* to have a tantrum. I slammed my fork down in the middle of supper on the second day and yelled, "If you don't stop fighting, I'm going to kill myself. Yammer, yammer, nag, nag!" And I put my fingers in my ears and squeezed my eyes tight shut and screamed so the whole county could hear, "Shut *up!*" And then I lost my breath and began to turn blue. Daddy hastily apologized to everyone, and Mother said she was sorry for carrying on so about a trinket that had nothing but sentimental value—she was just vexed with herself for being careless, that was all, and she wasn't going to say another word about it.

I never heard so many references to stealing and cake, and even to Oklahoma (ordinarily no one mentioned Oklahoma once in a month of Sundays) and the ten-cent store as I did throughout those next days. I myself once made a ghastly slip and said something to Stella about "the five-and-dime." "The five-and-*dime!*" she exclaimed. "Where'd you get *that* kind of talk? Do you by any chance have reference to the *ten-cent store?*"

The worst of all was Friday night—the very night before I was to meet Lottie Jump—when Judge Bay came to play two-handed pinochle with Daddy. The Judge, a giant in intimidating haberdashery—for some reason, the white piping on his vest bespoke, for me, handcuffs and prison bars—and with an aura of disapproval for almost everything on earth except what pertained directly to himself, was telling Daddy, before they began their game, about the infamous vandalism that had been going on among the college students. "I have reason to believe that there are girls in this gang as well as boys," he said. "They ransack vacant houses and take everything. In one house on Pleasant Street, up there by the Catholic Church, there wasn't anything to take, so they took the kitchen sink. Wasn't a question of taking everything *but*—they took the kitchen sink."

"What ever would they want with a kitchen sink?" asked my mother.

"Mischief," replied the Judge. "If we ever catch them and if they come within my jurisdiction, I can tell you I will give them no quarter. A thief, in my opinion, is the lowest of the low."

Mother told about the chocolate cake. By now, the fiction was so factual in my mind that each time I thought of it I saw a funny-paper bum in baggy pants held up by rope, a hat with holes through which tufts of hair stuck up, shoes from which his toes protruded, a disreputable stubble on his face; he came up beneath the open window where the devil's food was cooling and he stole it and hotfooted it for the woods, where his companion was frying a small fish in a beat-up skillet. It never crossed my mind any longer that Lottie Jump had hooked that delicious cake.

Judge Bay was properly impressed. "If you will steal a chocolate cake, if you will steal a kitchen sink, you will steal diamonds and money. The small child who pilfers a penny from his mother's pocketbook has started down a path that may lead him to holding up a bank."

It was a good thing I had no homework that night, for I could not possibly have concentrated. We were all sent to our rooms, because the pinochle players had to have absolute quiet.

I spent the evening doing cross-stitch. I was making a bureau runner for a Christmas present; as in the case of the Christmas card, I had no one to give it to, but now I decided to give it to Lottie Jump's mother. Stella was reading *Black Beauty,* crying. It was an interminable evening. Stella went to bed first; I saw to that, because I didn't want her lying there awake listening to me talking in my sleep. Besides, I didn't want her to see me tearing open the cardboard box—the one in the shape of a church, which held my Christmas Sunday School offering. Over the door of the church was this shaming legend: "My mite for the poor widow." When Stella had begun to grind her teeth in her first deep sleep, I took twenty cents away from the poor widow, whoever she was (the owner of the kitchen sink, no doubt), for the trolley fare, and secreted it and the remaining three pennies in the pocket of my middy. I wrapped the money well in a handkerchief and buttoned the pocket and hung my skirt over the middy. And then I tore the paper church into bits—the heavens opened and Judge Bay came toward me with a double-barreled shotgun— and hid the bits under a pile of pajamas. I did not sleep one wink. Except that I must have, because of the stupendous nightmares that kept wrenching the flesh off my skeleton and caused me to come close to perishing of thirst; once I fell out of bed and hit my head on Stella's ice skates. I would have waked her up and given her a piece of my mind for leaving them in such a lousy place, but then I remembered: I wanted *no* commotion of any kind.

I couldn't eat breakfast and I couldn't eat lunch. Old Johnny-on-the-spot Jack kept saying, "*Poor* Polecat. Polecat wants her fish for dinner." Mother made an abortive attempt to take my temperature. And when all that hullabaloo subsided, I was nearly in the soup because Mother asked me to mind Tess while she went to the sanitarium to see Mrs. Rogers, who, all of a sudden, was too sick to have anyone but grownups near her. Stella couldn't stay with the baby, because she had to go to ballet, and Jack couldn't, because he had to go up to the mesa and empty his traps. ("No, they *can't* wait. You want my skins to rot in this hot-one-day-cold-the-next weather?") I was arguing and whining when the telephone rang. Mother went to answer it and came back with a look of great sadness; Mrs. Rogers, she had learned, had had another hemorrhage. So Mother would not be going to the sanitarium after all and I needn't stay with Tess.

By the time I left the house, I was as cross as a bear. I felt awful about the widow's mite and I felt awful for being mean about staying with Tess, for Mrs. Rogers was a kind old lady, in a cozy blue hug-me-tight and an old-fangled boudoir cap, dying here all alone; she was a friend of Grandma's and had lived just down the street from her in Missouri, and all in the world Mrs. Rogers wanted to do was go back home and lie down in her own big bedroom in her own big, high-ceilinged house and have Grandma and other members of the Eastern Star come in from time to time to say hello. But they wouldn't let her go home; they were going to kill or cure her. I could not help feeling that my hardness of heart and evil of intention had had a good deal to do with her new crisis; right at the very same minute I had been saying "Does that old Mrs. Methuselah *always* have to spoil my fun?" the poor wasted thing was probably coughing up her blood and saying to the nurse, "Tell Emily Vanderpool not to mind me, she can run and play."

I had a bad character, I know that, but my badness never gave me half the enjoyment Jack and Stella thought it did. A good deal of the time I wanted to eat lye. I was certainly having no fun now, thinking of Mrs. Rogers and of depriving that poor widow of bread and milk; what if this penniless woman without a husband had a dog to feed, too? Or a baby? And besides, I didn't want to go downtown to steal anything from the ten-cent store; I didn't want to see Lottie Jump again—not really, for I knew in my bones that that girl was trouble with a capital T. And still, in our short meeting she had mesmerized me; I would think about her style of talking and the expert way she had made off with the perfume flask and the cake (how had she carried the cake through the streets without being noticed?) and be bowled over, for the part of me that did not love God was a black-hearted villain. And apart from these considerations, I had some sort of idea that if I did not keep my appointment with Lottie Jump, she would somehow get revenge; she had seemed a girl of purpose. So, revolted and fascinated, brave and lily-livered, I plodded along through the snow in my flopping galoshes up toward the Chautauqua, where the trolley stop was. On my way, I passed Virgil Meade's house; there was not just a snowman, there was a whole snow family in the back yard, and Virgil himself was throwing a stick for his dog. I was delighted to see that he was alone.

Lottie, who was sitting on a bench in the shelter eating a Mr. Goodbar, looked the same as she had the other time except that she was wearing an amazing hat. I think I had expected her to have a black handkerchief over the lower part of her face or to be wearing a Jesse James waistcoat. But I had never thought of a hat. It was felt; it was the color of cooked meat; it had some flowers appliquéd on the front of it; it had no brim, but rose straight up to a very considerable height, like a monument. It sat so low on her forehead and it was so tight that it looked, in a way, like part of her.

"How's every little thing, bub?" she said, licking her candy wrapper.

"Fine, Lottie," I said, freshly awed.

A silence fell. I drank some water from the drinking fountain, sat down, fastened my galoshes, and unfastened them again.

"My mother's teeth grow wrong way to," said Lottie, and showed me what she meant: the lower teeth were in front of the upper ones. "That so-called trolley car takes its own sweet time. This town is blah."

To save the honor of my home town, the trolley came scraping and groaning up the hill just then, its bell clanging with an idiotic frenzy, and ground to a stop. Its broad, proud cowcatcher was filled with dirty snow, in the middle of which rested a tomato can, put there, probably, by somebody who was bored to death and couldn't think of anything else to do—I did a lot of pointless things like that on lonesome Saturday afternoons. It was the custom of this trolley car, a rather mysterious one, to pause at the shelter for five minutes while the conductor, who was either Mr. Jansen or Mr. Peck, depending on whether it was the A.M. run or the P.M., got out and stretched and smoked and spit. Sometimes the passengers got out, too, acting like sightseers whose destination was this sturdy stucco gazebo instead of, as it really was, the Piggly Wiggly or the Nelson Dry. You expected them to take snapshots of the drinking fountain or of the

Chautauqua meeting house up on the hill. And when they all got back in the car, you expected them to exchange intelligent observations on the aborigines and the ruins they had seen.

Today there were no passengers, and as soon as Mr. Peck got out and began staring at the mountains as if he had never seen them before while he made himself a cigarette, Lottie, in her tall hat (was it something like the Inspector's hat in the Katzenjammer Kids?), got into the car, motioning me to follow. I put our nickels in the empty box and joined her on the very last double seat. It was only then that she mapped out the plan for the afternoon, in a low but still insouciant voice. The hat—she did not apologize for it, she simply referred to it as "my hat"—was to be the repository of whatever we stole. In the future, it would be advisable for me to have one like it. (How? Surely it was unique. The flowers, I saw on closer examination, were tulips, but they were blue, and a very unsettling shade of blue.) I was to engage a clerk on one side of the counter, asking her the price of, let's say, a tube of Daggett & Ramsdell vanishing cream, while Lottie would lift a round comb or a barrette or a hair net or whatever on the other side. Then, at a signal, I would decide against the vanishing cream and would move on to the next counter that she indicated. The signal was interesting; it was to be the raising of her hat from the rear—"like I've got the itch and gotta scratch," she said. I was relieved that I was to have no part in the actual stealing, and I was touched that Lottie, who was going to do all the work, said we would "go halvers" on the take. She asked me if there was anything in particular I wanted—she herself had nothing special in mind and was going to shop around first—and I said I would like some rubber gloves. This request was entirely spontaneous; I had never before in my life thought of rubber gloves in one way or another, but a psychologist—or Judge Bay—might have said that this was most significant and that I was planning at that moment to go on from petty larceny to bigger game, armed with a weapon on which I wished to leave no fingerprints.

On the way downtown, quite a few people got on the trolley, and they all gave us such peculiar looks that I was chicken-hearted until I realized it must be Lottie's hat they were looking at. No wonder. I kept looking at it myself out of the corner of my eye; it was like a watermelon standing on end. No, it was like a tremendous test tube. On this trip—a slow one, for the trolley pottered through that part of town in a desultory, neighborly way, even going into areas where no one lived—Lottie told me some of the things she had stolen in Muskogee and here in Adams. They included a white satin prayer book (think of it!), Mr. Goodbars by the thousands (she had probably never paid for a Mr. Goodbar in her life), a dinner ring valued at two dollars, a strawberry emery, several cans of corn, some shoelaces, a set of poker chips, countless pencils, four spark plugs ("Pa had this old car, see, and it was broke, so we took 'er to get fixed; I'll build me a radio with 'em sometime—you know? Listen in on them ear muffs to Tulsa?"), a Boy Scout knife, and a Girl Scout folding cup. She made a regular practice of going through the pockets of the coats in the cloakroom every day at recess, but she had never found anything there worth a red cent and was about to give that up. Once, she had taken a gold pencil from a teacher's desk and had got caught—she was sure that this was one of the reasons she was only in the third grade. Of this unjust experience, she said, "The old hoot owl! If I was drivin' in a car on a lonesome stretch and she was settin' beside me, I'd wait till we got to a pile of gravel and then I'd stop and say, 'Git out, Miss Priss.' She'd git out, all right."

Since Lottie was so frank, I was emboldened at last to ask her what she had done with the cake. She faced me with her grin; this grin, in combination with the hat, gave me a surprise from which I have never recovered. "I ate it up," she said. "I went in your garage and sat on your daddy's old tires and ate it. It was pretty good."

There were two ten-cent stores side by side in our town, Kresge's and Woolworth's, and as we walked down the main street toward them, Lottie played with a Yo-Yo. Since the street was thronged with Christmas shoppers and farmers in for Saturday, this was no ordinary accomplishment; all in all, Lottie Jump was someone to be reckoned with. I cannot say that I was proud to be seen with her; the fact is that I hoped I would not meet anyone I knew, and I thanked my lucky stars that Jack was up in the hills with his dead skunks, because if he had seen her with that lid and that Yo-Yo, I would never have heard the last of it. But in another way I *was* proud to be with her; in a smaller hemisphere, in one that included only her and me, I was swaggering—I felt like Somebody, marching along beside this lofty Somebody from Oklahoma who was going to hold up the dime store.

There is nothing like Woolworth's at Christmastime. It smells of peanut brittle and terrible chocolate candy, Djer-Kiss talcum powder and Ben Hur Perfume—smells sourly of tinsel and waxily of artificial poinsettias. The crowds are made up largely of children and women, with here and there a deliberative old man; the women are buying ribbons and wrappings and Christmas cards, and the children are buying asbestos pot holders for their mothers and, for their fathers, suède bookmarks with a burnt-in design that says "A good book is a good friend" or "Souvenir from the Garden of the Gods." It is very noisy. The salesgirls are forever ringing their bells and asking the floor-walker to bring them change for a five; babies in go-carts are screaming as parcels fall on their heads; the women, waving rolls of red tissue paper, try to attract the attention of the harried girl behind the counter. ("Miss! All I want is this one batch of the red. Can't I just give you the dime?" And the girl, beside herself, mottled with vexation, cries back, "Has to be rung up, Moddom, that's the rule.") There is pandemonium at the toy counter, where things are being tested by the customers—wound up, set off, tooted, pounded, made to say "Maaaah-Maaaah!" There is very little gaiety in the scene and, in fact, those baffled old men look as if they were walking over their own dead bodies, but there is an atmosphere of carnival, nevertheless, and as soon as Lottie and I entered the doors of Woolworth's golden-and-vermilion bedlam, I grew giddy and hot—not pleasantly so. The feeling, indeed, was distinctly disagreeable, like the beginning of a stomach upset.

Lottie gave me a nudge and said softly, "Go look at the envelopes. I want some rubber bands."

This counter was relatively uncrowded (the seasonal stationery supplies—the Christmas cards and wrapping paper and stickers—were at a separate counter), and I went around to examine some very beautiful letter paper; it was pale pink and it had a border of roses all around it. The clerk here was a cheerful middle-aged woman wearing an apron, and she was giving all her attention to a seedy old man who could not make up his mind between mucilage and paste. "Take your time, Dad," she said. "Compared to the rest of the girls, I'm on my vacation." The old man, holding a tube in one hand and a bottle in the other, looked at her vaguely and said, "I want it for stamps. Sometimes I write a letter and stamp it and then don't mail it and steam the stamp off. Must have ninety cents' worth of stamps like that." The woman laughed. "I know what you mean," she said. "I get mad and write a letter and then I tear it up." The old man gave her a condescending look and said, "That so? But I don't suppose yours are of a political nature." He bent his gaze again to the choice of adhesives.

This first undertaking was duck soup for Lottie. I did not even have to exchange a word with the woman; I saw Miss Fagin lift up *that hat* and give me the high sign, and we moved away, she down one aisle and I down the other, now and again catching a glimpse of each other through the throngs. We met at the foot of the second counter, where notions were sold.

"Fun, huh?" said Lottie, and I nodded, although I felt wholly dreary. "I want some crochet hooks," she said. "Price the rickrack."

This time the clerk was adding up her receipts and did not even look at me or at a woman who was angrily and in vain trying to buy a paper of pins. Out went Lottie's scrawny hand, up went her domed chimney. In this way for some time she bagged sitting birds: a tea strainer (there was no one at all at that counter), a box of Mrs. Carpenter's All Purpose Nails, the rubber gloves I had said I wanted, and four packages of mixed seeds. Now you have some idea of the size of Lottie Jump's hat.

I was nervous, not from being her accomplice but from being in this crowd on an empty stomach, and I was getting tired—we had been in the store for at least an hour—and the whole enterprise seemed pointless. There wasn't a thing in her hat I wanted—not even the rubber gloves. But in exact proportion as my spirits descended, Lottie's rose; clearly she had only been target-practicing and now she was moving in for the kill.

We met beside the books of paper dolls, for reconnaissance. "I'm gonna get me a pair of pearl beads," said Lottie. "You go fuss with the hairpins, hear?"

Luck, combined with her skill, would have stayed with Lottie, and her hat would have been a cornucopia by the end of the afternoon if, at the very moment her hand went out for the string of beads, that idiosyncrasy of mine had not struck me full force. I had never known it to come with so few preliminaries; probably this was so because I was oppressed by all the masses of bodies poking and pushing me, and all the open mouths breathing in my face. Anyhow, right then, at the crucial time, I *had to be alone*.

I stood staring down at the bone hairpins for a moment, and when the girl behind the counter said, "What kind does Mother want, hon? What color is Mother's hair?" I looked past her and across at Lottie and I said, "Your brother isn't the only one in your family that doesn't have any brains." The clerk, astonished, turned to look where I was looking and caught Lottie in the act of lifting up her hat to put the pearls inside. She had unwisely chosen a long strand and was having a little trouble; I had the nasty thought that it looked as if her brains were leaking out.

The clerk, not able to deal with this emergency herself, frantically punched her bell and cried, "Floorwalker! Mr. Bellamy! I've caught a thief!"

Momentarily there was a violent hush—then such a clamor as you have never heard. Bells rang, babies howled, crockery crashed to the floor as people stumbled in their rush to the arena.

Mr. Bellamy, nineteen years old but broad of shoulder and jaw, was instantly standing beside Lottie, holding her arm with one hand while with the other he removed her hat to reveal to the overjoyed audience that incredible array of merchandise. Her hair was wild, her face a mask of innocent bewilderment, Lottie Jump, the scurvy thing, pretended to be deaf and dumb. She pointed at the rubber gloves and then she pointed at me, and Mr. Bellamy, able at last to prove his mettle, said "Aha!" and, still holding Lottie, moved around the counter to me and grabbed *my* arm. He gave the hat to the clerk and asked her kindly to accompany him and his redhanded catch to the manager's office.

I don't know where Lottie is now—whether she is on the stage or in jail. If her performance after our arrest meant anything, the first is quite as likely as the second. (I never saw her again, and for all I know she lit out of town that night on a freight train. Or perhaps her whole family decamped as suddenly as they had arrived; ours was a most transient population. You can be sure I made no attempt to find her again, and for months I avoided going anywhere near Arapahoe Creek or North Hill.) She never said a word but kept making signs with her fingers, ad-libbing the whole thing. They tested her hearing by shooting off a popgun right in her ear and she never batted an eyelid. They called up my father, and he came over from the Safeway on the double. I heard very little of what he said because I was crying so hard, but one thing I did hear him say was, "Well, young lady, I guess you've seen to it that I'll have to part company with my good friend Judge Bay." I tried to defend myself, but it was useless. The manager, Mr. Bellamy, the clerk, and my father patted Lottie on the shoulder, and the clerk said, "Poor, afflicted child." For being a poor, afflicted child, they gave her a bag of hard candy, and she gave them the most fraudulent smile of gratitude, and slobbered a little, and shuffled out, holding her empty hat in front of her like a beggar-man. I hate Lottie Jump to this day, but I have to hand it to her—she was a genius.

The floorwalker would have liked to see me sentenced to the reform school for life, I am sure, but the manager said that, considering this was my first offense, he would let my father attend to my punishment. The old-maid clerk, who looked precisely like Emmy Schmalz, clucked her tongue and shook her head at me. My father hustled me out of the office and out of the store and into the car and home, muttering the entire time; now and again I'd hear the words "morals" and "nowadays."

What's the use of telling you the rest? You know what happened. Daddy on second thoughts decided not to hang his head in front of Judge Bay but to make use of his friendship in this time of need, and he took me to see the scary old curmudgeon at his house. All I remember of that long declamation, during which the Judge sat behind his desk never taking his eyes off me, was the warning: "I want you to give this a great deal of thought, miss. I want you to search and seek in the innermost corners of your conscience and root out every bit of badness." Oh, *him!* Why, listen, if I'd rooted out all the badness in me, there wouldn't have been anything left of me. My mother cried for days because she had nurtured an outlaw and was ashamed to show her face at the neighborhood store; my father was silent, and he often looked at me. Stella, who was a prig, said, "And to think you did it at *Christmas*time!" As for Jack—well, Jack a couple of times did not know how close he came to seeing glory when I had a butcher knife in my hand. It was Polecat this and Polecat that until I nearly went off my rocker. Tess, of course, didn't know what was going on and asked so many questions that finally I told her to go to Helen Hunt Jackson in a savage tone of voice.

Good old Muff.

It is not true that you don't learn by experience. At any rate, I did that time. I began immediately to have two or three friends at a time—to be sure, because of the stigma on me, they were by no means the elite of Carlyle Hill Grade—and never again when that terrible need to be alone arose did I let fly. I would say, instead, "I've got a headache. I'll have to go home and take an aspirin," or "Gosh all hemlocks, I forgot—I've got to go to the dentist."

After the scandal died down, I got into the Camp Fire Girls. It was through pull, of course, since Stella had been a respected member for two years and my mother was a friend of the leader. But it turned out all right. Even Muff did not miss our periods of companionship, because about that time she grew up and started having literally millions of kittens.

In the Zoo

Keening harshly in his senility, the blind polar bear slowly and ceaselessly shakes his head in the stark heat of the July and mountain noon. His open eyes are blue. No one stops to look at him; an old farmer, in passing, sums up the old bear's situation by observing, with a ruthless chuckle, that he is a "back number." Patient and despairing, he sits on his yellowed haunches on the central rock of his pool, his huge toy paws wearing short boots of mud.

The grizzlies to the right of him, a conventional family of father and mother and two spring cubs, alternately play the clown and sleep. There is a blustery, scoundrelly, half-likable bravado in the manner of the black bear on the polar's left; his name, according to the legend on his cage, is Clancy, and he is a rough-and-tumble, brawling blowhard, thundering continually as he paces back and forth, or pauses to face his audience of children and mothers and release from his great, gray-tongued mouth a perfectly Vesuvian roar. If he were to be reincarnated in human form, he would be a man of action, possibly a football coach, probably a politician. One expects to see his black hat hanging from a branch of one of his trees; at any moment he will light a cigar.

The polar bear's next-door neighbors are not the only ones who offer so sharp and sad a contrast to him. Across a reach of scrappy grass and litter is the convocation of conceited monkeys, burrowing into each other's necks and chests for fleas, picking their noses with their long, black, finicky fingers, swinging by their gifted tails on the flying trapeze, screaming bloody murder. Even when they mourn—one would think the male orangutan was on the very brink of suicide—they are comedians; they only fake depression, for they are firmly secure in their rambunctious tribalism and in their appalling insight and contempt. Their flibbertigibbet gamboling is a sham, and, stealthily and shiftily, they are really watching the pitiful polar bear ("Back number," they quote the farmer. "That's *his* number all right," they snigger), and the windy black bear ("Life of the party. Gasbag. Low I.Q.," they note scornfully on his dossier), and the stupid, bourgeois grizzlies ("It's feed the face and hit the sack for them," the monkeys say). And they are watching my sister and me, two middle-aged women, as we sit on a bench between the exhibits, eating popcorn, growing thirsty. We are thoughtful.

A chance remark of Daisy's a few minutes before has turned us to memory and meditation. "I don't know why," she said, "but that poor blind bear reminds me of Mr. Murphy." The name "Mr. Murphy" at once returned us both to childhood, and we were floated far and fast, our later lives diminished. So now we eat our popcorn in silence with the ritualistic appetite of childhood, which has little to do with hunger; it is not so much food as a sacrament, and in tribute to our sisterliness and our friendliness I break the silence to say that this is the best popcorn I have ever eaten in my life. The extravagance of my statement instantly makes me feel self-indulgent, and for some time I uneasily avoid looking at the blind bear. My sister does not agree or disagree; she simply says that popcorn is the only food she has ever really liked. For a long time, then, we eat without a word, but I know, because I know her well and know her similarity to me, that Daisy is thinking what I am thinking; both of us are mournfully remembering Mr. Murphy, who, at one time in our lives, was our only friend.

This zoo is in Denver, a city that means nothing to my sister and me except as a place to take or meet trains. Daisy lives two hundred miles farther west, and it is her custom, when my every-other-year visit with her is over, to come across the mountains to see me off on my eastbound train. We know almost no one here, and because our stays are short, we have never bothered to learn the town in more than the most desultory way. We know the Burlington uptown office and the respectable hotels, a restaurant or two, the Union Station, and, beginning today, the zoo in the city park.

But since the moment that Daisy named Mr. Murphy by name our situation in Denver has been only corporeal; our minds and our hearts are in Adams, fifty miles north, and we are seeing, under the white sun at its pitiless meridian, the streets of that ugly town, its parks and trees and bridges, the bandstand in its dreary park, the roads that lead away from it, west to the mountains and east to the plains, its mongrel and multitudinous churches, its high school shaped like a loaf of bread, the campus of its college, an oasis of which we had no experience except to walk through it now and then, eyeing the woodbine on the impressive buildings. These things are engraved forever on our minds with a legibility so insistent that you have only to say the name of the town aloud to us to rip the rinds from our nerves and leave us exposed in terror and humiliation.

We have supposed in later years that Adams was not so bad as all that, and we know that we magnified its ugliness because we looked upon it as the extension of the possessive, unloving, scornful, complacent foster mother, Mrs. Placer, to whom, at the death of our parents within a month of each other, we were sent like Dickensian grotesqueries—cowardly, weak-stomached, given to tears, backward in school. Daisy was ten and I was eight when, unaccompanied, we made the long trip from Marblehead to our benefactress, whom we had never seen and, indeed, never heard of until the pastor of our church came to tell us of the arrangement our father had made on his deathbed, seconded by our mother on hers. This man, whose name and face I have forgotten and whose parting speeches to us I have not forgiven, tried to dry our tears with talk of Indians and of buffaloes; he spoke, however, at much greater length, and in preaching cadences, of the Christian goodness of Mrs. Placer. She was, he said, childless and fond of children, and for many years she had been a widow, after the lingering demise of her tubercular husband, for whose sake she had moved to the Rocky Mountains. For his support and costly medical care, she had run a boarding house, and after his death, since he had left her nothing, she was obliged to continue running it. She had been a girlhood friend of our paternal grandmother, and our father, in the absence of responsible relatives, had made her the beneficiary of his life insurance on the condition that she lodge and rear us. The pastor, with a frankness remarkable considering that he was talking to children, explained to us that our father had left little more than a drop in the bucket for our care, and he enjoined us to give Mrs. Placer, in return for her hospitality and sacrifice, courteous help and eternal thanks. "Sacrifice" was a word we were never allowed to forget.

And thus it was, in grief for our parents, that we came cringing to the dry Western town and to the house where Mrs. Placer lived, a house in which the square, uncushioned furniture was cruel and the pictures on the walls were either dour or dire and the lodgers, who lived in the upper floors among shadowy wardrobes and chiffoniers, had come through the years to resemble their landlady in appearance as well as in deportment.

After their ugly-colored evening meal, Gran—as she bade us call her—and her paying guests would sit, rangy and aquiline, rocking on the front porch on spring and summer and autumn nights, tasting their delicious grievances: those slights delivered by ungrateful sons and daughters, those imprudences committed by trolley-car conductors and uppity salesgirls in the ready-to-wear, all those slurs and calculated elbow-jostlings that were their daily crucifixion and their staff of life. We little girls, washing the dishes in the cavernous kitchen, listened to their even, martyred voices, fixed like leeches to their solitary subject and their solitary creed—that life was essentially a matter of being done in, let down, and swindled.

At regular intervals, Mrs. Placer, chairwoman of the victims, would say, "Of course, I don't care; I just have to laugh," and then would tell a shocking tale of an intricate piece of skulduggery perpetrated against her by someone she did not even know. Sometimes, with her avid, partial jury sitting there on the porch behind the bitter hopvines in the heady mountain air, the cases she tried involved Daisy and me, and, listening, we travailed, hugging each other, whispering, "I wish she wouldn't! Oh, how did she find out?" How *did* she? Certainly we never told her when we were snubbed or chosen last on teams, never admitted to a teacher's scolding or to the hoots of laughter that greeted us when we bit on silly, unfair jokes. But she knew. She knew about the slumber parties we were not invited to, the beefsteak fries at which we were pointedly left out; she knew that the singing teacher had said in so many words that I could not carry a tune in a basket and that the sewing superintendent had said that Daisy's fingers were all thumbs. With our teeth chattering in the cold of our isolation, we would hear her protestant, litigious voice defending our right to be orphans, paupers, wholly dependent on her—except for the really ridiculous pittance from our father's life insurance—when it was all she could do to make ends meet. She did not care, but she had to laugh that people in general were so small-minded that they looked down on fatherless, motherless waifs like us and, by association, looked down on her. It seemed funny to her that people gave her no credit for taking on these sickly youngsters who were not even kin but only the grandchildren of a friend.

If a child with braces on her teeth came to play with us, she was, according to Gran, slyly lording it over us because our teeth were crooked but there was no money to have them straightened. And what could be the meaning of our being asked to come for supper at the doctor's house? Were the doctor and his la-di-da New York wife and those pert girls with their solid-gold barrettes and their Shetland pony going to shame her poor darlings? Or shame their poor Gran by making them sorry to come home to the plain but honest life that was all she could provide for them?

There was no stratum of society not reeking with the effluvium of fraud and pettifoggery. And the school system was almost the worst of all: if we could not understand fractions, was that not our teacher's fault? And therefore what right had she to give us F? It was as plain as a pikestaff to Gran that the teacher was only covering up her own inability to teach. It was unlikely, too—highly unlikely—that it was by accident that time and time again the free medical clinic was closed for the day just as our names were about to be called out, so that nothing was done about our bad tonsils, which meant that we were repeatedly sick in the winter, with Gran fetching and carrying for us, climbing those stairs a jillion times a day with her game leg and her heart that was none too strong.

Steeped in these mists of accusation and hidden plots and double meanings, Daisy and I grew up like worms. I think no one could have withstood the atmosphere in that house where everyone trod on eggs that a little bird had told them were bad.

They spied on one another, whispered behind doors, conjectured, drew parallels beginning "With all due respect . . ." or "It is a matter of indifference to *me* but . . ." The vigilantes patrolled our town by day, and by night returned to lay their goodies at their priestess's feet and wait for her oracular interpretation of the innards of the butcher, the baker, the candlestick maker, the soda jerk's girl, and the barber's unnatural deaf white cat.

Consequently, Daisy and I also became suspicious. But it was suspicion of ourselves that made us mope and weep and grimace with self-judgment. Why were we not happy when Gran had sacrificed herself to the bone for us? Why did we not cut dead the paper boy who had called her a filthy name? Why did we persist in our willful friendliness with the grocer who had tried, unsuccessfully, to overcharge her on a case of pork and beans?

Our friendships were nervous and surreptitious; we sneaked and lied, and as our hungers sharpened, our debasement deepened; we were pitied; we were shifty-eyed, always on the lookout for Mrs. Placer or one of her tattletale lodgers; we were hypocrites.

Nevertheless, one thin filament of instinct survived, and Daisy and I in time found asylum in a small menagerie down by the railroad tracks. It belonged to a gentle alcoholic ne'er-do-well, who did nothing all day long but drink bathtub gin in rickeys and play solitaire and smile to himself and talk to his animals. He had a little, stunted red vixen and a deodorized skunk, a parrot from Tahiti that spoke Parisian French, a woebegone coyote, and two capuchin monkeys, so serious and humanized, so small and sad and sweet, and so religious-looking with their tonsured heads that it was impossible not to think their gibberish was really an ordered language with a grammar that some day some philologist would understand.

Gran knew about our visits to Mr. Murphy and she did not object, for it gave her keen pleasure to excoriate him when we came home. His vice was not a matter of guesswork; it was an established fact that he was half-seas over from dawn till midnight. "With the black Irish," said Gran, "the taste for drink is taken in with the mother's milk and is never mastered. Oh, I

know all about those promises to join the temperance movement
and not to touch another drop. The way to hell is paved with
good intentions."

We were still little girls when we discovered Mr. Murphy,
before the shattering disease of adolescence was to make our
bones and brains ache even more painfully than before, and we
loved him and we hoped to marry him when we grew up. We
loved him, and we loved his monkeys to exactly the same degree
and in exactly the same way; they were husbands and fathers
and brothers, these three little, ugly, dark, secret men who
minded their own business and let us mind ours. If we stuck our
fingers through the bars of the cage, the monkeys would sometimes take them in their tight, tiny hands and look into our
faces with a tentative, somehow absent-minded sorrow, as if they
terribly regretted that they could not place us but were glad to
see us all the same. Mr. Murphy, playing a solitaire game of cards
called "once in a blue moon" on a kitchen table in his back yard
beside the pens, would occasionally look up and blink his beautiful blue eyes and say, "You're peaches to make over my wee
friends. I love you for it." There was nothing demanding in his
voice, and nothing sticky; on his lips the word "love" was jocose
and forthright, it had no strings attached. We would sit on either
side of him and watch him regiment his ranks of cards and stop
to drink as deeply as if he were dying of thirst and wave to his
animals and say to them, "Yes, lads, you're dandies."

Because Mr. Murphy was as reserved with us as the capu-
chins were, as courteously noncommittal, we were surprised one
spring day when he told us that he had a present for us, which
he hoped Mrs. Placer would let us keep; it was a puppy, for
whom the owner had asked him to find a home—half collie and
half Labrador retriever, blue-blooded on both sides.

"You might tell Mrs. Placer—" he said, smiling at the name,
for Gran was famous in the town. "You might tell Mrs. Placer,"
said Mr. Murphy, "that this lad will make a fine watchdog. She'll
never have to fear for her spoons again. Or her honor." The last
he said to himself, not laughing but tucking his chin into his
collar; lines sprang to the corners of his eyes. He would not let
us see the dog, whom we could hear yipping and squealing inside
his shanty, for he said that our disappointment would weigh on

his conscience if we lost our hearts to the fellow and then could not have him for our own.

That evening at supper, we told Gran about Mr. Murphy's present. A dog? In the first place, why a dog? Was it possible that the news had reached Mr. Murphy's ears that Gran had just this very day finished planting her spring garden, the very thing that a rampageous dog would have in his mind to destroy? What sex was it? A male! Females, she had heard, were more trustworthy; males roved and came home smelling of skunk; such a consideration as this, of course, would not have crossed Mr. Murphy's fuddled mind. Was this young male dog housebroken? We had not asked? That was the limit!

Gran appealed to her followers, too raptly fascinated by Mr. Murphy's machinations to eat their Harvard beets. "Am I being farfetched or does it strike you as decidedly queer that Mr. Murphy is trying to fob off on my little girls a young cur that has not been trained?" she asked them. "If it were housebroken, he would have said so, so I feel it is safe to assume that it is not. Perhaps cannot *be* housebroken. I've heard of such cases."

The fantasy spun on, richly and rapidly, with all the skilled helping hands at work at once. The dog was tangibly in the room with us, shedding his hair, scratching his fleas, shaking rain off himself to splatter the walls, dragging some dreadful carcass across the floor, chewing up slippers, knocking over chairs with his tail, gobbling the chops from the platter, barking, biting, fathering, fighting, smelling to high heaven of carrion, staining the rug with his muddy feet, scratching the floor with his claws. He developed rabies; he bit a child, two children! Three! Everyone in town! And Gran and her poor darlings went to jail for harboring this murderous, odoriferous, drunk, Roman Catholic dog.

And yet, astoundingly enough, she came around to agreeing to let us have the dog. It was, as Mr. Murphy had predicted, the word "watchdog" that deflected the course of the trial. The moment Daisy uttered it, Gran halted, marshaling her reverse march; while she rallied and tacked and reconnoitered, she sent us to the kitchen for the dessert. And by the time this course was under way, the uses of a dog, the enormous potentialities for investigation and law enforcement in a dog trained by Mrs. Placer,

were being minutely and passionately scrutinized by the eight
upright bloodhounds sitting at the table wolfing their brown
Betty as if it were fresh-killed rabbit. The dog now sat at attention beside his mistress, fiercely alert, ears cocked, nose aquiver,
the protector of widows, of orphans, of lonely people who had
no homes. He made short shrift of burglars, homicidal maniacs,
Peeping Toms, gypsies, bogus missionaries, Fuller Brush men
with a risqué spiel. He went to the store and brought back groceries, retrieved the evening paper from the awkward place the
boy had meanly thrown it, rescued cripples from burning houses,
saved children from drowning, heeled at command, begged, lay
down, stood up, sat, jumped through a hoop, ratted.

Both times—when he was a ruffian of the blackest delinquency
and then a pillar of society—he was full-grown in his prefigura-
tion, and when Laddy appeared on the following day, small,
unsteady, and whimpering lonesomely, Gran and her lodgers
were taken aback; his infant, clumsy paws embarrassed them, his
melting eyes were unapropos. But it could never be said of Mrs.
Placer, as Mrs. Placer her own self said, that she was a woman
who went back on her word, and her darlings were going to
have their dog, softheaded and feckless as he might be. All the
first night, in his carton in the kitchen, he wailed for his mother,
and in the morning, it was true, he had made a shambles of the
room—fouled the floor, and pulled off the tablecloth together
with a ketchup bottle, so that thick gore lay everywhere. At
breakfast, the lodgers confessed they had had a most amusing
night, for it had actually been funny the way the dog had been
determined not to let anyone get a wink of sleep. After that first
night, Laddy slept in our room, receiving from us, all through
our delighted, sleepless nights, pats and embraces and kisses and
whispers. He was our baby, our best friend, the smartest, prettiest,
nicest dog in the entire wide world. Our soft and rapid blandish-
ments excited him to yelp at us in pleased bewilderment, and
then we would playfully grasp his muzzle, so that he would snarl,
deep in his throat like an adult dog, and shake his head
violently, and, when we freed him, nip us smartly with great
good will.

He was an intelligent and genial dog and we trained him
quickly. He steered clear of Gran's radishes and lettuce after she

had several times given him a brisk comeuppance with a strap across the rump, and he soon left off chewing shoes and the laundry on the line, and he outgrew his babyish whining. He grew like a weed; he lost his spherical softness, and his coat, which had been sooty fluff, came in stiff and rusty black; his nose grew aristocratically long, and his clever, pointed ears stood at attention. He was all bronzy, lustrous black except for an Elizabethan ruff of white and a tip of white at the end of his perky tail. No one could deny that he was exceptionally handsome and that he had, as well, great personal charm and style. He escorted Daisy and me to school in the morning, laughing interiorly out of the enormous pleasure of his life as he gracefully cantered ahead of us, distracted occasionally by his private interest in smells or unfamiliar beings in the grass but, on the whole, engrossed in his role of chaperon. He made friends easily with other dogs, and sometimes he went for a long hunting weekend into the mountains with a huge and bossy old red hound named Mess, who had been on the county most of his life and had made a good thing of it, particularly at the fire station.

It was after one of these three-day excursions into the high country that Gran took Laddy in hand. He had come back spent and filthy, his coat a mass of cockleburs and ticks, his eyes bloodshot, loud *râles* in his chest; for half a day he lay motionless before the front door like someone in a hangover, his groaning eyes explicitly saying "Oh, for God's sake, leave me be" when we offered him food or bowls of water. Gran was disapproving, then affronted, and finally furious. Not, of course, with Laddy, since all inmates of her house enjoyed immunity, but with Mess, whose caddish character, together with that of his nominal masters, the firemen, she examined closely under a strong light, with an air of detachment, with her not caring but her having, all the same, to laugh. A lodger who occupied the back west room had something to say about the fire chief and his nocturnal visits to a certain house occupied by a certain group of young women, too near the same age to be sisters and too old to be the daughters of the woman who claimed to be their mother. What a story! The exophthalmic librarian—she lived in one of the front rooms—had some interesting insinuations to make about the deputy marshal, who had borrowed, significantly, she thought, a book on hypnotism. She also knew—she was, of course, in a most useful position in the town, and from her authoritative pen in the middle of the library her mammiform and azure eyes and her eager ears missed nothing—that the fire chief's wife was not as scrupulous as she might be when she was keeping score on bridge night at the Sorosis.

There was little at the moment that Mrs. Placer and her disciples could do to save the souls of the Fire Department and their families, and therefore save the town from holocaust (a very timid boarder—a Mr. Beaver, a newcomer who was not to linger long—had sniffed throughout this recitative as if he were smelling burning flesh), but at least the unwholesome bond between Mess and Laddy could and would be severed once and for all. Gran looked across the porch at Laddy, who lay stretched at full length in the darkest corner, shuddering and baying abortively in his throat as he chased jack rabbits in his dreams, and she said, "A dog can have morals like a human." With this declaration Laddy's randy, manly holidays were finished. It may have been telepathy that woke him; he lifted his heavy head from his paws, laboriously got up, hesitated for a moment, and then padded languidly across the porch to Gran. He stood docilely beside her chair, head down, tail drooping as if to say, "O.K., Mrs. Placer, show me how and I'll walk the straight and narrow."

The very next day, Gran changed Laddy's name to Caesar, as being more dignified, and a joke was made at the supper table that he had come, seen, and conquered Mrs. Placer's heart—for within her circle, where the magnanimity she lavished upon her orphans was daily demonstrated, Mrs. Placer's heart was highly thought of. On that day also, although we did not know it yet, Laddy ceased to be our dog. Before many weeks passed, indeed, he ceased to be anyone we had ever known. A week or so after he became Caesar, he took up residence in her room, sleeping alongside her bed. She broke him of the habit of taking us to school (temptation to low living was rife along those streets; there was a chow—well, never mind) by the simple expedient of chaining him to a tree as soon as she got up in the morning. This discipline, together with the stamina-building cuffs she gave his sensitive ears from time to time, gradually but certainly remade his character. From a sanguine, affectionate, easygoing Gael (with the fits of melancholy that alternated with the larkiness), he turned into an overbearing, military, efficient, loud-voiced Teuton. His bark, once wide of range, narrowed to one dark, glottal tone.

Soon the paper boy flatly refused to serve our house after Caesar efficiently removed the bicycle clip from his pants leg; the skin was not broken, or even bruised, but it was a matter of principle with the boy. The milkman approached the back door in a seizure of shakes like St. Vitus's dance. The metermen, the coal men, and the garbage collector crossed themselves if they were Catholics and, if they were not, tried whistling in the dark. "Good boy, good Caesar," they caroled, and, unctuously lying, they said they knew his bark was worse than his bite, knowing full well that it was not, considering the very nasty nip, requiring stitches, he had given a representative of the Olson Rug Company, who had had the folly to pat him on the head. Caesar did not molest the lodgers, but he disdained them and he did not brook being personally addressed by anyone except Gran. One night, he wandered into the dining room, appearing to be in search of something he had mislaid, and, for some reason that no one was ever able to divine, suddenly stood stock-still and gave the easily upset Mr. Beaver a long and penetrating look. Mr. Beaver, trembling from head to toe, stammered, "Why—er, hello there, Caesar, old boy, old boy," and Caesar charged. For a moment, it was touch and go, but Gran saved Mr. Beaver, only to lose him an hour later when he departed, bag and baggage, for the Y.M.C.A. This rout and the consequent loss of revenue would more than likely have meant Caesar's downfall and his deportation to the pound if it had not been that a newly widowed druggist, very irascible and very much Gran's style, had applied for a room in her house a week or so before, and now he moved in delightedly, as if he were coming home.

Finally, the police demanded that Caesar be muzzled and they warned that if he committed any major crime again—they cited the case of the Olson man—he would be shot on sight. Mrs. Placer, although she had no respect for the law, knowing as much as she did about its agents, obeyed. She obeyed, that is, in part; she put the muzzle on Caesar for a few hours a day, usually early in the morning when the traffic was light and before the deliveries had started, but the rest of the time his powerful jaws and dazzling white saber teeth were free and snapping. There was between these two such preternatural rapport, such an impressive conjugation of suspicion, that he, sensing the approach of a policeman, could convey instantly to her the immediate necessity of clapping his nose cage on. And the policeman, sent out on the complaint of a terrorized neighbor, would be greeted by this law-abiding pair at the door.

Daisy and I wished we were dead. We were divided between hating Caesar and loving Laddy, and we could not give up the hope that something, some day, would change him back into the loving animal he had been before he was appointed vice-president of the Placerites. Now at the meetings after supper on the porch he took an active part, standing rigidly at Gran's side except when she sent him on an errand. He carried out these assignments not with the air of a servant but with that of an accomplice. "Get me the paper, Caesar," she would say to him, and he, dismayingly intelligent and a shade smart-alecky, would open the screen door by himself and in a minute come back with the *Bulletin*, from which Mrs. Placer would then read an item, like the Gospel of the day, and then read between the lines of it, scandalized.

In the deepening of our woe and our bereavement and humiliation, we mutely appealed to Mr. Murphy. We did not speak outright to him, for Mr. Murphy lived in a state of indirection, and often when he used the pronoun "I," he seemed to be speaking of someone standing a little to the left of him, but we went to see him and his animals each day during the sad summer, taking what comfort we could from the cozy, quiet indolence of his back yard, where small black eyes encountered ours politely and everyone was half asleep. When Mr. Murphy inquired about Laddy in his bland, inattentive way, looking for a stratagem whereby to shift the queen of hearts into position by the king, we would say, "Oh, he's fine," or "Laddy is a nifty dog." And Mr. Murphy, reverently slaking the thirst that was his talent and his concubine, would murmur, "I'm glad."

We wanted to tell him, we wanted his help, or at least his

sympathy, but how could we cloud his sunny world? It was awful to see Mr. Murphy ruffled. Up in the calm clouds as he generally was, he could occasionally be brought to earth with a thud, as we had seen and heard one day. Not far from his house, there lived a bad, troublemaking boy of twelve, who was forever hanging over the fence trying to teach the parrot obscene words. He got nowhere, for she spoke no English and she would flabbergast him with her cold eye and sneer, *"Tant pis."* One day, this boorish fellow went too far; he suddenly shot his head over the fence like a jack-in-the-box and aimed a water pistol at the skunk's face. Mr. Murphy leaped to his feet in a scarlet rage; he picked up a stone and threw it accurately, hitting the boy square in the back, so hard that he fell right down in a mud puddle and lay there kicking and squalling and, as it turned out, quite badly hurt. "If you ever come back here again, I'll kill you!" roared Mr. Murphy. I think he meant it, for I have seldom seen an anger so resolute, so brilliant, and so voluble. "How dared he!" he cried, scrambling into Mallow's cage to hug and pet and soothe her. "He must be absolutely mad! He must be the Devil!" He did not go back to his game after that but paced the yard, swearing a blue streak and only pausing to croon to his animals, now as frightened by him as they had been by the intruder, and to drink straight from the bottle, not bothering with fixings. We were fascinated by this unfamiliar side of Mr. Murphy, but we did not want to see it ever again, for his face had grown so dangerously purple and the veins of his forehead seemed ready to burst and his eyes looked scorched. He was the closest thing to a maniac we had ever seen. So we did not tell him about Laddy; what he did not know would not hurt him, although it was hurting us, throbbing in us like a great, bleating wound.

But eventually Mr. Murphy heard about our dog's conversion, one night at the pool hall, which he visited from time to time when he was seized with a rare but compelling garrulity, and the next afternoon when he asked us how Laddy was and we replied that he was fine, he tranquilly told us, as he deliberated whether to move the jack of clubs now or to bide his time, that we were sweet girls but we were lying in our teeth. He did not seem at all angry but only interested, and all the while he questioned us, he went on about his business with the gin and the hearts and spades and diamonds and clubs. It rarely happened that he won the particular game he was playing, but that day he did, and when he saw all the cards laid out in their ideal pattern, he leaned back, looking disappointed, and he said, "I'm damned." He then scooped up the cards, in a gesture unusually quick and tidy for him, stacked them together, and bound them with a rubber band. Then he began to tell us what he thought of Gran. He grew as loud and apoplectic as he had been that other time, and though he kept repeating that he knew *we* were innocent and he put not a shred of the blame on us, we were afraid he might suddenly change his mind, and, speechless, we cowered against the monkeys' cage. In dread, the monkeys clutched the fingers we offered to them and made soft, protesting noises, as if to say, "Oh, stop it, Murphy! Our nerves!"

As quickly as it had started, the tantrum ended. Mr. Murphy paled to his normal complexion and said calmly that the only practical thing was to go and have it out with Mrs. Placer. "At once," he added, although he said he bitterly feared that it was too late and there would be no exorcising the fiend from Laddy's misused spirit. And because he had given the dog to us and not to her, he required that we go along with him, stick up for our rights, stand on our own mettle, get up our Irish, and give the old bitch something to put in her pipe and smoke.

Oh, it was hot that day! We walked in a kind of delirium through the simmer, where only the grasshoppers had the energy to move, and I remember wondering if ether smelled like the gin on Mr. Murphy's breath. Daisy and I, in one way or another, were going to have our gizzards cut out along with our hearts and our souls and our pride, and I wished I were as drunk as Mr. Murphy, who swam effortlessly through the heat, his lips parted comfortably, his eyes half closed. When we turned in to the path at Gran's house, my blood began to scald my veins. It was so futile and so dangerous and so absurd. Here we were on a high moral mission, two draggletailed, gumptionless little girls and a toper whom no one could take seriously, partly because he was little more than a gurgling bottle of booze and partly because of the clothes he wore. He was a sight, as he always was when he was out of his own yard. There, somehow, in the carefree disorder, his clothes did not look especially strange, but on the streets of the town, in the barbershop or the post office or on Gran's path, they were fantastic. He wore a pair of hound's-tooth pants, old but maintaining a vehement pattern, and with them he wore a collarless blue flannelette shirt. His hat was the silliest of all, because it was a derby three sizes too big. And as if Shannon, too, was a part of his funny-paper costume, the elder capuchin rode on his shoulder, tightly embracing his thin red neck.

Gran and Caesar were standing side by side behind the screen door, looking as if they had been expecting us all along. For a moment, Gran and Mr. Murphy faced each other across the length of weedy brick between the gate and the front porch, and no one spoke. Gran took no notice at all of Daisy and me. She adjusted her eyeglasses, using both hands, and then looked down at Caesar and matter-of-factly asked, "Do you want out?"

Caesar flung himself full-length upon the screen and it sprang open like a jaw. I ran to meet him and head him off, and Daisy threw a library book at his head, but he was on Mr. Murphy in one split second and had his monkey off his shoulder and had broken Shannon's neck in two shakes. He would have gone on nuzzling and mauling and growling over the corpse for hours if Gran had not marched out of the house and down the path and slapped him lightly on the flank and said, in a voice that could not have deceived an idiot, "Why, Caesar, you scamp! You've hurt Mr. Murphy's monkey! Aren't you ashamed!"

Hurt the monkey! In one final, apologetic shudder, the life was extinguished from the little fellow. Bloody and covered with slather, Shannon lay with his arms suppliantly stretched over his head, his leather fingers curled into loose, helpless fists. His hind legs and his tail lay limp and helter-skelter on the path. And Mr. Murphy, all of a sudden reeling drunk, burst into the kind of tears that Daisy and I knew well—the kind that time alone could stop. We stood aghast in the dark-red sunset, killed by our horror and our grief for Shannon and our unforgivable disgrace. We stood upright in a dead faint, and an eon passed before Mr. Murphy picked up Shannon's body and wove away, sobbing, "I don't believe it! I don't *believe it!*"

The very next day, again at morbid, heavy sunset, Caesar

died in violent convulsions, knocking down two tall hollyhocks in his throes. Long after his heart had stopped, his right hind leg continued to jerk in aimless reflex. Madly methodical, Mr. Murphy had poisoned some meat for him, had thoroughly envenomed a whole pound of hamburger, and early in the morning, before sunup, when he must have been near collapse with his hangover, he had stolen up to Mrs. Placer's house and put it by the kitchen door. He was so stealthy that Caesar never stirred in his fool's paradise there on the floor by Gran. We knew these to be the facts, for Mr. Murphy made no bones about them. Afterward, he had gone home and said a solemn Requiem for Shannon in so loud a voice that someone sent for the police, and they took him away in the Black Maria to sober him up on strong green tea. By the time he was in the lockup and had confessed what he had done, it was far too late, for Caesar had already gulped down the meat. He suffered an undreamed-of agony in Gran's flower garden, and Daisy and I, unable to bear the sight of it, hiked up to the red rocks and shook there, wretchedly ripping to shreds the sand lilies that grew in the cracks. Flight was the only thing we could think of, but where could we go? We stared west at the mountains and quailed at the look of the stern white glacier; we wildly scanned the prairies for escape. "If only we were something besides kids! Besides girls!" mourned Daisy. I could not speak at all; I huddled in a niche of the rocks and cried.

No one in town, except, of course, her lodgers, had the slightest sympathy for Gran. The townsfolk allowed that Mr. Murphy was a drunk and was fighting Irish, but he had a heart and this was something that could never be said of Mrs. Placer. The neighbor who had called the police when he was chanting the *Dies Irae* before breakfast in that deafening monotone had said, "The poor guy is having some kind of a spell, so don't be rough on him, hear?" Mr. Murphy became, in fact, a kind of hero; some people, stretching a point, said he was a saint for the way that every day and twice on Sunday he sang a memorial Mass over Shannon's grave, now marked with a chipped, cheap plaster figure of Saint Francis. He withdrew from the world more and more, seldom venturing into the streets at all, except when he went to the bootlegger to get a new bottle to snuggle

into. All summer, all fall, we saw him as we passed by his yard,
sitting at his dilapidated table, enfeebled with gin, graying,
withering, turning his head ever and ever more slowly as he
maneuvered the protocol of the kings and the queens and the
knaves. Daisy and I could never stop to visit him again.

It went on like this, year after year. Daisy and I lived in a
mesh of lies and evasions, baffled and mean, like rats in a maze.
When we were old enough for beaux, we connived like sluts to
see them, but we would never admit to their existence until Gran
caught us out by some trick. Like this one, for example: Once,
at the end of a long interrogation, she said to me, "I'm more relieved than I can tell you that you *don't* have anything to do
with Jimmy Gilmore, because I happen to know that he is after
only one thing in a girl," and then, off guard in the loving
memory of sitting in the movies the night before with Jimmy,
not even holding hands, I defended him and defeated myself,
and Gran, smiling with success, said, "I *thought* you knew him.
It's a pretty safe rule of thumb that where there's smoke there's
fire." That finished Jimmy and me, for afterward I was nervous
with him and I confounded and alarmed and finally bored him
by trying to convince him, although the subject had not come
up, that I did not doubt his good intentions.

Daisy and I would come home from school, or, later, from
our jobs, with a small triumph or an interesting piece of news,
and if we forgot ourselves and, in our exuberance, told Gran,
we were hustled into court at once for cross-examination. Once,
I remember, while I was still in high school, I told her about
getting a part in a play. How very nice for me, she said, if that
kind of make-believe seemed to me worth while. But what was
my role? An old woman! A widow woman believed to be a
witch? She did not care a red cent, but she did have to laugh in
view of the fact that Miss Eccles, in charge of dramatics, had
almost run her down in her car. And I would forgive her, would
I not, if she did not come to see the play, and would not think
her eccentric for not wanting to see herself ridiculed in public?

My pleasure strangled, I crawled, joy-killed, to our third-
floor room. The room was small and its monstrous furniture was
too big and the rag rugs were repulsive, but it was bright. We

would not hang a blind at the window, and on this day I stood there staring into the mountains that burned with the sun. I feared the mountains, but at times like this their massiveness consoled me; they, at least, could not be gossiped about.

Why did we stay until we were grown? Daisy and I ask ourselves this question as we sit here on the bench in the municipal zoo, reminded of Mr. Murphy by the polar bear, reminded by the monkeys not of Shannon but of Mrs. Placer's insatiable gossips at their post-prandial feast.

"But how could we have left?" says Daisy, wringing her buttery hands. "It was the depression. We had no money. We had nowhere to go."

"All the same, we could have gone," I say, resentful still of the waste of all those years. "We could have come here and got jobs as waitresses. Or prostitutes, for that matter."

"I wouldn't have wanted to be a prostitute," says Daisy.

We agree that under the circumstances it would have been impossible for us to run away. The physical act would have been simple, for the city was not far and we could have stolen the bus fare or hitched a ride. Later, when we began to work as salesgirls in Kress's, it would have been no trick at all to vanish one Saturday afternoon with our week's pay, without so much as going home to say goodbye. But it had been infinitely harder than that, for Gran, as we now see, held us trapped by our sense of guilt. We were vitiated, and we had no choice but to wait, flaccidly, for her to die.

You may be sure we did not unlearn those years as soon as we put her out of sight in the cemetery and sold her house for a song to the first boob who would buy it. Nor did we forget when we left the town for another one, where we had jobs at a dude camp—the town where Daisy now lives with a happy husband and two happy sons. The succubus did not relent for years, and I can still remember, in the beginning of our days at the Lazy S 3, overhearing an edgy millionaire say to his wife, naming my name, "That girl gives me the cold shivers. One would think she had just seen a murder." Well, I had. For years, whenever I woke in the night in fear or pain or loneliness, I would increase my suffering by the memory of Shannon, and my tears were as bitter as poor Mr. Murphy's.

We have never been back to Adams. But we see that house plainly, with the hopvines straggling over the porch. The windows are hung with the cheapest grade of marquisette, dipped into coffee to impart to it an unwilling color, neither white nor tan but individual and spitefully unattractive. We see the wicker rockers and the swing, and through the screen door we dimly make out the slightly veering corridor, along one wall of which stands a glass-doored bookcase; when we were children, it had contained not books but stale old cardboard boxes filled with such things as W.C.T.U. tracts and anti-cigarette literature and newspaper clippings relating to sexual sin in the Christianized islands of the Pacific.

Even if we were able to close our minds' eyes to the past, Mr. Murphy would still be before us in the apotheosis of the polar bear. My pain becomes intolerable, and I am relieved when Daisy rescues us. "We've got to go," she says in a sudden panic. "I've got asthma coming on." We rush to the nearest exit of the city park and hail a cab, and, once inside it, Daisy gives herself an injection of adrenalin and then leans back. We are heart-broken and infuriated, and we cannot speak.

Two hours later, beside my train, we clutch each other as if we were drowning. We ought to go out to the nearest policeman and say, "We are not responsible women. You will have to take care of us because we cannot take care of ourselves." But gradually the storm begins to lull.

"You're sure you've got your ticket?" says Daisy. "You'll surely be able to get a roomette once you're on."

"I don't know about that," I say. "If there are any V.I.P.s on board, I won't have a chance. 'Spinsters and Orphans Last' is the motto of this line."

Daisy smiles. "I didn't care," she says, "but I had to laugh when I saw that woman nab the redcap you had signaled to. I had a good notion to give her a piece of my mind."

"It will be a miracle if I ever see my bags again," I say, mounting the steps of the train. "Do you suppose that black-guardly porter knows about the twenty-dollar gold piece in my little suitcase?"

"Anything's possible!" cries Daisy, and begins to laugh. She is so pretty, standing there in her bright-red linen suit and her black velvet hat. A solitary ray of sunshine comes through a broken pane in the domed vault of the train shed and lies on her shoulder like a silver arrow.

"So long, Daisy!" I call as the train begins to move.

She walks quickly along beside the train. "Watch out for pickpockets!" she calls.

"You, too!" My voice is thin and lost in the increasing noise of the speeding train wheels. "Goodbye, old dear!"

I go at once to the club car and I appropriate the writing table, to the vexation of a harried priest, who snatches up the telegraph pad and gives me a sharp look. I write Daisy approximately the same letter I always write her under this particular set of circumstances, the burden of which is that nothing for either of us can ever be as bad as the past before Gran mercifully died. In a postscript I add: "There is a Roman Catholic priest (that is to say, he is *dressed* like one) sitting behind me although all the chairs on the opposite side of the car are empty. I can only conclude that he is looking over my shoulder, and while I do not want to cause you any alarm, I think you would be advised to be on the lookout for any appearance of miraculous medals, scapulars, papist booklets, etc., in the shops of your town. It really makes me laugh to see the way he is pretending that all he wants is for me to finish this letter so that he can have the table."

I sign my name and address the envelope, and I give up my place to the priest, who smiles nicely at me, and then I move across the car to watch the fields as they slip by. They are alfalfa fields, but you can bet your bottom dollar that they are chocka-block with marijuana.

I begin to laugh. The fit is silent but it is devastating; it surges and rattles in my rib cage, and I turn my face to the window to avoid the narrow gaze of the Filipino bar boy. I must think of something sad to stop this unholy giggle, and I think of the polar bear. But even his bleak tragedy does not sober me. Wildly I fling open the newspaper I have brought and I pretend to be reading something screamingly funny. The words I see are in a Hollywood gossip column: "How a well-known starlet can get a divorce in Nevada without her crooner husband's consent, nobody knows. It won't be worth a plugged nickel here."

The Liberation

On the day Polly Bay decided to tell her Uncle Francis and his sister, her Aunt Jane, that in a week's time she was leaving their house and was going East to be married and to live in Boston, she walked very slowly home from Nevilles College, where she taught, dreading the startled look in their eyes and the woe and the indignation with which they would take her news. Hating any derangement of the status quo, her uncle, once a judge, was bound to cross-examine her intensively, and Aunt Jane, his perfect complement, would bolster him and baffle her. It was going to be an emotional and argumentative scene; her hands, which now were damp, would presently be dripping. She shivered with apprehension, fearing her aunt's asthma and her uncle's polemic, and she shook with rebellion, knowing how they would succeed in making her feel a traitor to her family, to the town, and to Colorado, and, obscurely, to her country.

Uncle Francis and Aunt Jane, like their dead kinsmen, Polly's father and her grandfather and her great-grandmother, had a vehement family and regional pride, and they counted it virtue in themselves that they had never been east of the Mississippi. They had looked on the departures of Polly's sisters and her cousins as acts of betrayal and even of disobedience. They had been distressed particularly by removals to the East, which were, they felt, iconoclastic and, worse, rude; how, they marveled, could this new generation be so ungrateful to those intrepid early Bays who in the forties had toiled in such peril and with such fortitude across the plains in a covered wagon and who with such perseverance had put down the roots for their traditions in this town that they had virtually made? Uncle Francis and Aunt Jane had done all in their power—through threats and sudden illnesses and cries of "Shame!"—to prevent these desertions, but, nevertheless, one by one, the members of the scapegrace generation had managed to fly, cut off without a penny, scolded to death, and spoken of thereafter as if they were unredeemed, treasonous, and debauched. Polly was the last, and her position, therefore, was the most uncomfortable of all; she and her aunt and uncle were the only Bays left in Adams, and she knew that because she was nearly thirty they had long ago stopped fearing that she, too, might go. As they frequently told her, in their candid way, they felt she had reached "a sensible age"—it was a struggle for them not to use the word "spinster" when they paid her this devious and crushing compliment. She knew perfectly well, because this, too, they spoke of, that they imagined she would still be teaching *Immensee* in German I years after they were dead, and would return each evening to the big, drafty house where they were born, and from which they expected to be carried in coffins ordered for them by Polly from Leonard Harper, the undertaker, whose mealy mouth and shifty eye they often talked about with detestation as they rocked and rocked through their long afternoons.

Polly had been engaged to Robert Fair for five months now and had kept his pretty ring in the desk in her office at college; she had not breathed a word to a soul. If she had spoken out when she came back from the Christmas holidays in her sister's Boston house, her uncle and aunt, with a margin of so much time for their forensic pleas before the college year was over, might have driven her to desperate measures; she might have had to flee, without baggage, in the middle of the night on a bus. Not wanting to begin her new life so haphazardly, she had guarded her secret, and had felt a hypocrite.

But she could not keep silent any longer; she had to tell them and start to pack her bags. She did not know how to present her announcement—whether to disarm them with joy or to stun them with a voice of adamant intention. Resenting the predicament, which so occupied her that her love was brusquely pushed aside, and feeling years younger than she was—an irritable adolescent, nerve-racked by growing pains—she now snatched leaves from the springtime bushes and tore them into shreds. It was late May and the purple lilacs were densely in blossom, offering their virtuous fragrance on the wind; the sun was tender on the yellow willow trees; the mountain range was blue and fair and free of haze. But Polly's senses were not at liberty today to take in these demure delights; she could not respond today at all to the flattering fortune that was to make her a June bride; she could not remember of her fiancé anything beyond his name, and, a little ruefully and a little cynically, she wondered if it was love of him or boredom with freshmen and with her aunt and uncle that had caused her to get engaged to him.

Although she loitered like a school child, she had at last to confront the house behind whose drawn blinds her aunt and uncle awaited her return, innocent of the scare they were presently to get and anticipating the modest academic news she brought each day to serve them with their tea. She was so un-willing that when she came in sight of the house she sat down on a bench at a trolley stop, under the dragging branches of a spruce tree, and opened the book her uncle had asked her to bring from the library. It was *The Heart of Midlothian.* She read with distaste; her uncle's pleasures were different from her own.

Neither the book, though, nor the green needles could hide from her interior eye that house where she had lived for seven years, since her father had died; her mother had been dead for many years and her sisters had long been gone—Fanny to Washington and Mary to Boston—but she had stayed on, quiet and unquestioning. Polly was an undemanding girl and she liked to teach and she had not been inspired to escape; she had had, until now, no reason to go elsewhere although, to be sure, these years had not been exclusively agreeable. For a short time, she had lived happily in an apartment by herself, waking each morn-ing to the charming novelty of being her own mistress. But Uncle Francis and Aunt Jane, both widowed and both bereft of their heartless children, had cajoled her and played tricks upon her will until she had consented to go and live with them. It was not so much because she was weak as it was because they were so extremely strong that she had at last capitulated out of fatigue and had brought her things in a van to unpack them, sighing, in two wallpapered rooms at the top of the stout brown house. This

odious house, her grandfather's, was covered with broad, unkempt shingles; it had a turret, and two bow windows within
which begonia and heliotrope fed on the powerful mountain
sun. Its rooms were huge, but since they were gorged with furniture and with garnishments and clumps and hoards of artifacts
of Bays, you had no sense of space in them and, on the contrary,
felt cornered and nudged and threatened by hanging lamps with
dangerous dependencies and by the dark, bucolic pictures of
Polly's forebears that leaned forward from the walls in their
insculptured brassy frames.

The house stood at the corner of Oxford Street and Pine,
and at the opposite end of the block, at the corner of Pine and
Plato (the college had sponsored the brainy place names), there
was another one exactly like it. It had been built as a wedding
present for Uncle Francis by Polly's grandfather, and here Uncle
Francis and his wife, Aunt Lacy, had reared an unnatural daughter and two unnatural sons, who had flown the coop, as he crossly
said, the moment they legally could; there was in his tone the
implication that if they had gone before they had come of age, he
would have haled them back, calling on the police if they
offered to resist. Uncle Francis had been born litigious; he had
been predestined to arraign and complain, to sue and sentence.

Aunt Jane and Uncle Richard had lived in Grandpa's
house, and their two cowed, effeminate sons had likewise vanished when they reached the age of franchise. When both Uncle
Richard and Aunt Lacy had been sealed into the Bay plot,
Uncle Francis had moved down the street to be with his sister for
the sake of economy and company, taking with him his legal
library, which, to this day, was still in boxes in the back hall, in
spite of the protests of Mildred, their truculent housekeeper.
Uncle Francis had then, at little cost, converted his own house
into four inconvenient apartments, from which he derived a
shockingly high income. A sign over the front door read, "The
Bay Arms."

Polly's parents' red brick house, across the street from Uncle
Francis's—not built but bought for them, also as a wedding
present—had been torn down. And behind the trolley bench on
which she sat there was the biggest and oldest family house of all,
the original Bay residence, a vast grotesquerie of native stone,

and in it, in the beginning of Polly's life, Great-grandmother had imperiously lived, with huge, sharp diamonds on her fichus and her velvet, talking without pause of red Indians and storms on the plains, because she could remember nothing else. The house was now a historical museum; it was called, not surprisingly, the Bay. Polly never looked at it without immediately remembering the intricate smell of the parlor, which had in it moss, must, belladonna, dry leaves, wet dust, oil of peppermint, and something that bound them all together—a smell of tribal history, perhaps, or the smell of a house where lived a half-cracked and haughty old woman who had come to the end of the line.

In those early days, there had been no other houses in this block, and the Bay children had had no playmates except each other. Four generations sat down to Sunday midday dinner every week at Great-grandmother's enormous table; the Presbyterian grace was half as long as a sermon; the fried rabbit was dry. On Christmas Eve, beneath a towering tree in Grandpa's house, sheepish Uncle Richard, as Santa Claus, handed round the presents while Grandpa sat in a central chair like a king on a throne and stroked his proud goatee. They ate turkey on Thanksgiving with Uncle Francis and Aunt Lacy, shot rockets and pinwheels off on the Fourth of July in Polly's family's back yard. Even now, though one of the houses was gone and another was given over to the display of minerals and wagon wheels, and though pressed-brick bungalows had sprung up all along the block, Polly never entered the street without the feeling that she came into a zone restricted for the use of her blood kin, for there lingered in it some energy, some air, some admonition that this was the territory of Bays and that Bays and ghosts of Bays were, and forever would be, in residence. It was easy for her to vest the wind in the spruce tree with her great-grandmother's voice and to hear it say, "Not a one of you knows the sensation of having a red Indian arrow whiz by your sunbonnet with wind enough to make the ribbons wave." On reflection, she understood the claustrophobia that had sent her sisters and cousins all but screaming out of town; horrified, she felt that her own life had been like a dream of smothering.

She was only pretending to read Walter Scott and the sun was setting and she was growing cold. She could not postpone any longer the discharge of the thunderbolt, and at last she weakly rose and crossed the street, feeling a convulsion of panic grind in her throat like a hard sob. Besides the panic, there was a heavy depression, an ebbing away of self-respect, a regret for the waste of so many years. Generations should not be mingled for daily fare, she thought; they are really contemptuous of one another, and the strong individuals, whether they belong to the older or the younger, impose on the meek their creeds and opinions, and, if they are strong enough, brook no dissent. Nothing can more totally subdue the passions than familial piety. Now Polly saw, appalled and miserably ashamed of herself, that she had never once insisted on her own identity in this house. She had dishonestly, supinely (thinking, however, that she was only being polite), allowed her aunt and uncle to believe that she was contented in their house, in sympathy with them, and keenly interested in the minutiae that preoccupied them: their ossifying arteries and their weakening eyes, their dizzy spells and migrant pains, their thrice-daily eucharist of pills and drops, the twinges in their old, uncovered bones. She had never disagreed with them, so how could they know that she did not, as they did, hate the weather? They assumed that she was as scandalized as they by Uncle Francis's tenants' dogs and children. They had no way of knowing that she was bored nearly to frenzy by their vicious quarrels with Mildred over the way she cooked their food.

In the tenebrous hall lined with closed doors, she took off her gloves and coat, and, squinting through the shadows, saw in the mirror that her wretchedness was plain in her drooping lips and her frowning forehead; certainly there was no sign at all upon her face that she was in love. She fixed her mouth into a bogus smile of courage, she straightened out her brow; with the faintest heart in the world she entered the dark front parlor, where the windows were always closed and the shades drawn nearly to the sill. A coal fire on this mild May day burned hot and blue in the grate.

They sat opposite each other at a round, splayfooted table under a dim lamp with a beaded fringe. On the table, amid the tea things, there was a little mahogany casket containing the props with which, each day, they documented their reminiscences of murders, fires, marriages, bankruptcies, and of the triumphs and the rewards of the departed Bays. It was open, showing cracked photographs, letters sallow-inked with age, flaccid and furry newspaper clippings, souvenir spoons flecked with venomous green, little white boxes holding petrified morsels of wedding cake. As Polly came into the room, Aunt Jane reached out her hand and, as if she were pulling a chance from a hat, she picked a newspaper clipping out of the box and said, "I don't think you have ever told Polly the story of the time you were in that train accident in the Royal Gorge. It's such a yarn."

Her uncle heard Polly then and chivalrously half rose from his chair; tall and white-haired, he was distinguished, in a dour way, and dapper in his stiff collar and his waistcoat piped with white. He said, "At last our strayed lamb is back in the fold." The figure made Polly shiver.

"How late you are!" cried Aunt Jane, thrilled at this small deviation from routine. "A department meeting?" If there had been a department meeting, the wreck in the Royal Gorge might be saved for another day.

But they did not wait for her answer. They were impelled, egocentrically and at length, to tell their own news, to explain why it was that they had not waited for her but had begun their tea. Uncle Francis had been hungry, not having felt quite himself earlier in the day and having, therefore, eaten next to nothing at lunch, although the soufflé that Mildred had made was far more edible than customary. He had several new symptoms and was going to the doctor tomorrow; he spoke with infinite peace of mind. Painstakingly then, between themselves, they discussed the advisability of Aunt Jane's making an appointment at the beauty parlor for the same hour Uncle Francis was seeing Dr. Wilder; they could in this way share a taxi. And what was the name of that fellow who drove the Town Taxi whom they both found so cautious and well-mannered? Bradley, was it? They might have him drive them up a little way into the mountains for the view; but, no, Francis might have got a bad report and Jane might be tired after her baking under the dryer. It would be better if they came straight home. Sometimes they went on in this way for hours.

Polly poured herself a cup of tea, and Aunt Jane said, as she had said probably three thousand times in the past seven years, "You may say what you like, there is simply nothing to take the place of a cup of tea at the end of the day."

Uncle Francis reached across the table and took the newspaper clipping from under his sister's hand. He adjusted his glasses and glanced at the headlines, smiling. "There was a great deal of comedy in that tragedy," he said.

"Tell Polly about it," said Aunt Jane. Polly knew the details of this story by heart—the number of the locomotive and the name of the engineer and the passengers' injuries, particularly her uncle's, which, though minor, had been multitudinous.

Amazing herself, Polly said, "Don't!" And, amazed by her, they stared.

"Why, Polly, what an odd thing to say!" exclaimed Aunt Jane. "My dear, is something wrong?"

She decided to take them aback without preamble—it was the only way—and so she said, "Nothing's wrong. Everything's right at last. I am going to be married ten days from today to a teacher at Harvard and I am going to Boston to live."

They behaved like people on a stage; Aunt Jane put her teacup down, rattling her spoon, and began to wring her hands; Uncle Francis, holding his butter knife as it were a gavel, glared.

"What are you talking about, darling?" he cried. "Married? What do you mean?"

Aunt Jane wheezed, signaling her useful asthma, which, however, did not oblige her. "Boston!" she gasped. "What ever for?"

Polly returned her uncle's magisterial look, but she did so obliquely, and she spoke to her cuffs when she said, "I mean 'married,' the way you were married to Aunt Lacy and the way Aunt Jane was married to Uncle Richard. I am in love with a man named Robert Fair and *he* is with *me* and we're going to be married."

"How lovely," said Aunt Jane, who, sight unseen, hated Robert Fair.

"Lovely perhaps," said Uncle Francis the magistrate, "and perhaps not. You might, if you please, do us the honor of enlightening us as to the qualifications of Mr. Fair to marry and export you. To the best of my knowledge, I have never heard of him."

"I'm quite sure we don't know him," said Aunt Jane; she coughed experimentally, but her asthma was still in hiding.

"No, you don't know him," Polly said. "He has never been in the West." She wished she could serenely drink her tea while she talked, but she did not trust her hand. Fixing her eyes on a maidenhair fern in a brass jardiniere on the floor, she told them how she had first met Robert Fair at her sister Mary's cottage in Edgartown the summer before.

"You never told us," said Uncle Francis reprovingly. "I thought you said the summer had been a mistake. Too expensive. Too hot. I thought you agreed with Jane and me that summer in the East was hard on the constitution." (She had; out of habit she had let them deprecate the East, which she had loved at first sight, had allowed them to tell her that she had had a poor time when, in truth, she had never been so happy.)

Shocked by her duplicity, Aunt Jane said, "We ought to have suspected something when you went back to Boston for Christmas with Mary instead of resting here beside your own hearth fire."

Ignoring this sanctimonius accusation, Polly continued, and told them as much of Robert Fair as she thought they deserved to know, eliding some of his history—for there was a divorce in it—but as she spoke, she could not conjure his voice or his face, and he remained as hypothetical to her as to them, a circumstance that alarmed her and one that her astute uncle sensed.

"You don't seem head over heels about this Boston fellow," he said.

"I'm nearly thirty," replied his niece. "I'm not sixteen. Wouldn't it be unbecoming at my age if I *were* lovesick?" She was by no means convinced of her argument, for her uncle had that effect on her; he could make her doubt anything—the testimony of her own eyes, the judgments of her own intellect. Again, and in vain, she called on Robert Fair to materialize in this room that was so hostile to him and, through his affection, bring a persuasive color to her cheeks. She did not question the power of love nor did she question, specifically, the steadfastness of her own love, but she did observe, with some dismay, that, far from conquering all, love lazily sidestepped practical problems; it was no help in this interview; it seemed not to cease but to be temporarily at a standstill.

Her uncle said, "Sixteen, thirty, sixty, it makes no difference. It's true I wouldn't like it if you were wearing your heart on your sleeve, but, my Lord, dear, I don't see the semblance of a light in your eye. You look quite sad. Doesn't Polly strike you as looking downright blue, Jane? If Mr. Fair makes you so doleful, it seems to me you're better off with us."

"It's not a laughing matter," snapped Aunt Jane, for Uncle Francis, maddeningly, had chuckled. It was a way he had in disputation; it was intended to enrage and thereby rattle his adversary. He kept his smile, but for a moment he held his tongue while his sister tried a different tack. "What I don't see is why you have to go to Boston, Polly," she said. "Couldn't he teach Italian at Nevilles just as well as at Harvard?"

Their chauvinism was really staggering. When Roddy, Uncle Francis's son, went off to take a glittering job in Brazil, Aunt Jane and his father had nearly reduced this stalwart boy to kicks and tears by reiterating that if there had been anything of worth or virtue in South America, the grandparent Bays would have settled there instead of in the Rocky Mountains.

"I don't think Robert would like it here," said Polly.

"What wouldn't he like about it?" Aunt Jane bridled. "I thought our college had a distinguished reputation. Your great-grandfather, one of the leading founders of it, was a man of culture, and unless I am sadly misinformed, his humanistic spirit is still felt on the campus. Did you know that his critical study of Isocrates is *highly* esteemed among classical scholars?"

"I mean I don't think he would like the West," said Polly, rash in her frustration.

She could have bitten her tongue out for the indiscretion, because her jingoistic uncle reddened instantly and menacingly, and he banged on the table and shouted, "How does he know he doesn't like the West? You've just told us he's never been farther west than Ohio. How does he dare to presume to damn what he doesn't know?"

"I didn't say he damned the West. I didn't even say he didn't like it. I said *I* thought he wouldn't."

"Then *you* are presuming," he scolded. "I am impatient with Easterners who look down their noses at the West and call us crude and barbaric. But Westerners who renounce and denounce and derogate their native ground are worse."

"Far worse," agreed Aunt Jane. "What can have come over you to turn the man you intend to marry against the land of your forebears?"

Polly had heard it all before. She wanted to clutch her head in her hands and groan with helplessness; even more, she wished that this were the middle of next week.

"We three are the last left of the Bays in Adams," pursued Aunt Jane, insinuating a quaver into her firm, stern voice. "And Francis and I will not last long. You'll only be burdened and bored with us a little while longer."

"We have meant to reward you liberally for your loyalty," said her uncle. "The houses will be yours when we join our ancestors."

In the dark parlor, they leaned toward her over their cups of cold tea, so tireless in their fusillade that she had no chance to deny them or to defend herself. Was there to be, they mourned, at last not one Bay left to lend his name and presence to municipal celebrations, to the laying of cornerstones and the opening of fairs? Polly thought they were probably already fretting over who would see that the grass between the family graves was mown.

Panicked, she tried to recall how other members of her family had extricated themselves from these webs of casuistry. Now she wished that she had more fully explained her circumstances to Robert Fair and had told him to come and fetch her away, for he, uninvolved, could afford to pay the ransom more easily than she. But she had wanted to spare him such a scene as this; they would not have been any more reticent with him; they would have, with this same arrogance—and this underhandedness—used their advanced age and family honor to twist the argument away from its premise.

Darkness had shrunk the room to the small circle where they sat in the thin light of the lamp; it seemed to her that their reproaches and their jeremiads took hours before they recommenced the bargaining Aunt Jane had started.

Reasonably, in a judicious voice, Uncle Francis said, "There is no reason at all, if Mr. Fair's attainments are as you describe, that he can't be got an appointment to our Romance Language Department. What is the good of my being a trustee if I can't render such a service once in a way?"

As if this were a perfectly wonderful and perfectly surprising solution, Aunt Jane enthusiastically cried, "But of course you can! That would settle everything. Polly can eat her cake and have it, too. Wouldn't you give them your house, Francis?"

"I'd propose an even better arrangement. Alone here, Jane, you and I would rattle. Perhaps we would move into one of my apartments and the Robert Fairs could have this house. Would that suit you?"

"It would, indeed it would," said Aunt Jane. "I have been noticing the drafts here more and more."

"I don't ask you to agree today, Polly," said Uncle Francis. "But think it over. Write your boy a letter tonight and tell him what your aunt and I are willing to do for him. The gift of a house, as big a house as this, is not to be scoffed at by young people just starting out."

Her "boy," Robert, had a tall son who in the autumn would enter Harvard. "Robert has a house," said Polly, and she thought of its dark-green front door with the brilliant brass trimmings; on Brimmer Street, at the foot of Beacon Hill, its garden faced the Charles. Nothing made her feel more safe and more mature than the image of that old and handsome house.

"He could sell it," said her indomitable aunt.

"He could rent it," said her practical uncle. "That would give you additional revenue."

The air was close; it was like the dead of night in a sealed room and Polly wanted to cry for help. She had not hated the West till now, she had not hated her relatives till now; indeed, till now she had had no experience of hate at all. Surprising as the emotion was—for it came swiftly and authoritatively—it nevertheless cleared her mind and, outraged, she got up and flicked the master switch to light up the chandelier. Her aunt and uncle blinked. She did not sit down again but stood in the doorway to deliver her valediction. "I don't want Robert to come here because I don't want to live here any longer. I want to live my own life."

"Being married is hardly living one's own life," said Aunt Jane.

At the end of her tether now, Polly all but screamed at them, "We *won't* live here and that's that! You talk of my presuming, but how can *you* presume to boss not only me but a man you've never even seen? I don't want your houses! I hate these houses! It's true—I hate, I despise, I abominate the West!"

So new to the articulation of anger, she did it badly and, ashamed to death, began to cry. Though they were hurt, they were forgiving, and both of them rose and came across the room, and Aunt Jane, taking her in a spidery embrace, said, "There. You go upstairs and have a bath and rest and we'll discuss it later. Couldn't we have some sherry, Francis? It seems to me that all our nerves are unstrung."

Polly's breath toiled against her sobs. but all the same she took her life in her hands and she said, "There's nothing further to discuss. I am leaving. I am not coming back."

Now, for the first time, the old brother and sister exchanged a look of real anxiety; they seemed, at last, to take her seriously; each waited for the other to speak. It was Aunt Jane who hit upon the new gambit. "I mean, dear, that we will discuss the wedding. You have given us very short notice but I daresay we can manage."

"There is to be no wedding," said Polly. "We are just going to be married at Mary's house. Fanny is coming up to Boston."

"Fanny has known all along?" Aunt Jane was insulted. "And all this time you've lived under our roof and sat at our table and never told *us* but told your sisters, who abandoned you?"

"Abandoned me? For God's sake, Aunt Jane, they had their lives to lead!"

"Don't use that sort of language in this house, young lady," said Uncle Francis.

"I apologize. I'm sorry. I am just so sick and tired of—"

"Of course you're sick and tired," said the adroit old woman. "You've had a heavy schedule this semester. No wonder you're all nerves and tears."

"Oh, it isn't that! Oh, leave me alone!"

And, unable to withstand a fresh onslaught of tears, she rushed to the door. When she had closed it upon them, she heard her aunt say, "I simply can't believe it. There must be some way out. Why, Francis, we would be left altogether *alone,*" and there was real terror in her voice.

Polly locked the door to her bedroom and dried her eyes and bathed their lids with witch hazel, the odor of which made her think of her Aunt Lacy, who, poor simple creature, had had to die to escape this family. Polly remembered that every autumn Aunt Lacy had petitioned Uncle Francis to let her take her children home for a visit to her native Vermont, but she had never been allowed to go. Grandpa, roaring, thumping his stick, Uncle Francis bombarding her with rhetoric and using the word "duty" repeatedly, Polly's father scathing her with sarcasm, Aunt Jane slyly confusing her with red herrings had kept her an exhausted prisoner. Her children, as a result, had scorned their passive mother and had wounded her, and once they finally escaped, they had not come back—not for so much as a visit. Aunt Lacy had died not having seen any of her grandchildren; in the last years of her life she did nothing but cry. Polly's heart ached for the plight of that gentle, frightened woman. How lucky *she* was that the means of escape had come to her before it was too late! In her sister's Boston drawing room, in a snowy twilight, Robert Fair's proposal of marriage had seemed to release in her an inexhaustible wellspring of life; until that moment she had not known that she was dying, that she was being killed—by inches, but surely killed—by her aunt and uncle and by the green yearlings in her German classes and by the dogmatic monotony of the town's provincialism. She shuddered to think of her narrow escape from wasting away in these arid foothills, never knowing the cause or the name of her disease.

Quiet, herself again, Polly sat beside the window and looked out at the early stars and the crescent moon. Now that she had finally taken her stand, she was invulnerable, even though she knew that the brown sherry was being put ceremoniously on a tray, together with ancestral Waterford glasses, and though she knew that her aunt and uncle had not given up—that they had, on the contrary, just begun. And though she knew that for the

last seven days of her life in this house she would be bludgeoned
with the most splenetic and most defacing of emotions, she knew
that the worst was over; she knew that she would survive, as her
sisters and her cousins had survived. In the end, her aunt and
uncle only *seemed* to survive; dead on their feet for most of their
lives, they had no personal history; their genesis had not been
individual—it had only been a part of a dull and factual plan.
And they had been too busy honoring their family to love it, too
busy defending the West even to look at it. For all their pride
in their surroundings, they had never contemplated them at all
but had sat with the shades drawn, huddled under the steel
engravings. They and her father had lived their whole lives on
the laurels of their grandparents; their goal had already been
reached long before their birth.

The mountains had never looked so superb to her. She
imagined a time, after Uncle Francis and Aunt Jane were dead,
when the young Bays and their wives and husbands might come
back, free at last to admire the landscape, free to go swiftly
through the town in the foothills without so much as a glance at
the family memorials and to gain the high passes and the peaks
and the glaciers. They would breathe in the thin, lovely air of
summits, and in their mouths there would not be a trace of the
dust of the prairies where, as on a treadmill, Great-grandfather
Bay's oxen plodded on and on into eternity.

The next days were for Polly at once harrowing and delight-
ful. She suffered at the twilight hour (the brown sherry had become a daily custom, and she wondered if her aunt and uncle
naïvely considered getting her drunk and, in this condition,
persuading her to sign an unconditional indenture) and all
through dinner as, by turns self-pitying and contentious, they
sought to make her change her mind. Or, as they put it, "come to
her senses." At no time did they accept the fact that she was
going. They wrangled over summer plans in which she was included; they plotted anniversary speeches in the Bay museum;
one afternoon Aunt Jane even started making a list of miners'
families among whom Polly was to distribute Christmas baskets.

But when they were out of her sight and their nagging
voices were out of her hearing, they were out of her mind, and in

it, instead, was Robert Fair, in his rightful place. She graded examination papers tolerantly, through a haze; she packed her new clothes into her new suitcases and emptied her writing desk completely. On these starry, handsome nights, her dreams were charming, although, to be sure, she sometimes woke from them to hear the shuffle of carpet slippers on the floor below her as her insomniac aunt or uncle paced. But before sadness or rue could overtake her, she burrowed into the memory of her late dream.

The strain of her euphoria and her aunt's and uncle's antipodean gloom began at last to make her edgy, and she commenced to mark the days off on her calendar and even to reckon the hours. On the day she met her classes for the last time and told her colleagues goodbye and quit the campus forever, she did not stop on the first floor of the house but went directly to her room, only pausing at the parlor door to tell Aunt Jane and Uncle Francis that she had a letter to get off. Fraudulently humble, sighing, they begged her to join them later on for sherry. "The days are growing longer," said Aunt Jane plaintively, "but they are growing fewer."

Polly had no letter to write. She had a letter from Robert Fair to read, and although she knew it by heart already, she read it again several times. He shared her impatience; his students bored him, too; he said he had tried to envision her uncle's house, so that he could imagine her in a specific place, but he had not been able to succeed, even with the help of her sister. He wrote, "The house your malicious sister Mary describes could not exist. Does Aunt Jane *really* read Ouida?"

She laughed aloud. She felt light and purged, as if she had finished a fever. She went to her dressing table and began to brush her hair and to gaze, comforted, upon her young and loving face. She was so lost in her relief that she was pretty, and that she was going to be married and was going away, that she heard neither the telephone nor Mildred's feet upon the stairs, and the housekeeper was in the room before Polly had turned from her pool.

"It's your sister calling you from Boston," said Mildred with ice-cold contempt; she mirrored her employers. "I heard those operators back East giving themselves *some* airs with their la-di-da way of talking."

Clumsy with surprise and confusion (Mary's calls to her were rare and never frivolous), and sorry that exigency and not calm plan took her downstairs again, she reeled into that smothering front hall where hat trees and cane stands stood like people. The door to the parlor was closed, but she knew that behind it Aunt Jane and Uncle Francis were listening.

When Mary's far-off, mourning voice broke to Polly the awful, the impossible, the unbelievable news that Robert Fair had died that morning of the heart disease from which he had intermittently suffered for some years, Polly, wordless and dry-eyed, contracted into a nonsensical, contorted position and gripped the telephone as if this alone could keep her from drowning in the savage flood that had come from nowhere.

"Are you there, Polly? Can you hear me, darling?" Mary's anxious voice came louder and faster. "Do you want me to come out to you? Or can you come on here now?"

"I can't come now," said Polly. "There's nothing you can do for me." There had always been rapport between these sisters, and it had been deeper in the months since Robert Fair had appeared upon the scene to rescue and reward the younger woman. But it was shattered; the bearer of ill tidings is seldom thanked. "How can you help me?" Polly demanded, shocked and furious. "You can't bring him back to life."

"I can help bring you back to life," her sister said. "You must get out of *there*, Polly. It's more important now than ever."

"Do you think that was why I was going to marry him? Just to escape this house and this town?"

"No, no! Control yourself! We'd better not try to talk any more now—you call me when you can."

The parlor door opened, revealing Uncle Francis with a glass of sherry in his hand.

"Wait, Mary! Don't hang up!" Polly cried. There was a facetious air about her uncle; there was something smug. "I'll get the sleeper from Denver tonight," she said.

When she hung up, her uncle opened the door wider to welcome her to bad brown sherry; they had not turned on the lights, and Aunt Jane, in the twilight, sat in her accustomed place.

"Poor angel," said Uncle Francis.

"I am so sorry, so very sorry," said Aunt Jane.

When Polly said nothing but simply stared at their impassive faces, Uncle Francis said, "I think I'd better call up Wilder. You ought to have a sedative and go straight to bed."

"I'm going straight to Boston," said Polly.

"But why?" said Aunt Jane.

"Because he's there. I love him and he's there."

They tried to detain her; they tried to force the sherry down her throat; they told her she must be calm and they asked her to remember that at times like this one needed the love and the support of one's blood kin.

"I am going straight to Boston," she repeated, and turned and went quickly up the stairs. They stood at the bottom, calling to her: "You haven't settled your affairs. What about the bank?" "Polly, get hold of yourself! It's terrible, I'm heartbroken for you, but it's not the end of the world."

She packed nothing; she wanted nothing here—not even the new clothes she had bought in which to be a bride. She put on a coat and a hat and gloves and a scarf and put all the money she had in her purse and went downstairs again. Stricken but diehard, they were beside the front door.

"Don't go!" implored Aunt Jane.

"You need us now more than ever!" her uncle cried.

"And we need you. Does that make no impression on you, Polly? Is your heart that cold?"

She paid no attention to them at all and pushed them aside and left the house. She ran to the station to get the last train to Denver, and once she had boarded it, she allowed her grief to overwhelm her. She felt chewed and mauled by the niggling hypochondriacs she had left behind, who had fussily tried to appropriate even her own tragedy. She felt sullied by their disrespect and greed.

How lonely I have been, she thought. And then, not fully knowing what she meant by it but believing in it faithfully, she said half aloud, "I am not lonely now."

A Reading Problem

One of the great hardships of my childhood—and there were many, as many, I suppose, as have ever plagued a living creature—was that I could never find a decent place to read. If I tried to read at home in the living room, I was constantly pestered by someone saying, "For goodness' sake, Emily, move where it's light. You're going to ruin your eyes and no two ways about it," or "You ought to be outdoors with the other youngsters getting some roses in your cheeks." Of course, I knew how to reply to these kill-joy injunctions; to the first I said, "They're *my* eyes," and to the second, "Getting some brains in my head is more important than getting any so-called roses in my cheeks." But even when I had settled the hash of that Paul Pry—Mother, usually, but sometimes a visiting aunt, or even a bossy neighbor— I was cross and could no longer concentrate. The bedroom I shared with my sister Stella was even worse, because Stella was always in it, making an inventory of her free samples out loud, singing Camp Fire Girl songs, practicing ballet steps and giggling whenever she made a mistake; she was one of the most vacant people I have ever known.

At one certain time of year, I could read up in the mountains, in any number of clearings and dingles and amphitheaters, and that was in the fall. But in the winter it was too cold, and in the spring there were wood ticks, and in the summer there were snakes. I had tried a pinewoods I was very fond of for several weeks one summer, but it was no good, because at the end of every paragraph I had to get up and stamp my feet and shout and describe an agitated circle on the ground with a stick to warn the rattlers to stay away from me.

The public library was better, but not much. The librarian,

Mrs. Looby, a fussbudgety old thing in a yellow wig and a hat planted with nasturtiums, was so strict about the silent rule that she evicted children who popped their gum or cracked their knuckles, and I was a child who did both as a matter of course and constantly. Besides, she was forever coming into the children's section like a principal making rounds, and leaning over you to see what you were reading; half the time she disapproved and recommended something else, something either so dry you'd go to sleep reading it or so mushy you'd throw up. Moreover, our dog, Reddie, loved to follow me to the library, and quite often, instead of waiting outside under the lilac bush, as he was supposed to do, he would manage to get in when someone opened the door. He didn't come to see me; he came to tease Mrs. Looby, who abominated anything that walked on four legs. He would sit on his haunches in front of her desk, wagging his tail and laughing, with his long pink tongue hanging out. "Shoo!" Mrs. Looby would scream, waving her hands at him. "Emily Vanderpool, you get this pesky dog of yours out of here this minute! The very idea! Quick, Emily, or I'll call the dogcatcher! I'll call the dogcatcher. I will positively call the dogcatcher if a dog ever comes into my library again." I had to give up the library altogether after one unlucky occasion when Reddie stood on his hind legs and put his paws on top of her high desk. She had had her back to him, and, thinking she heard a customer, she turned, saying in her library whisper, "Good afternoon, and what may I do for you this afternoon?" and faced the grinning countenance of my dog. That time, in her wrath and dismay, she clutched her head in her hands and dislodged her hat and then her wig, so that a wide expanse of baldness showed, and everyone in the children's section dived into the stacks and went all to pieces.

For a while after that, I tried the lobby of the downtown hotel, the Goldmoor, where the permanent residents, who were all old men, sat in long-waisted rocking chairs, rocking and spitting tobacco juice into embossed cuspidors and talking in high, offended, lonesome voices about their stomach-aches and their insomnia and how the times had changed. All in the world the old duffers had left was time, which, hour after hour, they had to kill. People like that, who are bored almost to extinction, think that everyone else is, too, and if they see someone reading a book, they say to themselves, "I declare, here's somebody worse off than I am. The poor soul's really hard up to have to depend on a book, and it's my bounden Christian duty to help him pass the time," and they start talking to you. If you want company on the streetcar or the bus or the interurban, open a book and you're all set. At first, the old men didn't spot me, because I always sat in one of the two bow windows in a chair that was half hidden by a potted sweet-potato plant, which, according to local legend, dated from the nineteenth century—and well it might have, since it was the size of a small-size tree. My chair was crowded in between this and a table on which was a clutter of seedy Western souvenirs—a rusted, beat-up placer pan with samples of ore in it, some fossils and some arrowheads, a toma-hawk, a powder horn, and the shellacked tail of a beaver that was supposed to have been trapped by a desperado named Mountain Jim Nugent, who had lived in Estes Park in the seventies. It was this tabletop historical museum that made me have to give up the hotel, for one day, when I was spang in the middle of *Hans Brinker*, two of the old men came over to it to have a whining, cantankerous argument about one of the rocks in the placer pan, which one maintained was pyrites and the other maintained was not. (That was about as interesting as their conversations ever got.) They were so angry that if they hadn't been so feeble I think they would have thrown the rocks at each other. And then one of them caught sight of me and commenced to cackle. "Lookit what we got here," he said. "A little old kid in a middy reading windies all by her lonesome."

I had been taught to be courteous to my elders, so I looked up and gave the speaker a sickly smile and returned to my book, which now, of course, I could not follow. His disputant became his ally, and they carried on, laughing and teasing me as if I were a monkey that had suddenly entered their precincts for the sole purpose of amusing them. They asked me why I wasn't at the movies with my sweetheart, they asked me how I'd like to be paddled with that stiff old beaver tail of Mountain Jim's, and they asked me to sing them a song. All the other old men, de-lighted at this small interruption in their routine of spitting and complaining, started rubbernecking in my direction, grinning and chuckling, and a couple of them came shuffling over to watch the fun. I felt as if I had a fever of a hundred and five, because of the blush that spread over my entire person, including my insides. I was not only embarrassed, I was as mad as anything to be hemmed in by this phalanx of giggling old geezers who looked like a flock of turkey gobblers. "Maybe she ran away from home," said one of them. "Hasn't been any transients in this hotel since that last Watkins fella. Fella by the name of Fletcher. Is your name Fletcher, Missy?" Another said, "I think it's mighty nice of her to come and pay us a call instead of going to the show with her best beau," and when a third said, "I bet I know where there's a Hershey bar not a thousand miles from here," I got up and, in a panic, ducked through the lines and fled; taking candy from a strange old man was the quickest way to die like a dog from poison.

So the hotel after that was out. Then I tried the depot, but it was too dirty and noisy; a couple of times I went and sat in the back of the Catholic church, but it was dark there, and besides I didn't feel right about it, because I was a United Presbyterian in good standing. Once, I went into the women's smoking room in the library at the college, but it was full of worried-looking old-maid summer-school students who came back year after year to work on their Master's degrees in Education, and they asked me a lot of solemn questions, raising their voices as if I were deaf. Besides, it was embarrassing to watch them smoke; they were furtive and affected, and they coughed a good deal. I could smoke better than that and I was only ten; I mean the one time I had smoked I did it better—a friend and I each smoked a cubeb she had pinched from her tubercular father.

But at last I found a peachy place—the visitors' waiting room outside the jail in the basement of the courthouse. There were seldom any visitors, because there were seldom any prisoners, and when, on rare occasions, there were, the visitors were too edgy or too morose to pay any heed to me. The big, cool room had nothing in it but two long benches and a wicker table, on which was spread out free Christian Science literature. The sheriff, Mr. Starbird, was very sympathetic with me, for he liked to read himself and that's what he did most of the time (his job was a snap; Adams was, on the whole, a law-abiding town) in his office that adjoined the waiting room; he read and read, not lifting his eyes from Sax Rohmer even when he was rolling a cigarette. Once, he said he wished his own daughters, Laverne, thirteen, and Ida, sixteen, would follow my example, instead of, as he put it, "rimfirin' around the county with paint on their faces and spikes on their heels and not caring two hoots for anything on God's green earth except what's got on pants." Mr. Starbird and I became good friends, although we did not talk much, since we were busy reading. One time, when we were both feeling restless, he locked me up in a cell so I could see how it felt; I kind of liked it. And another time he put handcuffs on me, but they were too big.

At the time I discovered the jail, in the first hot days in June, I was trying to memorize the books of the Bible. If I got them by heart and could name them off in proper order and without hesitating or mispronouncing, I would be eligible to receive an award of a New Testament at Sunday School, and if there was one thing I liked, it was prizes. So every day for several weeks I spent the whole afternoon more or less in jail, reading whatever fun thing I had brought along (*Rebecca of Sunnybrook Farm, Misunderstood Betsy, Trudy Goes to Boarding School*) and then working away at I Samuel, II Samuel, I Kings, II Kings, whispering so as not to disturb Mr. Starbird. Sometimes, on a really hot day, he would send out for two bottles of Dr. Pepper.

One blistering Saturday, when I was as limp as a rag after walking through the sun down the hill and into the hot valley where the courthouse was, I got to the stairs leading to the waiting room and was met by the most deafening din of men yelling and bars rattling and Mr. Starbird hollering "Quiet there, you bastards!" at the top of his voice. I was shocked and scared but very curious, and I went on down the steps, hearing the vilest imaginable language spewing out from the direction of the cells. I had just sat down on the edge of one of the benches and was opening *Tom Sawyer Abroad* when Mr. Starbird, bright red in the face, came in, brushing his hands. Two sweating deputies followed him. "Not today, Emily," said Mr. Starbird when he saw me. "We got some tough customers today, worse luck. And me with a new Fu."

The prisoners were moonshiners, he told me as he led me

by the arm to the stairs, whose still up in the mountains had been discovered, because they had drunk too much of their own rotgut and had got loose-tongued and had gone around bragging at the amusement park up at the head of the canyon. There were five of them, and they had had to be disarmed of sawed-off shotguns, although, as Mr. Starbird modestly pointed out, this wasn't much of a job, since they had been three sheets in the wind. "Whew!" said the sheriff. "They got a breath on 'em like the whole shootin' match of St. Louis before the Volstead Act." I told him I didn't mind (it would give me considerable prestige with my brother and my friends to be on hand if one of them should try to make a break, and I would undoubtedly get my name in the paper: "Emily Vanderpool, daughter of Mr. and Mrs. Peter Vanderpool, witnessed the attempted escape of the desperate criminals. Emily is to receive an award at the United Presbyterian Church on July 29th"), but Mr. Starbird told me, a little sharply, to go on now, and I had no choice but to go.

Go where? I had exhausted every possibility in town. I thought of going to the Safeway, where my father was the manager, and asking him if I could read in his office, but I knew how that would go over on a busy Saturday when the farmers and the mountain people were in town buying potatoes and side meat; my father didn't have Mr. Starbird's temperament. Then, vaguely, I considered the front porch of a haunted house at the top of Carlyle Hill but rejected it when I remembered a recent rumor that there was a nest of bats under the eaves; I didn't want them in my hair, using my pigtails to swing on. I wasn't too sure I could read anyhow, because I was so excited over the prisoners, but it was far too hot to roller-skate, too hot to explore the dump—too hot, indeed, for anything but sitting quietly beside the lockup.

I started in the direction of home in a desultory way, stopping at every drinking fountain, window-shopping, going methodically through the ten-cent stores, looking for money in the gutters. I walked down the length of the main street, going toward the mountains, over whose summits hung a pale heat haze; the pavement was soft, and when it and the shimmering sidewalk ended, I had to walk in the red dirt road, which was so dusty that after a few steps my legs, above the tops of my socks, looked burned—not sunburned, *burned*.

At the outskirts of town, beside the creek, there was a tourist camp where funny-looking people pitched tents and filled up the wire trash baskets with tin cans; sometimes, on a still night, you could hear them singing state songs, and now and again there was the sound of an accordion or a harmonica playing a jig. Today there was only one tent up in the grounds, a sagging, ragged white one, and it looked forlorn, like something left behind. Nearby was parked a Model T, dark red with rust where its sky-blue paint had worn off, and to it was attached a trailer; I knew how hot the leather seat of that car would be and I could all but hear the sun beating on the top of it like hailstones. There wasn't a soul in sight, and there wasn't a sound nearby except for a couple of magpies ranting at each other in the trees and the occasional digestive croak of a bullfrog. Along the creek, there was a line of shady cottonwoods, and I decided to rest there for a while and cool off my feet in the water.

After I had washed as well as I could, I leaned back against the tree trunk, my feet still in the water, and opened the Bible to the table of contents, and then I closed my eyes so that I wouldn't cheat; I started reciting, softly and clearly and proud of myself. I had just got to Ezra, having gone so far very fast without a hitch, when a noise caused me to fling back my eyelids and to discover that a man's big foot in a high buttoned shoe had materialized on the ground beside me. Startled, I looked up into the bearded face of a tall man in black clothes (black suit, black string tie, black-rimmed eyeglasses, black hat—the hat was dented in such a way that it looked like a gravy boat) and into the small brown eyes of a girl about Stella's age, who wore a tennis visor and a long, dirty white thing that looked like her nightgown.

"Greetings, Christian soldier," said the man, in a deep, rich Southern accent, and he offered me a large, warty hand. "Evangelist Gerlash is the name, and this is my girl, Opal."

Opal put her hand on my head and said, "Peace."

"Same to you," I said awkwardly, and took my feet out of the water. "You can have this tree if you want. I was just leaving."

I started to get up, but Evangelist Gerlash motioned me to stay where I was, and he said, "It uplifts my heavy heart and it uplifts Opal's to find a believer in our wanderings through this godless world. All too seldom do we find a person applying themself to the Book. Oh, sister, keep to this path your youthful feet have started on and shun the Sodoms *and* the Gomorrahs *and* the Babylons!"

My youthful feet were so wet I was having a struggle to put on my socks, and I thought, Peace! That's all he knows about it. There's not an inch of peace or privacy in this whole town.

"Seek truth and *not* the fleshpots!" said the man. "Know light, *not* license! 'A little child shall lead them,' says the Book you hold in your small hands, as yet unused to woman's work. Perhaps *you* are that very child."

"Amen," said Opal, and with this they both sat down, tailor-fashion, on the bank of the stream. For some time, nothing more was said. The Gerlashes complacently scrutinized me, as if I were the very thing they had been looking for, and then they looked at each other in a congratulatory way, while I, breaking out in an itching rash of embarrassment, tried to think of an urgent bit of business that would excuse me from their company without being impolite. I could think only of the dentist or of a dancing class, but I was dressed for neither; some weeks before, my Uncle Will M'Kerrow, who lived in Ridley, Missouri, had gone to a sale at the Army and Navy store in St. Joe and had bought presents for me and my brother and my two sisters, and today I was wearing mine—khaki knickers and a khaki shirt and a cavalry hat. I had perked up the hat by twining a multicolored shoelace around the band; the other shoelace I had cut in two to tie the ends of my pigtails; over my heart was sewn a red "C," a school letter that I had got in the spring for collateral reading. The dentist, Dr. Skeen, a humorist, would have died laughing if he had seen me in these A.E.F. regimentals, and Miss Jorene Roy, the dancing teacher, would have had kittens. Although the Gerlashes had no way of knowing the personality of either of them, I was so unskillful at useful lies, and believed so firmly that my mind could be read, that I did not dare pretend I was going to have a cavity filled or to assume the five ballet positions. I said nothing and waited for an inspiration to set me free.

People who talked Bible talk like this made me ashamed for them.

Evangelist Gerlash was immensely tall, and his bones had only the barest wrapper of flesh; he made me think of a tree with the leaves off, he was so angular and gnarled, and even his skin was something like bark, rough and pitted and scarred. His wild beard was the color of a sorrel horse, but his long hair was black, and so were the whiskers on the backs of his hands that imperfectly concealed, on the right one, a tattoo of a peacock. His intense and watchful brown eyes were flecked with green, and so were Opal's. Opal's hair was the color of her father's beard and it fell ropily to her shoulders; it needed a good brushing, and probably a fine comb wouldn't have done it any harm.

Presently, the evangelist took his beard between his hands and squeezed as if he were strangling it, and he said, "We have had a weary journey, sister."

"You said a mouthful," said Opal, and hugely yawned.

"We come all the way from Arkansas this trip," said her father. "We been comin' since May."

"I liked it better last summer," said Opal, "up in Missouri and Iowa. I don't like this dry. Mountains give me the fantods." She looked over her shoulder up at the heat-hidden range and shuddered violently.

"We been roving like gypsies of the Lord, warning the wicked and helping the sick," her father went on. "We are pleased to meet up with a person who goes to the source of goodness and spiritual health. In other words, we are glad to make the acquaintance of a *friend*." And, still wringing his beard, he gave me an alarming smile that showed a set of sharp, efficient teeth. "Yes, sir, it gladdens me right down to the marrowbone to see a little girl on a summer day reading the word of God instead of messing with the vanities of this world *or* robbing the honest farmer of his watermelon *or* sassing her Christian mother."

"We stopped in nineteen towns and preached up a storm," said Opal. "You got any gum on you?"

Fascinated by the Gerlashes, although the piety the evangelist assigned to me discomforted me, since I was no more reading the Bible than your cat, I took a package of Beech-Nut out of the pocket of my knickers, and along with it came my hand-me-down Ingersoll that hadn't run for two years. Opal took a stick of gum, and her father, with his eye on my watch, said, "Don't mind if I do," and also took a stick. "That's a dandy timepiece you got there. Remember that nice old gold turnip I used to have, Opie?"

"Yeah," said Opal scornfully. "I remember you hocked that nice old gold turnip."

"Possessions are a woe and a heavy load of sin," said her father, and reached out for my watch. But after he had held it to his ear and fiddled with the stem for a while, he gave it back, saying, "*Was* a dandy timepiece. Ain't nothing now but a piece of tin and isinglass." Then he returned to his thesis. "I reckon this is the one and only time I or Opal has come across a person, let alone a child, drinking at the wellspring of enlightenment." And he gave me his hand to shake again.

"Amen," said Opal.

There followed a drawling antiphonal recitative that related the Gerlash situation. In the winter, they lived in a town called Hoxie, Arkansas, where Evangelist Gerlash clerked in the Buttorf drugstore and preached and baptized on the side. ("Hoxie may be only a wide space in the road," said Opal, "but she don't have any homely mountains.") Mrs. Gerlash, whom Abraham had untimely gathered to his bosom the winter before, had been a hymn singer and an organ player and had done a little preaching herself. Opal, here, had got the word the day she was born, and by the time she was five and a half years old she could preach to a fare-thee-well against the Catholics and the Wets. She was also an A-1 dowser and was renowned throughout the Wonder State. In the summer, they took to the road as soon as Opal was out of school, and went camping and preaching and praying (and dowsing if there was a call for it) and spreading the truth all over the country. Last year, they had gone through the Middle West up as far as Chicago (here Opal, somewhat to her father's impatience, digressed to tell me the story of Mrs. O'Leary's cow), and the year before they had gone through New England; on earlier trips they had covered Florida and Georgia. One of these days, they were going to set up shop in New York City, though they understood the tourist-camp situation there was poor. Sometimes they found hospitality and sometimes they didn't, depending on the heathens per capita. Sometimes the Christian citizens lent them a hall, and they put up a sign on the front door saying, "The Bible Tabernacle." Often, in such a receptive community, they were invited to supper and given groceries by the believers. But sometimes they had to do their saving of souls in a public park or in a tourist camp. ("Not much business in this one," said Opal, gazing ruefully at their solitary tent.) Mr. Buttorf, the druggist in Hoxie, always said he wasn't going to keep Gerlash one more day if he didn't quit this traipsing around three months of the year, but the Lord saw to it that right after Labor Day Buttorf came to his senses and hired him again. They had arrived in Adams this morning, and if they found fertile ground, they meant to stay a week, sowing the seeds of righteousness. Evangelist Gerlash would be much obliged to learn from me what sort of town this was; he said he guessed nobody could give him the lay of the land—spiritually speaking—any better than a Bible-reading girl like me.

"But first," he said, "tell Opal and I a little something about yourself, sister." He took a black notebook out of the pocket of his black coat and took a stubby pencil out of his hatband, licked it, and began to ask me questions. All the time he was taking down my dossier, Opal rocked gently back and forth, hugging herself and humming "Holy, Holy, Holy." I was much impressed by her, because her jaws, as she diligently chewed her gum, were moving in the opposite direction to her trunk; I was sure she would be able to pat her head and rub her stomach at the same time.

It never occurred to me that I didn't have to answer questions put to me by adults (except for the old men in the Gold-moor, who were not serious)—even strange ones who had dropped out of nowhere. Besides, I was always as cooperative as possible with clergymen, not knowing when my number might come up. The evangelist's questions were harmless enough, but some of them were exceedingly strange. In between asking my name and my age and my father's occupation, he would say, "Which do you think is the Bible Sabbath—Saturday or Sunday?" and "Do you know if the Devil is a bachelor or is he a married man?" When to these hard, interesting questions I replied that I did not know, Opal left off her humming and said, "Amen."

When he had got from me all the data he wanted, he said, "I bet you this here town is a candidate for brimstone. I bet you it's every bit as bad as that one out on the plains we were at for two weeks in a hall. Heathens they were, but *scared,* so they give us a hall. That Mangol."

"Mudhole is what I call it," said Opal.

Her father chuckled. "Opal makes jokes," he explained. Then he said, "That was the worst town we come across in all our travels, sister, and somewheres on me I've got a clipping from the Mangol daily showing what I told the folks down there. I wouldn't be surprised if the same situation was here in Adams, being in the same state with Mangol and not any too far away from Mangol and having that college that is bound to sow free-thinking. Forewarned is forearmed is what I always say. I may have a good deal of hard work to do here." He began to fish things out of his pockets, and you never saw such a mess—a knife, a plug of chewing tobacco, a thin bar of soap, envelopes with arithmetic on them, a handkerchief I am not going to describe, any number of small pamphlets and folded-up handbills. Finally, he handed me a clipping. It said,

ANOTHER SOUR, GASSY STOMACH
VICTIM SAYS GASTRO-PEP
GAVE RELIEF

There was a picture of an indignant-looking man with a pointed head and beetling brows and a clenched jaw, who testified:

"For 3 years I had been a Great Victim of stomach gas and indigestion," said Mr. Homer Wagman, prominent Oklahoma citizen of 238 Taos Street, Muskogee. "My liver was sluggish, I would get bloated up and painful and had that tired dragged out feeling all the time. Recently a friend told me about Gastro-Pep so I decided to give it a trial. After taking 3 bottles of this medicine my WHOLE SYSTEM has gone through such a change that I can hardly believe it! Now my gas and stomach discomfort are relieved and I can eat my meals without suffering. I sleep like a schoolboy." Advt.

I did not know what I was reading, but I didn't like it anyway, since it had so nasty a sound; I didn't mind hearing about broken legs or diphtheria, but I hated any mention of anyone's insides. I started to read it for the second time, trying to think of something intelligent or complimentary to say to Evangelist Gerlash, and I must have made a face, because he leaned over me, adjusting his glasses, and said, "Oops! Hold on! Wrong write-up," and snatched the clipping out of my hand. I'm not absolutely sure, but I think Opal winked at me. Her father shuffled through his trash again and finally handed me another clipping, which, this time, was not an advertisement. The headline was

GERLASH LOCATES HELL IN
HEART OF CITY OF MANGOL

and the story beneath it ran:

"Hell is located right in the heart of the city of Mangol but will not be in operation until God sets up His Kingdom here in the earth," declared Evangelist Gerlash last night to another capacity crowd in the Bible Tabernacle.

"There are some very bad trouble spots in the city of Mangol that no doubt would be subjects of Hell right now," continued the evangelist and said, "but there are so many good people and places in this city that overshadow the bad that God has decided to postpone Hell in Mangol until the time of the harvest and the harvest, God says, 'is the end of the world' (Matthew 13:39).

"Hell, when started by God with eternal fire that comes from God out of Heaven and ignites the entire world, including this city, will be an interesting place. It will be a real play of fireworks, so hot that all the elements of earth will melt; too hot all over to find a place for any human creature to live. God is not arranging this fireworks for any human creature and therefore, if you or I ever land in this place, it is because we choose to go there."

Evangelist Gerlash and his daughter, Opal Gerlash, 12, of Hoxie, Arkansas, have been preaching on alternate nights for the last week at the Bible Tabernacle, formerly the Alvarez Feed and Grain store, at 1919 Prospect Street. Tonight Opal Gerlash will lecture on the subject, "Are You Born Again by Jumping, Rolling, Shouting, or Dancing?"

I read this with a good deal more interest than I had read of Mr. Wagman's renascence, although as Evangelist Gerlash's qualifications multiplied, my emotion waned. I had assumed from the headline, which made the back of my neck prickle, that he had some hot tips on the iniquities of that flat, dull little prairie town of Mangol that now and again we drove through when we were taking a trip to the southwest; the only thing I had ever noticed about it was that I had to hold my nose as we went through it, because the smell of sugar beets was so powerfully putrid. The city of Mangol had a population of about six hundred.

Nevertheless, though the evangelist did not scare or awe me, I had to be polite, and so, handing back the clipping, I said, "When do you think the end of the world is apt to be?" Opal had stopped her humming and swaying, and both she and her father were staring at me with those fierce brown eyes.

"In the autumn of the world," said Evangelist Gerlash sepulchrally, and Opal said, as she could be counted on to do, "Amen."

"Yeah, I know," I said. "But what autumn? What year?" He and Opal simultaneously bowed their heads in silent prayer. Both of them thoughtfully chewed gum.

Then Opal made a speech. "The answer to this and many other questions will be found in Evangelist Gerlash's inspirational hundred-and-twelve-page book entitled *Gerlash on the Bible*. Each and every one of you will want to read about the seven great plagues to smite the people of the world just before the end. Upon who will they fall? Have they begun? What will it mean to the world? In this book, on sale for the nominal sum of fifty cents or a half dollar, Evangelist Gerlash lets the people in on the ground floor regarding the law of God." From one of the deep sleeves of her kimono—for that was what that grimy garment was—Opal withdrew a paper-bound book with a picture of her father on the front of it, pointing his finger at me.

"Fifty cents, a half dollar," said the author, "which is to say virtually free, gratis, and for nothing."

Up the creek a way, a bullfrog made a noise that sounded distinctly like "Ger-lash."

"What makes Mangol so much worse than any place else?" I asked, growing more and more suspicious now that the conversation had taken so mercantile a turn.

But the Gerlashes were not giving out information free. "You will find the answer to this and many other questions in the book," said Opal. "Such as 'Can Wall Street run God's Business?' "

"Why does the Devil go on a sit-down strike for a thousand years?" said her father.

"What?" said I.

"Who will receive the mark of the beast?" said Opal.

"Repent!" commanded Evangelist Gerlash. "Watch! Hearken!"

"Ger-lash," went the bullfrog.

"Will hell burn forever?" cried Opal. "Be saved from the boiling pits! Take out insurance against spending eternity on a griddle!"

"Thy days are numbered," declared her father.

Opal said, "Major Hagedorn, editor of the Markston *Standard,* in his editorial said, 'This man Gerlash is as smart as chain lightning and seems to know his Bible forwards and backwards.' " All this time, she was holding up the book, and her father, on the cover of it, was threatening to impale me on his accusing finger.

"Perhaps our sister doesn't have the wherewithal to purchase this valuable book, or in other words the means to her salvation," he said, at last, and gave me a look of profound sadness, as if he had never been so sorry for anyone in his life. I said it was true I didn't have fifty cents (who ever heard of anyone ten years old going around with that kind of money?), and I offered to trade my Bible for *Gerlash on the Bible,* since I was interested in finding out whether the Devil was a bachelor or had a wife. But he shook his head. He began to throttle his beard again, and he said, "Does a dove need a kite? Does a giraffe need a neck? Does an Eskimo need a fur coat? Does Gerlash need a Bible?"

"Gerlash is a regular walking encyclopedia on the Bible," said Opal.

"One of the biggest trouble spots in the world is Mangol, Colorado," said Evangelist Gerlash. "No reason to think for a minute the contamination won't spread up here like a plague of locusts. Don't you think you had ought to be armed, Christian soldier?"

"Yes, I do," I said, for I had grown more and more curious. "But I don't have fifty cents."

"Considering that you are a Christian girl and a Bible reader," said the man, "I think we could make a special price for you. I reckon we could let you have it for twenty-five cents. O.K., Opal?"

Opal said rapidly, "Gastro-Pep contains over thirty ingredients. So it is like taking several medicines at once. And due to the immense volume in which it sells, the price of Gastro-Pep is reasonable, so get it now. Tonight!"

Evangelist Gerlash gave his daughter a sharp look. And, flustered, she stammered, "I mean, owing to the outstanding nature of Gerlash's information, the price of this *in*valuable book is a mere nothing. The truth in this book will stick and mark you forever."

"You want this book bad, don't you, sister Emily Vanderpool?" asked her father. "You are a good girl, and good girls are entitled to have this book, which is jam-packed with answers to the questions that have troubled you for years. You can't tell me your mammy and pappy are so mean that they wouldn't give their little girl a quarter for *Gerlash on the Bible*. Why don't you skedaddle over to home and get the small sum of twenty-five cents off your Christian ma?" He opened his notebook and checked my address. "Over to 126 Belleview Avenue."

"I'm hungry," said Opal. "I could eat me a horse."

"Never mind you being hungry," said her father, with a note of asperity in his mushy voice. "Don't you doubt me, sister Vanderpool," he went on, "when I tell you your innocent life is in danger. Looky here, when I got a call to go and enlighten the children of darkness in Mangol, just down the line from here, I got that call like a clap of thunder and I knew I couldn't waste no time. I went and I studied every den of vice in the city limits and some outside the city limits. It's bad, sister. For twenty-five cents, you and your folks can be prepared for when the Mangolites come a-swarming into this town." He glanced again at his notebook. "While you're getting the purchase price of my book, please ask your pure-hearted mother if I might have the loan of her garage to preach the word of God in. Are you folks centrally located?"

"My brother's got his skunk skins drying in it," I said. "You couldn't stand the smell."

"Rats!" said Evangelist Gerlash crossly, and then sternly he said, "You better shake a leg, sister. This book is offered for a limited time only."

"I can't get a quarter," I said. "I already owe her twenty cents."

"What're you going to have for supper?" asked Opal avidly. "I could eat a bushel of roasting ears. We ain't had a meal in a dog's age—not since that old handout in Niwot."

"Alas, too true," said her father. "Do you hear that, my sister Emily? You look upon a hungry holy man of God and his girl who give to the poor and save no crust for himself. Fainting for the want of but a crumb from the rich man's groaning board, we drive ourself onwards, bringing light where there is darkness and comfort where there is woe. Perhaps your good Christian mother and father would give us an invite to their supper tonight, in exchange for which they and theirs would gladly be given this priceless book, free of charge, signed by hand."

"Well, gosh," I said, working my tennis shoes on over my wet socks, "I mean . . . Well, I mean I don't know."

"Don't know what?" said that great big man, glowering at me over the tops of his severe spectacles. "Don't you go and tell me that a good Bible-reading girl like you has got kin which are evolutionists and agnostics and infidels who would turn two needy ministers of God away from their door. To those who are nourished by the Law of the Lord, a crust now and then is sufficient to keep body and soul together. I don't suppose Opal and I have had hot victuals for a good ten days, two weeks." A piteous note crept into his versatile voice, and his brown eyes and his daughter's begot a film of tears. They did look awfully hungry, and I felt guilty the way I did when I was eating a sandwich and Reddie was looking up at me like a martyr of old.

"Didn't she say her daddy ran a grocery store?" asked Opal, and her father, consulting my vital statistics, smiled broadly.

"There's nothing the matter with *your* ears, Opie," he said. And then, to me, "How's about it, sister? How's about you going down to this Safeway store and getting Opal and I some bread and some pork chops and like that?"

"Roasting ears," said Opal. "And a mushmelon."

It had suddenly occurred to me that if I could just get up and run away, the incident would be finished, but Evangelist Gerlash was clairvoyant, and, putting two firmly restraining hands on my shoulders and glaring at me straight in the eye, he said, "We don't have a thing in the world tonight to do but show up at 125 Belleview Avenue round about suppertime."

"I'd rather cook out," said Opal. "I'd rather she brought the groceries." Her father bent his head into his hands, and there was a great sob in his voice when he said, "I have suffered many a bitter disappointment in this vale of tears, but I suppose the bitterest is right now here in Adams, Colorado, where, thinking I had found a child of light, she turned out to be a mocker, grinding under her heel shod in gold the poor and the halt. Oh, sister, may you be forgiven on the Day of Judgment!"

"Whyn't you go get us some eats?" said Opal, cajoling. "If you get us some eats, we won't come calling. If we come calling, like as not we'll spend the night."

"Haven't slept in a bed since May," said her father, snuffling.

"We don't shake easy," said Opal, with an absolutely shameless grin.

My mother had a heart made of butter, and our spare room was forever occupied by strays, causing my father to scold her to pieces after they'd gone, and I knew that if the Gerlashes showed up at our house (and plainly they would) with their hard-luck story and their hard-luck looks and all their devices for saving souls, she would give them houseroom and urge them to stay as long as they liked, and my father would not simmer down for a month of Sundays.

So I got up and I said, "All right, I'll go get you a sack of groceries." I had a nebulous idea that my father might let me

buy them on time or might give me a job as a delivery boy until
I had paid for them.

To my distress, the Gerlashes got up, too, and the evangelist
said, "We'll drive you down to Main Street, sister, and sit outside, so there won't be no slip-up."

"It's Saturday!" I cried. "You can't find a place to park."

"Then we'll just circle round and round the block."

"But I can't get into a car with strangers," I protested.

"Strangers!" exclaimed Evangelist Gerlash. "Why, sister,
we're friends now. Don't you know all about Opal and I? Didn't
we lay every last one of our cards on the table right off the bat?"
He took my arm in his big, bony hand and started to propel me
in the direction of the Ford, and just then, like the Mounties to
the rescue, up came Mr. Starbird's official car, tearing into the
campgrounds and stopping, with a scream from the brakes,
right in front of me and the Gerlashes. A man in a deputy's
uniform was in the front seat beside him.

"Why, Emily," said Mr. Starbird as he got out of the car and
pushed his hat back from his forehead. "I thought you went on
home after that ruckus we had. You'll be glad to hear those
scalawags are going off to the pen tomorrow, so you can come
back to jail any time after 10 A.M."

Opal giggled, but her father shivered and looked as if a
rabbit had just run over his grave. 'We're getting outa here," he
said to her under his breath, and started at a lope toward his car.

"That's them all right," said the man in the deputy's uniform. "They set up shop in the feed store, and when they wasn't
passing out mumbo-jumbo about the world going up in fire-
crackers, they was selling that medicine. Medicine! Ninety percent wood alcohol and ninety percent fusel oil. Three cases of
jake-leg and God knows how many workers passed out in the
fields."

Mr. Starbird and the deputy had closed in on the Gerlashes.
Mr. Starbird said, "I don't want any trouble with you, mister. I
just want you to get out of Adams before I run you out on a rail.
We got plenty of our own preachers and plenty of our own
bootleggers, and we don't need any extra of either one. Just
kindly allow me to impound this so-called medicine and then

you shove. What kind of a bill of goods were they trying to sell you, Emily, kid?"

The deputy said, "That's another of their lines. We checked on them after they left Mangol, checked all the way back to Arkansas. They get some sucker like a kid or an idiot and give them this spiel and promise they'll go to heaven if they'll just get them some grub or some money or my Aunt Geraldine's diamond engagement ring or whatever."

I said nothing. I was thrilled, and at the same time I was mortally embarrassed for the Gerlashes. I was sorry for them, too, because, in spite of their predicament, they looked more hungry than anything else.

Opal said, "If we went to jail, we could eat," but her father gave her a whack on the seat and told her, "Hush up, you," and the procession, including myself, clutching my Bible and *Tom Sawyer Abroad*, moved toward the tent and the Model T. The sheriff took two cases of medicine out of the tent and put them in his car, and then we stood there watching the Gerlashes strike camp and put all their bivouac gear into the trailer. They worked swiftly and competently, as if they were accustomed to sudden removals. When they were finished, Opal got into the front seat and started to cry. "God damn it to hell," said the child preacher. "Whyn't we ever have something to eat?"

Mr. Starbird, abashed by the dirty girl's tears, took out his wallet and gave her a dollar. "Don't you spend a red cent of it in Adams," he said. "You go on and get out of town and then get some food."

Evangelist Gerlash, having cranked the car, making a noise like a collision, climbed into the driver's seat, and grinned at the sight of the dollar. "I have cast my bread upon the waters and I am repaid one hundredfold," he said. "And you, in casting your bread upon the waters, you, too, will be repaid one hundred-fold."

"Amen," said Opal, herself again, no longer crying.

"Now beat it," said Mr. Starbird.

"And give Mangol a wide berth," said the deputy.

The car shook as if it were shaking itself to death, and it coughed convulsively, and then it started up with a series of jerks and detonations, and disappeared in a screen of dust and black smoke.

Mr. Starbird offered to give me a lift home, and I got into the front seat beside him while the deputy from Mangol got in the back. On the way up the hill, Mr. Starbird kept glancing at me and then smiling.

"I've never known a girl quite like you, Emily," he said. "Memorizing the books of the Bible in the hoosegow, wearing a buck-private hat."

I blushed darkly and felt like crying, but I was pleased when Mr. Starbird went on to say, "Yes, sir, Emily, you're going to go places. What was the book you were reading down at my place when you were wearing your father's Masonic fez?" I grew prouder and prouder. "It isn't every girl of ten years of age who brushes up against some moonshiners with a record as long as your arm in the very same day that a couple of hillbilly fakers try to take her for a ride. Why, Emily, do you realize that if it hadn't of been for you, we might not have got rid of those birds till they'd set up shop and done a whole lot of mischief?"

"Really?" I said, not quite sure whether he was teasing me, and grinned, but did so looking out the window, so Mr. Starbird wouldn't see me.

Was I lucky that day! On the way home, I saw about ten people I knew, and waved and yelled at them, and when I was getting out in front of my house, Virgil Meade, with whom I had had an on-again off-again romance for some time and to whom I was not currently speaking, was passing by and he heard the sheriff say, "Come on down to jail tomorrow and we'll get some Dr. Pepper."

The sheriff's invitation gave me great prestige in the neighborhood, but it also put an end to my use of the jail as a library, because copycats began swarming to the courthouse and making so much racket in the waiting room that Mr. Starbird couldn't hear himself think, let alone follow Fu Manchu. And after a few weeks he had to post a notice forbidding anyone in the room except on business. Privately, he told me that he would just as lief let me read in one of the cells, but he was afraid word would leak out and it might be bad for my reputation. He was as sorry, he said, as he could be.

He wasn't half as sorry as I was. The snake season was still on in the mountain; Mrs. Looby hated me; Aunt Joey was visiting, and she and Mother were using the living room to cut out Butterick patterns in; Stella had just got on to pig Latin and never shut her mouth for a minute. All the same, I memorized the books of the Bible and I won the New Testament, and I'll tell you where I did my work—in the cemetery, under a shady tree, sitting beside the grave of an infant kinswoman of the sheriff, a late-nineteenth-century baby called Primrose Starbird.

A Summer Day

He wore hot blue serge knickerbockers and a striped green shirt, but he had no shoes and he had no hat and the only things in his pants pockets were a handkerchief that was dirty now, and a white pencil from the Matchless Lumber Company, and a card with Mr. Wilkins' name printed on it and his own, Jim Little-field, written on below the printing, and a little aspirin box. In the aspirin box were two of his teeth and the scab from his vaccination. He had come on the train barefoot all the way from Missouri to Oklahoma, because his grandmother had died and Mr. Wilkins, the preacher, had said it would be nice out here with other Indian boys and girls. Mr. Wilkins had put him on the through train and given the nigger man in the coach half a dollar to keep an eye on him, explaining that he was an orphan and only eight years old. Now he stood on the crinkled cinders beside the tracks and saw the train moving away like a fast little fly, and although Mr. Wilkins had promised on his word of honor, there was no one to meet him.

There was no one anywhere. He looked in the windows of the yellow depot, where there was nothing but a fat stove and a bench and a tarnished spittoon and a small office where a tele-graph machine nervously ticked to itself. A freshly painted hand-car stood on a side track near the water tower, looking as if no one were ever going to get into it again. There wasn't a sound, there wasn't even a dog or a bee, and there was nothing to look at except the bare blue sky and, across the tracks, a field of stubble that stretched as far as year after next beyond a rusty barbed-wire fence. Right by the door of the depot, there was an oblong piece of tin, which, shining in the sun, looked cool, al-though, of course, Jim knew it would be hot enough to bite your foot. It looked cool because it made him think of how the rain water used to shine in the washtubs in Grandma's back yard. On washday, when he had drawn buckets of it for her, it would sometimes splash over on his feet with a wonderful sound and a wonderful feeling. After the washing was on the line, she would black the stove and scrub the kitchen floor, and then she would take her ease, drinking a drink of blood-red sassafras as she sat rocking on the porch, shaded with wisteria. At times like that, on a hot summer day, she used to smell as cool as the underside of a leaf.

There was nothing cool here, so far as you could see. The paint on the depot was so bright you could read the newspaper by it in the dark. Jim could not see any trees save one, way yonder in the stubble field, and it looked poor and lean. In Missouri, there were big trees, as shady as a parasol. He remembered how he had sat on the cement steps of the mortuary parlor in the shade of the acacias, crying for his grandmother, whom he had seen in her cat-gray coffin. Mr. Wilkins had lipped some snuff and consoled him, talking through his nose, which looked like an unripe strawberry. "I don't want to be no orphan," Jim had cried, thinking of the asylum out by the fairground, where the kids wore gray cotton uniforms and came to town once a week on the trolley car to go to the library. Many of them wore glasses and some of them were lame. Mr. Wilkins had said, "Landagoshen, Jim boy, didn't I say you were going to be Uncle Sam's boy? Uncle Sam don't fool with orphans, he only takes care of *citizens*." On the train, a fat man had asked him what he was going to be when he grew up and Jim had said, "An aborigine." The man had laughed until he'd had to wipe his round face with a blue bandanna, and the little girl who was with him had said crossly, "What's funny, Daddy? What did the child say?" It had been cool before that, when he and Mr. Wilkins were waiting under the tall maple trees that grew beside the depot in Missouri and Mr. Marvin Dannenbaum's old white horse was drinking water out of the moss-lined trough. And just behind them, on Linden Street, Miss Bessie Ryder had been out in her yard picking a little mess of red raspberries for her breakfast. The dew would have still been on them when she doused them good with cream. Over the front of her little house there was a lattice where English ivy grew and her well was surrounded by periwinkle.

But Jim could not remember any of that coolness when he went out of the shade of the maples into the coach. Mrs. Wilkins had put up a lunch for him; when he ate it later, he found a dead ant on one of the peanut-butter sandwiches and the Baby Ruth had run all over the knobby apple. His nose had felt swollen and he'd got a headache and the green seat was as scratchy as a brush when he lay down and put his cheek on it. The train had smelled like the Fourth of July, like punk and lady crackers, and when it stopped in little towns, its rest was uneasy, for it throbbed and jerked and hissed like an old dog too feeble to get out of the sun. Once, the nigger man had taken him into the baggage car to look at some kind of big, expensive collie in a cage, muzzled and glaring fiercely through the screen; there were trunks and boxes of every shape, including one large, round one that the nigger man said held nothing but one enormous cheese from Michigan. When Jim got back to his seat, the fat man with the little girl had bought a box lunch that was put on the train at Sedalia, and Jim had watched them eat fried chicken and mustard greens and beet pickles and pone. The next time the train stopped, the nigger man had collected the plates and the silverware and had taken them into the station.

Jim had made the train wheels say "Uncle Sam, Uncle Sam," and then he hadn't been able to make them stop, even when he was half asleep. Mr. Wilkins had said that Uncle Sam wasn't one of your fair-weather friends that would let a Cherokee down when all his kin were dead. It was a blessing to be an Indian, the preacher had said, and Mrs. Wilkins had said, "It surely is, Jim boy. I'd give anything to be an Indian, just anything you can name." She had been stringing wax beans when she'd said that, and the ham hock she would cook with them had already been simmering on the back of the stove. Jim had wanted to ask her why she would like to be an Indian, but she'd seemed to have her mind on the beans, so he'd said nothing and stroked the turkey wing she used for brushing the stove.

It was hot enough to make a boy sick here in this cinder place, and Jim did not know what he would do if someone did not come. He could not walk barefoot all the way back to Missouri; he would get lost if he did not follow the tracks, and if he did follow them and a train came when he was drowsy, he might get scooped up by the cowcatcher and be hurled to kingdom come. He sat on his heels and waited, feeling the gray clinkers pressing into his feet, listening to the noontime sleep. Heat waves trembled between him and the depot and for a long time there was no sound save for the anxious telegraph machine, which was saying something important, although no one would heed. Perhaps it was about him—Jim! It could be a telegram from Mr. Wilkins saying for them to send him back. The preacher might have found a relation that Jim could live with. The boy saw, suddenly, the tall, white colonnade of a rich man's house by the Missouri River; he had gone there often to take the brown bread and the chili sauce Grandma used to make, and the yellow-haired lady at the back door of the big house had always said, "Don't you want to rest a spell, Jimmy, here where it's cool?" He would sit on a bench at the long table and pet the mother cat who slept on the windowsill and the lady would say, "You like my old puss-in-boots, don't you? Maybe you'd best come and live with me and her, seeing that she's already got your tongue." Sometimes this lady wore a lace boudoir cap with a blue silk bow on the front, and once she had given him a button with a pin that said, "LET'S CRACK THE VOLSTEAD ACT." The stubborn stutter of the machine could be a message from her, or maybe it was from Miss Bessie Ryder, who once had told his fortune with cards in a little room with pictures of Napoleon everywhere; the English ivy growing just outside made patterns on Napoleon's face, and in the little silver pitcher in the shape of Napoleon's head there was a blue anemone. Or it could be the Wilkinses themselves sending for him to come and live in the attic room, where there was the old cradle their baby had died in and a pink quilt on the bed with six-pointed stars.

Jim cried, catching his tears with his gentle tongue. Then, a long way off, a bell began to ring slowly and sweetly, and when it stopped, he heard an automobile coming with its bumptious cutout open. He went on crying, but in a different way, and his stomach thumped with excitement, for he knew it would be the people from the school, and suddenly he could not bear to have them find him. He ran the length of the depot and then ran back again, and then he hopped on one foot to the door and hopped on the piece of tin. He screamed with the awful, surprising pain. He sat down and seized his burned foot with both hands, and through his sobs he said, "Oh, hell on you, oh, Judas Priest!" He heard the car stop and the doors slam and he heard a lady say, "Wait a minute. Oh, it's all right." Jim shut his eyes as feet munched the cinders, closer and closer to him.

"Don't touch me!" he shrieked, not opening his eyes, and there was a silence like the silence after the district nurse in Missouri had looked down his throat. They did not touch him, so he stopped crying, and the lady said, "Why, the train must have come *long ago!* I will positively give that stationmaster a piece of my mind."

Jim opened his eyes. There was a big man, with very black hair, which fell into his face, wearing a spotted tan suit and a ring with a turquoise the size of a quarter. The woman had gold earrings and gold teeth, which she showed in a mechanical smile, and she wore a blue silk dress with white embroidery on the bertha. They both smelled of medicine. The man touched Jim on the arm where he had been vaccinated; baffled by everything in the world, he cried wildly. The woman bent down and said, "Well, well, well, there, there, there." Jim was half suffocated by the smell of medicine and of her buttery black hair. The man and woman looked at each other, and Jim's skin prickled because he knew they were wondering why he had not brought anything. Mr. Wilkins had said you didn't need to, not even shoes.

"Well, honey," said the lady, taking his hand, "we've come a long way all by our lonesome, haven't we?"

"A *mighty* long way," said the man, laughing heartily to make a joke of it. He took Jim's other hand and made him stand up, and then they started down the cinder path and around the corner of the depot to a tall, black touring car, which said on the door:

DEPARTMENT OF THE INTERIOR
INDIAN SERVICE

In the back seat there were two huge empty demijohns and a brand-new hoe.

"Hop in front, sonny," said the man. The black leather seat scorched Jim's legs, and he put his hand over his eyes to shut out the dazzle of the windshield.

"No shoes," said the woman, getting in beside him.

"Already noted," said the man. He got in, too, and his fat thigh was dampish at Jim's elbow.

Jim worried about the telegraph machine. Would it go on until someone came to listen to it or would it stop after a while like a telephone? It must be about him, because he was the only one who had got off the train here, and it must be from someone saying to send him back, because there was nothing else it could be about. His heart went as fast as a bobbin being filled and he wanted to throw up and to hide and to cram a million grapes into his mouth and to chase a scared girl with a garter snake, all at once. He thought of screaming bloody murder so that they would let him get out of the car, but they might just whip him for that, whip him with an inner tube or beat him over the head with the new hoe. But he wouldn't stay at the school! If there was no other way, he would ride home on a freight car, like a hobo, and sleep in the belfry of the church under the crazy bell. He would escape tonight, he told himself, and he pressed his hand on his heart to make it quiet down.

From the other side of the depot, you could see the town. A wide street went straight through the level middle of it, and it had the same kind of stores and houses and lampposts that any other town had. The trees looked like leftovers, and the peaked brown dogs slinked behind the trash cans in an ornery way. The man started the car, and as they drove up the main street, Jim could tell that the men sitting on the curb were Indians, for they had long pigtails and closed-up faces. They sat in a crouch, with their big heads hanging forward and their flat-fingered hands motionless between their knees. The women who were not fat were as lean and spry as katydids, and all of them walked up and down the main street with baskets full of roasting ears on one arm and babies on the other. The wooden cupola on the red brick courthouse was painted yellow-green and in the yard men lay with their hats over their eyes or sat limply on the iron benches under the runty trees, whose leaves were gray with dust or lice. A few children with ice-cream cones skulked in the door-ways, like abused cats. Everyone looked ailing.

The man from the school gestured with the hand that wore the heavy turquoise, and he said, "Son, this is your ancestors' town. This here is the capital of the Cherokee nation."

"You aren't forgetting the water, are you, Billings?" said the woman in a distracted way, and when the man said he was not, she said to Jim, "Do you know what 'Cherokee' means?"

"No," said Jim.

The woman looked over his head at the man. "Goodness knows, we earn our bread. What can you do with Indians if they don't know they're Indians?"

"I always knew I was an Indian," said the man.

"And so did I," said the woman. "Always."

Jim sat, in this terrible heat and terrible lack of privacy, between their mature bodies and dared not even change the position of his legs, lest he hit the gearshift. He felt that they were both looking at him as if a rash were coming out on his face and he wished they would hurry and get to the school, so that he could start escaping. At the thought of running away after the sun was down and the animals and robbers started creeping in the dark, his heart started up again, like an engine with no one in charge.

The car stopped at a drugstore, and the man got out and heaved the demijohns onto the sidewalk. In the window of the store was a vast pink foot with two corn plasters and a bunion plaster. Next door was an empty building and on its window lights were pasted signs for J. M. Barclay's Carnival Show and for Copenhagen snuff and for Clabber Girl baking powder. The carnival sign was torn and faded, the way such signs always are, and the leg of a red-haired bareback rider was tattered shabbily. How hot a carnival would be, with the smell of dung and pop-corn! Even a Ferris wheel on a day like this would be no fun. Awful as it was here, where the sun made a sound on the roof of the car, it would be even worse to be stuck in the highest seat of a Ferris wheel when something went wrong below. A boy would die of the heat and the fear and the sickness as he looked down at the distant ground, littered with disintegrated popcorn balls.

The lady beside Jim took a handkerchief out of her white linen purse, and as she wiped the sweat away from her upper lip, he caught a delicate fragrance that made him think of the yellow-haired lady in Missouri and he said, "I want to write a letter as soon as I get there."

"Well, we'll see," the woman said. "Who do you want to write to?" But the man came back, so Jim did not have to answer. The man staggered, with his stomach pushed out, under the weight of the demijohn, and as he put it in the back seat, he said savagely, "I wish one of those fellers in Washington would have to do this a couple, three times. Then maybe the Department would get down to brass tacks about that septic tank."

"The Department!" ejaculated the woman bitterly.

The man brought the other jug of water, and they drove off again, coming presently to a highway that stretched out long and white, and as shining as the piece of tin at the depot. They passed an old farm wagon with a rocking chair in the back, in which a woman smaller and more withered than Jim's grandmother sat, smoking a corncob pipe. Three dark little children were sitting at her feet, lined up along one edge of the wagon with their chins on the sideboard, and they stared hard at the Indian Service car. The one in the middle waved timidly and then hid his head in his shoulder, like a bird, and giggled.

"Creeks!" cried the woman angrily. "Everywhere we see Creeks these days! What will become of the Cherokees?"

"Ask the boy what his blood is," said the man.

"Well, Jim," said the woman, "did you hear what Mr. Standing-Deer said?"

"What?" said Jim and turned convulsively to look at the man with that peculiar name.

"Do you remember your mother and father?" said the woman.

"No, they were dead."

"How did they die?"

"I don't know. Of the ague, maybe."

"He says they may have died of the ague," said the woman to Mr. Standing-Deer, as if he were deaf. "I haven't heard that word 'ague' for years. Probably he means flu. Do you think perhaps this archaism is an index to the culture pattern from which he comes?"

Mr. Standing-Deer made a doglike sound in his throat. "Ask me another," he said. "I don't care about his speech at this stage of the game—it's the blood I'm talking about."

"Were Mama and Daddy both Indians?" ask the woman kindly.

"I don't care!" Jim said. He had meant to say "I don't know," but he could not change it afterward, because he commenced to cry again so hard that the woman patted his shoulder and did not ask him any more questions. She told him that her name was Miss Hornet and that she had been born in Chickasha and that she was the little boys' dormitory matron and that Mr. Standing-Deer was the boys' counselor. She said she was sure Jim would like it at the school. "Uncle Sam takes care of us all just as well as he can, so we should be polite to him and not let him see that we are homesick," she said, and Jim, thinking of his getaway this night, said softly, "Yes'm, Mr. Wilkins already told me."

After a time they turned into a drive, at the end of which was a big, white gate. Beyond it lay terraced lawns, where trees grew beside a group of buildings. It was hushed here, too. In spots, the grass was yellow, and the water in the ditch beyond the gate was slow. There was a gravelly space for kids to play in, but there were no kids there. There were a slide and some swings and a teeter-totter, but they looked as deserted as bones, and over the whole place there hung a tight feeling, as if a twister were coming. Once, when a twister had come at home, all the windows in Mr. Dannenbaum's house had been blown out, and it had taken the dinner off some old folks' table, and when Jim and his grandmother went out to look, there was the gravy bowl sitting on top of a fence post without a drop gone out of it.

Jim meant to be meek and mild until the sun went down, so that they would not suspect, and when Mr. Standing-Deer got out to open the gate, he said quietly to Miss Hornet, "Are the children all asleep now?"

"Yes, we are all asleep now," she said. "Some of us aren't feeling any too well these hot days." Jim stole an anxious glance at her to see if she were sick with something catching, but he could tell nothing from her smooth brown face.

The buildings were big and were made of dark stone, and because the shades were down in most of the windows, they looked cool, and Jim thought comfortably of how he would spend this little time before nightfall and of all the cool things there would be inside—a drink of water and some potted ferns and cold white busts of Abraham Lincoln and George Washington and rubber treads on the stairs, like those in the public school back in Missouri. Mr. Standing-Deer stopped the car by one of the smaller buildings, whose walls were covered with trumpet creeper. There had been trumpet creeper at Grandma's, too, growing over the backhouse, and a silly little girl named Lady had thought the blossoms were really trumpets and said the fairies could hear her playing "The Battle Hymn of the Republic" on them. She was the girl who had said she had found a worm in a chocolate bar and a tack in a cracker. With Lady, Jim used to float nasturtium leaves on the rain water in the tubs, and then they would eat them as they sat in the string hammock under the shade of the sycamores.

It was true that there were ferns in the hall of the small building, and Jim looked at them greedily, though they were pale and juiceless-looking and grew out of a sagging wicker-covered box. To the left of the door was an office, and in it, behind a desk, sat a big Indian woman who was lacing the fingers of one hand with a rubber band. She was wearing a man's white shirt and a necktie with an opal stickpin, and around her fat waist she wore a broad beaded belt. Her hair was braided around her head, and right at the top there was a trumpet flower, looking perfectly natural, as if it grew there.

"Is this the new boy?" she said to Miss Hornet.

"Who else would it be, pray tell?" said Miss Hornet crossly.

"My name is Miss Dreadfulwater," said the woman at the desk in an awful, roaring voice, and then she laughed and grabbed Jim's hand and shouted, "And you'd better watch your step or I'll dreadfulwater *you*."

Jim shivered and turned his eyes away from this crazy woman, and he heard his distant voice say, "Did you get Mr. Wilkins' telegram?"

"Telegram?" boomed Miss Dreadfulwater, and laughed uproariously. "Oh, sure, we got his telegram. Telegram and long-distance telephone call. Didn't you come in a de-luxe Pullman drawing room? And didn't Uncle Sam his own self meet you in the company limousine? Why, yes, sir, Mr. Wilkins, and Uncle Sam and Honest Harold in Washington, and all of us here have just been thinking about hardly anything else but Jim Little-field."

Mr. Standing-Deer said wearily, "For Christ's sake, Sally, turn on the soft music. The kid's dead beat."

"I'm dead beat, too, Mr. Lying-Moose and Miss Yellow-Jacket, and I say it's too much. It's too much, I say. There are six more down in this dormitory alone, and that leaves, altogether, eight well ones. And the well ones are half dead on their feet at that, the poor little old buzzards."

There was something wrong with Miss Dreadfulwater that Jim could not quite understand. He would have said she was drunk if she hadn't been a woman and a sort of teacher. She took a card out of the desk and asked him how old he was and if he had been vaccinated and what his parents' names were. He wanted a drink of water, or wanted at least to go and smell the ferns, but he dared not ask and stood before the desk feeling that he was already sick with whatever it was the others were sick with. Mr. Standing-Deer took a gun out of his coat pocket and put it on the desk and then he went down the hall, saying over his shoulder, "I guess they're all too sick to try and fly the coop for a while."

"How old was your mother when she died?" said Miss Dreadfulwater.

"Eighteen and a half," said Jim.

"How do you know?" she said.

"Grandma told me. Besides, I knew."

"You *knew?* You remember your mother?"

"Yes," said Jim. "She was a Bolshevik."

Miss Dreadfulwater put down her Eversharp and looked straight into his eyes. "Are you crazy with the heat or am I?" she said.

He rather liked her, after all, and so he smiled until Miss Hornet said, "Hurry along, Sally, I haven't got all day."

"O.K., O.K., Queenie. I just wanted to straighten out this about the Bolshevik."

"Oh, do it later," said Miss Hornet. "You know he's just making up a story. They all do when they first come."

Miss Dreadfulwater asked some more questions—whether his tonsils were out, who Mr. Wilkins was, whether Jim thought he was a full-blood or a half-breed or what. She finished finally and put the card back in the drawer, and then Miss Hornet said to Jim, "What would you like to do now? You're free to do whatever you like till suppertime. It's perfectly clear that you have no unpacking to do."

"Did he come just like this?" said Miss Dreadfulwater, astonished. "Really?"

Miss Hornet ignored her and said, "What would you like to do?"

"I don't know," Jim said.

"Of course you do," she said sharply. "Do you want to play on the slide? Or the swings? None of the other children are out, but I should think a boy of eight could find plenty of ways to amuse himself."

"I can," he said. "I'll go outside."

"He ought to go to bed," said Miss Dreadfulwater. "You ought to put him to bed right now if you don't want him to come down with it."

"Be still, Sally," said Miss Hornet. "You run along now, Jim."

Although Jim was terribly thirsty, he did not stop to look for a drinking fountain or even to glance at the ferns. The composition floor was cool to his feet, but when he went out the door the heat came at him like a slapping hand. He did not mind it, because he would soon escape. The word "escape" itself refreshed him and he said it twice under his breath as he walked across the lawn.

In back of the building, there was a good-sized tree and a boy was sitting in the shade of it. He wore a green visor, and he was reading a book and chewing gum like sixty.

Jim walked up to him and said, "Do you know where any water is?"

The boy took off the visor, and Jim saw that his eyes were

bright red. They were so startling that he could not help staring. The boy said, "The water's poisonous. There's an epidemic here."

Jim connected the poisonous water and the sickness in the dormitory with the boy's red eyes, and he was motionless with fear. The boy put his gum on his lower lip and clamped it there with his upper teeth, which were striped with gray and were finely notched, like a bread knife. "One died," he said, and laughed and rolled over on his stomach.

At the edge of the lawn beyond all the buildings, Jim saw a line of trees, the sort that follow a riverbank, and he thought that when it got dark, that was where he would go. But he was afraid, and even though it was hot and still here and he was thirsty, he did not want the day to end soon, and he said to the ugly, laughing boy, "Isn't there any good water at all?"

"There is," said the boy, sitting up again and putting his visor on, "but not for Indians. I'm going to run away." He popped his gum twice and then he pulled it out of his mouth for a full foot and swung it gently, like a skipping rope.

Jim said, "When?"

"When my plans are laid," said the boy, showing all his strange teeth in a smile that was not the least friendly. "You know whose hangout is over there past the trees?"

"No, whose?"

"Clyde Barrow's," whispered the boy. "Not long ago, they came and smoked him out with tommy guns. That's where I'm going when I leave here."

For the first time, Jim noticed the boy's clothes. He wore blue denim trousers and a blue shirt to match, and instead of a belt, he wore a bright-red sash, about the color of his eyes. It was certainly not anything Jim had ever seen any other boy wear, and he said, pointing to it, "Is that a flag or something?"

"It's the red sash," replied the boy. "It's a penalty. You aren't supposed to be talking to me when I have it on." He gave Jim a nasty, secret smile and took his gum out of his mouth and rolled it between his thumb and forefinger. "What's your name, anyway?" he asked.

"Jim Littlefield."

"That's not Indian. My name is Rock Forward Mankiller.

My father's name is Son-of-the-Man-Who-Looked-Like-a-Bunch-of-Rags-Thrown-Down. It's not that long in Navajo."

"Navajo?" asked Jim.

"Hell, yes. I'm not no Cherokee," said the boy.

"What did you do to make them put the red sash on you?" Jim asked, wishing to know, yet not wanting to hear.

"Wouldn't you like to know?" said Rock Forward and started to chew his gum again. Jim sat down in the shade beside him and looked at his burned foot. There was no blister, but it was red and the skin felt drawn. His head ached and his throat was sore, and he wanted to lie down on his stomach and go to sleep, but he dared not, lest he be sleeping when the night came. He felt again the burden of the waiting silence; once a fool blue jay started to raise the roof in Clyde Barrow's woods and a couple of times he heard a cow moo, but the rest of the time there was only this hot stillness in which the red-eyed boy stared at him calmly.

"What do they do if you escape and they catch you?" Jim asked, trembling and giving himself away.

"Standing-Deer comes after you with his six-gun, and then you get the red sash," said Rock Forward, eyeing him closely. "You can't get far unless you lay your plans. I know what you're thinking about, Littlefield. All new kids do. I'm wise to it." He giggled and stretched his arms out wide, and once again he showed his sickening teeth.

The desire to sleep was so strong that Jim was not even angry with Rock Forward, and he swayed to and fro, half dozing, longing to lie full length on a bed and dimly to hear the sounds the awake people made through a half-open door. Little, bright-colored memories came to him pleasantly, like the smallest valentines. The reason he knew that his mother had been a Bolshevik was that she'd had a pair of crimson satin slippers, which Grandma had kept in a drawer, along with her best crocheted pot holders and an album of picture postal cards from Gettysburg. The lovely shoes were made of satin and the heels were covered with rhinestones. The shiny cloth, roughened in places, was the color of Rock Forward's eyes and of his sash. Jim said, "No kidding, why do you have to wear the red sash?"

"I stole Standing-Deer's gun, if you want to know, and I said, 'To hell with Uncle Sam.' "

Jim heard what the boy said but he paid no mind, and he said, not to the boy or to anyone, "I'll wait till tomorrow. I'm too sleepy now."

Nor did Rock Forward pay any heed to Jim. Instead, he said, turning his head away and talking in the direction of the outlaw's hangout, "If I get sick with the epidemic and die, I'll kill them all. Standing-Deer first and Dreadfulwater second and Hornet third. I'll burn the whole place up and I'll spit everywhere."

"Do you have a father?" said Jim, scarcely able to get the words out.

"Of course I have a father," said Rock Forward in a sudden rage. "Didn't I just tell you his name? Didn't you know he was in jail for killing a well-known attorney in Del Rio, Texas? If he knew I was here, he'd kill them all. He'd take this red sash and tear it to smithereens. I'm no orphan and I'm not a Cherokee like the rest of you either, and when I get out of here, Standing-Deer had just better watch out. He'd just better watch his p's and q's when I get a six-gun of my own." Passionately, he tore off his visor and bent it double, cracking it smack down the middle of the isinglass, and then, without another word, he went running off in the direction of the line of trees, the ends of the red sash flapping at his side.

Jim was too sleepy to care about anything now—now that he had decided to wait until tomorrow. He did not even care that it was hot. He lay down on the sickly grass, and for a while he watched a lonesome leaf-cutter bee easing a little piece of plantain into its hole. He hoped they would not wake him up and make him walk into the dormitory; he hoped that Mr. Standing-Deer would come and carry him, and he could see himself with his head resting on that massive shoulder in the spotted coat. He saw himself growing smaller and smaller and lying in a bureau drawer, like Kayo in the funny papers. He rustled in his sleep, moving away from the sharp heels of the red shoes, and something as soft and deep and safe as fur held him in a still joy.

The Philosophy Lesson

Cora Savage watched the first real snowfall of the year through the long, trefoiled windows of the studio where the Life Class met. It was a high, somber room in one of the two square towers of the auditorium, which, because of some personal proclivity of the donor, were exorbitantly Gothic and had nothing to do with the other buildings on the campus, which were serene and low and Italian Renaissance. Here, in this chilly room, three mornings a week from nine until twelve, twenty-seven students met in smocks to render Cora, naked, on canvases in oil, and on sheets of coarse-grained paper in charcoal, seriously applying those principles of drawing they had learned, in slide talks, in their lecture classes. But just as Cora had predicted to her anxious United Presbyterian mother, the students took no more account of Cora than if she had been a plaster cast or an assemblage of apples and lemons for a still-life study. At first, the class had been disquieted by her inhuman ability to remain motionless so long, and they chattered about it among themselves as if she had no ears to hear. Their instructor, Mr. Steele, a fat and comfort-loving man who spent a good part of the three hours seated on a padded bench, reading and, from time to time, brewing coffee for himself on a hot plate behind a screen, told them bluffly that since this talent of hers could not possibly last, they should take advantage of it while it did. Thereafter, they ceased to speak of her except in the argot of their craft. Mr. Steele, deep in Trollope, was polite if they sought him out for help, and, once an hour, he made a tour of the room, going from easel to easel commenting kindly but perfunctorily.

Cora rested only twice in the three hours. After she struck the pose at nine, she waited, in heavy pain, for the deep bell to ring in the chapel tower, signaling the passage of fifty minutes. When she stepped off the dais with the first peal and came to recognizable life again by putting on her blue flannel wrapper, a tide of comfort immediately and completely washed away the cramps and tingles in her arms and legs. For ten minutes, then, she sat on the edge of her platform, smoking cigarettes, which, because of her fatigue, made her agreeably dizzy and affected her eyes so that the light altered, shifting, like the light on the prairies, from sage-green to a submarine violet, to saffron, to the color of a Seckel pear. When the bell rang again, on the hour, she turned herself to stone. She did not talk to the students, unless they spoke first to her, nor did she look at their drawings and paintings until afterward, when everyone was gone and she stepped out from behind her screen, fully dressed. Then she wandered about through the thicket of easels and saw the travesties of herself, grown fat, grown shriveled, grown horsefaced, turned into Clara Bow. The representations of her face were, nearly invariably, the faces of the authors of the work. Her complete anonymity to them at once enraged and fascinated her.

As she posed, she stared through those high, romantic windows at the sky and the top of a cottonwood tree. Usually, because the tension of her muscles would not allow her to think or to pursue a fantasy to its happy ending, she counted slowly by ones, to a hundred, and she had become so precise in her timing that five minutes passed in each counting: ten hundreds, a thousand, and then the bell commenced to ring. Often she felt she must now surely faint or cry out against the pain that began midway through the first hour, began as an itching and a stinging in the part of her body that bore the most weight and then gradually overran her like a disease until the whole configuration of bone and muscle dilated and all her pulses throbbed. Nerves jerked in her neck and a random shudder seized her shoulder blades and sometimes, although it was cold in the studio, all her skin was hot and her blood roared; her heart deafened her. If she had closed her eyes, she would have fallen down—nothing held her to her position except the scene through the windows, an abridgment of the branches of the cottonwood tree whose every twig and half-dead leaf she knew by heart so that she still saw it, if her mind's eye wandered. She knew the differences of the sheen on its bark in rain and in sun and how the dancing of the branches varied with the winds; she waited for birds and squirrels, and if they came, she lost track of her numbers and the time went quickly. She had grown fond of the tree through knowledge of it and at noon, when she left the building—this beautiful release was like the first day after an illness and all the world was fresh—she greeted it as if it were her possession, and she thought how pleasant it would look when its leaves came back to it in April.

Thus, while she recognized the chills and fevers and the pins and needles that bedeviled her, she remained detached from them as if their connection with her was adventitious and the real business at hand was the thorough study of her prospect of bits of wood and bits of cloud, and counting to tell the hours.

On the day of the first snowfall, though, she did not deny her discomfort, she simply and truly did not feel it and, although she was pinioned, she drifted in a charming ease, a floating, as if she hovered, slowly winding, like the flakes themselves. The snow began in the second hour, just as she resumed her pose, one in which she held a pole upright like a soldier with a spear. It was the most unmerciful attitude she had yet held, for all her weight lay on her right heel, which seemed to seek a grafting with the dais, and the arm that held the pole swelled until she imagined in time it would be so bellied out that her vaccination scar would appear as an umbilical indentation. For the first time she had felt put upon, and during her first rest she had been angry with the students and with Mr. Steele, who took it for granted that she was made of a substance different from theirs. And, when a girl in Oxford glasses and a spotless green linen smock, radiating good will, came to sit for a moment on the dais and said admiringly, "That would *kill* me! Are you going to do this professionally?" she was the more affronted; the servant whose ambitions go beyond his present status does not wish to be complimented on the way he polishes the silver.

When the snow came, the studio was dematerialized. The storm began so suddenly, with so little warning from the skies, that for a moment Cora doubted its existence, whirling there in the cottonwood, and thought that her eyes had invented it out of a need to vary their view. She loved the snow. When she had first heard of heaven, she had thought it would be a place where snow was forever falling and forever concealing the harshness of the world. And she had never remembered, when she was a child, from one year to the next how cold snow was; always, when the first flakes flew, she had run out in her bare feet, expecting the miraculous purity to be as soft as a cat, and then she ran back into the house to lie on the floor in the front hall, giggling with surprise.

In Missouri, by the river, the snow was as hard as a floor, but now and then a soft place would take her unawares and she would go in up to the top of her galoshes, and then she was a mess, her astrakhan coat covered with snow, her tasseled yellow mittens soaking wet. They went, she and her father and her brother Randall, for the Christmas greens each year, for holly and ground hemlock and partridge berry to put in the long, cold summer parlor where a green carpet spread like a lawn. The purple light of early Christmas morning came through the scrim curtains as the Savage children, Cora and Randall, Abigail and Evangeline, opened their presents. Often snow fell on Christmas day, shutting them in, protecting them, putting a spell on them. The little girls, wearing new tam-o'-shanters, wearing the bracelets and rings and fake wrist watches sent by cousins, surrounded by double-jointed dolls and sets of colored pencils, pig banks, patent-leather pocketbooks, jackstones, changeable taffeta hair ribbons, teased their poor brother with his ungainly boy's things— tool chests, fishing gear, the year he was eight, a .22.

The snow had been best, perhaps, most elegant there in Missouri. There had been times when Grandmother Savage had driven over from Kavanagh to call; she had an old-fashioned sleigh with rakish curled runners. In the little parlor, what Mr. Savage derisively called "the pastor's parlor," they drank hot cocoa from fat, hand-painted cups, bordered with a frieze of asters. And all the while the snow was coming down.

More elegant in Missouri, but it had been more keenly exciting here in Adams. Randall and Cora (by now Cora was a tomboy and disdained her older sisters) often took their sleds over the practice ski jumps in the foothills behind the college. The wind was knocked out of them as they hit the ground and once Cora lost control and went hurtling into a barbed-wire fence. It seemed to her, on reflection, that she had slowly revolved on her head, like a top, for a long time before the impact. Then, too frightened to move lest she find she could not, she had lain there waiting for her brother. Blood, in niggardly drops, from the wounds in her forehead stained the snow. Afterward, she had been afraid of the ski jumps and had only coasted down a steep hill that terminated in a cemetery; but this was dangerous enough, and reckless children sometimes crashed into the spiked palings of the iron fence and broke their heads wide open. There were so many of these accidents and the injuries were often so nearly serious that a city ordinance was passed, forbidding anyone to slide down that street. Then, added to the danger, there was the additional thrill of possibly being caught by the police and put into jail. One hid oneself and one's sled behind the spooky little stone house at the graveyard's edge, where the caretaker kept his lawn mover and gardening tools, and waited for the Black Maria. But it never came.

Cora was pleased today that probably she alone in the studio had seen what was happening outside. The students were intent on their work, applying to each other for criticism or for pallette knives, measuring parts of Cora with pencils held at arm's length as they squinted and grimaced; sometimes, to her mistrust, they came quite close to examine the shape of a muscle or the color of a shadow on her skin. For the time being, the snow was a private experience; perhaps everything at this moment proceeded from her own mind, even this grubby room with its forest of apparatus and its smell of banana oil, even all these people. She thought of Bishop Berkeley, whom Dr. Bosch had assigned to the class in Introduction to Philosophy; she thought of the way Berkeley had dismantled the world of its own reality and had made each idiom of it into an idea in the mind of God. "Or in his own mind," said Dr. Bosch dryly, for he had no use for the Bishop. This morning, Cora had much use for him, and she concluded that she would be at peace forever if she could believe that she existed only for herself and possibly for a superior intelligence and that no one existed for her save when he was tangibly present.

As she pondered this quieting phenomenon (it just might work, she just might tutor herself to believe in such sublimity), the door to the studio opened and she turned away from the window. A latecomer entered, a boy in a sheep-lined mackinaw and a freshman beanie; his ashen corduroy trousers, freckled with oil paint, were tucked into the tops of his yellow field boots. His name was Ernie Wharton and he had been in high school with Cora; in the beginning, she had resented him and had disliked hearing that familiar voice she had heard the year before in Spanish II. Once she had even been in a play with him and on several evenings after rehearsal he had walked her home and they had talked at length at the foot of the steps on Benedict Street, where the smell of lilacs nearly led her to infatuation. But they had only gone on talking learnedly of *The Ode on Intimations of Immortality*, which both of them admired. On the first day of the Life Class, he, too, had been embarrassed, and had looked only at the model's feet and at her face, but in time he merged into the general background and was no more specific to her than any of the others.

Panting, as if he had been running, red from the cold, his canine face (the face of an amiable dog, a border collie) wore a look of befuddlement and at first Cora thought it stemmed from worry over his being so late, but she knew this could not be true, for Mr. Steele paid no heed at all to the arrival and departure of his students. Indeed, he did not so much as look up from *Framley Parsonage* when the outside air came rushing through the door, up the spiral staircase. No one gave Ernie's entrance more than passing recognition, no one but Cora, at whom he looked directly and whom he seemed to address, as if he had come to bring this news exclusively to her. "Somebody just committed suicide on the Base Line," he said.

In their incredulity, the class fell over itself, dropped pencils, splashed turpentine, tore paper, catapulted against their easels, said, "Oh, damn it." Then they surrounded Ernie, who stood against the door as if he did not mean to stay but was only a courier stopping at one of the many stations on his route. Although no one was looking at her, Cora continued to hold her pose and to look at the snow in her tree, but she listened and, now and then, stole a glance at the narrator's face, awry with dismay and with a sort of excruciated pleasure in the violent finality of the act he described. A second-year pre-medical student, two hours before, had been run over by the morning mail train coming from Denver. He had driven his car to the outskirts of town and there it had been found at a crossing, its motor still running. The engineer had seen the body on the tracks but he had had no time to stop the train, and the man had been broken to pieces. Wharton had gone out there (they were fraternity brothers; the president had called him just as he was leaving for class) and had seen the butchered mess, the head cut loose, the legs shivered, one hand, perched like a bird, on a scrub oak. His name was Bernard Allen, said Ernie, and he had been one prince of a fellow.

Bernard Allen!

The girl in Oxford glasses went pale and said, "My godfather, I knew *him!* I went to the Phi Gam tea dance with him Friday."

(Friday? thought Cora. But that was the night he and Maisie Perrine went horseback riding. That was the night I saw his white hair shining like this snow as I looked out my bedroom window toward the boarding house where Maisie lives next door to us. I, spying at all hours of the day and night, spying and tortured at what I saw, saw Bernard Allen's blue Cord town car draw up to Mrs. Mullen's house at midnight last Friday. Bernard and Maisie must have been to a dance, for Maisie was wearing a long dress of gold lamé and her sable coat. "I'll be waiting on the porch. Don't be long," said Maisie. They kissed connubially. "I hate to have you take off that gorgeous dress," said Bernard, and she replied, "I'd look good riding a horse in this, wouldn't I?" He let her out of the car and took her to the door and then he drove away. Half an hour later he was back and Maisie, in riding clothes, ran down the sagging steps of Mrs. Mullen's front porch. Where would they find a stable open at this time of night? They could. They would. For they had claimed the pot of gold and were spending it all on everything their hearts desired, on clothes and cars and bootleg whiskey. Probably one of them kept a string of blooded horses somewhere with a stableman so highly paid that he did not mind being waked up in the middle of the night. "Why didn't you bring Luster?" asked

Maisie. "Because he doesn't like the moon." Luster was his dog, a golden retriever. They drove away then in the direction of Left Hand Canyon. I suppose eventually I went to sleep.)

Forgetting now that Ernie Wharton's facts were immediate and that, because he had been united with the dead boy in a secret order, his was the right to tell the tale and to lead the speculation—forgetting this, the art students shrilly turned to the girl in Oxford glasses. Had he been strange, they asked her, had he seemed cracked?

"He was like everybody else," she said, "like all pre-meds. You know, a little high-hat the way they all are because they know those six-dollar words."

She did not like to speak ill of the dead, she said, but, frankly, Bernard had been the world's worst dancer and, as she looked back on it, she thought he had probably been tight. Not that that made any difference, she quickly added, because she was broad-minded, but it might throw some light on his suicide. Maybe he was drunk this morning. It was unlikely, she supposed, that he would have been drinking at eight-thirty in the morning. Still, you never could tell. She could not think of anything else about him. Except that he had this pure white hair—not blond, not towheaded; he had had a grandfather's white hair. It had been a blind date and a very short one, for they'd only gone to the dance and that was over at six and then she had gone right home to dress for the SAE formal. It had been just one of those dates that fills an afternoon and comes to nothing, when you get along all right, but you aren't much interested. Christmas, though, it gave her the creeps.

All the time the girl talked, Ernie stared at her, dumb-struck with rage. How *dare* she be so flip, said his frosty eyes. Presently, because her facts were thin, the students returned to him and they interrogated him closely as if he were a witness in a court of law. What had they done with the car? How long was it before the police arrived? Where did the guy come from? Had his family been told? At first, Ernie answered factually but ab-stractedly and then, hectored by a repetition of the same ques-tions, he grew impatient and, turning wrathfully on the girl in the green smock, he shouted, "I'm not sure you knew him at all. He was engaged. He was engaged to be married to Maisie Perrine, and they announced it at the Chi Psi dance about three hours after you claim to have been at a tea dance with him."

The girl laughed lightly. "Keep your shirt on, sonny. That doesn't cut any ice. Can't you be engaged to somebody and take somebody else to a tea dance?"

Ernie said, "Not if you're so deep you end up by killing yourself."

"Oh, bushwa," said the girl and went back to her easel, but she was the only one who did, and among the others a moral debate began: whether suicide *did* demonstrate depth, whether suicide was an act of cowardice or of bravery.

Cora no longer listened. She was thinking of Maisie Perrine and wondering whether her yellow Cadillac roadster was there now at the crossing, its top whitened with snow, the windshield wipers going. Maybe she did not know yet and was still in class, still undisheveled in her orderly, expensive clothes, her sumptuous red hair shining, her fine hand taking down notes on Middle English marketplace romances. What would happen when she heard? And where was Luster, where was Bernard Allen's fond golden dog?

And what was the misery that had brought the boy to suicide? Rich, privileged, in love, he and his girl had seemed the very paradigm of joy. Why had he done it? And yet, why not? Why did not she, who was seldom happy, do it herself? A darkness beat her like the wings of an enormous bird and frantic terror of the ultimate hopelessness shook her until the staff she held slipped and her heart seemed for a moment to fail. She began to sweat and could feel the drops creeping down her legs. The bell rang and her pole went clattering to the floor, knocking over a portrait on an easel nearby, and all the students, still talking of the death that morning, looked up with exclamations of shock, but she could tell by their faces that none of them had been thinking her thoughts, that she alone, silent and stationary there on the dais, had shared Bernard Allen's experience and had plunged with him into sightlessness. No. No, wait a minute. Each mortal in the room must, momentarily, have died. But just as the fledgling artists put their own faces on their canvases, so they had perished in their own particular ways.

The snow was a benison. It forgave them all.

MANHATTAN ISLAND

Children Are Bored on Sunday

Through the wide doorway between two of the painting galleries, Emma saw Alfred Eisenburg standing before "The Three Miracles of Zenobius," his lean, equine face ashen and sorrowing, his gaunt frame looking undernourished, and dressed in a way that showed he was poorer this year than he had been last. Emma herself had been hunting for the Botticelli all afternoon, sidetracked first by a Mantegna she had forgotten, and then by a follower of Hieronymus Bosch, and distracted, in an English room as she was passing through, by the hot invective of two ladies who were lodged (so they bitterly reminded one another) in an outrageous and expensive mare's-nest at a hotel on Madison. Emma liked Alfred, and once, at a party in some other year, she had flirted with him slightly for seven or eight minutes. It had been spring, and even into that modern apartment, wherever it had been, while the cunning guests, on their guard and highly civilized, learnedly disputed on aesthetic and political subjects, the feeling of spring had boldly invaded, adding its nameless, sentimental sensations to all the others of the buffeted heart; one did not know and never had, even in the devouring raptures of adolescence, whether this was a feeling of tension or of solution—whether one flew or drowned.

In another year, she would have been pleased to run into Alfred here in the Metropolitan on a cold Sunday, when the galleries were thronged with out-of-towners and with people who dutifully did something self-educating on the day of rest. But this year she was hiding from just such people as Alfred Eisenburg, and she turned quickly to go back the way she had come, past the Constables and Raeburns. As she turned, she came face to face with Salvador Dali, whose sudden countenance, with its unlikely mustache and its histrionic eyes, familiar from the photographs in public places, momentarily stopped her dead, for she did not immediately recognize him and, still surprised by seeing Eisenburg, took him also to be someone she knew. She shuddered and then realized that he was merely famous, and she penetrated the heart of a guided tour and proceeded safely through the rooms until she came to the balcony that overlooks the medieval armor, and there she paused, watching two youths of high-school age examine the joints of an equestrian's shell.

She paused because she could not decide what to look at now that she had been denied the Botticelli. She wondered, rather crossly, why Alfred Eisenburg was looking at it and why, indeed, he was here at all. She feared that her afternoon, begun in such a burst of courage, would not be what it might have been; for this second's glimpse of him—who had no bearing on her life—might very well divert her from the pictures, not only because she was reminded of her ignorance of painting by the presence of someone who was (she assumed) versed in it but because her eyesight was now bound to be impaired by memory and conjecture, by the irrelevant mind-portraits of innumerable people who belonged to Eisenburg's milieu. And almost at once, as she had predicted, the air separating her from the schoolboys below was populated with the images of composers, of painters, of writers who pronounced judgments, in their individual argot, on Hindemith, Ernst, Sartre, on Beethoven, Rubens, Baudelaire, on Stalin and Freud and Kierkegaard, on Toynbee, Frazer, Thoreau, Franco, Salazar, Roosevelt, Maimonides, Racine, Wallace, Picasso, Henry Luce, Monsignor Sheen, the Atomic Energy Commission, and the movie industry. And she saw herself moving, shaky with apprehensions and martinis, and with the belligerence of a child who feels himself laughed at, through the apartments of Alfred Eisenburg's friends, where the shelves were filled with everyone from Aristophanes to Ring Lardner, where the walls were hung with reproductions of Seurat, Titian, Vermeer, and Klee, and where the record cabinets began with Palestrina and ended with Copland.

These cocktail parties were a modus vivendi in themselves for which a new philosophy, a new ethic, and a new etiquette had had to be devised. They were neither work nor play, and yet they were not at all beside the point but were, on the contrary, quite indispensable to the spiritual life of the artists who went to them. It was possible for Emma to see these occasions objectively, after these many months of abstention from them, but it was still not possible to understand them, for they were so special a case, and so unlike any parties she had known at home. The gossip was different, for one thing, because it was stylized, creative (integrating the whole of the garrotted, absent friend), and all its details were precise and all its conceits were Jamesian, and all its practitioners sorrowfully saw themselves in the role of Pontius Pilate, that hero of the untoward circumstance. (It has to be done, though we don't want to do it; 'tis a pity she's a whore, when no one writes more intelligent verse than she.) There was, too, the matter of the drinks, which were much worse than those served by anyone else, and much more plentiful. They dispensed with the fripperies of olives in martinis and cherries in manhattans (God forbid! They had no sweet teeth), and half the time there was no ice, and when there was, it was as likely as not to be suspect shavings got from a bed for shad at the corner fish store. Other species, so one heard, went off to dinner after cocktail parties certainly no later than half past eight, but no one ever left a party given by an Olympian until ten, at the earliest, and then groups went out together, stalling and squabbling at the door, angrily unable to come to a decision about where to eat, although they seldom ate once they got there but, with the greatest formality imaginable, ordered several rounds of cocktails, as if they had not had a drink in a month of Sundays. But the most surprising thing of all about these parties was that every now and again, in the middle of the urgent, general conversation, this cream of the enlightened was horribly curdled, and an argument would end, quite literally, in a bloody nose or a black eye. Emma was always astounded when this happened and continued to think that these outbursts did not arise out of hatred or jealousy but out of some quite unaccountable quirk, almost a reflex, almost something physical. She never quite believed her eyes—that is, was never altogether convinced that they were really beating one another up. It seemed, rather, that this was only a deliberate and perfectly honest demonstration of what might have happened often if they had not so diligently dedicated themselves to their intellects. Although she had seen them do it, she did not and could nòt believe that city people clipped each other's jaws, for, to Emma, urban equaled urbane, and ichor ran in these Augustans' veins.

As she looked down now from her balcony at the atrocious iron clothes below, it occurred to her that Alfred Eisenburg had been just such a first-generation metropolitan boy as these two who half knelt in lithe and eager attitudes to study the glittering splints of a knight's skirt. It was a kind of childhood she could not imagine and from the thought of which she turned away in secret, shameful pity. She had been really stunned when she first came to New York to find that almost no one she met had gluttonously read Dickens, as she had, beginning at the age of ten, and because she was only twenty when she arrived in the city and unacquainted with the varieties of cultural experience, she had acquired the idea, which she was never able to shake entirely loose, that these New York natives had been deprived of this and many other innocent pleasures because they had lived in apartments and not in two- or three-story houses. (In the early years in New York, she had known someone who had not heard a cat purr until he was twenty-five and went to a houseparty on Fire Island.) They had played hide-and-seek dodging behind ash cans instead of lilac bushes and in and out of the entries of apartment houses instead of up alleys densely lined with hollyhocks. But who was she to patronize and pity them? Her own childhood, rich as it seemed to her on reflection, had not equipped her to read, or to see, or to listen, as theirs had done; she envied them and despised them at the same time, and at the same time she feared and admired them. As their attitude implicitly accused her, before she beat her retreat, she never looked for meanings, she never saw the literary-historical symbolism of the cocktail party but went on, despite all testimony to the contrary, believing it to be an occasion for getting drunk. She never listened, their manner delicately explained, and when she talked she was always lamentably off key; often and often she had been stared at and had been told, "It's not the same thing at all."

Emma shuddered, scrutinizing this nature of hers, which they all had scorned, as if it were some harmless but sickening reptile. Noticing how cold the marble railing was under her hands, she felt that her self-blame was surely justified; she came to the Metropolitan Museum not to attend to the masterpieces but to remember cocktail parties where she had drunk too much and had seen Alfred Eisenburg, and to watch schoolboys, and to make experience out of the accidental contact of the palms of her hands with a cold bit of marble. What was there to do? One thing, anyhow, was clear and that was that today's excursion into the world had been premature; her solitude must continue for a while, and perhaps it would never end. If the sight of someone so peripheral, so uninvolving, as Alfred Eisenburg could scare her so badly, what would a cocktail party do? She almost fainted at the thought of it, she almost fell headlong, and the boys, abandoning the coat of mail, dizzied her by their progress toward an emblazoned tabard.

In so many words, she wasn't fit to be seen. Although she was no longer mutilated, she was still unkempt; her pretensions needed brushing; her ambiguities needed to be cleaned; her evasions would have to be completely overhauled before she could face again the terrifying learning of someone like Alfred Eisenburg, a learning whose components cohered into a central personality that was called "intellectual." She imagined that even the boys down there had opinions on everything political and artistic and metaphysical and scientific, and because she remained, in spite of all her opportunities, as green as grass, she was certain they had got their head start because they had grown up in apartments, where there was nothing else to do but educate themselves. This being an intellectual was not the same thing as dilettantism; it was a calling in itself. For example, Emma did not even know whether Eisenburg was a painter, a writer, a composer, a sculptor, or something entirely different. When, seeing him with the composers, she had thought he was one of them; when, the next time she met him, at a studio party, she decided he must be a painter; and when, on subsequent occasions, everything had pointed toward his being a writer, she had relied altogether on circumstantial evidence and not on anything he had said or done. There was no reason to suppose that he had not looked upon her as the same sort of variable and it made their anonymity to one another complete. Without the testimony of an impartial third person, neither she nor Eisenburg would ever know the other's actual trade. But his specialty did not matter, for his larger designation was that of "the intellectual," just as the man who confines his talents to the nose and throat is still a doctor. It was, in the light of this, all the more extraordinary that they had had that lightning-paced flirtation at a party.

Extraordinary, because Emma could not look upon herself as an intellectual. Her private antonym of this noun was "rube," and to her regret—the regret that had caused her finally to disappear from Alfred's group—she was not even a bona-fide rube. In her store clothes, so to speak, she was often taken for an intellectual, for she had, poor girl, gone to college and had never been quite the same since. She would not dare, for instance, go up to Eisenburg now and say that what she most liked in the Botticelli were the human and compassionate eyes of the centurions' horses, which reminded her of the eyes of her own Great-uncle Graham, whom she had adored as a child. Nor would she admit that she was delighted with a Crivelli Madonna because the peaches in the background looked exactly like marzipan, or that Goya's little red boy inspired in her only the pressing desire to go out immediately in search of a plump cat to stroke. While she knew that feelings like these were not really punishable, she had not perfected the art of tossing them off; she was no flirt. She was a bounty jumper in the war between Great-uncle Graham's farm and New York City, and liable to court-martial on one side and death on the other. Neither staunchly primitive nor confidently *au courant*, she rarely knew where she was at. And this was her Achilles' heel: her identity was always mistaken, and she was thought to be an intellectual who, however, had not made the grade. It was no use now to cry that she was not, that she was a simon-pure rube; not a soul would believe her. She knew, deeply and with horror, that she was thought merely stupid.

It was possible to be highly successful as a rube among the Olympians, and she had seen it done. Someone calling himself Nahum Mothersill had done it brilliantly, but she often wondered whether his name had not helped him, and, in fact, she had sometimes wondered whether that had been his real name.

If she had been called, let us say, Hyacinth Derryberry, she believed she might have been able, as Mothersill had been, to ask who Ezra Pound was. (This struck her suddenly as a very important point; it was endearing, really, not to know who Pound was, but it was only embarrassing to know who he was but not to have read the "Cantos.") How different it would have been if education had not meddled with her rustic nature! Her education had never dissuaded her from her convictions, but certainly it had ruined the looks of her mind—painted the poor thing up until it looked like a mean, hypocritical, promiscuous malcontent, a craven and apologetic fancy woman. Thus she continued secretly to believe (but *never* to confess) that the apple Eve had eaten tasted exactly like those she had eaten when she was a child visiting on her Great-uncle Graham's farm, and that Newton's observation was no news in spite of all the hue and cry. Half the apples she had eaten had fallen out of the tree, whose branches she had shaken for this very purpose, and the Apple Experience included both the descent of the fruit and the consumption of it, and Eve and Newton and Emma understood one another perfectly in this particular of reality.

Emma started. The Metropolitan boys, who, however bright they were, would be boys, now caused some steely article of dress to clank, and she instantly quit the balcony, as if this unseemly noise would attract the crowd's attention and bring everyone, including Eisenburg, to see what had happened. She scuttered like a quarry through the sightseers until she found an empty seat in front of Rembrandt's famous frump, "The Noble Slav"— it was this kind of thing, this fundamental apathy to most of Rembrandt, that made life in New York such hell for Emma— and there, upon the plum velours, she realized with surprise that Alfred Eisenburg's had been the last familiar face she had seen before she had closed the door of her tomb.

In September, it had been her custom to spend several hours of each day walking in a straight line, stopping only for traffic lights and outlaw taxicabs, in the hope that she would be tired enough to sleep at night. At five o'clock—and gradually it became more often four o'clock and then half past three—she would go into a bar, where, while she drank, she seemed to be reading the

information offered by the *Sun* on "Where to Dine." Actually
she had ceased to dine long since; every few days, with effort,
she inserted thin wafers of food into her repelled mouth, flushing
the frightful stuff down with enormous drafts of magical, purify-
ing, fulfilling applejack diluted with tepid water from the tap.
One weighty day, under a sky that grimly withheld the rain, as
if to punish the whole city, she had started out from Ninetieth
Street and had kept going down Madison and was thinking, as
she passed the chancery of St. Patrick's, that it must be nearly
time and that she needed only to turn east on Fiftieth Street to
the New Weston, where the bar was cool, and dark to an almost
absurd degree. And then she was hailed. She turned quickly,
looking in all directions until she saw Eisenburg approaching,
removing a gray pellet of gum from his mouth as he came. They
were both remarkably shy and, at the time, she had thought they
were so because this was the first time they had met since their
brief and blameless flirtation. (How curious it was that she could
scrape off the accretions of the months that had followed and
could remember how she had felt on that spring night—as trembling, as expectant, as altogether young as if they had sat together
underneath a blooming apple tree.) But now, knowing that her
own embarrassment had come from something else, she thought
that perhaps his had, too, and she connected his awkwardness on
that September day with a report she had had, embedded in a
bulletin on everyone, from her sole communicant, since her retreat, with the Olympian world. This informant had run into
Alfred at a party and had said that he was having a very bad
time of it with a divorce, with poverty, with a tempest that had
carried off his job, and, at last, with a psychoanalyst, whose fees
he could not possibly afford. Perhaps the nightmare had been
well under way when they had met beside the chancery. Without
alcohol and without the company of other people, they had had
to be shy or their suffering would have shown in all its humiliating dishabille. Would it be true still if they should inescapably
meet this afternoon in an Early Flemish room?

Suddenly, on this common level, in this state of social dis-
placement, Emma wished to hunt for Alfred and urgently tell
him that she hoped it had not been as bad for him as it had been
for her. But naturally she was not so naïve, and she got up and

went purposefully to look at two Holbeins. They pleased her, as Holbeins always did. The damage, though, was done, and she did not really see the pictures; Eisenburg's hypothetical suffering and her own real suffering blurred the clean lines and muddied the lucid colors. Between herself and the canvases swam the months of spreading, cancerous distrust, of anger that made her seasick, of grief that shook her like an influenza chill, of the physical afflictions by which the poor victimized spirit sought vainly to wreck the arrogantly healthy flesh.

Even that one glance at his face, seen from a distance through the lowing crowd, told her, now that she had repeated it to her mind's eye, that his cheeks were drawn and his skin was gray (no soap and water can ever clean away the grimy look of the sick at heart) and his stance was tired. She wanted them to go together to some hopelessly disreputable bar and to console one another in the most maudlin fashion over a lengthy succession of powerful drinks of whisky, to compare their illnesses, to marry their invalid souls for these few hours of painful communion, and to babble with rapture that they were at last, for a little while, no longer alone. Only thus, as sick people, could they marry. In any other terms, it would be a *mésalliance,* doomed to divorce from the start, for rubes and intellectuals must stick to their own class. If only it could take place—this honeymoon of the cripples, this nuptial consummation of the abandoned—while drinking the delicious amber whisky in a joint with a jukebox, a stout barkeep, and a handful of tottering derelicts; if it could take place, would it be possible to prevent him from marring it all by talking of secondary matters? That is, of art and neurosis, art and politics, art and science, art and religion? Could he lay off the fashions of the day and leave his learning in his private entrepôt? Could he, that is, see the apple fall and not run madly to break the news to Newton and ask him what on earth it was all about? Could he, for her sake (for the sake of this pathetic rube all but weeping for her own pathos in the Metropolitan Museum), forget the whole dispute and, believing his eyes for a change, admit that the earth was flat?

It was useless for her now to try to see the paintings. She went, full of intentions, to the Van Eyck diptych and looked for a long time at the souls in Hell, kept there by the implacable, indifferent, and genderless angel who stood upon its closing mouth. She looked, in renewed astonishment, at Jo Davidson's pink, wrinkled, embalmed head of Jules Bache, which sat, a trinket on a fluted pedestal, before a Flemish tapestry. But she was really conscious of nothing but her desire to leave the museum in the company of Alfred Eisenburg, her cousin-german in the territory of despair.

So she had to give up, two hours before the closing time, although she had meant to stay until the end, and she made her way to the central stairs, which she descended slowly, in disappointment, enviously observing the people who were going up, carrying collapsible canvas stools on which they would sit, losing themselves in their contemplation of the pictures. Salvador Dali passed her, going quickly down. At the telephone booths, she hesitated, so sharply lonely that she almost looked for her address book, and she did take out a coin, but she put it back and pressed forlornly forward against the incoming tide. Suddenly, at the storm doors, she heard a whistle and she turned sharply, knowing that it would be Eisenburg, as, of course, it was, and he wore an incongruous smile upon his long, El Greco face. He took her hand and gravely asked her where she had been all this year and how she happened to be here, of all places, of all days. Emma replied distractedly, looking at his seedy clothes, his shaggy hair, the green cast of his white skin, his deep black eyes, in which all the feelings were disheveled, tattered, and held together only by the merest faith that change *had* to come. His hand was warm and her own seemed to cling to it and all their mutual necessity seemed centered here in their clasped hands. And there was no doubt about it; he had heard of her collapse and he saw in her face that she had heard of his. Their recognition of each other was instantaneous and absolute, for they cunningly saw that they were children and that, if they wished, they were free for the rest of this winter Sunday to play together, quite naked, quite innocent. "What a day it is! What a place!" said Alfred Eisenburg. "Can I buy you a drink, Emma? Have you time?"

She did not accept at once; she guardedly inquired where they could go from here, for it was an unlikely neighborhood for the sort of place she wanted. But they were *en rapport,* and he, wanting to avoid the grownups as much as she, said they would go across to Lexington. He needed a drink after an afternoon like this—didn't she? Oh, Lord, yes, she did, and she did not question what he meant by "an afternoon like this" but said that she would be delighted to go, even though they would have to walk on eggs all the way from the Museum to the place where the bottle was, the peace pipe on Lexington. Actually, there was nothing to fear; even if they had heard catcalls, or if someone had hooted at them, "Intellectual loves Rube!" they would have been impervious, for the heart carved in the bark of the apple tree would contain the names Emma and Alfred, and there were no perquisites to such a conjugation. To her own heart, which was shaped exactly like a valentine, there came a winglike palpitation, a delicate exigency, and all the fragrance of all the flowery springtime love affairs that ever were seemed waiting for them in the whisky bottle. To mingle their pain, their handshake had promised them, was to produce a separate entity, like a child that could shift for itself, and they scrambled hastily toward this profound and pastoral experience.

Beatrice Trueblood's Story

When Beatrice Trueblood was in her middle thirties and on the very eve of her second marriage, to a rich and reliable man—when, that is, she was in the prime of life and on the threshold of a rosier phase of it than she had ever known before—she overnight was stricken with total deafness.

"The vile unkindness of fate!" cried Mrs. Onslager, the hostess on whose royal Newport lawn, on a summer day at lunchtime, poor Beatrice had made her awful discovery. Mrs. Onslager was addressing a group of house guests a few weeks after the catastrophe and after the departure of its victim—or, more properly, of its victims, since Marten ten Brink, Mrs. Trueblood's fiancé, had been there, too. The guests were sitting on the same lawn on the same sort of dapper afternoon, and if the attitudes of some of Mrs. Onslager's audience seemed to be somnolent, they were so because the sun was so taming and the sound of the waves was a glamorous lullaby as the Atlantic kneaded the rocks toward which the lawn sloped down. They were by no means indifferent to this sad story; a few of them knew Marten ten Brink, and all of them knew Beatrice Trueblood, who had been Mrs. Onslager's best friend since their girlhood in St. Louis.

"I'm obliged to call it fate," continued Mrs. Onslager. "Because there's nothing wrong with her. All the doctors have reported the same thing to us, and she's been to a battalion of them. At first she refused to go to anyone on the ground that it would be a waste of money, of which she has next to none, but Jack and I finally persuaded her that if she didn't see the best men in the country and let us foot the bills, we'd look on it as unfriendliness. So, from Johns Hopkins, New York Hospital, the Presbyterian, the Leahy Clinic, and God knows where, the same account comes back: there's nothing physical to explain it, no disease, no lesion, there's been no shock, there were no hints of any kind beforehand. And *I'll* not allow the word 'psychosomatic' to be uttered in my presence—not in this connection, at any rate—because I know Bea as well as I know myself and she is not hysterical. Therefore, it has to be fate. And there's a particularly spiteful irony in it if you take a backward glance at her life. If ever a woman deserved a holiday from tribulation, it's Bea. There was first of all a positively hideous childhood. The classic roles were reversed in the family, and it was the mother who drank and the father who nagged. Her brother took to low life like a duck to water and was a juvenile delinquent before he was out of knickers—I'm sure he must have ended up in Alcatraz. They were unspeakably poor, and Bea's aunts dressed her in their hand-me-downs. It was a house of the most humiliating squalor, all terribly genteel. You know what I mean—the mother prettying up her drunkenness by those transparent dodges like 'Two's my limit,' and keeping the gin in a Waterford decanter, and the father looking as if butter wouldn't melt in his mouth when they were out together publicly, although everyone knew that he was a perfectly ferocious tartar. Perhaps it isn't true that he threw things at his wife and children and whipped them with a razor strop—he didn't have to, because he could use his tongue like a bludgeon. And then after all that horror, Bea married Tom Trueblood—really to escape her family, I think, because she couldn't possibly have loved him. I mean it isn't possible to love a man who is both a beast and a fool. *He* was drunker than her mother ever thought of being; he was obscene, he was raucous, his infidelities to that good, beautiful girl were of a vulgarity that caused the mind to boggle. I'll never know how she managed to live with him for seven mortal years. And then at last, after all those tempests, came Marten ten Brink, like redemption itself. There's nothing sensational in Marten, I'll admit. He's rather a stick, he was born rather old, he's rather jokeless and bossy. But, oh, Lord, he's so *safe*, he was so protective of her, and he is so scrumptiously rich! And two months before the wedding *this* thunderbolt comes out of nowhere. It's indecent! It makes me so angry!" And this faithful friend shook her pretty red head rapidly in indignation, as if she were about to hunt down fate with a posse and hale it into court.

"Are you saying that the engagement has been broken?" asked Jennie Fowler, who had just got back from Europe and to whom all this was news.

Mrs. Onslager nodded, closing her eyes as if the pain she suffered were unbearable. "They'd been here for a week, Marten and Bea, and we were making the wedding plans, since they were to be married from my house. And the very day after this gruesome thing happened, she broke the engagement. She wrote him a note and sent it in to his room by one of the maids. I don't know what she said in it, though I suppose she told him she didn't want to be a burden, something like that—much more gracefully, of course, since Bea *is* the soul of courtesy. But whatever it was, it must have been absolutely unconditional, because he went back to town before dinner the same night. The letter I got from him afterward scarcely mentioned it—he only said he was sorry his visit here had ended on 'an unsettling note.' I daresay he was still too shocked to say more."

"Hard lines on ten Brink," said Harry McEvoy, who had never married.

"What do you mean, 'hard lines on *ten Brink?*' " cried Mrs. Fowler, who had married often, and equally often had gone, livid with rage, to Nevada.

"Well, if he was in love with her, if he counted on this . . . Not much fun to have everything blow up in your face. Lucky in a way, I suppose, that it happened before, and not afterward."

The whole party glowered at McEvoy, but he was entirely innocent of their disapproval and of his stupidity that had provoked it, since he was looking through a pair of binoculars at a catboat that seemed to be in trouble.

"If he was in love with her," preached Mrs. Fowler rabidly, "he would have stuck by her. He would have refused to let her break the engagement. He would have been the one to insist on the specialists, he would have moved heaven and *earth,* instead of which he fled like a scared rabbit at the first sign of bad luck. I thought he was only a bore—I didn't know he was such a venomous pill."

"No, dear, he isn't that," said Priscilla Onslager. "Not the most sensitive man alive, but I'd never call him a venomous pill. After all, remember it was *she* who dismissed *him*."

"Yes, but if he'd had an ounce of manliness in him, he would have put up a fight. No decent man, no manly man, would abandon ship at a time like that." Mrs. Fowler hated men so passionately that no one could dream why she married so many of them.

"Has it occurred to any of you that she sent him packing because she didn't want to marry him?" The question came from Douglas Clyde, a former clergyman, whose worldliness, though it was very wise, had cost him his parish and his cloth.

"Certainly not," said Priscilla. "I tell you, Doug, I know Bea. But at the moment the important thing isn't the engagement, because I'm sure it could be salvaged if she could be cured. And how's she to be cured if nothing's wrong? I'd gladly have the Eumenides chase me for a while if they'd only give her a rest."

Jack Onslager gazed through half-closed eyes at his wholesome, gabbling wife—he loved her very much, but her public dicta were always overwrought and nearly always wrong—and then he closed his eyes tight against the cluster of his guests, and he thought how blessed it would be if with the same kind of simple physical gesture one could also temporarily close one's ears. One could decline to touch, to taste, to see, but it required a skill he had not mastered to govern the ears. Those stopples made of wax and cotton would be insulting at a party; besides, they made him claustrophobic, and when he used them, he could hear the interior workings of his skull, the boiling of his brains in his brainpan, a rustling behind his jaws. He would not like to go so far as Beatrice had gone, but he would give ten years of his life (he had been about to say he would give his eyes and changed it) to be able, when he wanted, to seal himself into an impenetrable silence.

To a certain extent, however, one could insulate the mind against the invasion of voices by an act of will, by causing them to blur together into a general hubbub. And this is what he did now; in order to consider Mrs. Trueblood's deafness, he deafened himself to the people who were talking about it. He thought of the day in the early summer when the extraordinary thing had taken place.

It had been Sunday. The night before, the Onslagers and their houseparty—the young Allinghams, Mary and Leon Herbert, Beatrice and ten Brink—had gone to a ball. It was the kind of party to which Onslager had never got used, although he had been a multimillionaire for twenty years and not only had danced through many such evenings but had been the host at many more, in his own houses or in blazoned halls that he had hired. He was used to opulence in other ways, and took for granted his boats and horses and foreign cars. He also took for granted, and was bored by, most of the rites of the rich: the formal dinner parties at which the protocol was flawlessly maneuvered and conversation moved on stilts and the food was platitudinous; evenings of music to benefit a worthy cause (How papery the turkey always was at the buffet supper after the Grieg!); the tea parties to which one went obediently to placate old belles who had lost their looks and their husbands and the roles that, at their first assembly, they had assumed they would play forever. Well-mannered and patient, Onslager did his duty suavely, and he was seldom thrilled.

But these lavish, enormous midsummer dancing parties in the fabulous, foolish villas on Bellevue Avenue and along the Ocean Drive did make his backbone tingle, did make him glow. Even when he was dancing, or proposing a toast, or fetching a wrap for a woman who had found the garden air too cool, he always felt on these occasions that he was static, looking at a colossal *tableau vivant* that would vanish at the wave of a magic golden wand. He was bewitched by the women, by all those *soignée* or demure or jubilant or saucy or dreaming creatures in their caressing, airy dresses and their jewels whose priceless hearts flashed in the light from superb chandeliers. They seemed, these dancing, laughing, incandescent goddesses, to move in inaccessible spheres; indeed, his wife, Priscilla, was transfigured, and, dancing with her, he was moon-struck. No matter how much he drank (the champagne of those evenings was invested with a special property—one tasted the grapes, and the grapes had come from celestial vineyards), he remained sober and amazed and, in

spite of his amazement, so alert that he missed nothing and re-
corded everything. He did not fail to see, in looks and shrugs
and the clicking of glasses, the genesis of certain adulteries, and
the demise of others in a glance of contempt or an arrogant withdrawal. With the accuracy of the uninvolved bystander, he heard
and saw among these incredible women moving in the aura of
their heady perfume their majestic passions—tragic heartbreak,
sublime fulfillment, dangerous jealousy, the desire to murder.
When, on the next day, he had come back to earth, he would
reason that his senses had devised a fiction to amuse his mind,
and that in fact he had witnessed nothing grander than flirtations and impromptu pangs as ephemeral as the flowers in the
supper room.

So, at the Paines' vast marble house that night, Onslager,
aloof and beguiled as always, had found himself watching
Beatrice Trueblood and Marten ten Brink with so much interest
that whenever he could he guided his dancing partner near
them, and if they left the ballroom for a breath of air on a bench
beside a playing fountain, or for a glass of champagne, he managed, if he could do so without being uncivil to his interlocutor
and without being observed by them, to excuse himself and follow. If he had stopped to think, this merciful and moral man
would have been ashamed of his spying and eavesdropping, but
morality was irrelevant to the spell that enveloped him. Besides,
he felt invisible.

Consequently, he knew something about that evening that
Priscilla did not know and that he had no intention of telling
her, partly because she would not believe him, partly because
she would be displeased at the schoolboyish (and parvenu) way
he put in his time at balls. The fact was that the betrothed were
having a quarrel. He heard not a word of it—not at the dance,
that is—and he saw not a gesture or a grimace of anger, but he
nevertheless knew surely, as he watched them dance together,
that ten Brink was using every ounce of his strength not to shout,
and to keep in check a whole menagerie of passions—fire-breath-
ing dragons and bone-crushing serpents and sabertoothed tigers—
and he knew also that Beatrice was running for dear life against
the moment when they would be unleashed, ready to gobble her
up. Her broad, wide-eyed, gentle face was so still it could have

been a painting of a face that had been left behind when the woman who owned it had faded from view, and Bea's golden hand lay on ten Brink's white sleeve as tentatively as a butterfly. Her lover's face, on the other hand, was—Onslager wanted to say "writhing," and the long fingers of the hand that pressed against her back were splayed out and rigid, looking grafted onto the sunny flesh beneath the diaphanous blue stuff of her dress. He supposed that another observer might with justification have said that the man was animated and that his fiancée was becomingly engrossed in all he said, that ten Brink was in a state of euphoria as his wedding approached, while Beatrice moved in a wordless haze of happiness. He heard people admiringly remark on the compatibility of their good looks; they were said to look as if they were "dancing on air"; women thanked goodness that Mrs. Trueblood had come at last into a safe harbor, and men said that ten Brink was in luck.

As soon as the Onslagers and their guests had driven away from the ball and the last echo of the music had perished and the smell of roses had been drowned by the smell of the sea and the magic had started to wane from Onslager's blood, he began to doubt his observations. He was prepared to elide and then forget his heightened insights, as he had always done in the past. The group had come in two cars, and the Allinghams were with him and Priscilla on the short ride home. Lucy Allingham, whose own honeymoon was of late and blushing memory, said, with mock petulance, 'I thought *young* love was supposed to be what caught the eye. But I never saw anything half so grand and wonderful as the looks of those two." And Priscilla said, "How true! How magnificently right you are, Lucy! They were radiant, both of them."

Late as it was, Priscilla proposed a last drink and a recapitulation of the party—everyone had found it a joy—but ten Brink said, "Beatrice and I want to go down and have a look at the waves, if you don't mind," and when no one minded but, on the contrary, fondly sped them on their pastoral way, the two walked down across the lawn and presently were gone from sight in the romantic mist. Their friends watched them and sighed, charmed, and went inside to drink a substitute for nectar.

Hours later (he looked at his watch and saw that it was close on five o'clock), Jack woke, made restless by something he had sensed or dreamed, and, going to the east windows of his bedroom to look at the water and see what the sailing would be like that day, he was arrested by the sight of Beatrice and Marten standing on the broad front steps below. They were still in their evening clothes. Beatrice's stance was tired; she looked bedraggled. They stood confronting each other beside the balustrade; ten Brink held her shoulders tightly, his sharp, handsome (but, thought Onslager suddenly, Mephistophelean) face bent down to hers.

"You mustn't think you can shut your mind to these things," he said. "You can't shut your ears to them." Their voices were clear in the hush of the last of the night.

"I am exhausted with talk, Marten," said Beatrice softly. "I will not hear another word."

An hour afterward, the fairest of days dawned on Newport, and Jack Onslager took out his sloop by himself in a perfect breeze, so that he saw none of his guests until just before lunch, when he joined them for cocktails on the lawn. Everyone was there except Beatrice Trueblood, who had slept straight through the morning but a moment before had called down from her windows that she was nearly ready. It was a flawless day to spend beside the sea: the chiaroscuro of the elm trees and the sun on the broad, buoyant lawn shifted as the sea winds disarrayed the leaves, and yonder, on the hyacinthine water, the whitecaps shuddered and the white sails swelled; to the left of the archipelago of chairs and tables where they sat, Mrs. Onslager's famous rosary was heavily in bloom with every shade of red there was and the subtlest hues of yellow, and her equally famous blue hydrangeas were at their zenith against the house, exactly the color of this holiday sky, so large they nodded on their stems like drowsing heads.

The Allinghams, newly out of their families' comfortable houses in St. Louis and now living impecuniously in a railroad flat in New York that they found both adventurous and odious, took in the lawn and seascape with a look of real greed, and even of guile, on their faces, as if they planned to steal something or eat forbidden fruit.

In its pleasurable fatigue from the evening before and too much sleep this morning, the gathering was momentarily disinclined to conversation, and they all sat with faces uplifted and eyes closed against the sun. They listened to the gulls and terns shrieking with their evergreen gluttony; they heard the buzz-saw rasp of outboard motors and the quick, cleaving roar of an invisible jet; they heard automobiles on the Ocean Drive, a power mower nasally shearing the grass at the house next door, and from that house they heard, as well, the wail of an infant and the panicky barking of an infant dog.

"I wish this day would never end," said Lucy Allingham. "This is the kind of day when you want to kiss the earth. You want to have an affair with the sky."

"Don't be maudlin, Lucy," said her husband. "And above all, don't be inaccurate." He was a finicking young cub who had been saying things like this all weekend.

Onslager's own wife, just as foolishly given to such figures of speech but with a good deal more style, simply through being older, said, "Look, here comes Beatrice. She looks as if her eyes were fixed on the Garden of Eden before the Fall and as if she were being serenaded by angels."

Marten ten Brink, an empiricist not given to flights of fancy, said, "Is that a depth bomb I hear?"

No one answered him, for everyone was watching Beatrice as she came slowly, smiling, down the stone steps from the terrace and across the lawn, dulcifying the very ground she walked upon. She was accompanied by Mrs. Onslager's two Siamese cats, who cantered ahead of her, then stopped, forgetful of their intention, and closely observed the life among the blades of grass, then frolicked on, from time to time emitting that ugly parody of a human cry that is one of the many facets of the Siamese cat's scornful nature. But the insouciant woman paid no attention to them, even when they stopped to fight each other, briefly, with noises straight from Hell.

"You look as fresh as dew, dear," said Priscilla. "Did you simply sleep and sleep?"

"Where on earth did you get that fabric?" asked Mrs. Herbert. "Surely not here. It must have come from Paris. Bea, I do declare your clothes are always the ones I want for myself."

"Sit here, Beatrice," said ten Brink, who had stood up and was indicating the chair next to himself. But Beatrice, ignoring him, chose another chair. The cats, still flirting with her, romped at her feet; one of them pretended to find a sporting prey between her instep and her heel, and he pounced and buck-jumped silently, his tail a fast, fierce whip. Beatrice, who delighted in these animals, bent down to stroke the lean flanks of the other one, momentarily quiescent in a glade of sunshine.

"What do you think of the pathetic fallacy, Mrs. Trueblood?" said Peter Allingham, addressing her averted head. "Don't you think it's pathetic?" By now, Onslager was wishing to do him bodily harm for his schoolmasterish teasing of Lucy.

"Monkeys," murmured Beatrice to the cats. "Darlings."

"Beatrice!" said Marten ten Brink sharply, and strode across to whisper something in her ear. She brushed him away as if he were a fly, and she straightened up and said to Priscilla Onslager, "Why is everyone so solemn? Are you doing a charade of a Quaker meeting?"

"Solemn?" said Priscilla, with a laugh. "If we seem solemn, it's because we're all smitten with this day. Isn't it supreme? Heaven can't possibly be nicer."

"Is this a new game?" asked Beatrice, puzzled, her kind eyes on her hostess's face.

"Is what a new game, dear?"

"What *is* going on?" She had begun to be ever so slightly annoyed. "Is it some sort of silence test? We're to see if we can keep still till teatime? Is it that? I'd be delighted—only, for pity's sake, tell me the rules and the object."

"Silence test! Sweetheart, you're still asleep. Give her a martini, Jack," said Priscilla nervously, and to divert the attention of the company from her friend's quixotic mood she turned to ten Brink. "I believe you're right," she said, "I believe they're detonating depth bombs. Why on Sunday? I thought sailors got a day of rest like everybody else."

A deep, rumbling subterranean thunder rolled, it seemed, beneath the chairs they sat on.

"It sounds like ninepins in the Catskills," said Priscilla.

"I never could abide that story," said Mary Herbert. "Or the Ichabod Crane one, either."

Jack Onslager, his back toward the others as he poured a drink for Beatrice, observed to himself that the trying thing about these weekends was not the late hours, not the overeating and the overdrinking and the excessive batting of tennis balls and shuttlecocks; it was, instead, this kind of aimless prattle that never ceased. There seemed to exist, on weekends in the country, a universal terror of pauses in conversation, so that it was imperative for Mary Herbert to drag in Washington Irving by the hair of his irrelevant head. Beatrice Trueblood, however, was not addicted to prattle, and he silently congratulated her on the way, in the last few minutes, she had risen above their fatuous questions and compliments. That woman was as peaceful as a pool in the heart of a forest. He turned to her, handing her the drink and looking directly into her eyes (blue and green, like an elegant tropic sea), and he said, "I have never seen you looking prettier."

For just a second, a look of alarm usurped her native and perpetual calm, but then she said, "So you're playing it, too. I don't think it's fair not to tell me—unless this is a joke on me. Am I 'it'?"

At last, Jack was unsettled; Priscilla was really scared; ten Brink was angry, and, getting up again to stand over her like a prosecuting attorney interrogating a witness of bad character, he said, "You're not being droll, Beatrice, you're being tiresome."

Mrs. Onslager said, "Did you go swimming this morning, lamb? Perhaps you got water in your ears. Lean over—see, like this," and she bent her head low to the left and then to the right while Beatrice, to whom these calisthenics were inexplicable, watched her, baffled.

Beatrice put her drink on the coffee table, and she ran her forefingers around the shells of her ears. What was the look that came into her face, spreading over it as tangibly as a blush? Onslager afterward could not be sure. At the time he had thought it was terror; he had thought this because, in the confusion that ensued, he had followed, sheeplike with the others, in his wife's lead. But later, when he recaptured it for long reflection, he thought that it had not been terror, but rather that Priscilla in naming it that later was actually speaking of the high color of her own state of mind, and that the look in Beatrice's eyes and on her mouth had been one of revelation, as if she had opened a door and had found behind it a new world so strange, so foreign to all her knowledge and her experience and the history of her senses, that she had spoken only approximately when, in a far, soft, modest voice, she said, "I am deaf. That explains it."

When Onslager had come to the end of his review of those hours of that other weekend and had returned to the present one, he discovered that he had so effectively obliterated the voices around him that he now could not recall a single word of any of the talk, although he had been conscious of it, just as some part of his mind was always conscious of the tension and solution of the tides.

"But you haven't told us yet how she's taking it now," Mrs. Fowler was saying.

"I can't really tell," replied Priscilla. "I haven't been able to go to town to see her, and she refuses to come up here—the place probably has bad associations for her now. And I'm no good at reading between the lines of her letters. She has adjusted to it, I'll say that." Priscilla was thoughtful, and her silence commanded her guests to be silent. After a time, she went on, "I'll say more than that. I'll say she has adjusted too well for my liking. There is a note of gaiety in her letters—she is almost jocose. For example, in the last one she said that although she had lost Handel and music boxes and the purring of my Siamese, she had gained a valuable immunity to the voices of professional Irishmen."

"Does she mention ten Brink?" asked someone.

"Never," said Priscilla. "It's as if he had never existed. There's more in her letters than the joking tone. I wish I could put my finger on it. The closest I can come is to say she sounds *bemused.*"

"Do you think she's given up?" asked Jennie Fowler. "Or has she done everything there is to be done?"

"The doctors recommended psychiatry, of course," said Priscilla, with distaste. "It's a dreary, ghastly, humiliating thought, but I suppose—"

"I should think you *would* suppose!" cried Mrs. Fowler. "You shouldn't leave a stone unturned. Plainly someone's got to *make* her go to an analyst. They're not that dire, Priscilla. I've heard some very decent things about several of them."

"It won't be I who'll make her go," said Priscilla, sighing. "I disapprove too much."

"But you don't disapprove of the medical people," persisted Jennie. "Why fly in the face of their prescription?"

"Because . . . I *couldn't* do it. Propose to Beatrice that she is mental? I can't support the thought of it."

"Then Jack must do it," said the managerial divorcée. "Jack must go straight down to town and get her to a good man and then patch up things with Marten ten Brink. I still detest the sound of him, but *de gustibus,* and I think she ought to have a husband."

The whole gathering—even the cynical ex-pastor—agreed that this proposal made sense, and Onslager, while he doubted his right to invade Bea's soft and secret and eccentric world, found himself so curious to see her again to learn whether some of his conjectures were right that he fell in with the plan and agreed to go to New York in the course of the week. As, after lunch, they dispersed, some going off for *boccie* and others to improve their shining skin with sun, Douglas Clyde said sotto voce to Onslager, "Why doesn't it occur to anyone but you and me that perhaps she doesn't *want* to hear?"

Startled, the host turned to his guest. "How did you know I thought that?"

"I watched you imitating deafness just now," said the other. "You looked beatific. But if I were you, I wouldn't go too far."

"Then you believe . . . contrary to Priscilla and her Eumenides . . . ?"

"I believe what you believe—that the will is free and very strong," Clyde answered, and he added, "I believe further that it can cease to be an agent and become a despot. I suspect hers *has.*"

Mrs. Trueblood lived in the East Seventies, in the kind of apartment building that Jack Onslager found infinitely more melancholy than the slum tenements that flanked and faced it in the sultry city murk of August. It was large and new and commonplace and jerry-built, although it strove to look as solid as

Gibraltar. Its brick façade was an odious mustardy brown. The doorman was fat and choleric, and when Onslager descended from his cab, he was engaged in scolding a band of vile-looking little boys who stood on the curb doubled up with giggles, now and again screaming out an unbelievable obscenity when the pain of their wicked glee abated for a moment. A bum was lying spread-eagled on the sidewalk a few doors down; his face was bloody but he was not dead, for he was snoring fearsomely. Across the street, a brindle boxer leaned out a window, his fore-paws sedately crossed on the sill in a parody of the folded arms of the many women who were situated in other windows, irascibly agreeing with one another at the tops of their voices that the heat was hell.

But the builders of the house where Mrs. Trueblood lived had pretended that none of this was so; they had pretended that the neighborhood was bourgeois and there was no seamy side, and they had commemorated their swindle in a big facsimile of rectitude. Its square foyer was papered with a design of sanitary ferns upon a field of hygenic beige; two untruthful mirrors mir-rored each other upon either lateral wall, and beneath them stood love seats with aseptic green plastic cushions and straight blond legs. The slow self-service elevator was an asphyxiating chamber with a fan that blew a withering sirocco; its tinny walls were embossed with a meaningless pattern of fleurs-de-lis; light, dim and reluctant, came through a fixture with a shade of some ersatz material made esoterically in the form of a starfish. As Onslager ascended to the sixth floor at a hot snail's pace, hearing alarming *râles* and exhalations in the machinery, he was fretful with his discomfort and fretful with snobbishness. He deplored the circumstances that required Beatrice, who was so openhearted a woman, to live in surroundings so mean-minded; he could not help thinking sorrowfully that the ideal place for her was Marten ten Brink's house on Fifty-fifth Street, with all its depths of richness and its sophisticated planes. The bastard, he thought, taking Jennie Fowler's line—why did he let her down? And then he shook his head, because, of course, he knew it hadn't been like that.

This was not his first visit to Beatrice. He and Priscilla had been here often to cocktail parties since she had lived in New

York, but the place had made no impression on him; he liked cocktail parties so little that he went to them with blinders on and looked at nothing except, furtively, his watch. But today, in the middle of a hostile heat wave and straight from the felicities of Newport, he was heavyhearted thinking how her apartment was going to look; he dreaded it; he wished he had not come. He was struck suddenly with the importunity of his mission. How had they *dared* be so possessive and dictatorial? And why had *he* been delegated to urge her to go to a psychiatrist? To be sure, his letter to her had said only that since he was going to be in the city, he would like to call on her, but she was wise and sensitive and she was bound to know that he had come to snoop and recommend. He was so embarrassed that he considered going right down again and sending her some flowers and a note of apology for failing to show up. She could not know he was on his way, for it had not been possible to announce himself over the house telephone—and how, indeed, he wondered, would she know when her doorbell rang?

But when the doors of the elevator slid open, he found her standing in the entrace of her apartment. She looked at her watch and said, "You're punctual." Her smiling, welcoming face was cool and tranquil; unsmirched by the heat and the dreariness of the corridor and, so far as he could judge, by the upheaval of her life, she was as proud and secret-living as a flower. He admired her and he dearly loved her. He cherished her as one of life's most beautiful appointments.

"That you should have to come to town on such a day!" she exclaimed. "I'm terribly touched that you fitted me in."

He started to speak; he was on the point of showering on her a cornucopia of praise and love, and then he remembered that she would not hear. So, instead, he kissed her on either cheek and hoped the gesture, mild and partial, obscured his turmoil. She smelled of roses; she seemed the embodiment of everything most pricelessly feminine, and he felt as diffident as he did at those lovely summer balls.

Her darkened, pretty sitting room—he should not have been so fearful, he should have had more faith in her—smelled of roses, too, for everywhere there were bowls of them from Priscilla's garden, brought down by the last weekend's guests.

"I'm terribly glad you fitted me in," repeated Beatrice when she had given him a drink, and a pad of paper and a pencil, by means of which he was to communicate with her (she did this serenely and without explanation, as if it were the most natural thing in the world), "because yesterday my bravura began to peter out. In fact, I'm scared to death."

He wrote, "You shouldn't be alone. Why not come back to us? You know nothing would please us more." How asinine, he thought. What a worthless sop.

She laughed. "Priscilla couldn't bear it. Disaster makes her cry, good soul that she is. No, company wouldn't make me less scared."

"Tell me about it," he wrote, and again he felt like a fool.

It was not the deafness itself that scared her, she said—not the fear of being run down by an automobile she had not heard or violated by an intruder whose footfall had escaped her. These anxieties, which beset Priscilla, did not touch Beatrice. Nor had she yet begun so very much to miss voices or other sounds she liked; it was a little unnerving, she said, never to know if the telephone was ringing, and it was strange to go into the streets and see the fast commotion and hear not a sound, but it had its comic side and it had its compensations—it amused her to see the peevish snapping of a dog whose bark her deafness had forever silenced, she was happy to be spared her neighbors' vociferous television sets. But she was scared all the same. What had begun to harry her was that her wish to be deaf had been granted. This was exactly how she put it, and Onslager received her secret uneasily. She had not bargained for banishment, she said; she had only wanted a holiday. Now, though, she felt that the Devil lived with her, eternally wearing a self-congratulatory smile.

"You are being fanciful," Onslager wrote, although he did not think she was at all fanciful. "You can't wish yourself deaf."

But Beatrice insisted that she *had* done just that.

She emphasized that she had *elected* to hear no more, would not permit of accident, and ridiculed the doting Priscilla's sentimental fate. She had done it suddenly and out of despair, and she was sorry now. "I am ashamed. It was an act of cowardice," she said.

"How cowardice?" wrote Onslager.

"I could have broken with Marten in a franker way. I could simply have told him I had changed my mind. I didn't have to make him mute by making myself deaf."

"Was there a quarrel?" he wrote, knowing already the question was superfluous.

"Not *a* quarrel. An incessant wrangle. Marten is jealous and he is indefatigably vocal. I wanted terribly to marry him—I don't suppose I loved him very much but he seemed good, seemed safe. But all of a sudden I thought, I cannot and I will not listen to another word. And now I'm sorry because I'm so lonely here, inside my skull. Not hearing makes one helplessly egocentric."

She hated any kind of quarrel, she said—she shuddered at raised voices and quailed before looks of hate—but she could better endure a howling brawl among vicious hoodlums, a shrill squabble of shrews, a degrading jangle between servant and mistress, than she could the least altercation between a man and a woman whose conjunction had had as its origin tenderness and a concord of desire. A relationship that was predicated upon love was far too delicate of composition to be threatened by cross-purposes. There were houses where she would never visit again because she had seen a husband and wife in ugly battle dress; there were restaurants she went to unwillingly because in them she had seen lovers in harsh dispute. How could things ever be the same between them again? How could two people possibly continue to associate with each other after such humiliating, disrobing displays?

As Beatrice talked in discreet and general terms and candidly met Jack Onslager's eyes, in another part of her mind she was looking down the shadowy avenue of all the years of her life. As a girl and, before that, as a child, in the rambling, shambling house in St. Louis, Beatrice in her bedroom doing her lessons would hear a rocking chair on a squeaking board two flights down; this was the chair in which her tipsy mother seesawed, dressed for the street and wearing a hat, drinking gin and humming a Venetian barcarole to which she had forgotten the words. Her mother drank from noon, when, with lamentations, she got up, till midnight, when, the bottle dry, she fell into a groaning, nightmare-ridden unconsciousness that resembled the condition immediately preceding death. This mortal sickness was terrifying; her removal from reality was an ordeal for everyone, but not even the frequent and flamboyant threats of suicide, the sobbed proclamations that she was the chief of sinners, not all the excruciating embarrassments that were created by that interminable and joyless spree, were a fraction as painful as the daily quarrels that commenced as soon as Beatrice's father came home, just before six, and continued, unmitigated, until he—a methodical man, despite his unfathomable spleen—went to bed, at ten. Dinner, nightly, was a hideous experience for a child, since the parents were not inhibited by their children or the maid and went on heaping atrocious abuse upon each other, using sarcasm, threats, lies—every imaginable expression of loathing and contempt. They swam in their own blood, but it was an ocean that seemed to foster and nourish them; their awful wounds were their necessities. Freshly appalled each evening, unforgiving, disgraced, Beatrice miserably pushed her food about on her plate, never hungry, and often she imagined herself alone on a desert, far away from any human voice. The moment the meal was finished, she fled to her schoolbooks, but even when she put her fingers in her ears, she could hear her parents raving, whining, bullying, laughing horrible, malign laughs. Sometimes, in counterpoint to this vendetta, another would start in the kitchen, where the impudent and slatternly maid and one of her lovers would ask *their* cross questions and give crooked answers.

In spite of all this hatefulness, Beatrice did not mistrust marriage, and, moreover, she had faith in her own even temper. She was certain that sweetness could put an end to strife; she believed that her tolerance was limitless, and she vowed that when she married there would be no quarrels.

But there were. The dew in her eyes as a bride gave way nearly at once to a glaze when she was a wife. She left home at twenty, and at twenty-one married Tom Trueblood, who scolded her for seven years. Since she maintained that it took two to make a quarrel, she tried in the beginning, with all the cleverness and fortitude she had, to refuse to be a party to the storms that rocked her house and left it a squalid shambles, but her silence only made her husband more passionately angry, and at last, ripped and raw, she had to defend herself. Her dignity trampled to death, her honor mutilated, she fought back, and felt estranged from the very principles of her being. Like her parents, Tom Trueblood was sustained by rancor and contentiousness; he really seemed to love these malevolent collisions which made her faint and hot and ill, and he seemed, moreover, to regard them as essential to the married state, and so, needing them, he would not let Beatrice go but tricked and snared her and strewed her path with obstacles, until finally she had been obliged to run away and melodramatically leave behind a note.

Beatrice was a reticent woman and had too much taste to bare all these grubby secret details, but she limned a general picture for Onslager and, when she had finished, she said, "Was it any wonder, then, that when the first blush wore off and Marten showed himself to be cantankerous my heart sank?"

Onslager had listened to her with dismay. He and Priscilla were not blameless of the sin she so deplored—no married people were—but their differences were minor and rare and guarded, their sulks were short-lived. Poor, poor Beatrice, he thought. Poor lamb.

He wrote, "Have you heard from Marten?"

She nodded, and closed her eyes in a dragging weariness. "He has written me volumes," she said. "In the first place, he doesn't believe that I am deaf but thinks it's an act. He says I am indulging myself, but he is willing to forgive me if I will only come to my senses. Coming to my senses involves, among other things, obliterating the seven years I lived with Tom—I told you he was madly jealous? But how do you amputate experience? How do you eliminate what intransigently *was*?"

"If that's Marten's line," wrote Onslager, revolted by such childishness, "obviously you can't give him a second thought. The question is what's to be done about *you?*"

"Oh, I don't know, I *do* not know!" There were tears in her voice, and she clasped her hands to hide their trembling. "I am afraid that I am too afraid ever to hear again. And you see how I speak as if I had a choice?"

Now she was frankly wringing her hands, and the terror in her face was sheer. "My God, the mind is diabolical!" she cried. "Even in someone as simple as I."

The stifling day was advancing into the stifling evening, and Jack Onslager, wilted by heat and unmanned by his futile pity, wanted, though he admired and loved her, to leave her. There was nothing he could do.

She saw this, and said, "You must go. Tomorrow I am starting with an analyst. Reassure Priscilla. Tell her I know that everything is going to be all right. I know it not because I am naïve but because I *still* have faith in the kindness of life." He could not help thinking that it was will instead of faith that put these words in her mouth.

And, exteriorly, everything was all right for Beatrice. Almost at once, when she began treatment with a celebrated man, her friends began to worry less, and to marvel more at her strength and the wholeness of her worthy soul and the diligence with which she and the remarkable doctor hunted down her troublesome quarry. During this time, she went about socially, lent herself to conversation by reading lips, grew even prettier. Her analysis was a dramatic success, and after a little more than a year she regained her hearing. Some months later, she married a man, Arthur Talbot, who was far gayer than Marten ten Brink and far less rich; indeed, a research chemist, he was poor. Priscilla deplored this aspect of him, but she was carried away by the romance (he looked like a poet, he adored Beatrice) and at last found it in her heart to forgive him for being penniless.

When the Talbots came to Newport for a long weekend not long after they had married, Jack Onslager watched them both with care. No mention had ever been made by either Jack or Beatrice of their conversation on that summer afternoon, and when his wife, who had now become a fervent supporter of psychiatry, exclaimed after the second evening that she had never seen Beatrice so radiant, Onslager agreed with her. Why not? There would be no sense in quarreling with his happy wife. He himself had never seen a face so drained of joy, or even of the memory of joy; he had not been able to meet Bea's eyes.

That Sunday—it was again a summer day beside the sea— Jack Onslager came to join his two guests, who were sitting alone on the lawn. Their backs were to him and they did not hear his approach, so Talbot did not lower his voice when he said to his wife, "I have told you a thousand times that my life has to be exactly as I want it. So stop these hints. *Any* dedicated scientist worth his salt is bad-tempered."

Beatrice saw that her host had heard him; she and Onslager travailed in the brief look they exchanged. It was again an enrapturing day. The weather overhead was fair and bland, but the water was a mass of little wrathful whitecaps.

Between the Porch and the Altar

At five in the morning in February, it is darker than at midnight. The streets are empty of automobiles; the latest readers have gone to bed and the earliest risers are only just opening their eyes. The few people abroad are swift and furtive, like creatures who must quit a place before the sun shines forth. At that hour, their business seems mysterious and even shady, although they are not cutthroats or thieves but only watchmen and charwomen and night waitresses on their way home to dine at sunrise. So uncluttered are the streets, so starkly direct is the walk of the people that anyone whose custom it is to get up much later, at the normal hour, feels when he goes out that he intrudes upon a scene of bare but important privacy. And a light, springing on abruptly to make a staring eye in a blackened building, may stir him with embarrassment and wonder as if this were an alarm or an esoteric signal of hostility.

It was cold and the girl was hungry. She paused in the vestibule of the apartment building and half turned to unlock the outer door again and go back to her warm bed. But as she lingered, she observed a bright blue star high over the houses opposite and the sight inexplicably gave her resolution, even though its color was so pure and frigid that it made her all the more conscious of the cold. She drew on her gloves and went out, shocked by a biting gust of wind which passed her by like a big rapid bird. She turned the corner and hurried along Sixth Avenue on her way to the first mass.

Although the star, which was now behind her, had had a decisive effect on her, it had not dispelled her apprehension and her distrust of the unfamiliar streets. While her feet were steady enough, her breath was erratic and her ears were fanciful, making her think she heard sinister noises behind the blank faces of the buildings. She looked straight ahead, fearful of what she might see in the dark doorways and even in the interiors of delicatessens and bakery shops whose cheerless windows were dimly silvered by the street lights. And still, discomforting as it was, she took a certain pleasure in her uneasiness, feeling that even the most accidental castigation was excellent at the beginning of Lent.

On the corner of Thirteenth Street, there was a large secondhand shop whose windows she had many times studied with an incredulous amusement, so dreadful were the objects shown there: funeral wreaths made of human hair, armadillo baskets, back-scratchers that looked like sets of bad teeth, ceramic vessels of an unimaginable function. The antelope with eaten ears and rubbed-off hide, the alabaster boar and the complacent Chinese philosopher made of porcelain stared out, looking, even at five in the morning, for someone to adopt them and give them a good home.

Within the doorway of the shop, a drunken beggar sprawled like a lumpy rug, his feet in ruptured tennis shoes thrust out onto the sidewalk. He was not asleep. Under a cap set raffishly at an angle on his head, he regarded the girl's approach with an eye made visible to her by the arc light at the intersection. Paradoxically, her pace slowed down as her terror rose, and the man had risen to his feet before she was abreast of him. The smell of whisky was so strong that it was like a taste in her mouth. He stretched forth his hand and whined, "Lady, I'm hungry, lady."

She did not carry a purse, but in her pocket were two dimes and a quarter. She intended to put the quarter into the poor box and the dimes in the candle offering, for she wished to light a candle for the repose of her mother's soul and another for the safe-keeping of two friends, captive in China by the Japanese. Although it was only a fraction of a minute that she debated, a succession of images with an individual emotion attending each revolved through her mind. She saw the poor box in the dim vestibule of the lower church and heard her quarter click upon the other coins. This box was stationed beside the holy-water font, near the statue of Our Lord between whose palely gleaming feet someone placed fresh flowers each day. Then she saw her mother lying in the limbo of her last hours, unsightly, unconsoled, and heard the sonorous matter-of-factness of her Protestant relatives to whom this transformation, so unbearable to her, was neither strange nor dreadful. It was not that they did not grieve their kinswoman, but it was that they had many times before known death and had learned, through its reiteration, that it was no wonder. She, still bedewed with baptism, had knelt and the blue beads of her rosary slipped through her fingers until her mother's soul abandoned its wrecked flesh. She had been, she remembered, in the middle of the fourth decade when her aunt, vigilant at the bedside, had whispered, "She is gone now." And she remembered how the odor of belladonna had obtruded so in her devotions that part of her mind pronounced the word over and over as if it belonged to a litany.

Then she tried to fancy her friends as they might be in prison and could not, could only see them before their fireplace on a winter day of the year before. She had come to tea and had stayed on for sherry. She sat on a maroon sofa; a little dog slept with his chin on her arm, whimpering once in a dream. There was shortbread to go with the wine and as she ate a piece she realized that it was the texture rather than the taste that made it her favorite pastry. In an easy silence that came in the conversation, she saw her reflection in the brass bedwarmer that hung beside the fireplace, and this blurred travesty of her face had the power, as the star had done this morning, to make her suddenly purposeful, and she told her friends goodbye that day, although they did not leave for another week.

In the early desolation of this present year, she felt tenderness muffling her like smoke and smaller, general pictures showed themselves to her: a clean room, a forced branch of apple blossoms, her mother's silver-backed hairbrush, her friends' passport pictures.

No time at all had passed. She saw the beggar's lips part again. She could not find her voice, and one bold self chided her for her nervousness, for this was no extraordinary occurrence. On the contrary, the rarest day in New York was the one on which one was not asked for money by a fellow like this or by a senile tart or by a belligerent child. She could pass by, or she could say she had no money. But mechanically she had paused—she was not yet a craftsman in the selection of experience and her days were often a chain of pauses—and the man took advantage of her hesitance, saying, with his vague face close to hers, "Lady, was you ever hungry?" Her fear of him was obliterated by an abstract but brilliant anger, for his question was beside the point, unfair, a contemptible trick. She almost spoke her indignation aloud and then her anger burnt itself out; she controlled herself stiffly like a soldier: on this grave day she should not presume to judge. And into the cold hand, she put the quarter and one of the dimes. The man muttered something but she did not hear what he said and she went on hastily. In the windows of a flower shop, she saw her shadow drift through pots of white azaleas. When she turned the corner at Sixteenth Street, she slowed down, for two nuns walked slowly ahead of her. Her hunger returned with savage force.

The entrance to the Jesuits' church was dark. Its black iron gates were open only a crack. A nightlike and velvety blackness stood solidly between the columns on the porch of the upper church. The stone steps leading downward seemed colder than the sidewalks, and the holy water was cold. It teemed with the ripples of fingers that had been dipped there before her own, and the touch of it on her forehead was icy. Today, between the wounded feet, were dark roses. One of the sisters touched the feet and then pressed her fingers to her lips.

The mass had not begun. The girl said her prayers, but she could not concentrate, for her mind was occupied with what she would do with her last dime. Who was the neediest, she questioned: the poor, the dead, or the oppressed? Truly, she had to admit that she loved the poor less than her mother and her friends, and yet, for this very reason—for a willful sacrifice—should she not put the dime into the poor box? Then she thought, but I have given already to the poor. Lout, wastrel that he was, he was poor and it is not the duty, nor even the right, of the almsgiver to distinguish between degrees of poverty. But between her mother and her friends, how should she choose? Should one pray for someone's long life here or for someone else's shortened term in Purgatory? It occurred to her to offer her mass for her mother and light the candle for the prisoners. This seemed like a compromise and did not satisfy her, yet there was no alternative.

Four nuns were in the pew ahead of her and, finishing their prayers, they sat back and simultaneously opened their missals. On the right hand of one, she saw a wedding ring. She had never before been close enough to a nun to notice this, and she wondered when it was that the badge of their eternal marriage was placed upon them and if they really did feel unity with God at that moment or felt, instead, hushed isolation. The words of the Gospel today were: *Lay up to yourselves treasures in heaven: where neither the rust nor the moth doth consume, and where thieves do not break through nor steal. For where thy treasure is, there is thy heart also.* The words, now that she had seen the wedding ring, seemed richer and more profoundly exciting than they had done before, and for a moment she was almost idolatrous, worshipful, almost, of the fair-skinned sisters in their tower of ivory and their house of gold. And then she recoiled, for under the coif of one she saw black stubble.

The church was full, principally of old people who slept so little that rising for the earliest mass on Ash Wednesday was no great hardship. Most of them were telling their beads and only a few had missals. An aged man behind her said his Aves aloud in a harsh, sibilant voice and his false teeth clicked on one another in counterpoint to the measured whispers of his wooden beads. A bald young seminarian entered the sanctuary to light the candles on the altar. He genuflected gracefully and liquidly like a dancer, and the hand with which he crossed himself was as long and white and as shapely as one painted by El Greco. He was incongruously beautiful in his surroundings, for the lower church was ugly and in bad taste. The statues were gaudy, even in this shadowy light, and the crucifix was sentimental. In all the accouterments of the sanctuary, there was a mixture of modern leanness and Victorian laciness. The seminarian alone seemed a product of inspiration.

At last the bell rang and the celebrant with his altar boys entered the sanctuary. The girl prayed that nothing would mar the spirit of penance which she carried like a fragile light; she closed her eyes to the nun's neck and begged forgiveness for her fault-finding. All through the mass, while she fixed her attention on her mother—imagining her face, disembodied, hovering in a crowd of other faces in Purgatory, which she saw as an echoing marble hall—she wondered if she had not committed an act of betrayal, both to the beggar to whom she gave unwillingly and to the parish poor, deprived of her offering through her cowardice. Although she knew that her confusion would be understood and unraveled by the counsel of a confessor, she went, half dazed, to the communion rail and received, she felt, with an imperfect heart. Afterwards, her thanksgiving was more full of petition than of gratitude: I humbly beseech guidance and my whole heart desires wisdom and stern purpose. Reason reiterated to her that she had properly allocated her good will: money to the poor, a mass for the dead, a candle for the oppressed. Yet she was not assured in her heart and she prayed with a dry compulsion.

When she had received the cross of ashes on her forehead, she went directly to the altar of St. Francis Xavier at the back of the church. The cups for the candles were blood-red; the flames cast a sheen on the closed tabernacle. She knelt down to pray the saint to watch over her friends. As she stood up to take the taper to light her candle, she saw an old woman coming from the vestibule. She pretended not to see, for she recognized the old crone who was always there before the sun and the Jesuits discovered her. At later masses she begged on the sidewalk. The girl had already lighted the taper and was looking for a fresh cup when the woman reached the altar.

Blear-eyed, unctuous, crafty, she slithered to her knees. "God bless you, dearie," she began, her face touching the skirt of the girl's coat. The dime was in the pocket on that side, and it was as if the woman smelled it with her long nose or heard it with her ear beneath her sour gray hair or felt it on her furrowed cheek. It was impossible to ignore her, and the girl could think of no way to resolve this preposterous dilemma. Her hand still held the taper and her eyes still roved the tiers of candles seeking an unlighted one.

It seemed some time before the old woman spoke again. Behind them, people were moving about, unconcerned with anything but the small devotional tasks they had set themselves.

Some were making the stations of the cross, some prayed at the Lady altar, others gazed meditatively at the crucifix. The bald young beadle had come again into the sanctuary and was preparing the altar for the next mass. Everything happening in the church was pious and usual, save for the squalid commerce at St. Francis' altar. The ceiling seemed oppressively low; she was reminded of a dreary train shed.

When the woman spoke again, her voice was more eager and hopeful. She nodded toward the candles and said, "They're every one of them lit already and they won't bring the new ones round till after the eight o'clock." How well she knew the habits of this church's servants! She had probably studied them for months, huddling in shadows behind the grating that enclosed the baptismal font or in the corner where the statue of St. Ignatius stood. The girl saw that what she said was true and she blew out the taper and replaced it. But she was determined to make the offering and she stepped down to go to another altar. The old woman took hold of her coat and peered straight into her face, shamelessly. She said, "You're young and pretty, girlie." The oblique entreaty weakened her, embarrassed her movement like a web, and finally she put her hand into her pocket and took out the dime. Before the clever, metropolitan fingers had enclosed the alms, the girl had gone, running down Sixteenth Street to the corner of Sixth Avenue. The streets were lighter now, and the big star had begun to pale. Shopkeepers were putting trash on the sidewalks; news vendors were cutting the ropes that bound the morning papers; a melancholy white horse ambled down the street dragging a milk truck after him.

When the coffee was nearly ready and her rooms were full of its fragrance, the girl looked at her forehead in the bathroom mirror and saw that the Jesuit had marked her clearly. She washed away the ashes, leaving herself alone possessed of the knowledge of her penance.

I Love Someone

My friends have gone now, abandoning me to the particular pallor of summer twilight in the city. How long the daytime loiters, how noisily the children loiter with it! I hear their reedy voices splintering like glass in the streets as they tell their mothers no, they *won't* come in, and call up to the filmed windows of the tenements on the avenue, "Marian!" or "Harold!" dropping, invariably, the final consonant. Abashed by my own indolence, I wish to scold them for theirs, to ask them sharply, as if I were their teacher, "Who on earth is Harol?" I hear their baseballs thudding against the walls of shops, hear their feet adroitly skipping rope, hear them singing songs from *South Pacific*, hear a sudden, solo scream for which there is neither overture nor finale: the moment it is formed, it is finished like a soap bubble. Listening to them half against my will, I think how strong a breed they are, how esoteric a society with their shrouded totems and taboos. What is the meaning of this statement I hear, shouted in singsong suddenly, "My mother is in the bathroom shooting dice"? Or ponder this: a day or so ago, I saw a legend on the sidewalk that haunts me; within a fat, lopsided heart were chalked the words "I LOVE SOMEONE." I thought at the time how artful this confession was that concealed the identity both of the lover and of the beloved. In an adult (in myself, say) it would have been a boast or a nervous lie, but in the child who wrote the words, it was no more than an ironic temporizing.

My impatience with the children tonight is not real; I am lorn for other reasons as I sit here in the heat and in the mauve light, facing an empty evening, realizing too late that I should have provided myself with company and something to do. It has been a melancholy day and the events of it have enervated me: I simply sit, I simply stare at a bowl of extraordinary roses. Harriet Perrine and Nancy Lang and Mady Hemingway and I went this afternoon to the funeral of our dear friend, Marigold Trask. Famously beautiful, illustrious for her charm and her stylish wit, inspired with joy, Marigold killed herself with sodium amytal last Thursday night, leaving bereft a husband and two young sons. The five of us had been fast friends since school days and the death has shocked us badly; in an odd way, it has also humiliated us and when we lunched today before the service (held in a non-religious "chapel" fitted out with an electric organ and bogus Queen Anne chairs) we did not speak of Marigold at all but talked as we had talked before, when she was alive and with us. We talked of plays and clothes and we plumbed the depths of the scandals that deluged the world outside our circle. We behaved, even now that it had happened, as if nothing unsightly would ever happen to any of us. But afterward, after we had seen the gray-gloved lackeys close her casket and carry her out to the hearse, we came up here to my apartment and with our drinks we did discuss at length the waste and the folly and the squalor of her suicide. There was a note of exasperation in the tone of all our voices. "If people would only wait!" cried Nancy Lang. "Everything changes in time."

"If it was Morton, she could have divorced him," said Mady. "*We* would have stuck by."

"I don't think it was Morton," said Harriet and we all nodded. Morton was a stick and none of us liked him, but he was not at all the sort of man who would drive a woman to *that*. To lovers, yes, and trips alone, but not to *that*. Then Harriet proposed, "It could have been the Hungarian."

"Oh, but that's been over for months," said Mady. "Besides, *she* chucked *him*." Mady is an orthodox woman. Her mind is as literal as her modern house.

Nancy said, "It must have been something much deeper. If it wasn't, then it was simply beastly of her to do this to the boys."

We talked then of the effects of such catastrophes on children, and though we spoke wholly in banalities (we are not women with original minds; we "keep up" and that's the most that can be said of us) and were objective, I could not help thinking that the others felt it would have been better if, assuming that one of us had had to take the overdose of sleeping pills, it had been I. For I have never married and my death would discommode no one. My friends would miss me, it is true: to put it bluntly, they would have no one to coddle and champion in a world unfit for solitary living. They are devoted to me, I am sure, and in their way they love me, but they are not *concerned*. They cannot be, for there is no possible way for them really to know me now; it would embarrass them, as married women, to confront the heart of a spinster which is at once impoverished and prodigal, at once unloving and lavishly soft. Therefore, out of necessity, they have invented their own image of me, and I fancy that if I tried to disabuse them of their notions, they would think I was hallucinated; in alarm they would get me to a really good doctor as quickly as possible.

Harriet, who is a tireless and faulty analyst of character, often explains in my presence that I am "one of those beings whom nothing, but nothing, can bring down to earth." Does she mean by this that I am involved in nothing? Or does she derive her ethereal vision of me from the fact that I never appear to change? My moods don't show and perhaps this gives me a blandness that, for some reason, she associates with the upper air. I never make drastic changes in my life; I seldom rearrange my furniture; I have worn the same hairdress for twenty years. Harriet lives in a state of daily surprise but surprise only for things and scenes and people that do not alter in the least. She begins her day by marveling that her egg is, in color and constituents, exactly the same as the egg of yesterday and of the day before and that tomorrow the same phenomenon will greet her happy, natural eyes. Whenever she goes into the Frick to look at her favorite pictures, she stands awed before the El Greco "St. Jerome," her hands clasped rapturously, her whole being seeming to cry out in astonishment, "Why, it's still here!"

But I am grateful that Harriet and Nancy and Mady have embedded me in a myth. This sedative conviction of theirs, that ichor runs in my veins and that mine is an operating principle of the most vestal kind, has kept me all these years (I am forty-three) from going into hysteria or morbidity or hypochondria or any other sort of beggary by which even the most circumspect spinster of means is tempted. I have no entourage of coat-carrying young men and drink is not a problem; the causes I take up are time-honored and uncontroversial: I read aloud to crippled children but I do not embroil myself in anything remotely ideological. I know that my friends have persuaded themselves that I once had a love affair that turned out badly—upon this universal hypothesis rests perhaps as much as half the appeal of unmarried women who show no signs of discontent, and there is no tact more beatifying than that which protects a grief that is never discussed. Now and again it amuses me to wonder what their conjectures are. I daresay that when they speculate, they kill off my lover in splendor, in a war, perhaps, or in a tuberculosis sanitarium. I can all but hear them forearming their dinner guests before I arrive: "Jenny Peck has never married, you know. She had one of those really tragic things when she was very young, so totally devastating that she has never said a word about it even to her closest friends."

But the fact is that there has been nothing in my life. I have lived the whole of it in the half-world of brief flirtations (some that have lasted no longer than the time it takes to smoke a cigarette under the marquee of a theater between the acts), of friendships that have perished of the cold or have hung on, desiccated, outliving their meaning and never once realizing the possibility of love. I have dwelt with daydreams that through the years have become less and less high-reaching, so apathetic, indeed, that now I would rather recite the names of the forty-eight states to myself than review one of those skimpy fictions. From childhood I have unfailingly taken all the detours around passion and dedication; or say it this way, I have been a pilgrim without faith, traveling in an anticipation of loss, certain that the grail will have been spirited away by the time I have reached my journey's end. If I did not see in myself this skepticism, this unconditional refusal, this—I admit it—contempt, I would find it degrading that no one has ever proposed marriage to me. I do not wish to refuse but I do not know how to accept. In my ungivingness, I am more dead now, this evening, than Marigold Trask in her suburban cemetery.

But my reflexes are still lively and my nerves are spry, and sometimes I can feel the pain through the anesthetic. Then it is on certain mornings I will not wake, although my dreams, abstract and horrible, pester me relentlessly and raucously. The sarcasm of my dreams! All night long my secret mind derides and crucifies me, "Touché!" All the same, I do not consciously nurse the wound. Be caught red-eyed by my friends? It would never do, for their delusion is my occupation: *cogitant, ergo sum*. Unlike Marigold, I will never unsettle these affectionate women, for whatever would I do without them? I would not know how to order my existence if they did not drop in on me after a gallery or a matinee, have me to dine when the extra man is either "interesting" or "important" (the Egyptologists I have listened to! The liberals with missions! Shall I forget until my dying day the herpetologist that Mady once produced who talked to me of cobras throughout the fish?), have me to come for long weekends in the summer, send me flowers and presents of perfume in clever bottles, lend me their husbands for lunch, treat me, in general, like someone of royal blood suspended in an incurable but unblemishing disease.

Thus it is I sit and meditate in the ambiguous light while beyond me and below me the city children vehemently play at stick-ball, postponing their supper hour just as I postpone mine. I know that I should stir. I must take the glasses and the ashtrays to the kitchen and rinse them out because my silent and fastidious maid, who comes to me by the day, would be alarmed if I departed from my custom. I must eat what she has prepared for me, I must read, must bathe, must read again, and finally turn off my light and commence my nightmares in the heat that lies like jelly on the city. But thinking of myself, of Marigold (how secretly she did it!), of the anonymous child who told the world he loved someone, I am becalmed and linger exactly where I am, unable to give myself a purpose for doing anything.

By now my friends are at home in Fairfield County. All three of them are ardent gardeners, and presently they will be minding their tomato vines and weeding between their rows of corn. I imagine their cool, rose-laden drawing rooms where, later, they will join their husbands for cocktails. Is it too late for me to ring up someone and propose dinner and an air-conditioned movie? Much too late. Much too late. Idiotically, I say the phrase aloud, compulsively repeat it several times and try to think how my lips look as I protract the word "much."

Gradually the words lose their meaning and I am speaking gibberish. *Now* what would they think of me, babbling like a cretin? I have just set my tongue against the roof of my mouth to say "late" for the dozenth time when a bumble of voices invades my open windows. The clamor, as of an angry, lowing multitude, is closer than the street sounds and I sit up, startled. Perhaps it is a party in the garden next door; but the voices are harsh and there is no laughter. The sound echoes as if a mass of people were snarling at the bottom of a pit; muted, they are nevertheless loud—and loud, the words are nevertheless indistinguishable. For a minute I remain, true to my character, remote from the tumult; but then, because there is neither pause nor change and because the sound is so close at hand, I grow ever so slightly afraid. Still, I do not move, not even to switch on a light, until suddenly, like the report of a gun, an obscenity explodes in the hot dusk. The voice that projects it is an adolescent boy's and it is high and helpless with outrage. I rise and stand quivering before my chair and then I move across the carpet and open the door to my bedroom.

As I hesitate, I once again take note of the glasses and the ashtrays. And once again, although my heart is pounding rapidly now with a fear that is gathering itself into a shape, I think, quite separately, of Marigold and I wonder if she knew when it was coming. *It!* Shocked at my circumvention, I revise: when *death* was coming. But does that improve the sentence? *It* means as much to me as *death* does—or, for that matter, *life*. I go further and I say, "I wonder if she finally knew why she wanted nothing else?" For I, you see, dwelling upon the rim of life, see everyone in the arena as acting blindly. I would know, but did Marigold? Does the bullfighter know, until he is actually in danger, that the danger itself is his master? Not the glory, not the ladies' roses, or the pageant, or the accolades, but the flashing glimpse of the evil and the random and the unknown? Far from the stage and safe, I, who never act on impulse, know nearly precisely the outcome of my always rational behavior. It makes me a woman without hope; but since there is no hope there is also no despair.

I lean from my bedroom window and discover the source of the noises in the courtyard of this respectable apartment house: a huddle of boys stands in the service entry where the gate has not yet been locked. They are of all sizes and all shapes and colors, and I recognize them at once as a roving band of youthful hoodlums whose viciousness I have read about in the tabloids. All their faces wear the same expression of mingled rage and fascination, and all their eyes are fixed on something I cannot see. There are twenty-odd of them and it is from them that comes this steady snarl. I lean out farther and at my end of the areaway I see a pair of boys fighting. The fight is far advanced, for one of them, big and black-haired, has the other down on the cement. Blood comes from his wide mouth, open in a gasp, and his hands flutter weakly against his assailant's shoulders. The engagement is silent. Stunned by its cynicism, I try to pity the loser but I cannot, for his defeat has made him hideous. Strands of his brown hair lie like scattered rags on the cement in a parody of a halo.

Now other tenants are aroused and come to their windows to look in revulsion and indignation. Above me a man shouts down, "I am going to call the police!" But the fight continues, silently and maliciously, and the boys in the gateway ignore my neighbor, who grows very angry and cries, "Get out of this court! I have a gun here!"

But still they pay no attention. At last the boy on his back closes his eyes and utters some soft sentence that is evidently his surrender, for the other, giving him one last brutish punch in the ribs, gets up, staggering a little. Now that the excitement is over, the audience instantly quits the gateway; they vanish swiftly in a body, every man jack of them, and do not even glance back. But the victor lingers like an actor on a stage as if he were expecting applause, and seeing that the boys are gone, he looks up at the windows of the apartments. Perhaps he is seeking the man who threatened him with the law; perhaps he wants to challenge *him*. But he finds, instead, myself and as he looks at me, his feral face breaks into a shameless smile. I suppose he is eighteen or nineteen, but the wickedness in his little black eyes and his scarlet mouth is as old as the hills. He wears a thin mustache, so well groomed and theatrical that it appears to adhere to his lip with gum. He looks at me and then looks down at the other boy, who is just now getting to his feet, and then looks up at me again and shrugs his shoulders. Is he asking me to confirm the justice of his violence? Or the beauty of it? Or the passion?

The blood is driven crudely to my face and I turn from the window. It is my intention at first to lie down on my bed and, if I can, to close my inner eye to what I have just seen. But instead, as will-less as a somnambulist, I go to my door and take the elevator down and let myself out into the street where there is no longer any tumult but, rather, a palpable and sneaky hush. I feel watched and mind-read. With no conscious plan, I walk quickly down the street past the dull buildings with their mongrel doors and their minuscule plots of gritty privet, walking toward the avenue where I reason the boys have gone. A squad car drives slowly by and a bored policeman throws his cigarette stub from the window.

My aim is now articulate. I realize that I want to see the ruffians face to face, both the undefeated and the overthrown, to see if I can penetrate at last the mysterious energy that animates everyone in the world except myself.

But I do not reach the avenue. Halfway there, I glance down at the sidewalk and I see that swollen heart with its fading proclamation, I LOVE SOMEONE. As easily it could read, beneath a skull and crossbones, I HATE SOMEONE. Now there is no need to investigate further; the answer is here in the obvious, trumpery scrawl, and I go back to my apartment and gather up the glasses and the ashtrays.

My friends and I have managed my life with the best of taste and all that is lacking at this banquet where the appointments are so elegant is something to eat.

Cops and Robbers

The child, Hannah, sitting hidden on the attic steps, listened as her mother talked on the telephone to Aunt Louise.

"Oh, there's no whitewashing the incident. The child's hair is a sight, and it will be many moons, I can tell you, before I'll forgive Hugh Talmadge. But listen to me. The worst of it is that this baby of five has gone into a decline like a grown woman— like you or me, dear, at our most hysterical. Sudden fits of tears for no apparent reason and then simply hours of brooding. She won't eat, she probably doesn't sleep. I can't stand it if she's turning mental."

The door to the bedroom, across the hall, was half open, and through the crack of the door at the foot of the attic steps Hannah saw that in the course of the night her parents had disarrayed the pale-green blanket cover and now, half off the bed, drooping and askew, it looked like a great crumpled new leaf, pulled back here and there to show the rosy blankets underneath. In the bedroom it is spring, thought Hannah, and outdoors it is snowing on the Christmas trees; that is a riddle.

Her mother lay in the center of the big bed, which was as soft and fat as the gelded white Persian cat who dozed at her side, his scornful head erect, as if he were arrested not so much by sleep as by a coma of boredom and disgust. A little earlier, before he struck this pose, he had sniffed and disdained the bowl of cream on his mistress's breakfast tray, and when she had tried to cajole him into drinking it, he had coolly thrashed his tail at her. In the darkness of her enclosure, Hannah yearned, imagining herself in the privileged cat's place beside her mother, watching the mellowing, pillowing, billowing snow as it whorled down to meet the high tips of the pine trees that bordered the frozen formal garden. If she were Nephew, the cat, she would burrow into the silky depths of the bed up to her eyes and rejoice that she was not outside like a winter bird coming to peck at suet and snowy crumbs at the feeding station.

It was ugly and ungenerous here where she was, on the narrow, splintery stairs, and up in the attic a mouse or a rat scampered on lightly clicking claws between the trunks; some hibernating bees buzzed peevishly in their insomnia. Stingy and lonesome like old people, the shut-ins worried their grievances stealthily. And Hannah, spying and eavesdropping (a sin and she knew it), felt the ends of her cropped hair and ran a forefinger over her freshly combed boy's cut—the subject of her mother's conversation. Something like sleep touched her eyeballs, though this was early morning and she had not been awake longer than an hour. But it was tears, not drowsiness, that came. They fell without any help from her; her cheeks did not rise up as they usually did when she cried, to squeeze themselves into puckers like old apples, her mouth did not open in a rent of woe, no part of her body was affected at all except the eyes themselves, from which streamed down these mothering runnels.

"*Why did he do it?*" Her mother's question into the telephone was an impatient scream. "Why do men do half the things they do? Why does Arthur treat you in public as if you were an enlisted man? I swear I'll someday kill your rear admiral for you. Why does Eliot brag to Frances that he's unfaithful? Because they're sadists, every last one of them. I am very anti-man today."

"What is anti-man?" whispered Hannah.

The stools on either side of the fireplace in the den were ottomans, and sometimes Hannah and her mother sat on them in the late afternoon, with a low table between them on which were set a Chinese pot of verbena tisane, two cups, and a plate of candied orange rind. At the thought of her mother's golden hair in the firelight, and the smell of her perfume in the intimate warmth, and the sound of her voice saying, "Isn't this gay, Miss Baby?" the tears came faster, for in her heavy heart Hannah felt certain that now her hair was cut off, her mother would never want to sit so close to her again. Unable to see through the narrow opening of the door any longer, she leaned her face against the wall and felt her full tears moistening the beaver-board as she listened to her mother's recital of Saturday's catastrophe.

"On the face of it, the facts are innocent enough. He took her to town on Saturday to buy her a pair of shoes, having decided for his own reasons that I have no respect for my children's feet—the shoes he got are too odious, but that's another story. Then when he brought her back, here she was, cropped, looking like a rag doll. He said she'd begged to have it done. Of course she'd done nothing of the kind. To put the most charitable construction on the whole affair, I *could* say that when he went into the barbershop to have his own hair cut, he'd had a seizure of amnesia and thought he had Andy with him, or Johnny, or Hughie, and decided to kill two birds with one stone. And then afterward he was afraid of what I'd say and so cooked up this canard—and more than likely bribed her to bear him out. The way men will weasel out of their missteps! It isn't moral. It shocks me."

He did *not* think I was Andy or Johnny or Hughie, Hannah said to herself. In the barbershop at her father's club there had been no one but grown men and a fat stuffed skunk that stood in front of the mirror between two bottles of bay rum, its leathery nose pointed upward as if it were trying to see the underside of its chin in the looking glass. Through a steaming towel, her father had muttered, "Just do as I say, Homer, cut it off," and the barber, a lean man with a worried look on his red face, flinched, then shrugged his shoulders and began to snip off Hannah's heavy curls, frowning with disapproval and remarking once under his breath that women, even though they were five years old, were strictly forbidden on these premises. On the drive home, her peeled head had felt cold and wet, and she had not liked the smell that gauzily hovered around her, growing more cloying as the heater in the car warmed up. At a red light, her father had turned to her and, patting her on the knee, had said, "You look as cute as a button, young fellow." He had not seemed to hear her when she said, "I do not. I'm not a young fellow," nor had he noticed when she moved over against the door, as far away from him as she could get, hating him bitterly and hating her nakedness. Presently, he'd turned on the radio to a news broadcast and disputed out loud with the commentator.

Hannah, left all alone, had stared out the window at the wolfish winter. In one snow-flattened field she saw tall flames arising from a huge wire trash basket, making the rest of the world look even colder and whiter and more unkind. Her father scowled, giving the radio what for, swearing at the slippery roads—carrying on an absent-minded tantrum all by himself. Once, halted by a woman driver whose engine was stalled, he'd said, "Serves her right. She ought to be home at this time of day tending to business." As they turned in their own drive, he said a lie: "That was a fine idea of yours to have your hair cut off." She had never said any such thing; all she had said, when they were having lunch in a brown, cloudy restaurant, was that she would rather go to the barbershop with him than wait at Grandma's. But she had not contradicted him, for he did not countenance contradiction from his children. "I'm an old-fashioned man," he announced every morning to his three sons and his two daughters. "I am the autocrat of this breakfast table." And though he said it with a wink and a chuckle, it was clear that he meant business. Johnny, who was intellectual, had told the other children that an autocrat was a person like Hitler, and he had added sarcastically, "That sure is something to brag about, I must say."

The voice speaking into the phone took on a new tone, and Hannah, noticing this, looked out through the crack again. "What? Oh, please don't change the subject, pet, I really want your help. It isn't a trifle, it's terribly important, I really think it is the *final* effrontery. . . . All right, then, if you promise that we can come back to it." With her free hand, Hannah's mother lightly stroked the cat, who did not heed, and she lay back among her many pillows, listening to her sister but letting her eyes rove the room as if she were planning changes in its decoration. "Yes, I did hear it but I can't remember where," she said inattentively. Then, smiling in the pleasure of gossip, forgetting herself for a moment, she went on, "Perhaps I heard it from Peggy the night she came to dinner with that frightful new man of hers. That's it—it was from *him* I heard it, and automatically discounted it for no other reason than that I took an instantaneous dislike to him. If he is typical of his department, the C.I.A. must be nothing more or less than the Gestapo."

Hannah's head began to ache and she rolled it slowly, look-

ing up the steep, ladderlike steps into the shadowy attic. She was
bored now that the talk was not of her, and she only half heard
her mother's agile voice rising, descending, laughing quickly,
pleading, "Oh, no! It's not *pos*sible!" and she sucked her fingers,
one by one. Her tears had stopped and she missed them as she
might have missed something she had lost. Like her hair, like all
her golden princess curls that the barber had gazed at sadly as
they lay dead and ruined on the tiled floor.

Now that Hannah's hair was short, her days were long: it
was a million hours between breakfast and lunch, and before, it
had been no time at all, because her mother, still lying in her
oceanic bed, had every morning made Hannah's curls, taking her
time, telling anyone who telephoned that she would call back,
that just now she was busy "playing with this angel's hair."

Today was Wednesday, and Hannah had lived four lifetimes
since Saturday afternoon. Sunday had been endless, even though
her brothers and her sister had been as exciting as ever, with
their jokes and contests and their acrobatics and their game of
cops-and-robbers that had set the servants wild. But even in their
mad preoccupation it had been evident that the sight of Hannah
embarrassed them. "The baby looks like a skinned cat," said
Andy, and Hughie said, "It was a dopey thing to do. The poor
little old baby looks like a mushroom." The parents did nothing
to stop this talk, for all day long they were fighting behind the
closed door of the den, not even coming out for meals, their
voices growing slower and more sibilant as they drank more. "I
hate them," Johnny had said in the middle of the long, musty
afternoon, when the cops were spent and the robbers were sick
of water-pistol fights. "When they get stinking, I hate them,"
said Johnny. "I bet a thousand dollars he had had a couple when
he had them cut the baby's hair." Janie shouted, "Oh, that baby,
baby, baby, baby! Is that goofy baby the only pebble on the
beach? Why do they have to mess up Sunday fighting over her?
I'm going crazy!" And she ran around in a circle like a dog,
pulling at her hair with both hands.

On Monday morning, when Hannah's father took the older
children off to Marion Country Day School on his way to the
city, she had nearly cried herself sick, feeling that this Monday

the pain of their desertion was more than she could bear. She would not let go of Janie's hand, and she cried, "You'll be sorry if you come back and find I'm dead!" Janie, who was ten and hot-blooded—she took after Daddy, who had Huguenot blood—had slapped Hannah's hand and said, "The nerve of some people's children!" Hannah had stood under the porte-cochere, shivering in her wrapper and slippers, until the car went out the driveway between the tulip trees; she had waved and called, "Goodbye, dearest Janie and Johnny and Andy and Hughie!" Only Johnny had looked back; he rolled down the window and leaned out and called, "Ta-ta, half pint." They were all too old and busy to pay much attention to her, though often they brought her presents from school—a jawbreaker or a necklace made of paper clips. The four older children were a year apart, starting with John, who was thirteen, and ending with Janie, and when family photographs were taken, they were sometimes lined up according to height; these were called "stairstep portraits," and while Hannah, of course, was included, she was so much smaller than Janie that she spoiled the design, and one time Uncle Harry, looking at a picture taken on Palm Sunday when all five children were sternly holding their palms like spears, had said, pointing to Hannah, "Is that the runt of the litter or is it a toy breed?" Andy, who was Uncle Harry's pet, said, "We just keep it around the house for its hair. It's made of spun gold, you know, and very invaluable." This evidently was something the barber had not known, for he had swept the curls into a dustpan and thrown them into a chute marked "Waste." She wondered how long they would keep her now that her sole reason for existence was gone.

In other days, after Daddy and the children left and the maids began their panicky, silent cleaning, flinging open all the windows to chill the house to its heart, Hannah would run upstairs to the big bedroom to sit on the foot of the bosomy bed and wait while her mother drank her third cup of coffee and did the crossword puzzle in the *Tribune*. When she was stuck for a definition, she would put down her pencil and thoughtfully twist the diamond ring on her finger; if it caught the sun, Hannah would close her eyes and try to retain the flashing swords of green and purple, just as she unconsciously tried to seal forever in her memory the smell of the strong Italian coffee coming in a thin black stream out of the silver pot. Hannah remembered one day when her mother said to the cat, "What is that wretched four-letter word that means 'allowance for waste,' Nephew? We had it just the other day." Finally, when the puzzle was done and Edna had taken away the tray, she stretched out her arms to Hannah, who scrambled into her embrace, and she said, "I suppose you want your tawny tresses curled," and held her at arm's length and gazed at her hair with disbelieving eyes. "Bring us the brush, baby." All the while she brushed, then combed, then made long, old-fashioned sausage curls, turning and molding them on her index finger, she talked lightly and secretly about the dreams she had had and Christmas plans and what went on inside Nephew's head and why it was that she respected but could not bear Andy's violin teacher. She included Hannah, as if she were thirty years old, asking for her opinion or her corroboration of something. "Do you agree with me that Nephew is the very soul of Egypt? Or do you think there are Chinese overtones in his style?" After telling a dream (her dreams were full of voyages; one time she sailed into Oslo in Noah's ark and another time she went on the *Queen Mary* to Southampton in her night clothes without either luggage or a passport), she said, "What on earth do you suppose that means, Hannah? My id doesn't seem to know where it is at." Bewitching, indecipherable, she always dulcified this hour with her smoky, loving voice and her loving fingers that sometimes could not resist meandering over Hannah's head, ruining a curl by cleaving through it as she exclaimed, "Dear Lord, I never saw such stuff as this!" Actually, her own hair was the same vivacious color and the same gentle texture as Hannah's, and sometimes her hands would leave the child's head and go to her own, to stroke it slowly.

Lately now, for this last month, when the afternoons were snug and short and the lamps were turned on early and the hearth fires smelled of nuts, there had been another hour as well when Hannah and her hair had been the center of attention. Every day at half past two, she and her mother drove in the toylike English car over to Mr. Robinson Fowler's house, three miles away, on the top of a bald and beautiful hill from which it was possible, on a clear day, to see the beaches of Long Island. In a big, dirty studio, jammed with plaster casts and tin cans full of turpentine and stacked-up canvases and nameless metal odds and ends, Mr. Fowler, a large, quiet man who mumbled when he talked, was painting a life-size portrait of Hannah and her mother. Her mother, wearing a full skirt of scarlet felt and a starched white Gibson-girl shirt and a black ribbon in her hair, sat on a purple Victorian sofa, and Hannah, in a blue velvet jacket trimmed with black frogs and a paler-blue accordion-pleated skirt, stood leaning against her knee. In the picture, these colors were all different, all smudgy and gray, and the point of this, said Mr. Fowler, was to accent the lambencies of the hair. Before they took their pose, all the morning's careful curls were combed out, for Mr. Fowler wanted to paint Hannah's hair, he murmured in his closed mouth, "in a state of nature." Occasionally, he emerged from behind his easel and came across to them with his shambling, easygoing, friendly gait, to push back a lock of hair that had fallen over Hannah's forehead, and the touch of his fingers, huge as they were, was as light as her mother's.

Hannah liked the heat of the studio, and the smell of the tea perpetually brewing on an electric grill, and the sight of the enormous world of hills and trees and farms and rivers through the enormous windows, and she liked the quiet, which was broken only once or twice in the course of the hour's sitting by an exchange of a casual question and answer between Mr. Fowler and her mother, half the time about her hair. "It must never be cut," said the painter one day. "Not a single strand of it." After the sitting was over and Hannah and her mother had changed back into their regular clothes, Mr. Fowler drew the burlap curtains at the windows and turned on the soft lamps. Then he and her mother sat back in two scuffed leather armchairs drinking whisky and talking in a leisurely way, as if all the rest of the time in the world were theirs to enjoy in this relaxed geniality. Hannah did not listen to them. With her cup of mild, lemony tea, she sat on a high stool before a blackboard at the opposite end of the room and drew spider webs with a nubbin of pink chalk. Mr. Fowler and her mother never raised their voices or threw things at each other or stormed out of the room, banging doors and Hannah was sorry when it was time to go home where that kind of thing went on all the time, horrifying the house-maids, who never stayed longer than two months at the most, although the cook, who had a vicious tongue herself, had been with them ever since Johnny could remember.

The picture, when it was finished, was going to hang in the drawing room over an heirloom lowboy, where now there hung a pair of crossed épées, used by Hannah's father and his adversary in a jaunty, bloody *Studentenmensur* at Freiburg the year he went abroad to learn German. The lilac scar from the duel was a half moon on his round right cheek.

Now the picture would never be finished, since Hannah's corn-tassel hair was gone, and the sunny hour at the start of the day and the teatime one at the end were gone with it.

Hannah, sitting on the attic stairs, began to cry again as she thought of the closed circle of her days. Even her sister's and her brothers' return from school was not the fun it had been before; her haircut had become a household issue over which all of them squabbled, taking sides belligerently. Janie and Andy main-tained it did not matter; all right, they said, what if the baby did look silly? After all, she didn't go to school and nobody saw her. Johnny and Hughie and the cook and the maids said that it did matter, and Johnny, the spokesman for that camp, railed at his father behind his back and called him a dastard. But all the same, no one paid any attention to Hannah; when they spoke of "the baby," they might have been speaking of the car or a piece of furniture; one would never have known that she was in the room, for even when they looked directly at her, their eyes seemed to take in something other than Hannah. She felt that she was already shrinking and fading, that all her rights of being seen and listened to and caressed were ebbing away. Chilled and exposed as she was, she was becoming, nonetheless, invisible.

The tears came less fast now, and she heard her mother say, "How can I *help* looking at it closely? I shall eventually have to go to an analyst, as you perfectly well know, if I am to continue this marriage until the children are reasonably grown.

But in the meantime, until I get my doctor, who can I talk to but you? I wouldn't talk to you if you weren't my sister, because I don't think you're discreet at all." Sad, in her covert, Hannah saw that her mother was now sitting up straight against the headboard and was smoking a cigarette in long, meditative puffs; the smoke befogged her frowning forehead.

"Forget it, darling," she continued. "I know you are a tomb of silence. Look, do let me spill the beans and get it over with. It will put me into a swivet, I daresay, and I'll have to have a drink in my bath, but the way I feel, after these nights I've had, that's in the cards anyhow. . . . Oh, Christ, Louise, don't preach to me!"

Briefly, she put down the telephone and dragged Nephew to her side. Then she resumed, "Excuse me. I was adjusting my cat. Now, dear, right now, you can forget my 'charitable construction' because, of course, that's rot. At this juncture, neither one of us does anything by accident. I cannot believe that criminals are any more ingenious than wives and husbands when their marriages are turning sour. Do you remember how fiendish the Irelands were?

"Well, the night before the haircutting, we had a row that lasted until four, starting with Rob and going on from him to all the other men I know—he thinks it's bad form (and that's exactly how he puts it) that I still speak fondly of old beaux. He suspects me of the direst things with that poor pansy the decorators sent out to do the carpets on the stairs, and he's got it firmly rooted in his mind that Rob and I are in the middle of a red-hot affair. He doesn't know the meaning of friendship. He's got a sand dune for a soul. He suggested loathsomely that Rob and I were using Hannah as a blind—oh, his implications were too cynical to repeat.

"All this went on and on until I said that I would leave him. You know *that* old blind alley where any feint is useless because when five children are involved, one's hands are tied. Unless one can be proved mad. If only I could be! I would give my eyes to be sent away for a while to some insane asylum like that one Elizabeth loved so.

"It was hideous—the whole battle. We were so squalid with

drink. We drink prodigiously these days. The ice ran out and we didn't even take time to go get more, so we drank whisky and tap water as if we were in a cheap hotel, and I kept thinking, How lowering this is. But I couldn't stop. This was the worst quarrel we've ever had—by far the most fundamental. The things we said! We could have killed each other. In the morning, not even our hangovers could bring us together. And let me tell you, they were shattering. If I hadn't known I had a hangover, I would have sent for an ambulance without thinking twice. Hugh sidled around like a wounded land crab and swore he had fractured his skull. Fortunately, the children, all except the baby, had been asked to the Fosters' to skate, so at least we didn't have to put up appearances—we do that less and less as it is. But finally we began to pull ourselves together about noon with Bloody Marys, and when he proposed that he take Hannah into town and buy her lunch and some shoes, I almost forgave him everything. I was so delighted to have the house to myself. I would not rise to that bait about my neglecting the welfare of my children's feet. All I could think of was just being alone.

"I should have known. I think I might have sensed what was up if I hadn't been so sick, because as they were about to leave, the baby asked why I hadn't curled her hair and Hugh said, 'You leave that to me today.' Now, looking back on it, I can see that he rolled his eyes in that baleful, planning way of his and licked one corner of his mouth. But even if I had noticed, I still would never have dreamed he would be so vile.

"It goes without saying that we have been at swords' points ever since, and it doesn't help matters to see the child so woebegone, wearing this look of 'What did I do to deserve this?' How can one explain it away as an accident to a child when one perfectly knows that accident is not involved? Her misery makes me feel guilty. I am as shy of her as if I had been an accessory. I can't console her without spilling all the beans about Hugh. Besides, you can't say to a child, 'Darling, you are only a symbol. It was really *my* beautiful hair that was cut off, not yours.' . . .

"Rob *crushed?* Oh, for God's sake, no, not crushed—that's not Rob's style. He's outraged. His reaction, as a matter of fact, annoys me terribly, for he takes the whole thing as a personal affront and says that if Hugh had wanted to make an issue of my afternoons in his studio, he should have challenged him to a duel with the Freiburg swords. His theory, you see, is that Hugh has been smoldering at the thought of these testimonials of his manliness being replaced by the portrait. Rob claims that Hugh hates art—as of course he does—and that it's the artist in him, Rob, not the potential rival, that he is attacking. Needless to say, this gives him a heaven-sent opportunity to berate me for living in the camp of the enemy. He was horrid on Monday. He called me an opportunist and a brood mare. It depresses me that Rob, who is so intuitive about most things, can't see that *I* am the victim, that *my* values have been impugned. Today I hate all men.

"What am I going to do? What *can* I do? I'm taking her this afternoon to Angelo to see what he can salvage out of the scraps that are left. I'll get her a new doll—one with short hair. That's all I can do now. The picture will never be finished, so the dueling swords will stay where they are. And I will stay where I am— Oh, there's no end! Why on earth does one have children?"

For a minute or two her mother was silent, leaning back with her eyes closed, listening to Aunt Louise. Hannah no longer envied the cat curled into her mother's arm; she hated his smug white face and she hated her mother's sorrowful smile. Hot and desolate and half suffocated, she wished she were one of the angry bees. If she were a bee, she would fly through the crack of the attic door and sting Nephew and her mother and her father and Janie and Andy and Mr. Fowler. "Zzzzzzz," buzzed the child to herself.

After the telephone conversation was over and her mother had got up and gone to run her bath, Hannah let herself silently out the door into the hall and went downstairs to the kitchen. The cook was dicing onions, weeping. "There's my baby," she said as Hannah came to stand beside her, "my very own baby." She put down her knife and wiped her hands and her eyes on her apron and scooped Hannah up in a bear hug.

"I love you, Mattie," said Hannah.

The cook's teary face looked surprised and she put the child down and said, "Run along now, kiddikins—Mattie's got work to do."

Hannah went into the den and kneeled on the window seat to watch the snow settling deeply on the branches of the trees. "I love you, snow," she said. It fell like sleep.

The Captain's Gift

Though it is wartime, it is spring, so there are boys down in the street playing catch. Babies and dogs are sunning in the square and here and there among them, on green iron benches under the trees, rabbis sit reading newspapers. Some stout women and some thin little girls have brought crusts of bread in paper bags and are casting crumbs to the pigeons. There is a fire in one of the wire trash baskets and bits of black ash fly upward, but there is no wind at all to carry them off and they slowly descend again. Out of the windows of the maternity hospital, new mothers, convalescent, wearing flowered wrappers, lean to call to their friends who stand in little clumps on the sidewalk, waving their arms and shouting up pleasantries and private jokes in Yiddish. They are loath to end the visit, but finally they must, for unseen nurses speak to the women at the windows and they retire, crying good-humored farewells and naming each friend by name: Good-bye, Uncle Nathan! Goodbye, Mama! Goodbye, Isabel! Goodbye, Mrs. Leibowitz! Goodbye! In the pushcarts at the curbstone are lilacs and mountain laurel, pots of grape hyacinth and petunias for window boxes; between sales the venders rearrange their buckets and talk with the superintendents of the apartment buildings who idle, smoking, in the cellar entries where they lean against the tall ash cans. Six blocks away, the clock at St. Marks-in-the-Bouwerie strikes four.

Mrs. Chester Ramsey, the widow of the general, has one of the very few private houses in the neighborhood. At the window of her drawing room on the second floor, she is writing letters at a little desk that looks like a spinet. Now and then, pausing for a word, she glances through the marquisette curtains that blur the scene below and impart to it a quality she cannot name but which bewitches her at this time of day, especially in the spring. It separates her while it does not take her quite away; she becomes of and not of the spectacle. And then, too, it makes her nostalgic for the days, long ago, when young matrons, her friends, strolled through the square under their parasols, when trim French nursemaids wheeled babies, whose names she knew, in English prams; and little girls in sailor hats walked briskly with their governesses to confirmation class; when she herself was well-known there and was greeted and detained innumerable times in her passage through the flower-lined walks.

But there is no bitterness at all in her reflection; indeed, she enjoys the lazy turmoil of the anonymous crowd below. Often, on a nice day like this if no one is coming in to tea, she goes out to sit on one of the benches, and it is always thrillingly strange to her that no one notices her, even though she wears the sort of clothes her mother might have done when she was an old lady: a black taffeta dress with a long skirt and a tightly buttoned, high-necked jacket with a garnet brooch at the throat, a small velvet hat, black silk gloves. She is not in the least unconscious of her appearance, but she does not hope to be greeted with a flurry of surprise; rather, its absence is what she looks forward to, and she is like a child, who, dressed in her mother's clothes, is accepted as a grown-up. She is no more eccentric than the bearded rabbis or the brown gypsy women who occasionally waddle along the paths with their greasy striped skirts and their waist-long strings of beads. Sometimes, sitting there, she feels that she is invisible. Surely, she thinks, the people would remark on her if they could see her; they would certainly realize that in her reside memories of this square and this neighborhood older than some of the plane trees. She is surprised and not resentful that none of them knows that she alone belongs here.

The lady's friends and relatives, who live uptown, year after year try to dislodge her from her old and inconvenient house. It is, they feel nervously, much too close to Third Avenue with its swarming, staggering riffraff, and living alone as she does with only two faithful maids (one of whom is deaf) and a choreman, she would be quite defenseless if burglars came. Moreover, the fire department has condemned her house as well as many others in the block, and they shudder to think of Mrs. Ramsey's being trapped in her bedroom at the back of the second floor, far from help. There is no question about it: she would be burned in her bed. But she baffles them with what they say is a paradox. She says, "I have never liked change, and now I am too old for it." They protest, unable sometimes to keep the note of exasperation out of their voices, that change is exactly what they want to preserve her from. They predict, with statistics to back them up, that the neighborhood will go still further downhill and soon will be another Delancey Street. She returns that, while she is touched by their solicitude, she has no wish to move. She is, she thanks them, quite at home. Finally they have to give up and when they have accepted defeat with a sigh, they begin to admire her stubbornness all over again, and to say it is really heroic the way she has refused to acknowledge the death of the past. The ivory tower in which she lives is impregnable to the ill-smelling, rude-sounding, squalid-looking world which through the years has moved in closer and closer and now surrounds her on all sides. Incredibly, she has not been swallowed up. She has not gone out of her way to keep the streets in their place, but the streets have simply not dared to encroach upon her dignity. Take the matter of the smells, for example. Her visitors, stepping out of their taxis before her door, are almost overpowered by the rank, unidentifiable emanations from cellars and open windows: food smells (these people think of nothing but food) that are so strong and so foreign and so sickening that they call to mind the worst quarters of the worst Near Eastern cities. And yet, the moment the door of Mrs. Ramsey's house closes upon them, shutting out the laden atmosphere, they have forgotten the stink which a moment before they had thought unforgettable, and are aware only of aged potpourri, of lemon oil, and of desiccated lavender in linen closets.

Despite her refusal to leave her inaccessible slums, Mrs. Ramsey passes hardly a day without at least one caller, for she remains altogether charming, preserving the grace of manner and the wit that marked her at her first Assembly almost sixty years ago. She has not, that is, kept even a suggestion of her beauty. The flesh has worn away from her crooked bones and her white hair is yellowish and rather thin; she has a filmy cataract over one eye, and in her skinny little face, her large nose has an

Hebraic look. Indeed, though she was famous for her looks, no one on first meeting her ever says, "She must have been a beauty in her day." It is quite impossible to reconstruct her as she might have been since there is nothing to go on; the skeleton seems quite a badly botched job, and the face has no reminder in it of a single good feature. One supposes, in the end, that she was one of those girls whose details are not independently beautiful, but who are, nevertheless, a lovely composition. General Ramsey, on the other hand, five years dead, was a handsome man at the very end of his life, and the portrait painted just before his final illness shows him to be keen-eyed, imposing, with a long, aristocratic head on a pair of military shoulders, heavily adorned.

A stranger, having heard of Mrs. Ramsey's charm, thinks when he first sees her that it must lie in a tart wit since she looks too droll, too much like a piquant chipmunk, to have a more expansive feminine elegance. But while the wit is there, bright and Edwardian, this is not the chief of her gifts. Rather, it is her tenderness and pity, her delicate and imaginative love, her purity that make her always say the right thing. She is so wise a husbandman, so economical, that her smallest dispensations and her briefest words are treasure. She has neither enemies nor critics, so that like an angel she is unendangered by brutality or by "difficult situations." Even her sorrow at her husband's death and her loneliness afterward seemed only to make sweeter her sweet life. She is an innocent child of seventy-five.

Among her friends, Mrs. Ramsey numbers many well-bred young men who, before the war, came to her house for tea or for lunch on Sunday. Now they are all in uniform and many of them are overseas, but they write to her frequently and she replies, in a wavy old-fashioned hand, on V-mail blanks. In spite of this substitution of the blanks for her own monogrammed letter paper, in spite of the military titles and the serial numbers which she copies down in the little box at the top of the page, in spite of the uniforms which she cannot help seeing in the square, and the newspapers and the War Bond drives, the blackout curtains at her windows and the buckets of sand in her fourth-floor corridor and the ration books, Mrs. Ramsey is the one person, her friends say, to whom the cliché may accurately be applied: "She does not know there is a war on." Her daughter, who is a

Red Cross supervisor and who comes in uniform once a week to dine with her mother, says she is "too good to be true," that she is a perfect asylum, that in her house one can quite delude oneself into believing that this tranquillity extends far beyond her doorstep, beyond the city, throughout the world itself, and that the catastrophes of our times are only hypothetical horrors. Her granddaughters, who are Waves, her grandson Ramsey who is an instructor in a pre-flight school, her son who manufactures precision instruments and has bought fifty thousand dollars' worth of bonds, her son-in-law, the military attaché, her daughter-in-law who works at the blood bank, all say the same thing of her. They say they frightfully pity people who cannot have a holiday from the war in her house. She continues to speak of Paris as if the only reason she does not go there is that she is too old and her health is too unsteady; she hopes that one of her favorite young men, wounded at Anzio, will enjoy Easter in Italy and she assumes that he will go to Rome to hear the Pope. She speaks of Germany and Japan as if they were still nothing more than two foreign countries of which she has affectionate memories. It is true that at times her blandness becomes trying. For example, if someone speaks of the mistakes of Versailles, she quite genuinely believes he refers to the way the flower beds are laid out in the palace gardens and she agrees warmly that they could have been ever so much nicer. But one has no business to be annoyed with her. Since there are so few years left to her (and since there is now no danger of our being bombed) it would be an unkind and playful sacrilege to destroy her illusion that the world is still good and beautiful and harmonious in all its parts. She need never know how barbarically civilization has been betrayed.

How refreshing must be her letters to the soldiers! She neither complains of their hardships nor gushes over their bravery. It must be marvelous, indeed, to know that there is someone across whose lips the phrase "the four freedoms" has never passed, someone whose vocabulary is innocent of "fascism," someone who writes calm reminiscences in her letters (even so! on the printed V-mail form!) of summer band concerts in Saratoga Springs, of winter dinner parties at the Murray Hill, which, in reality as fusty as an old trunk, she thinks is still the smartest hotel in town. Mothers of the soldiers are overjoyed: she is their link with the courtly past, she is Mrs. Wharton at first hand.

Mrs. Ramsey has written five letters to soldiers and sailors and a sixth is begun. But her eyes have started to burn, and since it is anyhow nearly time for tea, she rises from her desk and prepares to go to her bedroom to freshen up for her guests, who today will be one of her granddaughters and the fiancée of one of her young admirers. She looks down once more into the little park and thinks that it is the loveliest in the city. It reminds her of Bloomsbury Square. There she used to sit waiting for her husband while he copied out notes and lists of things in the British Museum whenever they visited London. One of his avocations, perhaps the mildest of them all, had been a study of English ballads and he kept notebooks full of their variants. Great as was her delight in his society, she was always glad when he stayed away a long time, for she loved sitting there alone, heedless of anything but the simple fact of her being there. Perhaps it is the memory of those days that now motivates her occasional afternoon in the square, for the atmosphere is just as foreign and her presence seems just as unusual as it used to be in London. The difference is that in London she had been a visitor from a distant country while here she is a visitor from a distant time. As she looks down she sees a little boy in a beret like a French sailor's. He is carrying a string shopping bag with a long loaf of bread sticking out of it. He walks beside his enormous mother who wears a red snood over a bun of hair as big as the loaf of bread in the bag. Mrs. Ramsey, for no reason, thinks how dearly she loves Europe and how sorry she is that there is no time left for her to go abroad again. If she were just a few years younger, she would be envious of the boys to whom she has been writing her letters.

She has just turned toward the door when she hears, far off, the bell at the street entrance and she makes a convulsive little gesture with her hand, afraid that the girls have come already and she is not prepared. She opens the door and waits beside it, listening, and then, hearing Elizabeth coming up the stairs alone, she steps out into the hall and calls down, "I am just going to dress, Elizabeth. Who was at the door?"

The plump middle-aged maid is deaf and she has not heard. She comes into sight on the stairs; she is carrying a parcel and, seeing her mistress, she says, "The special-delivery man brought it, Mrs. Ramsey, and I thought you would like to have it at once since it comes from overseas." She hands over the package, adding, "From Captain Cousins."

Mrs. Ramsey returns to the drawing room, saying to the maid, "Oh, I shan't wait to open *this!* If I am late and don't have time to dress, I am sure the young ladies won't mind." The maid beams, delighted with the look of pleasure in Mrs. Ramsey's face, and retires quietly as though she were leaving a girl to read her sweetheart's letter.

The little old lady sits down on a yellow and pink striped love seat, holding the box in her hands, but she does not immediately open it. She sits remembering her grandson, Arthur Cousins, of all the young men, her favorite. He looks much as the General did as a youth and it is this resemblance, probably, that so endears him to her. She recalls him in exquisite detail and his image takes her breath away. He is as tall, as fair, as red-cheeked as a Swede. Before he went away, when he used to come to see her, he always seemed sudden and exotic, making her drawing room look dusky. Whenever she saw him and now whenever she thinks of him, she remembers, rapturously, the hot beaches of Naples, the blinding winter sun at Saint Moritz, the waves of heat rising from the gravel slope before the Pitti Palace. The sunlight he calls up is not parching but wonderfully rich and heady. His mind is as luminous as his skin and his hair; and he is so happy! She thinks of him leaning forward in his chair at a recital to watch a woman playing a lute, bending her head down to look at it with love, as if she were looking into a child's face; his lips are parted and his eyes shine. She sees him sitting beside her in church and she remembers the days when he was an altar boy. The very package that she holds seems to give off a warmth of summertime and she touches it lightly here and there with her fingertips.

Arthur, first in England, then in France and then in Italy, has sent not only countless letters to his grandmother, but presents as well. Under the General's portrait, in a Chinese chest to which she wears the key on a gold chain round her neck, the letters lie in ribbon-bound packets and so do the gifts, still in their tissue-paper wrappings. From London, he sent Irish linen handkerchiefs and heliotrope sachets and a small pink marble shepherdess; from Paris, gloves and a silver box for oddments; from Italy, a leather writing case and two paste-studded shell combs. His affectionate letters, which she reads and rereads through a magnifying glass on a mother-of-pearl handle, tell of his homesickness, of his unwillingness to be so far away from her. He writes that, on his return, they must go again, as they did on the last day of his last furlough, round Central Park in a carriage. "Only with you, my darling Grandma, is this not just a stunt," he writes. They must, he goes on, dine at the Lafayette where the *moules marinières* have been celebrated from her day until his; she must allow him to come every day to tea and must tell him stories of her girlhood. He knows that he will find her exactly the same as she was when he told her goodbye.

On the last little square photograph headed "Somewhere in Germany" he had written, "I am sending you the best present that I have found for you yet. It is something that Helena Rubinstein (as if you knew who she is!) would give a fortune for, but I'm not going to tell you what it is. I like thinking of you trying to guess as you sit there among all your lares and penates and your fresh flowers."

Mrs. Ramsey, repeating to herself the phrase "fresh flowers," regrets that she has not sent out for some lilacs, for the only things in bloom are two white African violets on the sideboard. She feels a little guilty as though she has betrayed Arthur's picture of her and she thinks of what her daughter, Arthur's mother, said at dinner last night, "With you, Arthur will not change because you are unchangeable. But in his letters to me, he is becoming more and more unrecognizable."

She had forbidden her daughter to pursue this subject: there was a hint of disloyalty in her voice, or was it a hint of fear? The whole last sentence of Arthur's letter now reechoes in her mind and a slight cloud comes over her face. She feels a touch of cold and decides that she must tell Elizabeth to lay a fire after all. When one is very old and fleshless, one is like a thermometer, registering the least change in temperature.

But the fire must wait until she has opened her present. She smiles. She knows who Helena Rubinstein is, but it pleases her that Arthur thinks she does not. Perhaps it is a bottle of some rare scent that would so much gratify both of them. The clock at St. Mark's strikes the quarter hour and she goes to her desk and brings back a pair of scissors. She is so happy that she does not any longer try to imagine what is inside; she rather hopes she has not guessed rightly, that it is not scent, that it will take her completely by surprise.

Under the outer wrappings there is a shoe box, and in the box, a parcel in tissue paper, tied with a piece of string. It is something shapeless and, even when she has taken it out and has held it a moment in her old wrinkled hands, she cannot tell what it is. It is not a bottle and not a box or a case; it is rather heavy but its heaviness is of a curious kind: it seems to be a mass of something. She delays no longer and snips the string. There in her lap lies a braid of golden hair. At the top it is ruffled a little as though a girl, just fallen asleep, had tossed once or twice on her pillow; the rest of it is smooth, down to the end, which is tied with a little pink bow. It has been cut off cleanly at the nape of the neck, and it is so long that it must have hung below her waist. It is thick and it seems still so vital in the light that streams through the windows that Mrs. Ramsey feels its owner is concealed from her only by a vapor, that her head is here beside her on the love seat: she is hidden from Mrs. Ramsey just as Mrs. Ramsey is hidden from the people in the square.

She pushes the tissue paper with the handle of the scissors and the braid slips to the gray carpet and lies there shining like a living snake. Now the old lady clasps her hands together to end their trembling, and looking at the African violets she admits to some distant compartment of her mind the fact that they are dying and must be removed tomorrow. She speaks aloud in the empty room. "How unfriendly, Arthur!" she says. "How unkind!" And as if there were a voice in the hair at her feet, she distinctly hears him saying, "There's a war on, hadn't you heard?"

The End of a Career

By those of Angelica Early's friends who were given to hyperbole, she was called, throughout her life, one of the most beautiful women in the world's history. And those of more restraint left history out of their appraisal but said that Mrs. Early was certainly one of the most beautiful of living women. She had been, the legend was, a nymph in her cradle (a doting, bibulous aunt was fond, over cocktails, of describing the queenly baby's pretty bed—gilded and swan-shaped, lined with China silk of a blue that matched the infant eyes, and festooned with Mechlin caught into loops with rosettes), and in her silvery coffin she was a goddess. At her funeral, her friends mourned with as much bitterness as sorrow that such a treasure should be consigned to the eyeless and impartial earth; they felt robbed; they felt as if one of the wonders of the world had been demolished by wanton marauders. "It's wrong of God to bury His own masterpiece," said the tipsy aunt, "and if that's blasphemy, I'll take the consequences, for I'm not at all sure I want to go on living in a world that doesn't contain Angelica."

Between her alpha and omega, a span of fifty years, Mrs. Early enjoyed a shimmering international fame that derived almost entirely from the inspired and faultless *esprit de corps* of her flesh and her bones and her blood; never were the features and the colors of a face in such serene and unassailable agreement, never had a skeleton been more singularly honored by the integument it wore. And Angelica, aware of her responsibility to her beholders, dedicated herself to the cultivation of her gift and the maintenance of her role in life with the same chastity and discipline that guide a girl who has been called to the service of God.

Angelica's marriage, entered upon when she was twenty-two and her husband was ten years older, puzzled everyone, for Major Clayton Early was not a connoisseur of the complex civilization that had produced his wife's sterling beauty but was, instead, concerned with low forms of plant life, with primitive societies, and with big game. He was an accomplished huntsman—alarming heads and horns and hides covered the walls of his den, together with enlarged photographs of himself standing with his right foot planted firmly upon the neck of a dead beast—and an uneducated but passionate explorer, and he was away most of the time, shooting cats in Africa or making and recording observations in the miasmas of Matto Grosso and the mephitic verdure of the Malay Peninsula. While he was away, Angelica, too, was away a good deal of the time—on islands, in Europe, upstate, down South—and for only a few months of the year were they simultaneously in residence in a professionally and pompously decorated maisonette that overlooked Central Park. When Major Early was in town, he enjoyed being host to large dinner parties, at which, more often than not, he ran off reels on reels of crepuscular and agitated movies that showed savages eating from communal pots, savages dancing and drumming, savages in council, savages accepting the white man's offerings of chewing gum and mechanical toys; there were, as well, many feet of film devoted to tarantulas, apes, termite mounds, and orchidaceous plants. His commentary was obscure, for his vocabulary was bestrewn with crossword-puzzle words. Those evenings were so awful that no one would have come to them if it had not been for Angelica; the eye could stray from a loathsome witch doctor on the screen and rest in comfort and joy on her.

Some people said that Early was a cynic and some said that he was a fool to leave Angelica unguarded, without children and without responsibility, and they all said it would serve him right if he returned from one of his safaris to find himself replaced. Why did a man so antisocial marry at all, or, if he must marry, why not take as his wife some stalwart and thick-legged woman who would share his pedantic adventures—a champion skeet shooter, perhaps, or a descendant of Western pioneers? But then, on the other hand, why had Angelica married *him?* She never spoke of him, never quoted from his letters—if there were any letters—and if she was asked where he was currently traveling, she often could not answer. The speculation upon this vacant alliance ceased as soon as Early had left town to go and join his guides, for once he was out of sight, no one could remember much about him beyond a Gallic mustache and his ponderous jokes as his movies jerked on. Indeed, so completely was his existence forgotten that matchmakers set to work as if Angelica were a widow.

They did not get far, the matchmakers, because, apart from her beauty, there was not a good deal to be said about Angelica. She had some money—her parents had left her ample provision, and Early's money came from a reliable soap—but it was not enough to be of interest to the extremely rich people whose yachts and châteaux and boxes at the opera she embellished. She dressed well, but she lacked the exclusive chic, the unique fillip, that would have caused her style in clothes to be called *sui generis* and, as such, to be mentioned by the press. Angelica was hardly literate; the impressions her girlish mind had received at Miss Hewitt's classes had been sketched rather than etched, but she was not stupid and she had an appealing, if small and intermittent, humor. She was not wanting in heart and she was quick to commiserate and give alms to the halt and the lame and the poor, and if ugliness had been a disease or a social evil, she would, counting her blessings, have lent herself to its extirpation. She wasn't a cat, she wasn't a flirt or a cheat, wasn't an imbecile, didn't make *gaffes;* neither, however, alas, was she a wit, or a catalyst, or a transgressor to be scolded and punished and then forgiven and loved afresh. She was simply and solely a beautiful woman.

Women, on first confronting Angelica Early, took a backward step in alarm and instinctively diverted the attention of their husbands or lovers to something at the opposite end of the room. But their first impression was false, for Angelica's beauty was an end in itself and she was the least predatory of women. The consequence of this was that she had many women friends, or at any rate she had many hostesses, for there was no more splendid and no safer ornament for a dinner table than Angelica.

The appointments of these tables were often planned round her, the cynosure, and women lunching together had been known to debate (with their practical tongues in their cheeks but without malice) whether Waterford or Venetian glass went better with her and whether white roses or red were more appropriate in juxtaposition to her creamy skin and her luminous ash-blond hair. She was forever in demand; for weeks before parties and benefit balls hostesses contended for her presence; her status— next to the host—in protocol was permanent; little zephyrs of excitement and small calms of awe followed her entrance into a drawing room. She was like royalty, she was a public personage, or she was, as the aunt was to observe at her funeral, like the masterpiece of a great master. Queens and pictures may not, in the ordinary sense, have friends, but if they live up to their reputations, they will not want for an entourage, and only the cranks and the sightless will be their foes. There were some skeptics in Angelica's circle, but there were no cranks, and in speaking of her, using the superlatives that composed their native tongue, they called her adorable and indispensable, and they said that when she left them, the sun went down.

Men, on first gazing into those fabulous eyes, whose whites had retained the pale, melting blue of infancy, were dizzied, and sometimes they saw stars. But their vertigo passed soon, often immediately, although sometimes not until after a second encounter, planned in palpitations and bouts of fever, had proved flat and inconsequential. For a tête-à-tête with Angelica was marked by immediacy; she did not half disclose a sweet and sad and twilit history, did not make half promises about a future, implied the barest minimum of flattery and none at all of amorousness, and spoke factually, in a pleasant voice, without nuance and within the present tense. Someone had said that she was *sec*—a quality praiseworthy in certain wines but distinctly not delicious in so beautiful a woman. All the same, just as she had many hostesses, so she had many escorts, for her presence at a man's side gave him a feeling of achievement.

Angelica was not, that is, all façade—her eyes themselves testified to the existence of airy apartments and charming gardens behind them—but she was consecrated to her vocation and she had been obliged to pass up much of the miscellany of life that irritates but also brings about the evolution of personality; the unmolested oyster creates no pearl. Her heart might be shivered, she might be inwardly scorched with desire or mangled with jealousy and greed, she might be benumbed by loneliness and doubt, but she was so unswerving in her trusteeship of her perfection that she could not allow anxiety to pleat her immaculate brow or anger to discolor her damask cheeks or tears to deflower her eyes. Perhaps, like an artist, she was not always grateful for this talent of beauty that destiny had imposed upon her without asking leave, but, like the artist, she knew where her duty lay; the languishing and death of her genius would be the languishing and death of herself, and suicide, though it is often understandable, is almost never moral.

The world kindly imagined that Mrs. Early's beauty was deathless and that it lived its charmed life without support. If the world could have seen the contents of her dressing table and her bathroom shelves! If the world could have known the hours devoured by the matutinal ritual! Angelica and her reverent English maid, Dora, were dressed like surgeons in those morning hours, and they worked painstakingly, talking little, under lights whose purpose was to cast on the mirrors an image of ruthless veracity. The slightest alteration in the color of a strand of hair caused Angelica to cancel all engagements for a day or two, during which time a hairdresser was in attendance, treating the lady with dyes and allaying her fears. A Finn daily belabored her with bundles of birch fagots to enliven her circulation; at night she wore mud on her face and creamed gloves on her hands; her hair was treated with olive oil, lemon juice, egg white, and beer; she was massaged, she was vibrated, she was steamed into lassitude and then stung back to life by astringents; she was brushed and creamed and salted and powdered. All this took time, and, more than time, it took undying patience. So what the world did not know but what Angelica and her maid and her curators knew was that the blood that ever so subtly clouded her cheeks with pink and lay pale green in that admirable vein in her throat was kept in motion by a rapid pulse whose author was a fearful heart: If my talent goes, I'm done for, says the artist, and Angelica said, if I lose my looks, I'm lost.

So, even as she attentively lent the exquisite shell of her ear to her dinner partner, who was telling her about his visit to Samothrace or was bidding her examine with him his political views, even as she returned the gaze of a newcomer whose head was over his heels, even as she contributed to the talk about couturiers after the ladies had withdrawn, Angelica was thinking, in panic and obsession, of the innumerable details she was obliged to juggle to sustain the continuity of her performance.

Modern science has provided handsome women—and especially blondes, who are the most vulnerable—with defenses against many of their natural enemies: the sun, coarsening winds, the rude and hostile properties of foreign waters and foreign airs. But there has not yet been devised a way to bring to his knees the archfiend Time, and when Angelica began to age, in her middle forties, she went to bed.

Her reduction of the world to the size of her bedroom was a gradual process, for her wilting and fading was so slow that it was really imperceptible except to her unflinching eyes, and to Dora's, and to those of an adroit plastic surgeon to whose unadvertised sanitarium, tucked away in a rural nook in Normandy, she had retreated each summer since she was forty to be delivered of those infinitesimal lines and spots in her cheeks and her throat that her well-lighted mirror told her were exclamatory and shameful disfigurements. Such was the mystery that shrouded these trips to France that everyone thought she must surely be going abroad to establish a romantic ménage, and when she paused in Paris on her return to New York, she was always so resplendent that the guesses seemed to be incontrovertibly confirmed; nothing but some sort of delicious fulfillment could account for her subtlety, her lovely, tremulous, youthful air of secret memories. Some of her friends in idle moments went so far as to clothe this lover with a fleshy vestment and a personality and a nationality, and one of the slowly evolved myths, which was eventually stated as fact, was that he was a soul of simple origin and primal magnetism—someone, indeed, like Lady Chatterley's lover.

Angelica would suddenly appear in Paris at the beginning of September with no explanation of the summer or of that happy condition of her heart that was all but audible as a carol, and certainly was visible in her shimmering eyes and her glowing skin. She lingered in Paris only long enough to buy her winter wardrobe, to upset the metabolism of the men she met, to be, momentarily, the principal gem in the diadem of the international set, and to promise faithfully that next year she would join houseparties and cruises to Greece, would dance till dawn at *fêtes champêtres,* and would, between bullfights, tour the caves of Spain. She did not, of course, keep her promises, and the fact is that she would have disappointed her friends if she had. At these times, on the wing, it was as if she had been inoculated with the distillation of every fair treasure on earth and in heaven, with the moon and the stars, with the seas and the flowers, and the rainbow and the morning dew. Angelica was no longer *sec,* they said; they said a new dimension had brought her to life. Heretofore she had been a painted ship upon a painted ocean and now she was sailing the crests and the depths, and if her adventurous voyage away from the doldrums had come late in life, it had not come too late; the prime of life, they said, savoring their philosophy and refurbishing their cliché, was a relative season. They loved to speculate on why her lover was unpresentable. Wiseacres proposed, not meaning it, that he was a fugitive from the Ile du Diable; others agreed that if he was not Neanderthal (in one way or another) or so ignobly born that not even democracy could receive him into its generous maw—if he was not any of these things, he must be intransigently married. Or could he perhaps be one of those glittering Eastern rulers who contrived to take an incognito holiday from their riches and their dominions but could not, because of law and tradition, ever introduce Angelica into their courts? Once or twice it was proposed that Angelica was exercising scruples because of her husband, but this seemed unlikely; the man was too dense to see beyond his marriage feasts of Indians and his courtship of birds.

Who ever the lover was and whatever were the terms of their liaison, Angelica was plainly engaged upon a major passion whose momentum each summer was so forcefully recharged that it did not dwindle at all during the rest of the year. Now she began to be known not only as the most beautiful but as one of the most dynamic of women as well, and such was the general enthusiasm for her that she was credited with *mots justes* and insights and ingenious benevolences that perhaps existed only in the infatuated imaginations of her claque. How amazingly Angelica had changed! And how amazingly wrong they all were! For *not* changing had been her lifelong specialty, and she was the same as ever, only more so. Nevertheless, the sort of men who theretofore had cooled after their second meeting with her and had called her pedestrian or impervious or hollow now continued to fever and fruitlessly but breathlessly to pursue her. Often they truly fell in love with her and bitterly hated that anonymous fellow who had found the wellspring of her being.

Inevitably the news of her friends' speculations drifted back to her in hints and slips of the tongue. Angelica's humor had grown no more buxom with the passage of the years, and she was not amused at the enigma she had given birth to by immaculate conception. She took herself seriously. She was a good creature, a moral and polite woman, but she was hindered by unworldliness, and she was ashamed to be living a fiction. She was actually guilt-ridden because her summertime friend was not an Adonis from the Orient or a charming and ignorant workingman but was, instead, Dr. Fleege-Althoff, a monstrous little man, with a flat head on which not one hair grew and with the visage of a thief—a narrow, feral nose, a pair of pale and shifty and omniscient eyes, a mouth that forever faintly smiled at some cryptic, wicked jest. There was no help for it, but she was ashamed all the same that it was pain and humiliation, not bliss and glorification, that kept her occupied during her annual retreat. The fact was that she earned her reputation and her undiminishing applause and kept fresh the myth in which she moved by suffering the surface skin of her face to be planed away by a steel-wire brush, electrically propelled; the drastic pain was sickening and it lasted long, and for days—sometimes weeks—after the operation she was so unsightly that her looking glass, which, morbidly, she could not resist, broke her heart. She lay on a chaise in a darkened bedroom of that quiet, discreet sanitarium, waiting, counting the hours until the scabs that encrusted her flensed skin should disappear. But even when this dreadful mask was gone, she was still hideous, and her eyes and her mouth, alone untouched, seemed to reproach her when she confronted her reflection, as red and shining as if she had been boiled almost to death. Eight weeks later, though, she was as beautiful as she had been at her zenith, and the doctor, that ugly man, did not fail, in bidding her goodbye, to accord himself only a fraction of the credit and assign the rest to her Heavenly Father. Once, he had made her shiver when, giving her the grin of a gargoyle, he said, "What a face! Flower of the world! Of all my patients, you are the one I do not like to flail." Flail! The word almost made her retch, and she envisioned him lashing her with little metal whips, and smiling.

During the time she was at the sanitarium (a tasteful and pleasant place, but a far cry from the pastoral bower her friends imagined), she communicated with no one except her maid and with the staff, who knew her, as they knew all the other ladies, by an alias. She called herself Mrs. London, and while there was no need to go so far, she said she came from California. It was a long and trying time. Angelica had always read with difficulty and without much pleasure, and she inevitably brought with her the wrong books, in the hope, which she should long since have abandoned, that she might improve her mind; she could not pay attention to Proust, she was baffled by the Russians, and poetry (one year she brought "The Faerie Queene"!) caused her despair. So, for two and a half months, she worked at needlepoint and played a good deal of solitaire and talked to Dora, who was the only confidante she had ever had, and really the only friend. They had few subjects and most of them were solemn—the philosophy of cosmetics, the fleetingness of life. The maid, if she had a life of her own, never revealed it. Sometimes Angelica, unbearably sad that she had been obliged to tread a straight-and-narrow path with not a primrose on it, would sigh and nearly cry and say, "What have I done with my life?" And Dora, assistant guardian of the wonder, would reply, "You have worked hard, madame. Being beautiful is no easy matter." This woman was highly paid, but she was a kind woman, too, and she meant what she said.

It was Angelica's hands that at last, inexorably, began to tell the time. It seemed to her that their transfiguration came overnight, but of course what came overnight was her realization that the veins had grown too vivid and that here and there in the interstices of the blue-green, upraised network there had appeared pale freckles, which darkened and broadened and multiplied; the skin was still silken and ivory, but it was redundant and lay too loosely on her fingers. That year, when she got to the sanitarium, she was in great distress, but she had confidence in her doctor.

Dr. Fleege-Althoff, however, though he was sincerely sorry, told her there was nothing he could do. Hands and legs, he said, could not be benefited by the waters of the fountain of youth. Sardonically, he recommended gloves, and, taking him literally, she was aghast. How could one wear gloves at a dinner table? What could be more parvenu, more telltale, than to lunch in gloves at a restraurant? Teasing her further, the vile little man proposed that she revive the style of wearing mitts, and tears of pain sprang to Angelica's eyes. Her voice was almost petulant when she protested against these grotesque prescriptions. The doctor, nasty as he was, was wise, and in his unkind wisdom, accumulated through a lifetime of dealing with appearances, said, "Forgive my waggery. I'm tired today. Go get yourself loved, Mrs. London. I've dealt with women so many years that I can tell which of my patients have lovers or loving husbands and which have not—perhaps it will surprise you to know that very few of them have. Most have lost their men and come to me in the hope that the excision of crow's-feet will bring back the wanderers." He was sitting at his desk, facing her, his glasses hugely magnifying his intelligent, bitter eyes. "There is an aesthetic principle," he pursued, "that says beauty is the objectification of love. To be loved is to be beautiful, but to be beautiful is not necessarily to be loved. Imagine that, Mrs. London! Go and find a lover and obfuscate his senses; give him a pair of rose-colored glasses and he'll see your hands as superb—or, even better, he won't see your hands at all. Get loved by somebody—it doesn't matter who—and you'll get well."

"Get well?" said Angelica, amazed. "Am I ill?"

"If you are not ill, why have you come to me? I am a doctor," he said, and with a sigh he gestured toward the testimonials of his medical training that hung on the walls. The doctor's fatigue gave him an air of melancholy that humanized him, despite his derisive voice, and momentarily Angelica pitied him in his ineluctable ugliness. Still, he was no more solitary in his hemisphere than she was in hers, and quickly she slipped away from her consideration of him to her own woe.

"But even if I weren't married, how could I find a lover at my age?" she cried.

He shook his head wearily and said, "Like most of your countrywomen, you confound youth with value, with beauty, with courage—with everything. To you, youth and age are at the two poles, one positive, the other negative. *I* cannot tell you what to do. I am only an engineer—I am not the inventor of female beauty. I am a plastic surgeon—I am not God. All you can do now is cover your imperfections with *amour-propre*. You are a greedy woman, Mrs. London—a few spots appear on your hands and you throw them up and say 'This is the end.' What egotism!"

Angelica understood none of this, and her innocent and humble mind went round and round among his paradoxes, so savagely delivered. How could she achieve *amour-propre* when what she had most respected in herself was now irretrievably lost? And if she had not *amour-propre,* how could she possibly find anyone else to love her? Were not these the things she should have been told when she was a girl growing up? Why had no one, in this long life of hers, which had been peopled by such a multitude, warned her to lay up a store of good things against the famine of old age? Now, too late, she wrung her old-woman hands, and from the bottom of her simple heart she lamented, weeping and caring nothing that her famous eyes were smeared and their lids swollen.

At last the doctor took pity on her. He came around to her side of the desk and put his hands kindly on her shaking shoulders. "Come, Mrs. London, life's not over," he said. "I've scheduled your planing for tomorrow morning at nine. Will you go through with it or do you want to cancel?"

She told him, through her tears, that she would go through with the operation, and he congratulated her. "You'll rise from these depths," he said. "You'll learn, as we all learn, that there are substantial rewards in age."

That summer, Dr. Fleege-Althoff, who had grave problems of his own (he had a nagging wife; his only child, a son, was schizophrenic) and whose understanding was deep, did what he could to lighten Angelica's depression. He found that she felt obscurely disgraced and ashamed, as if she had committed a breach of faith, had broken a sacred trust, and could not expect anything but public dishonor. She had never been a happy woman, but until now she had been too diligent to be unhappy; the experience of unhappiness for the first time when one is growing old is one of the most malignant diseases of the heart. Poor soul! Her person was her personality. Often, when the doctor had finished his rounds, he took Angelica driving in the pretty countryside; she was veiled against the ravages of the sun and, he observed, she wore gloves. As they drove, he talked to her and endeavored to persuade her that for each of the crucifixions of life there is a solace. Sometimes she seemed to believe him.

Sometimes, believing him, she took heart simply through the look of the trees and the feel of the air, but when they had returned to the sanitarium and the sun had gone down and she was alone with her crumpled hands—with her crumpled hands and her compassionate but helpless maid—she could not remember any of the reasons for being alive. She would think of what she had seen on their drive: children playing with boisterous dogs; girls and young men on horses or bicycles, riding along the back roads; peasant women in their gardens tending their cabbages and tending their sunning babies at the same time. The earth, in the ebullience of summertime, seemed more resplendent and refreshed than she could ever remember it. Finally, she could not bear to look at it or at all those exuberant young human beings living on it, and began to refuse the doctor's invitations.

You might think that she would have taken to drink or to drugs, but she went on in her dogtrot way, taking care of her looks, remembering how drink hardens the skin and how drugs etiolate it.

That year, when Angelica arrived in Paris on her way back to New York, she was dealt an adventitious but crippling blow of mischance from which she never really recovered. She had arrived in midafternoon, and the lift in her hotel was crowded with people going up to their rooms after lunch. She had been one of the first to enter the car and she was standing at the back. At the front, separated from her by ten people or more, were two young men who had been standing in the lobby when she came into the hotel. They were Americans, effeminate and a little drunk, and one of them said to the other, "She must have been sixty—why, she could have been seventy!" His companion replied, "Twenty-eight. Thirty at the most." His friend said, "You didn't see her hands when she took off her gloves to register. They were old, I tell you. You can always tell by the hands."

Luckily for Angelica and luckily for them, the cruel, green boys got off first; as she rode up the remaining way to her floor, she felt dizzy and hot. Unused as she had been most of her life to emotion, she was embraced like a serpent by the desire to die (that affliction that most of us have learned to cope with through its reiteration), and she struggled for breath. She walked down the corridor to her room jerkily; all her resilience was gone. Immediately she telephoned the steamship line and booked the first passage home she could get. For two days, until the boat sailed, she lay motionless on her bed, with the curtains drawn, or she paced the floor, or sat and stared at her culprit hands. She saw no one and she spoke to no one except Dora, who told all the friends who called that her mistress was ill.

When these friends returned from Europe, and others from the country, they learned, to their distress and puzzlement, that Angelica was not going out at all, nor was she receiving anyone. The fiction of her illness, begun in Paris, gained documentation and became fact, until at last no one was in doubt: she had cancer, far too advanced for cure or palliation; they assumed she was attended by nurses. Poor darling, they said, to have her love affair end this way! They showered her with roses, telephoning their florists before they went out to lunch; they wrote her tactful notes of sympathy, and it was through reading these that she guessed what they thought was the reason for her retirement.

The maisonette seemed huge to her, and full of echoes; for the first time since she had married, she began to think about her husband and, though he was a stranger, to long for his return. Perhaps he could become the savior Fleege-Althoff had told her to seek. But she was not strong enough to wait for him. The drawing room was still in its summer shrouds; the umbrageous dining room was closed. At first, she dined in the library, and then she began to have dinner on a tray in her bedroom, sitting before the fire. Soon after this, she started keeping to her bedroom and, at last, to her bed, never rising from it except for her twice-daily ritualistic baths. Her nightdresses and bed jackets were made by the dressmaker she had always used to supplement her Paris wardrobe; she wore her jewels for the eyes of her maid and her masseuse—that is, she wore earrings and necklaces, but she never adorned her hands. And, as if she were dying in the way they thought, she wrote brave letters to her friends, and sometimes, when her loneliness became unbearable, she telephoned them and inquired in the voice of an invalid about their parties and about the theater, though she did not want to hear, but she refused all their kind invitations to come and visit, and she rang off saying, "Do keep in touch."

For a while, they did keep in touch, and then the flowers came less and less often and her mail dwindled away. Her panic gave way to inertia. If she had been able to rise from her bed, she would have run crying to them, saying, "I was faithful to your conception of me for all those years. Now take pity on me— reward me for my singleness of purpose." They would have been quick to console her and to laugh away her sense of failure. (She could all but hear them saying, "But my dear, how absurd! Look at your figure! Look at your face and your hair! What on earth do you mean by killing yourself simply because of your hands?") But she had not the strength to go to them and receive their mercy. They did not know and she could not tell them. They thought it was cancer. They would never have dreamed it was despair that she groped through sightlessly, in a vacuum everlasting and black. Their flowers and their letters and their telephone calls did not stop out of unkindness but out of forgetfulness; they were busy, they were living their lives.

Angelica began to sleep. She slept all night and all day, like a cat. Dreams became her companions and sleep became her food. She ate very little, but she did not waste away, although she was weakened—so weakened, indeed, that sometimes in her bath she had attacks of vertigo and was obliged to ring for Dora. She could not keep her mind on anything. The simplest words in the simplest book bewildered her, and she let her eyes wander drowsily from the page; before she could close the book and set it aside, she was asleep.

Just before Christmas, the drunken aunt, Angelica's only relative, came back to town after a lengthy visit to California. She had not heard from Angelica in months, but she had not been alarmed, for neither of them was a letter writer. The first evening she was back, she dined with friends and learned from them of her niece's illness; she was shocked into sobriety and bitterly excoriated herself for being so lazy that she had not bothered to write. She telephoned the doctor who had taken care of Angelica all her life and surprised him by repeating what she had heard—that the affliction had been diagnosed as cancer. At first, the doctor was offended that he had not been called in, and then, on second thought, he was suspicious, and he urged the aunt to go around as soon as she could and make a report to him.

The aunt did not warn Angelica that she was coming. She arrived late the next afternoon, with flowers and champagne and, by ill chance, a handsome pair of crocheted gloves she had picked up in a shop in San Francisco. She brought, as well, a bottle of Scotch, for her own amusement. The apartment was dark and silent, and in the wan light the servants looked spectral. The aunt, by nature a jovial woman—she drank for the fun of it—was oppressed by the gloom and went so quickly through the shadowy foyer and so quickly up the stairs that she was out of breath when she got to the door of Angelica's room. Dora, who had come more and more to have the deportment of a nurse, opened the door with nurselike gentleness and, seeing that her patient was, for a change, awake, said with nurselike cheer, "You have company, madame! Just look at what Mrs. Armstrong has brought!" She took the flowers to put in water and the champagne to put on ice, and silently left the room.

The moment Angelica saw her aunt, she burst into tears and held out her arms, like a child, to be embraced, and Mrs. Armstrong began also to cry, holding the unhappy younger woman in her arms. When the hurricane was spent and the ladies had regained their voices, the aunt said, "You must tell me the whole story, my pet, but before you do, you must give me a drink and open your present. I do pray you're going to like them—they are so much *you*."

Angelica rang for glasses and ice, for the Scotch, and then she undid the ribbon around the long box. When she saw what was inside, all the blood left her face. "Get out!" she said to her aunt, full of cold hatred. "Is that why you came—to taunt me?"

Amazed, Mrs. Armstrong turned away from a book she had been examining on a table in the window and met her niece's angry gaze.

"*I* taunt you?" she cried. "Why, darling, are you out of your mind? If you don't like the gloves, I'll give them to someone else, but don't—"

"Yes, do that! Give them to some young beautiful girl whose hands don't need to be hidden." And she flung the box and the gloves to the floor in an infantile fury. Twisting, she bent herself into her pillows and wept again, heartbrokenly.

By the end of the afternoon, Mrs. Armstrong's heart was also broken. She managed, with taste and tact, aided by a good deal of whisky, to ferret out the whole story, and, as she said to her dinner companion later on, it was unquestionably the saddest she had ever heard. She blamed herself for her obtuseness and she blamed Major Early for his, and, to a lesser extent, she blamed Angelica's friends for never realizing that they, with their constant and superlative praise of her looks, had added to her burden, had forced her into so conventional a life that she had been removed from most of experience. "The child has no memories!" exclaimed Mrs. Armstrong, appalled. "She wouldn't know danger if she met it head on, and she certainly wouldn't know joy. We virtually said to her, 'Don't tire your pretty eyes with looking at anything, don't let emotion harm a hair of your lovely head.' We simply worshipped and said, 'Let us look at you, but don't you look at us, for we are toads.' The ghastly thing is that there's nothing to be salvaged, and even if some miracle of surgery could restore her hands to her, it would do no good, for her disillusion is complete. I think if she could love anyone, if that talent were suddenly to come to her at this point in her life, she would love her ugly man in Normandy, and would love him *because* he was ugly."

When Angelica had apologized to her aunt for her tantrum

over the gloves, she had then got out of bed and retrieved them and, in the course of her soliloquy, had put them on and had constantly smoothed them over each finger in turn as she talked.

She was still wearing the gloves when Dora came in to run her evening bath and found that her heart, past mending, had stopped.

Obelisk